On a Distant Shore

Ann E Brockbank

First published in Great Britain as a paperback in 2016

Front cover by © R W Floyd, from an original oil painting

ISBN-10:1539912027
ISBN-13:9781539912026

For Wendy,

for her friendship, support and kindness

Also by Ann E Brockbank

Mr de Sousa's Legacy

The Blue Bay Café

ACKNOWLEDGMENTS

I couldn't have written this book without the help and support of some very special people. Firstly to Cathy, who not only puts the commas in the right places, but also reins in my creative spelling. I thank you for your time, friendship and expertise. Your sensitive editorial suggestions are always wise, and your honesty and encouragement have improved the book enormously. Also to my very special friend Wendy, for taking the time to read my finished manuscript. Your invaluable and astute advice is always welcome. Special thanks to Roger for answering random queries about apostrophes. I am enormously grateful to you all.

To my beloved partner Rob - your love and encouragement keeps me writing, and your beautiful artwork always adds a special quality to my novels. Thanks also to my friend and fellow author Sarah for your encouragement and advice whilst writing this third book. Huge thanks to Andrew and all the booksellers in Truro Waterstones. Your love, loyalty and support, makes me realise how lucky I am to know you all. To the amazing staff at Poldhu Café - I thank you for your support, and for letting me hog your beachside tables for hours whilst sustaining me with the most wonderful frothy coffee.

To my darling late husband Peter - we had some wonderful adventures together, the first one being in Poros, where this novel is set. You were there at the start of my writing journey and you always believed in me. You are in my heart forever. I am deeply indebted to the late great Winston Graham, whose novels brought me to live in Cornwall and inspired me to write. Most importantly, I'd like to thank every single reader who has spent their hard-earned money on this book. Without you, I'd be a very miserable writer without an audience. I am especially grateful to the readers who take the time to write a review, your kind words and support inspire me to keep writing.

1
Gweek, Cornwall

Already anxious due to the raised voices from the ongoing argument in the front seats, the flash of lightning preceded by a loud thunder crack only maximized Laura's concern. Flinching with every harsh word exchanged, she cowered in the back seat of the stuffy car, hugging her favourite dolly for comfort. Not even this dreadful storm quelled the quarrel, which had blown up at Athens airport, continued throughout the flight to Gatwick and had escalated on the long drive down to Cornwall.

In desperation she clasped her hands to her ears to muffle the sound as the car bumped its way over the debris of tree branches littering the country lane down to Gweek. Dusk was falling, making the journey more hazardous. It had been a long, tiring day and the noise of the storm had brought the argument up another octave. As they neared the house at Tolman Cross, Laura relaxed slightly - home was only minutes away now. Quickly pushing her doll into her bag, she sat up alert, ready to make a swift exit from the car.

'You disgust me Steve, you really do,' Laura's mother hissed. 'How could you do this to me? With *her,* of all people! I will not tolerate your indiscretions any more, and I will *not* forgive you this time.'

Steve sighed heavily. 'Oh give it a rest Claire.'

Laura's eyes darted between them, as she nibbled nervously at her bottom lip.

Steve narrowed his eyes as he caught Laura's countenance in the rear view mirror. 'And you can take that innocent look off your face Laura Tempest. If you hadn't repeated those stupid things to Mummy, she wouldn't be so cross with me. This is *your* fault!'

Laura's lip trembled.

'How dare you blame the child for your

misdemeanours!' Claire lashed out at him with her hand. Then as she turned to reassure Laura, a blinding flash of forked lightning struck a tree, splitting it before their eyes. Before Steve could brake, the tree hit the car with a tremendous crack, stopping the vehicle dead on impact.

Covering her head with her arms to shield the tiny particles of glass which pelted Laura's body, an overwhelming smell of earth and oil began to fill her nostrils.

The occupants in the front seats were obscured by the massive tree, and above the sound of the storm, she could hear her mother moaning in agony.

'Mummy,' she whimpered, as she attempted to wriggle towards her, but a shard of jagged metal tore the skin on her thigh. Blood oozed through her yellow summer trousers with rapid speed. Horrified, she began to scream uncontrollably.

Advancing headlights illuminated the carnage inside the car, increasing Laura's distress. She watched a man, a stranger, run frantically around the car, banging on the windows, trying desperately to open the crushed doors, prompting Laura to scream again for her mother.

A gust of sweet night air swept through the car as the stranger yanked the hatchback open. He scrambled in, punched one of the rear seats forward and dragged the terrified child from the wreckage of the car.

Overwhelmed with fear and pain, Laura fainted in the stranger's arms as he carried her bloodstained body back up the hill towards Tolman house to raise the alarm.

2
Poros, Greece

Poros was a volcanic island, formed through the union of two smaller islands and separated from the Peloponnese and its wonderful fragrant lemon groves by an extremely narrow channel, just wide enough to let the coastal steamers through.

It was a truly beautiful island, but Eva Barzini was admiring a different view. After carefully applying her 'signature' blood red lipstick in front of the full length mirror, she pressed her lips together on a tissue as she admired the curves and contours of her own naked body. Very soon her shape would change with the bambino growing inside her, and with it, her situation in life.

She wriggled into her black dress, smoothing it down like a second skin. The neckline was low to accentuate her best assets, but the length skimmed her knees, for no one looked at her legs. Licking her fingers, she teased wisps of her short glossy black hair until it framed her face. The look was complete. Her Italian mama would be proud of her.

Stepping out onto her wrought iron balcony, above the Barzini Ice Palace Gelateria, she surveyed the scene before her. Poros was an island of olives, figs and pistachios, with golden sandy bays, pine trees and warm crystal-clear water. Wherever you looked, bright crimson bougainvillaea adorned walls, while scarlet geraniums tumbled in abundance from ornate balconies. It was truly picturesque, a haven for artists and holidaymakers alike, but Eva hated her life there. Nothing could move her heart. All she yearned for was to have enough money to return to Cattolica, Italy, where her late mama had been born.

Eva loathed all of the twenty-one years she'd spent here, but now things were about to change. Confidently placing her hand on where her bambino was growing, no more than a thumbnail in size at the moment, she congratulated herself that her plan was coming to fruition. Very soon her life would change forever.

The Flying Dolphin ferry from Athens sounded its horn as it sailed into view, bringing the next batch of tourists to the island. The heat of the day would either bring them scurrying to Alexis Petrou's Taverna, or to the Ice Palace to buy gelato. She sighed impatiently. Since her mama died two years ago, serving gelato with her hateful brothers Marcos and Franco was not her idea of fun.

'Hello gorgeous,' a voice sighed appreciatively from below.

Eva glanced down her nose at the mop of unruly hair, which unmistakably belonged to Andreas Dopas, Akis and Marion's son from the Post Office next door. He was an unattractive lad, short and stocky with a monobrow, pockmarked skin and a generous mouth, which when he smiled, appeared to reach from ear to ear.

Eva shot him a look of contempt, crossed her arms and looked away.

Unperturbed at her response, or lack of it, Andreas grinned, lit a cigarette, took a long drag, and blew smoke rings seductively towards her. As she wafted the smoke away, she saw his father Akis emerge from the Post Office. In the next moment he'd delivered a resounding crack to Andreas's head.

'You idle good-for-nothing layabout. Where the hell have you been?' Akis yelled.

Eva's lip curled in mild amusement, as Andreas fell clumsily against the wall, shielding his head from the blows.

'I've been looking for you all morning.' After another smack, Akis pushed a telegram towards him. 'Here, take this to the Tempest's and be quick about it.'

'What, now? To Amora Cove? In this heat?'

'*Now*!' he snarled.

Andreas snatched the telegram from his hand, ducking

to avoid the next blow and skulked off towards the harbour.

As soon as the ferry docked, the passengers, mostly tourists, surged forward and made their way towards the nearest taverna. Alexis Petrou stood with his tea-towel draped over his left shoulder, and his arms open wide, welcoming strangers like old friends as they walked down the gangplank.

At the Taverna, Charles Tempest sat under the shade of his panama hat, with a cup of strong Greek coffee and a day old copy of The Telegraph. Although Charles was one of the wealthiest people on the island, owning almost all of the shops and tavernas in the harbour, he was a good landlord and always found time to drink coffee and pass the time of day with the locals.

At sixty-seven he was a tall, lean, handsome dapper man for his age, always immaculately dressed in a starched linen suit. Unperturbed by the advancing crowds which had broken the peace of the morning, he quietly ignored them as they noisily studied the menus.

As she ushered holidaymakers into the Ice Palace, Eva smiled inwardly at the sight of Charles Tempest. Little did he know of the fun she'd enjoyed with his wayward son over the last month, and how much her bambino would benefit from their fortune!

As Andreas uncoupled the mooring rope for his boat, the temperature had risen to thirty-one degrees. The last thing he wanted to do was sail out to the Tempest's villa with a telegram. Besides that, he was desperate to find his friend Nikos, to plan tomorrow's eighteenth birthday party for Yiannis Kiassos. He'd just turned to climb down into his vessel when he noticed, to his sheer delight, Charles Tempest sitting in the Taverna.

'It'll be quiet without the family Charles. Have you had word that they're home yet?' asked Alexis, as he placed another cup of coffee down on the table for him.

Charles nodded slowly. 'It is quiet, yes. Having a nine

year old granddaughter about the place can certainly tire you out. We didn't expect them to stay the whole month. We thought it was only for a couple of weeks. I love having Laura here, but Gwen tires of her so quickly. As to your other question, no, I haven't heard from them yet. They said they would send a telegram as soon as they got back home, but I should think they will be busy unpacking.'

'Excuse me Mr Tempest.' Andreas appeared smelling of sweat and tobacco, waving the dog-eared telegram in the air. 'This came for you.'

Charles peered over his spectacles at him, nodded and took the telegram from his hand, thanking him with a few drachmas.

'No problem,' Andreas said, feeling very pleased with himself.

'Talk of the devil eh?' He waved the telegram at Alexis. Charles took a sip of coffee, leant back in his chair and opened the telegram. His face paled as he read:

CONTACT JACK RYDER STOP URGENT STOP GRAVE NEWS STOP.

Leaving his coffee and paper in situ, Charles stood, violently scraping the chair legs on the wooden floor, then ran towards the Post Office.

'*This* was wired through from my solicitor over three hours ago. Why have I only just received it?' Charles demanded, shaking the telegram at Marion Dopas.

She flushed intensely. 'We couldn't find Andreas,' she murmured.

Charles regarded her reproachfully, as he pushed past her towards the dusty phone booth in the corner of the shop.

Marion opened her mouth to protest, then seeing the grave look on Tempest's face, skulked through to the back to eavesdrop the phone call.

Filled with dread, Charles dialled the number.

Kostas was clearing the tables when Charles emerged

ashen faced from the Post Office. Swiftly moving to his side, he asked softly, 'Whatever is the matter?'

Charles dragged his trembling fingers through his grey hair and for a long moment he was rendered speechless, then in a voice almost inaudible he said, 'There's... there's been an accident, a fatal car accident. My granddaughter Laura is the only survivor!'

With a protective arm on his shoulder, Kostas led him back to his seat as he called out to his father Alexis for a brandy. Sitting with him, he asked softly, 'Is your granddaughter injured?'

Charles nodded grimly. 'A cut to the leg and bruises apparently, she was very lucky. ' He laughed without humour. 'That's if you can call losing your parents lucky.' He pushed himself away from the table and stood. 'I must go and tell Gwen immediately. We shall have to leave for England in the morning.'

'Drink this first Mr Tempest,' Kostas said, thrusting a glass of brandy into his hand. 'You've had a terrible shock and it'll steady your nerves.'

Charles declined. 'Thank you, but I must go. I have a great deal to do. Please excuse me.' His voice was choked with emotion.

Kostas called after him, 'If there is anything we can do?'

Charles acknowledged him with a wave, and then shouted back, 'Yes, there is something Kostas. Please ask Yiannis to come over when he has a moment?'

Kostas nodded. 'Consider it done.'

3

Gweek was drenched in brilliant sunlight the morning after the storm, but the curtains at Creek House, along with all other houses in the tiny Cornish village, remained closed in respect. Gweek was in mourning for Claire and Steven Tempest.

The Western Morning Newspaper had reported the tragedy, so the noise from the normally busy boatyard seemed muted today. The local shop had been busy with people all morning, though few were buying goods. Most had clustered together to share their dismay. The lunch-time customers at The Black Swan sat in sombre silence around the bar. Many had worked through the night, helping the emergency services in their vain attempt to free the Tempests from their compressed car. Three trees in all had fallen and blocked the lane leading into the village that night. The unusual summer storm, coupled with high winds, were always a threat to vulnerable trees full of leaf at this time of year. It was indeed a sad day - the little family had been popular with all the residents, and everyone felt for little Laura and her loss.

The phone rang in Creek House, just as Sarah Haynes walked through the hall. She placed her Vogue magazine on the telephone table and adjusted her cardigan which was draped casually about her shoulders. 'Gweek 445631,' she said brightly.

'Sarah…. I've just read the news. Please tell me Laura is all right.'

Sarah's heart flipped at the sound of this voice from the past.

'Please Sarah, I need to know.'

Nervously she cleared her voice as she cupped the mouthpiece with her hand. 'You really shouldn't have rung. You promised.'

'I'm so sorry Sarah, but I need to know if Laura is okay.

You have to understand that!'

Her mouth went suddenly dry, as she listened to his heartfelt plea.

'Please Sarah.'

She swallowed hard. 'There is no need to worry. I've spoken to Jack Ryder, the Tempest's solicitor. He's been with her most of the night. He told me that apart from a cut to the leg, she came through quite unscathed.'

She heard him exhale.

'What will happen to her now?'

'Charles and Gwen are flying over from Greece. I suspect they will take her back with them. Look, I'm sorry. I really will have to go.'

'Thank you Sarah.' His voice was thick with emotion.

'Goodbye,' she said quietly, placing the receiver back on the hook.

She walked to the front door and stepped outside, gulping at the air to steady her jangled nerves. When calmness ensued, she glanced across Gweek Quay Boatyard and down towards the river. It was midday. The river was at its fullest. A full moon would preside over the tiny river village tonight. She cast her mind back to another full moon, almost ten years ago. Her eyes drifted to Hilltop House, the Tempest's residence, and then she closed her eyes in remembrance. She could smell the mossy undergrowth from that cold night. She remembered that bright yellow moon. She also remembered the secrets and lies it brought. Nothing was ever the same again after that night.

*

Word of the tragedy spread throughout the Island of Poros like wildfire. When Yiannis moored at Amora Cove, he bore many messages of condolence.

Charles was there to meet him on the beach - his face pinched, grey with grief. He had known Yiannis since birth. He'd been good friends with his father Kikos for many years before that. Although there was a vast class difference between them, Charles looked on Yiannis as his own son. And since his own father's death, Yiannis looked to Charles for help and guidance.

'When do you leave for England?' Yiannis asked, placing his hand gently on Charles's arm.

'Tomorrow morning.'

'Can I do anything?'

Charles nodded gratefully. 'We'll leave the motor boat in the harbour. If you would bring her back here, I would be very grateful.'

Yiannis nodded. 'Will you be gone long?'

His shoulders sank. 'It all depends on Laura's injuries. '

He looked downwards deep in thought, idly moving the shingle underfoot with the toe of his shoe.

'I'll keep an eye on things here for you. Don't worry about a thing. Will you bring little Laura home?'

Charles nodded. 'We're all the family she has now, except for my daughter-in-law's mother, but she has been quite ill for some time and not able to help. I shall leave a message with Akis at the Post Office when we decide to return. We'll probably need help with our luggage.'

'Okay, no problem.'

Charles glanced up at the villa. 'What on earth are we going to do with a nine year old child, Yiannis?'

'I'll help you as much as I can.'

Charles nodded and patted him warmly on the shoulder.

As Yiannis took his leave, Charles called him back. 'Wait a moment. I almost forgot.'

Yiannis waited.

'Happy eighteenth birthday my boy,' he said, pressing a white envelope into his hand.

Yiannis, deeply moved by the gesture, thanked him sincerely.

'I take it you will be closing the Athena Taverna tomorrow?' he asked inquisitively.

Yiannis's eyes glistened as he nodded. 'I don't think

papa would mind me closing for one night if he had been alive, do you?'

Charles smiled gently. 'I'm sure he wouldn't. Enjoy yourself Yiannis my boy.'

Yiannis watched for a moment as Charles walked wearily up the beach steps towards Villa Amora, then stepped into his boat.

*

It was seven a.m. and the sound of a small vessel, as it motored slowly through the narrow waterway between the harbour and the lemon groves, caught Eva's attention. She watched intently as it moored between the line of blue and white fishing boats. One of its occupants, a tall elegant woman in her late sixties, dressed in a Chanel suit, alighted from the vessel. The woman patted her hair to make sure her chignon was still tidy then made her way towards the Post Office, whilst her husband was left to lift a range of matching tan leather bags and suitcases out onto the harbour side.

From her balcony, Eva watched his struggle. She gently touched her stomach. This was her chance. She rushed inside, glanced at her reflection in her bedroom mirror, smoothed her hands down her tight black dress, tied a chiffon scarf to her neck, then ran downstairs into the morning sunshine.

'Mr Tempest,' Eva called out, as she ran towards him. 'Please let me help with those.' She picked up three of the smallest bags.

Charles looked up at her with tired, distant eyes. 'Thank you Eva, that's very kind of you. How are you my dear?'

Eva nodded. 'I'm fine thank you Mr Tempest. How are you? I was so sorry to hear about the accident,' she said tenderly, as she fell into step with him.

'Oh I'm bearing up Eva. It's the little one I feel sorry for.'

'Oh yes your poor granddaughter?'

'We're leaving for England now,' he answered sadly. 'Poor little mite. It's only four years since she lost her father, my only son, now the poor lamb has lost her mother too!'

Eva stumbled slightly, dropping one of the cases.

Charles halted momentarily. 'Sorry my dear, are they too heavy for you? Give them back to me.'

Trying to compose herself, she quickly answered, 'No, I'm fine I can manage. I'm sorry, but what did you mean she lost her father four years ago? Forgive me, but I thought he died in the car crash yesterday!'

Charles sighed and shook his head. 'My son Stephen died in April 1974 of a brain tumour!' He blinked a stray tear from his eyes.

A prickle of panic swept over Eva. Unable to keep the alarm from her voice she said, 'I.. I don't understand. Who was it that died yesterday then?'

Briefly taken aback, he answered calmly. 'It was my daughter-in-law Claire and her second husband, whom she married a couple of years ago. You met them surely, when they were here just recently?'

Eva could barely register what Charles was saying, as her head tried to make sense of everything. 'But, but Akis Dopas said it was Claire and Steven Tempest!'

Charles looked at her darkly. His facial muscles tensed at the angst in her voice.

Eva quickly checked herself. 'Sorry Mr Tempest. That must have sounded dreadful. Forgive my insensitivity.'

Charles sighed deeply. 'It's all right my dear. Yes, Akis was correct. My daughter-in-law's second husband was also called Steven Tempest, absolutely no relation though! Same name, but a different spelling! His Christian name was spelt with a 'v' instead of a 'ph' as was my son's.' He paused for a moment and laughed gently. 'He and my son had actually been friends since their school days, and I can tell you it caused no amount of confusion, especially at parent evenings and school report times!' he said reflectively. 'Anyway he kept in touch with Claire after my son's funeral and well, the rest is history, as they say.'

Stunned into silence Eva began to feel very ill.

'You've gone very pale my dear, are you all right?'

She swallowed hard and nodded. 'Excuse me.' She dropped the cases and walked away.

In the distance, the ferry cruised through the shimmering haze towards the harbour of waiting passengers. Charles looked towards the Post Office for his wife.

In the coolness of the Ice Palace, Eva slumped into a chair. Perspiration prickled her scalp as she held her head in her hands. How could this be? What had she done? Bearing the Tempest's grandchild was to have been her meal ticket out of here. But she had fallen pregnant to a 'nobody', an imposter! Her plan was in ruins.

*

An hour later when Eva emerged from gelateria for a breath of air and to collect her thoughts, Andreas ran towards her.

'Hey Eva?' He gazed lovingly into her eyes. 'What are you doing tonight?'

She gave a dismissive snarl as she pushed past him. 'Whatever it is, it won't be with you! Now get lost.'

Unperturbed he licked his lips. 'No Eva, wait a minute. It's Yiannis's eighteenth birthday party.'

Eva turned back with interest. 'Is it now?' Eva had always had designs on the handsome Yiannis Kiassos, though her past efforts to seduce him had been fruitless. 'And tell me, is Yiannis celebrating?' she enquired nonchalantly, picking at an imaginary piece of fluff from her dress.

Andreas grinned widely. 'You bet. There's a surprise party for him at Alexis.' He nodded towards the taverna next door.

'I see,' she breathed softly, her eyes twinkling mischievously. 'Well I may just have a birthday surprise for him myself!'

'Yeah?' he said eagerly. '…and what about me Eva?'

She pursed her lips. 'What about you?'

'Have you any surprises for me?'

She laughed derisively. 'In your dreams Andreas.'

Andreas pulled a wide grin as he dropped to his knees in mock prayer. 'Oh yes, Eva, you're in my dreams every night.'

Eva made an impatient clicking sound with her tongue as she walked away. This might just be the answer to her predicament.

.

4

The Athena Taverna was set back a couple of hundred yards from the bustle of the busy harbour of Poros, nestled at the far end of the village square known as the Plaka. An ancient plane tree threw dappled shade onto the large heavy iron studded doors, which opened inwards to reveal a gravel courtyard full of gardenias, camellias, hanging vines and terracotta pots full of jasmine.

Twelve tables set with crisp white cloths and red candle lanterns, surrounded a small raised wooden circle in the middle of the yard, where most evenings diners and waiters alike danced an impromptu 'tatavliano', a dance known for its gradual acceleration of tempo. A large charcoal grill ran the length of the far wall and normally glowed and smoked with the aroma of sizzling meat and swordfish steaks. To the left of the courtyard, stood a bar that extended through to the back of the building to a small seating area where the old men from the days of the 'Kepheneion' still gathered together to read, argue and gossip. Whilst high up in the corner of this room, an old dusty black and white television played continually to an uninterested audience.

The Athena Taverna had been in the Kiassos family for three generations. Opened first as a Kepheneion in 1944 it became a sanctuary for the local men of the village, where women were banned so they could read, drink, and listen to the wireless in peace.

Kikos Kiassos took over when his father died in 1959 and turned the Kepheneion into a taverna to catch the growing trade of Athenians who had begun to spend their holidays on the island. The taverna had prospered for a while until Kikos began to gamble. He would lay a wager on almost anything, from beetle racing to the date of the first storm in September. He was notorious for challenging his customers to toss a coin with him at the end of the meal to see who paid the bill. Sometimes he was lucky, but more often than not, he lost! His salvation was to be an English girl called Suzanne Paynter.

Suzanne breezed into his life like a breath of fresh air, planning only to spend a few days on Poros. She'd been in the middle of an island hopping holiday -working wherever she could. She fell in love, first, with the peaceful charm of this beautiful island, and then with the handsome, but hapless, Kikos. He was utterly bewitched by her freshness, beauty, and sheer enthusiasm for work. Within a few short weeks she had turned his fortunes around and stolen his heart. He soon proposed to her, and on the twenty first of September 1962 almost a year to the day she arrived, Suzanne presented Kikos with a son Yiannis, an heir for his now thriving empire.

A voice suddenly roused Yiannis from his reverie.

'Come on Yiannis, what are you doing? I thought you were closing the Taverna tonight?' Kostas said impatiently, as he watched his friend gather the remaining tablecloths.

'I'll just clear this lot,' Yiannis answered quickly.

Yiannis and Kostas had been friends all their lives, they were almost like brothers. They had grown at the same rate and were exactly five foot eleven inches and much the same build. They were both darkly handsome, but Yiannis had a most unusual attribute, he had pellucid aquamarine eyes that sparkled like jewels when he smiled his warm generous smile. Yiannis also had an unusual strawberry shaped birthmark under his right eye, which, as he got older, added to his good looks. In his youth he'd been teased mercilessly about it, causing him great distress, but now, he rather enjoyed his little bit of individuality.

Yiannis had been solely in charge of the Athena since his father had died six months ago. He had no other family. His mother died in childbirth when he was ten, the child died one hour after birth. His devastated father never married again.

'For goodness sake Yiannis, stop daydreaming and get a move on or you'll be nineteen before we have a chance to celebrate your eighteenth!' Kostas moaned.

'Sorry, I was just thinking about Papa. He had so looked forward to this day. Remember when he used to say, "There will be such a celebration on your eighteenth birthday Yiannis. Everyone will be here to see me hand over my empire." Now look!' He sighed. 'No celebration and no Papa, just the taverna.'

Andreas and Nicos appeared at that moment to join Kostas. 'Who says there's no celebration?' Andreas nudged Nicos. 'We have such a surprise for you!'

Yiannis rolled his eyes in trepidation.

'Let's just say you're going to get the mother of all birthday presents!'

Yiannis threw them a pensive look, as they whispered a private joke to each other. He locked the door to the bar and quickly checked to see all was clean and ready for the morning. As he stuffed the money from the till into his back pocket he turned to find Andreas's grandfather, Papa Andreas, shuffling through the Taverna gates.

'Oh no!' He quickly moved over to Papa Andreas as he was settling down at the table. 'We are closed old man!' He received no response. 'Papa Andreas, I'm sorry but I'm closed!'

The old man coughed then spat into the filthy piece of rag he produced from his pocket, took off his grease-stained hat, placed it on the table, and ordered coffee.

Yiannis shot a look of desperation towards his friends as the old man stared at the whitewashed walls of the Taverna, the rims of his empty eyes hung red, gaping with age. His tanned leathery skin hung in folds on his face, and he smelt of decaying vegetation.

'Andreas, help me out here, he's your grandfather!'

Andreas grimaced. 'I'm not touching him, he stinks! Just leave him.'

'I can't just leave him,' he hissed, fumbling in his

pocket for his keys. He walked back to the bar.

Andreas groaned impatiently. 'I'm not waiting any longer here, I'm dying of thirst. I'll see you lot at Alexis'.

The two other boys watched enviously as Andreas walked towards the harbour in the evening sunshine.

Nicos licked his lips thirstily. 'I must admit I could do with a drink as well. Kostas, go and get Yiannis. We're going to be here all night at this rate.'

Kostas laughed when he entered the bar. 'Yiannis, what *are* you doing?'

Yiannis poured the thick brown liquid into the tiny cup. 'It's for Papa Andreas.' He gestured to the cup. 'We'll leave him to it. He'll go away if there is no one here to serve him later. Anyway what's the rush?'

Kostas grinned. 'Just hurry will you and don't ask stupid questions.'

Yiannis swiftly locked the bar door again, delivered the drink along with a glass of water to Papa Andreas and shouted in his ear, 'The taverna is closed now old man! Come and join us at Alexis when you have finished, but remember to close the main door when you leave, okay? I have to go now!'

Yiannis made his way to the door, but the old man picked up his stick and jabbed him on the leg with it, stopping Yiannis abruptly in his tracks.

'Boy,' he croaked. 'You'd do well to stay here tonight!'

Yiannis brushed at the dirty mark the stick had made on his trousers. 'It's my taverna. I'll do as I please. Now drink up and go.'

The old man screwed his face and chewed thoughtfully on his gums. 'I'm just warning you. You should listen to me. You'd do well to stay here tonight!' he warned. 'There'll be trouble afoot.'

Yiannis shook his head. 'Okay come on.' Yiannis said, as he pushed his friends towards the exit. 'Let's get out of here.'

'What was all that about?' Kostas asked.

'No idea,' Yiannis answered, trying to hide his unease.

*

The journey home to Cornwall had taken its toll on Charles and Gwen. They had first stopped off at their London house to pick up their car and almost immediately embarked on the drive down to Cornwall. Though Gwen had protested keenly, Charles insisted on stopping off at the Royal Cornwall Hospital in Truro to spend a few hours comforting Laura before making their way to Gweek.

Pouring himself a large whisky Charles settled down into the soft leather easy-chair. Gwen had taken herself off to bed with a headache, so he was alone with his thoughts. He cast an unhurried look around the sitting room. Claire and Steven had made a few changes to the room since their marriage. New curtains, rugs etc - but all in all it was much the same as when he and Gwen occupied Hilltop House. It was a shared house, big enough for two couples, which happened when Greece became too hot in the summer time. Though Steven wasn't his own kin, he had got on well enough with him when he took on the role of husband and father to his widowed daughter-in-law Claire and granddaughter Laura.

He glanced at the clock. It was eight p.m. and still relatively light. The cool late summer evening beckoned him outside. From the front door he had a high vantage point over the village. To the left of his front door stood Creek House, where his good friends Sarah and Gerald Haynes lived. It stood impressively, a little way back from the roadside and looked over the Old Corn Mill. Further down the road was Barleyfield Farm, where the Ferris-Nortons' had lived for generations. He smiled to himself - eight-year old Pippa, the youngest daughter of Edwin and Carol Ferris-Norton, had arrived on the doorstep at Hilltop House almost as soon as Charles and Gwen had pulled up in their car. Her small face was pinched with worry about her friend, as she handed a hand drawn card to Charles. 'Please could you give this to Laura, Mr

Tempest?' she said.

Charles took the card and nodded kindly at the child and Pippa turned and ran off in the direction of home.

He placed the card with all the other get well cards and messages of condolence, which he'd found on his doormat. Everybody was so kind.

Feeling stiff from travelling, he pushed himself to walk a little way over to the first bridge, stopping to look down on the rising tide. The smell of the sea filled the evening air with a soft tang of salt. Small rodents in the undergrowth scurried out of sight at the sound of his footsteps. There was a true calmness about Gweek, he had always thought so. Maybe they would come home now for good. Maybe Greece was not the place to bring up a child. Maybe she would fair better here. There were so many decisions they had to make he really didn't know where to start. He thought of Laura, sitting in her hospital bed. Quiet and frightened of what was to become of her. She claimed to remember nothing about the accident, though the doctors told them this was down to shock. They would have to be ready for the onslaught of what may occur in a few days time when the enormity of what had happened dawned on her.

5

The taverna was buzzing with holidaymakers, but Alexis found the time to come out of the kitchen to greet Yiannis when he arrived. 'Ah, the boy becomes a man today. Come, sit.' He beckoned them to a table. 'We have music and dancing, and oh yes,' he shot a dubious look at Andreas. 'I believe Andreas has arranged a special treat for you tonight! Kostas, get the drinks in.'

'But, it's my night off!' Kostas protested.

Alexis clicked his tongue in annoyance, Kostas knew better than to argue.

The taverna was full, even though it was coming to the end of the season. Alexis was in high spirits. The strains of the Bazooki moved the boys to get up and dance. For some reason Yiannis felt very drunk. Always a moderate drinker, he was blissfully unaware of the amount of vodka Andreas surreptitiously tipped into his drinks throughout the night. His friends revelled in his inebriation and watched with amusement his prowess on the dance floor. Very vocally Yiannis beckoned all and sundry to join him until they formed a large circle. Suddenly he was pushed into the middle, blindfolded and spun around.

'Hey what the…?' Yiannis protested as he was pushed back and forth and round and round until he fell to his knees. 'Enough, please, I feel terrible! Kostas, help me!' But Kostas had been called into the kitchen to deal with an electrical problem.

'Give him some air, he's passed out,' Nicos said, as he and Andreas dragged him to his feet, and led him out of the Taverna. As the dancing continued, Yiannis was dragged up a flight of stairs and dropped onto Eva's bedroom floor.

Punching her fists into her hips she wailed, 'What have you done to him?'

'We have just loosened him up for you,' Andreas

laughed, pulling Nicos out of the room.

Nicos hesitated at the door. 'I don't think we should leave him, he's out for the count!'

'Oh shut up you old woman. He'll have the time of his life when he comes round.' Andreas winked at Eva and shoved Nicos out of the door.

Alone now, a smile grew on Eva's lips. She pulled her dress up over her head and with a great deal of effort, managed to remove Yiannis's trousers.

The smell of cheap perfume brought Yiannis to half consciousness. The smell clung like a nasty taste to the back of his throat, triggering a wave of nausea. He snorted in disgust, pulling at the blindfold, which was adding to his queasiness. It would not move. His head rolled drunkenly to one side, and grit pressed into his cheek from a dirty carpet.

He became acutely aware that his skin was in contact with another naked body and struggled to sit up when he felt a weight press down on him.

'Lay still!' Eva pushed him backwards.

He vaguely recognised the husky voice through his inebriated state. 'Where on earth am I?' he said, frantically pulling again at the blindfold. As slight as she was, the weight of Eva's body pressing on his abdomen caused his stomach to erupt. He twisted violently sending her tumbling backwards as he vomited on the carpet. Momentarily shaken from his inebriated state he tore the blindfold from his eyes to see the blurred image of Eva crawling towards him.

'Oh my God, what am I doing here?' He wiped the vomit from his mouth. 'Where the hell are your mad brothers? They'll kill me if they find me here!'

Eva pouted seductively. 'It's okay Yiannis, they'll be gone for hours, just lay back and enjoy your birthday treat.'

'No Eva!' he yelled, pushing away from her. He staggered clumsily to his feet pulling his trousers up as he stood.

She caught him with his shirttail. 'What the hell is the matter with you? Come back!' 'Get off!' he snapped, angrily yanking his shirt from her grip.

As she let go, he staggered backwards and fell to the floor. He crawled dizzily across the threadbare carpet, grasping at the door handle to help pull himself back onto his feet.

Eva dashed to the door, quickly locking it.

'For Christ sake Eva, let me out of here.' He pushed her to one side.

Pressing herself against the door she fluttered her eyelashes. 'Yiannis darling, come back and let's make love again.'

Yiannis's eyes narrowed. 'Again?' he said flatly.

Eva gave a pained look. 'Oh, don't tell me you were too drunk to feel anything.' She smiled. 'Never mind, come back and we'll do it again, and this time you *will* remember.'

He shook his head. 'I may be horribly drunk, but I know when you're lying. Now let me out of this place.'

*

Outside, Andreas and Nicos gleefully glanced up at her window, straining to hear any exciting noises.

'Lucky bastard!' said Andreas jealously. 'I've been pursuing her for ages, but she won't have anything to do with me. Can't understand it really, someone as handsome as me!'

Nicos quirked an eyebrow at him and took a long drag on his cigarette. 'You should become a tour guide like me Andreas, the women practically beg you to make love to them.'

'No,' he answered forlornly. 'I only want one woman. She'll come round one day. You just see if she doesn't.'

'When hell freezes over maybe,' Nicos added sotto voce, picking a stray piece of tobacco from his lip.

Kostas joined Andreas and Nicos. 'Sorry about that, the electricity keeps tripping in the kitchen. 'Where's

Yiannis?'

'Losing his manhood I should think,' Andreas laughed, gesturing towards Eva's bedroom.

Kostas blanched. 'Please tell me you are joking?' He glanced first up at the bedroom then at the road. His face turned ashen. 'Oh my God, look!' The others stopped laughing and followed Kostas's gaze. 'If I'm not mistaken that's the Barzini brothers coming.'

'I'm off!' Nikos said. He drained his glass and knocked Kostas out of his way.

Kostas ran to the Ice Palace doorway.

He knew that if they found Yiannis with Eva they would kill him for sure. 'Yiannis get the hell out of there now, the Barzini brothers are coming.' He waited a moment then checked the street again. He could see Andreas running down the road in the same direction as Nicos. Kostas cursed them, but he knew he also had to make himself scarce. With one last warning yell to Yiannis, he ran down the side of the Post Office and up the whitewashed alleyway scattering pots of red geraniums in his wake. At the back of the Ice Palace he hid amidst the stinking dustbins. Clutching his hands to his heaving chest, he prayed that Yiannis had heard his warning.

No one crossed the Barzini brothers, he knew a few people who had found that out to their cost.

When Eva and Yiannis heard Kostas's warning, they both exchanged a look of horror. In one swift movement she pushed Yiannis in the direction of the balcony. 'Get out quick!' she ordered.

'What! Out of the window, are you mad? I'll break my neck!'

'They will break more than your neck if they find you here,' she hissed, closing the shutters behind him. Eva kicked her discarded dress under the bed, and pulled her dressing gown on.

The balcony floor felt rotten underfoot as Yiannis moved gingerly along it, clinging precariously to the side of the building. He peered over the wrought iron railings to see if the coast was clear, quickly pulling back as the brothers walked beneath him. With baited breath he waited until he heard them enter the Ice Palace, grasped the drainpipe and hurled himself over the balcony. Flakes of paint and rust crumbled in his hand as the brittle pipe groaned and cracked under his weight. A loud thwack occurred, as the pipe began to peel off the wall. Helplessly he grasped at the wall but lost his grip and fell with a thud to the ground. Within seconds, Kostas had leapt from behind the dustbins and dragged Yiannis to his feet.

'Oh no stop, I think I've broken something!' Yiannis cradled his rib cage.

Ignoring his pleas, Kostas looped Yiannis's grazed arm around his own neck and dragged him protesting up the alleyway away from the harbour front.

Marcos took the stairs two at a time, and burst into her room.

'Don't you ever knock on a lady's door?' Eva said, indignantly.

His huge six-foot frame seemed to fill the room as he sniffed the air and bared his gold teeth. 'Smells more like a whore's bedroom in here. What have you been up to, and why are you undressed? Have you got someone up here?' He lurched forward, grabbed her by the wrists, and shook her violently.

'No!' she said indignantly.

Marcos scowled and yanked the balcony doors open. His foot crunched on the remains of a terracotta pot, and then he saw the broken drainpipe hanging limply from the wall. Grasping her by the throat he yelled, 'Who has been here?'

Eva's scalp prickled with fear. 'Nobody!'

His lip curled. 'Liar!' he said, flinging her to the floor.

*

Eventually the boys came to rest on a small shingle beach. Standing amongst a row of beached fishing boats, they took a moment to catch their breath.

'Do you think we were followed?' Yiannis gasped.

Kostas shook his head. 'I think we're safe.'

'I need to lie down,' Yiannis groaned exhaustedly as he collapsed on the ground.

'Are you okay? You took a hell of a fall.'

'I'll live,' he slurred, wiping his bloody hands down his shirt.

They lay in silence for a few minutes staring into the huge vault of stars, as Yiannis fought an overwhelming desire to sleep.

'I'm sorry Yian. I swear I didn't know what they had planned for you.'

'What?' Yiannis dragged himself back to wakefulness.

'I wouldn't have let them do that to you if I had known.'

Yiannis sighed. 'I know my friend, I know.'

'So…..How did it go?' Kostas nudged him in the ribs.

'Ouch, watch what you're doing,' Yiannis said, hugging his aching torso. 'How did what go?'

'You know,' he nodded. 'How was it?'

'Don't ask, Kostas. I don't want to talk about it,' he groaned.

Kostas laughed. 'Okay. No problem.'

Yiannis yawned noisily. 'What happened to the others?

Kostas sat up and bristled. 'Huh, first sign of trouble and they were off like rats down a sewer.' He selected a stone to throw aimlessly into the sea. They both listened for the dull plop.

Laying a heavy hand on Kostas's shoulder, he said, 'At least I know I can always depend on you my friend. Thanks for warning me Kostas.'

The boys watched as a huge bank of black cloud began to gather momentum, swallowing up the starry night as it rolled in.

'There's a storm brewing,' Kostas said knowingly. 'The first of many!'

The sound of distant thunder filled the night air and large spots of rain began to splatter the baked earth around them.

'Home I think Yiannis,' Kostas said, pulling him to his feet. 'Shall I come back with you?'

Yiannis winced in pain. 'No, I'll be fine. I'll see you tomorrow my friend.' They shared a brotherly hug.

'You won't forget this birthday in a hurry!'

'No, I won't,' he answered darkly as he staggered home.

A bolt of lightning flashed across the length of the sky and suddenly the whole island was plunged into pitch-blackness. The only lights visible were from the fishing boat lanterns as they quickly made their way back to the shelter of the harbour. Within seconds the heavens opened and Yiannis ran to the shelter of his taverna. He reached for the handle on the huge studded doors and found it already open.

Yiannis collected his thoughts for a moment, trying to remember if he'd shut the door on the way out. Then he remembered. 'Damn the old man,' he cursed Papa Andreas, as he stepped into the gravel courtyard. Two steps into the yard, he tripped and fell to his knees. Though inebriated, Yiannis knew something was amiss. A cold shiver ran through his body as the hairs on the back of his head stood on end. As he groped around in the darkness, he found pieces of broken furniture everywhere. A flash of lightning momentarily revealed the terrible carnage before him, and the realisation that his livelihood was in tatters.

Fearfully, he picked his way through the debris, feeling his way towards the door to the bar - that too was hanging open. A mound of broken furniture wedged the door from behind. He pushed hard until it opened enough to squeeze through.

The room stank of spirits, as the remains of the broken bottles crunched underfoot. Although he could not see, his senses knew the devastation was shocking. He choked back angry tears, as he reached over the glass-strewn bar to find the box of candles. He emptied them out on the bar and produced a book of matches from his pocket. One by one, each lit candle revealed the appalling destruction about him. Suddenly he felt very sober.

6

The electricity was restored to the island just after five the next morning and dawn broke two hours later. The heavy rain in the night had washed the Plaka clean of the summer dust, leaving dripping vine leaves hanging limply above the Athena courtyard, glistening in the pale watery morning sun. The day felt refreshingly cool, but this went unnoticed by Yiannis as he ploughed on, as he had by candlelight, through the night, in a vain and desperate hope to clear the mess before morning.

Kostas arrived just as Yiannis was throwing the last of his broken furniture onto a pile in the back yard.

He stood open-mouthed. 'What the hell happened here?'

Yiannis wore a look of despair. 'You tell me. It's taken me all night to clear this lot. Why would anyone want to do this to me Kostas?'

'Oh Yian.' Kostas hugged his friend. 'Why didn't you come for me last night? You shouldn't have had to do all this alone! Have you anything left?'

Yiannis shook his head slowly. "Not a lot here, the bar, furniture, crockery, all smashed, but they didn't get to the cellar, thank goodness. At least I still have some stock left!'

'You don't think Papa Andreas did it do you?' Kostas asked curiously.

Yiannis smiled and shook his head. 'No, he would have been a bit annoyed that he couldn't get another drink after we left, but not that irked! Though he did try to warn me about trouble afoot, didn't he?' He bent down to pick up a broken bottle and shook it in the air. 'I wish I could get hold of whoever did this!' Just as he spoke, Marcos and Franco appeared at his door.

Yiannis felt a blind panic sweep over him. In a breathy whisper he said, 'They've come for me Kostas!'

Kostas moved protectively towards Yiannis, himself

quaking in the presence of these two thugs.

Yiannis felt the muscles of his body tighten and conscious that his bowels were about to turn to liquid. 'They're going to kill me Kostas. Eva must have said something.'

Marcos walked into the courtyard, stopped, looked down, and moved some debris with his foot. He fixed his menacing gaze on Yiannis as he moved closer. 'Well, well, well, what have we here? Storm damage?'

'Looks like a very dissatisfied customer to me,' Franco said dryly as he leant against the door smirking.

Yiannis cleared his throat. 'Is there something I could do for you? Because as you see I'm in a bit of a mess and I need to get on with clearing up, or I'll never get back in business.'

Marcos quirked an eyebrow as he surveyed the fragments of furniture and bottles around him. 'I think perhaps the question is, what can *we* do for you? Looks to me like you need this establishment protecting.' He grinned, revealing his gold front teeth.

Yiannis forced himself to speak. 'I'm sure that won't be necessary. Nothing like this has ever happened before. It was probably some drunken youths, chancing their luck on finding some money on the premises. Don't you agree Kostas?'

'Oh yes, absolutely,' Kostas answered, his voice a few octaves higher than normal.

Marcos smirked. 'Nevertheless, we'll keep a watch out for you over the next few weeks, to see how it goes.' He turned away and beckoned Franco out of the courtyard. 'Come come. Let the boys get on. It's shameful what people do to other people's property isn't it brother?'

As soon as they left, Yiannis's knees buckled. 'Sweet Jesus, I thought they had come for me. I think I was that close to having to change my underclothes,' he said, squeezing his thumb and finger together. 'Thanks for staying with me Kostas.'

'You're welcome,' Kostas grinned weakly, as he tried to generate some saliva in his dry mouth.

'Well, I may have got away with last night's little escapade, but it looks like I'm in for trouble if they start demanding protection money off me. I have a feeling they are not going to let this go.' He bit his lip nervously.

*

Eva stood at her balcony window and watched the sun glinting on the peaceful harbour. Her fingers tenderly soothed the raw bruised skin of her neck where Marcos had attacked her the previous evening. She shuddered when she recalled the violence he had inflicted on her. He had damn near strangled her. Like a man possessed he had pinned her to the wall and practically squeezed the life out of her. But she obstinately refused him any satisfaction. It certainly wasn't because she felt any regard for Yiannis, that she hadn't revealed his name, she just needed to form a plan before her news could no longer be concealed.

In the street below, she watched the morning unfold as the locals went about their everyday business. Alexis Petrou was dragging bins full of yesterday's rubbish to the skip. Old men with leathery skin led their braying donkeys down from the hillside with baskets full of lemons to sell at the market. Fishermen with their morning catch on the harbour walls, their crinkled eyes and lined faces shaded with the traditional blue peaked caps, crouched over mounds of orange fishing nets, mending and weaving with quick nimble fingers. Another hour would see the straggle of tourists sleepily leave their accommodation, eyes shaded from the brilliant morning sun, sluggishly making their way to the nearest taverna for breakfast.

On the path immediately beneath her, lay a mangy dog, its head resting on paws, lifting its sorrowful eyes occasionally, in anticipation of a free morsel from the taverna. Suddenly, footsteps and the familiar voices of her brothers made Eva glance to her right. She quickly pulled herself back from the window as they passed by.

A great yelp followed the gruff voice of Marcos, as he kicked the dog out of his path. 'Get out of the way, you flea bitten runt!'

The terrified animal was kicked the length of the dusty path and ran yelping to the protection of Alexis taverna, only to be set upon by a disgruntled cat who had been sleeping peacefully under the shade of a large wicker chair. The dog made a half hearted attempt at retaliation, growling and barking at the spitting animal, until Irene Petrou ran out of the kitchen, broom in hand and set about walloping the yelping dog until it eventually skulked away, whimpering pathetically. The cat, its fur fluffed out to twice its size, watched smugly at the dog's cowardly retreat, licked its coat indignantly, then began to settle back down to sleep, only to be unceremoniously jabbed with the broom and sent spitting and twitching into the middle of the road.

'Bloody animals!' Irene muttered, as she tucked the broom under her arm and brushed her hands down her apron, satisfied on a job well done.

Eva sighed with relief when she stepped back onto her balcony and saw her brothers walking in the direction of the market. At least she would have some peace for a while longer.

*

Charles opened the front door at Hilltop House and gestured for Laura to enter. Normally a talkative child, Laura had been understandably quiet on the journey home from hospital.

Gwen took off her coat and checked her appearance in the hall mirror.

'May I go to my room grandpa?' Laura asked, her eyes brimming with tears.

Noting her distress, Charles asked, 'Are you sure you want to be on your own?'

Laura nodded.

'I'll get granny to bring some hot chocolate up to you.'

He watched for a moment as Laura climbed the stairs and then noted that Gwen was putting her coat back on. 'Where are you going?'

'We don't have any hot chocolate - I shall have to go down to the shop now,' Gwen answered acidly. 'She isn't the only one who could do with a sit down and a drink you know!'

Charles held up his hands. 'It's not a problem. I'll go,' he said quietly.

The Gweek shop smelt delicious when Charles walked through the door. Rows of fresh home baked bread and cakes made his mouth water. At the counter he met Sarah Haynes.

She glanced at his full shopping basket and smiled. 'I can't resist all this lovely produce either.'

They both made their purchases and began to walk towards home together. At the bridge they both stood and looked down the river. The tide was out and the great expanse of mud flats glistened in the morning sunshine. 'Even without the water, Gweek always gives off a peaceful charm,' Charles said.

Sarah nodded. 'I know what you mean. How are things with little Laura?'

'We brought her home today. She is very quiet, which is to be expected.'

'What are your plans?'

'After she has had her stitches out next week, we'll take her back to Poros.'

'If there is anything I can do Charles, you only have to ask. I know Laura doesn't really know my Vanessa. Claire always favoured the Ferris-Norton girl Pippa for Laura to play with. But Vanessa is the same age as Laura, and if you feel she needs to be with children of her own age and nationality, just let me know.'

'It's a shame you and Claire didn't see eye to eye.'

Sarah smiled and looked down the river. 'She was wary of me. She always believed that I held a candle for your

Stephen.'

Charles's eyes twinkled. 'And did you?'

Sarah smiled sadly.

'We always hoped you would be our daughter-in-law someday. Stephen always regretted going off on that trip around the world. He should have taken you with him. We told him that at the time. But he wanted to 'find' himself.'

Sarah unconsciously twisted her wedding ring. 'It's all water under the bridge as they say.'

'And you Sarah - have you been happy with Gerald? I should think his disability has been a terrible strain on you all. But you have three fine children.'

'It is a strain yes. Gerald will never walk again after falling from that horse, but he has his own nurse, she does most things for him. He seems quite resigned to his fate. As for my children, yes they are my joy Charles. Slater can be a little troublesome sometimes, but he is at that difficult age, between boyhood and manhood. Taylor…' she grinned. '…he is the sweetest boy. I know you shouldn't have favourites, but he has a piece of my heart that Slater and Vanessa could never reach. Isn't that an awful thing to admit to anyone?'

Charles patted her on the shoulder. 'I know how you feel. Stephen was *my* world. It broke my heart to lose him so young. In fact young Taylor reminds me so much of Stephen at that age.'

Sarah's heart flipped slightly at his observation.

'Well, I must get on,' Charles said, 'I promised Laura a hot chocolate.'

7

The gravel courtyard of the Athena was once again adorned with terracotta pots full of jasmine and geraniums all basking under the warm October sky.

Yiannis's business was almost back to normal, thanks to a lot of hard work and help from Kostas, kindly loaned by Alexis. Yiannis was fortunate in that there were still a smattering of tourists at this time of year, eager to soak up the last of the summer sun. Thankfully too the locals had filtered back and he'd managed to recoup some of his losses since the break-in. There was of course still a great pile of damaged tables and chairs at the back of the taverna and it would probably take most of the winter months to repair them all, but for the moment, Yiannis would manage with what he had.

It had taken a couple of weeks after the break-in before Yiannis had dared to venture out at night to do some fishing, reluctant to leave the Taverna unattended in case he received a repeat visit. But as the days passed, even the threat of the Barzini brothers visiting him about his assignation with Eva had waned slightly, and Yiannis began to relax a little.

In the cool morning calmness of the Athena kitchen, Yiannis stood at his scrubbed table, skilfully gutting and preparing the fish he'd caught that morning, when a sudden noise from the courtyard broke his concentration. He paused to listen, as a pang of unease swept over him. It was far too early for customers or staff.

'Hello?' he called cautiously, no one answered. He raised the fish knife. 'Who's there?' Still no one answered. Just as he moved forward, a figure leapt into the kitchen.

'It's me,' Andreas roared.

Yiannis fell clumsily against the table, his hand grasping his heart to calm the palpitations.

Andreas grinned mischievously and slapped a dog-eared piece of paper on the slimy fish scale table. 'Message for you Yian,' he said, his eyes sweeping over the room in search of something to drink.

Yiannis scowled darkly, trying to recover his composure. He placed the fish knife down and wiped his hands down his apron. 'From whom?' he snapped angrily.

Andreas shrugged his shoulders, turned and walked back into the courtyard to sit down. Shifting the corner of the table-cloth, he rested his feet on the table. 'Where's Dimitra today?' he shouted, looking around for the chef.

'It's his day off. Jesus Andreas, how long have you had this?' Yiannis yelled, emerging from the kitchen.

'Err, sorry, I should have brought it a couple of days ago. I found it in my pocket this morning. It's not important is it?' He lit a cigarette and flicked the dead match into the nearest pot of geraniums.

'Yes it *is* important,' he said, dragging his apron from his waist. 'Get out of my way Andreas.'

'Where are you going? Aren't you going to offer me a drink?' Andreas shouted as Yiannis rushed out of the gate. 'Oh don't bother then, I'll get my own.' He heaved his legs off the table, selected a glass from behind the bar, and then helped himself to a bottle of imported brandy from the top shelf.

Yiannis checked his watch as he ran along the harbour front. The telegram had read:

BACK ON THE TWELFTH STOP TEN-THIRTY A.M. FERRY STOP. CHARLES TEMPEST STOP

'Damn Andreas!' The Tempest's motorboat was moored back at Amora Cove and the ferry was due in thirty minutes. As he passed Alexis Taverna he grabbed Kostas by the arm. 'I'm just borrowing Kostas,' he shouted to Alexis, dragging his bemused friend from his work.

'Not again!' Alexis protested. 'I've only just got him back!'

'We'll be half an hour at the most, I'll explain later,' he

shouted, as the pair ran off towards Yiannis's fishing boat.

Alexis stabbed his fists into his hips angrily. 'Huh!' he muttered to his wife Irene. 'The last time he borrowed Kostas he was gone two weeks!'

*

Inside the Ice Palace the Barzini family slept late, though not all peacefully. Eva had endured another disturbed night, and as usual, her stomach erupted into a metal bucket the moment she woke. Wiping her mouth with a handkerchief she rubbed the groaning cavern of her empty stomach cursing the child that grew inside her. She waited until the bout of nausea had passed then tiptoed out of her bedroom, bucket in hand and headed for the bathroom. As she entered the bathroom the stench of urine made her retch again. She tried to keep the place clean, but it was an ongoing battle with two great louts living in the same house.

Her stomach began to churn, saliva filled her mouth, and she vomited again. With trembling hands she swilled her mouth with water and reached for a towel to dry herself. Sitting on the edge of the bath, she lowered the towel from her face to find Marcos standing stony faced in front of her.

Eva's eyes widened, she rubbed her stomach and said, 'Something I ate must have upset me.'

Franco appeared from behind Marcos, glanced indifferently at them with his sharp piggy brown eyes. 'Shove off out of here you two, I need to go!' he growled as he dragged several pieces of torn newspaper from the nail at the back of the door.

Marcos ignored him, grabbed Eva by the hair, and twisted it until her face was almost touching his. 'Something you ate eh? Liar! ' His eyes blazed with fury.

Eva began to tremble uncontrollably.

'Whose bastard are you carrying?' he shouted savagely, pulling her hair so hard she could hear it tearing at the roots. 'Whose is it?'

'Stop, please, you're hurting me,' she squealed, as perspiration prickled her scalp.

'Tell me, or I'll beat it out of you!' he snarled.

Eva stared into his angry face, as he tightened his grip round her hair. She opened her mouth to speak, but all she emitted was a pitiful squeal.

'Whose is it?' he yelled, as he slammed her head against the bathroom wall. Eva screamed and muttered a name, then fell to the floor to the sound of Franco evacuating his bowels.

8

The ferry from Piraeus sailed into view just as Yiannis moored the Tempests' yacht against the quay. Both he and Kostas had tried in vain to start Charles's motorboat, so in the end they had no option but to bring the yacht to harbour.

When the ferry docked between the colourful flotilla of fishing and pleasure boats, Charles was first to disembark. He looked tired and weary.

'What a journey,' he said to Yiannis, fanning himself with his hat.

'It's good to have you back sir. I'm sorry I've had to bring the yacht.'

Charles crinkled his nose. 'Motorboat wouldn't start eh? Never mind.'

'Here let me help.' Yiannis reached for his luggage.

'It's okay, I can manage these. Would you mind getting Laura? She's on the seat over there, I'm afraid she has been terribly sick.'

The little girl had curled up on the hard wooden bench and didn't attempt to move when Yiannis approached her. Her red and white gingham dress was wet and stained with vomit and one brown sandal lay abandoned under the bench. Her long blonde hair clung to her clammy forehead and she clutched a teddy bear close to her tear-stained face. Her eyes opened when Yiannis gently slipped his hands under her body and lifted her gently into his arms, mindful of her still bandaged leg. She slipped her arms around his neck and snuggled into his chest, whimpering at being moved.

'It's okay little one, you're nearly home now.' Yiannis cooed softly, bending down to pick her shoe up before making his way carefully down the gangplank.

Kostas was helping Charles and Gwen to load their luggage into the yacht as Yiannis said tenderly, 'Okay

Laura, I'm just going to pass you back to your grandpa.'

Laura's body tensed in his arms. 'Oh no, please don't make me go on another boat.' She sobbed and tightened her grip around his neck. 'I'll be sick again!'

'Hush now, this one isn't like the big boat. It won't make you poorly, I promise,' Yiannis reassured her.

'It will!' she protested, clinging to him for protection.

Gwen dabbed herself with her handkerchief. 'Oh for goodness sake Charles, just get hold of the silly child. I want to get home!'

Yiannis kept a firm hold on Laura. 'If I may sir, I'll stay here with her for a while, just until she recovers a little and then I'll bring her along when you've had a chance to settle in.'

Charles hesitated and looked at Gwen who was busying herself with the cases. 'I'm sure you have better things to do Yiannis.'

'Nothing that can't wait.'

'Well, if you're sure.'

'Absolutely, I'll be along soon.'

Charles nodded thankfully and stepped down into the yacht. As he started the motor, Laura's tense body relaxed in Yiannis's arms as she turned to watch them sail away.

Yiannis placed her down and took her hand. 'Okay let's get you a drink. You will soon feel better.'

Settling her on a chair at the back of Alexis Taverna, Yiannis took a bottle of water from the refrigerator and poured it into the glass. He pulled a chair up and sat down next to her. 'Here you go, sip that slowly. It will take the nasty taste away.'

With her eyes full of tears she said, 'Grandma made me eat a barley sugar before we got on the boat. She said she didn't want me to be sick. But I don't like barley sugar. I told her, but she wouldn't listen.'

Yiannis smiled thinly as he poured some of the remaining water into a napkin and set about wiping the tear and vomit stains from her face and arms.

Laura sipped the water calmly, feeling totally at ease with this stranger. She watched him intently as the light caught his mesmerising blue eyes. It made them sparkle. He had a very nice friendly face, and Laura liked him instantly. When a gentle breeze lifted the dark glossy hair from his face, she noticed for the first time a dark mark under his right eye.

'What's that?' she said, placing her finger on the mark.

'It's a birthmark. Do you like it? It looks like a strawberry, yes?'

'Yes. Where's my birthmark?' she enquired.

'Well not everyone has one.'

'Why have you got one?'

'Well, it's so you will always recognise me.'

She looked at the mark for a few seconds then turned her attention to the colourful fishing boats in the harbour. She sat thoughtfully for a while, took another sip of the water then placed it carefully on the table and said, 'How will you recognise me if I don't have a strawberry on my face?'

Yiannis tenderly brushed the hair from her brow. 'No one could ever forget you. You're the prettiest little girl on the island! Isn't she Alexis?' He tossed the question to Alexis who was watching the two of them with mild curiosity.

Alexis flipped his tea towel over his shoulder and came to stand at their table. 'I've never seen a prettier little girl on the island. She's like a princess.'

Laura smiled, enjoying the attention.

'I'm honoured to have you in my restaurant,' Alexis said, bowing low to her.

Laura grinned and raised her eyebrows. 'I'm not a princess,' she whispered to Yiannis.

'You're our little princess,' he whispered. 'Now I'm going to take you home. Say goodbye to Alexis?' He lifted her off the chair.

'Bye bye,' she said sweetly, waving to Alexis, then

slipped her small hand into Yiannis's and skipped happily towards the harbour's edge.

'Do you feel better now?'

Laura nodded hesitantly.

'Good.'

He led her closer to the harbours edge. 'Here we go, this is my boat. She's called Moondancer.' He pointed to the sixteen foot blue and white fishing boat bobbing lazily in the crystal-clear water.

She faltered at the sight of it. 'I don't want to be sick in your lovely boat!' she said firmly.

'I promise you won't be,' he said, holding his hand to his heart. 'This is a special boat.'

Laura eyed him suspiciously. It looked like an ordinary boat to her! 'Why is it called Moondancer?'

'I'll tell you when you get in. Come on.' He lifted Laura into his arms and walked down the harbour steps, placing her very carefully into the boat so as not to rock it. He sat her down on the painted blue wooden slats that stretched the width of the boat then flipped the rope from its tie. 'There you go, steady as a rock, yes?'

Laura nodded, and hoped her stomach would behave.

'Ready?'

Laura shook her head as tears filled her eyes.

'No tears allowed in this boat! I need you to be able to see if anything is coming, and you won't be able to do that if you're crying, will you?'

Laura looked blankly at him.

'Okay, we're heading over there.' He pointed to the headland in front of them. 'Is anything coming?'

Laura looked around nervously and shook her head as Yiannis yanked the starter cord.

The outboard motor sprang into life and he carefully manoeuvred the boat away from the harbour wall. 'You okay?' he asked.

Laura nodded.

A few minutes into the journey a shoal of fish swam

aside the boat. 'Look!' Yiannis nodded towards them.

Cautiously she glimpsed over the side of the boat into the pellucid water to witness the psychedelic display of fish as they gyrated in unison, glinting like jewels as the sunlight caught them. Her eyes were full of excitement. 'Oh aren't they pretty?'

'They're escorting you home! I shall have to teach you how to catch them in a net so you can see them better. Would you like that?'

Laura looked thoughtful. 'Can we put them back after we catch them?'

'But of course.'

They passed the first headland and Laura watched in awe as the sea lapped and sucked against the rocky inlets. She glanced again at Yiannis and he smiled warmly at her.

'Would you like to steer?'

She shook her head violently.

'Why not?'

'I don't know how,' she said in earnest.

'It's easy, come, try.' He took her hand and steadied her as she moved from her seat to sit next to him. Then he placed her hand on the rudder with his own large hand on top of hers. 'There, you're the captain now, just keep this distance away from the rocks and you'll be fine, okay?'

'Yes,' she said, holding her breath. Sheer concentration etched her face as she bit her lip and held onto the rudder as though her life depended on it.

'Don't stop breathing,' he laughed.

'You do it now,' she said, letting go of the rudder.

'Is that it? Do I have to do all the work now?'

'Yes.' She folded her arms. 'You said you would tell me why your boat is called Moondancer,' she asked quizzically. 'It can't dance with the moon!' she added.

He patted the side of the boat. 'Oh yes it can! Sometimes when I'm out in her fishing at night and the moon is bright in the sky. That's when it happens. The moon sends a golden shaft of light across the sea like a river of gold. All it takes is a gentle movement from the Moondancer and suddenly the golden moonlight bursts into thousands of sparkling jewels, covering the surface of the sea.' He looked at Laura's mesmerised face and added, 'You can come with me one night if you want?'

She clasped her hand together. 'Oh when, tonight?'

'No little one, not tonight, we'll have to get you settled in first, but I promise I will speak to your grandpa and we can all go out one night soon.'

As they sailed closer to Amora Cove, Yiannis slowed the boat down as he approached the notorious Midnight Rocks, a large underwater shelf visible only in the daytime, where many an unsuspecting vessel had come to grief in the hours of darkness.

As the boat sailed slowly around the last headland, Yiannis cut the motor, as they both took in the splendour of the vista before their eyes. 'I always like to drift for a moment whenever I come over to Amora Cove. It is such a beautiful sight, is it not? I believe it is the most beautiful villa on the island.'

Laura glanced up at the villa. The last time she had been here was three weeks ago with her mother and Steve. That was when all the trouble had started. But Laura pushed that to the back of her mind. If she didn't think about it, maybe it would go away.

To the right of the beach, against the backdrop of emerald green Cyprus trees and a powder blue sky stood Villa Amora. The brilliant white building with its burnt orange tiled roof, speckled golden with lichen, dazzled in opulence under the late morning sun.

'Do you live here as well?' She turned to look at Yiannis.

'Unfortunately not.'

'Why?'

'Because I have a house and business near the harbour.'

'Can't you come and live here with us? Grandpa won't mind I'm sure.'

He laughed gently. 'No, but I will come and see you,' he added.

'Everyday?'

Knowing that he delivered fresh fish to Villa Amora most days, he answered confidently, 'I'll see what I can do.'

She smiled with satisfaction.

'Look, your grandpa's up there, wave to him.'

Charles stood on the sun terrace amongst a froth of crimson bougainvillaea and waved back. He beckoned Gwen out to join him.

'What is it? ' Gwen emerged from the villa with her arms full of dirty washing. 'I'm busy.'

'Look at these two.' Charles nodded to the tiny fishing boat anchored a few yards from the Midnight Rocks. The sickly little girl they had left an hour ago was now standing secure in the arms of Yiannis chatting and giggling excitedly.

'Well the little madam! She doesn't look very seasick now does she?'

Charles grimaced. 'Oh come now Gwen, you should be happy that she's laughing again, after the terrible time she's been through.'

Gwen's pursed her lips. 'Well, we have all been through terrible time. It's just something we will all have to learn to live with,' she answered shortly as she walked back into the villa.

'Grandpa, look at me!' Laura shouted excitedly.

Charles waved again, and made his way down to the beach.

'Grandpa I can sail, Yiannis showed me, didn't you Yiannis?'

Yiannis nodded as he tied the rope to the mooring ring. He lifted her carefully out of the boat and she stood and waited for him to follow. Quite naturally she slipped her hand in his and pulled him towards her Grandpa.

Charles swept her into his arms. 'Well I must say Laura

you're looking a lot better than when we left you!'

'I feel a lot better. Yiannis gave me a drink and showed me how to sail and told me about the fish and the moon that dances didn't you Yiannis?' she said in one breath.

'It looks like he cleaned you up as well,' Gwen said, descending the steps behind them.

'Yes, Yiannis washed my hands and face but my dress smells awful.' She reached round to the button fastening at the back. 'I want to take it off.'

'Wait a minute, you can take it off when we get you inside. Say goodbye to Yiannis, and thank him for looking after you.'

Laura ran to Yiannis and reached up to plant a warm soft kiss on his cheek. 'Thank you Yiannis, you're my best friend.'

Yiannis raised his eyebrow towards Charles. 'You're my best friend too little one.'

They watched as Laura skipped alongside Gwen. At the top of the steps she turned for a last wave.

Charles laughed. 'Well I don't know what you did Yiannis, but you've worked wonders. We could hardly get a word out of her. We were beginning to wonder what on earth we had taken on. I didn't know you had a way with children!'

'Neither did I!' Yiannis answered coyly. 'I've never been any good with them before. She just took to me for some reason, but I have to admit she's a lovely little girl - a real ray of sunshine.'

'A real handful as well I'll wager,' Charles mused. 'Tell me Yiannis, did she mention anything about the accident to you?'

'No, I didn't like to speak of it, for fear of upsetting her.'

'The doctors say she doesn't remember a thing about it. She hasn't even mentioned her parents!'

'She could be blocking it out. Some people do when they have been through a traumatic time!'

Charles sighed heavily. 'Well I'm not looking forward to the day she does remember, we're not counsellors! I don't know how we are going to cope.'

'Well if I can help in any way, you know where I am.'

'Thank you my boy, but I'm sure you have enough on your plate with the Athena.'

'Honestly it's no problem. If you need me, I'm here,' he said, climbing back into his boat.

'Will you bring us fish in the morning?'

'Of course. I'll call here first with my catch.'

Charles waved in acknowledgement and Yiannis set sail back towards the harbour.

9

Back at the Athena, Yiannis found Andreas sprawled across the steps leading up to the bar, having obviously fallen off one of the barstools.

'Oh no, I'd forgotten all about you!' he said, rolling him over with his foot. 'Get up Andreas I need to open the taverna.'

Andreas moaned and cradled the empty bottle in the crook of his arm.

Yiannis picked it up. 'Not my best cognac!' he said slapping him.

'Ouch, what's the matter, what are you hitting me for?' He curled himself up in a ball and belched noisily.

Not quite forgiving him for pushing him into the clutches of Eva Barzini, Yiannis aimed the hose pipe at Andreas, and turned on the tap.

Coughing and spluttering, Andreas pleaded for him to stop.

'Come on move!' Yiannis wrenched Andreas to his feet, marched him to the door, and pushed him into the street.

'Hey,' Andreas grumbled as he sat in the road. 'What sort of friend are you?'

'The sort who doesn't make you pay for drinking my finest cognac. Now, clear off, before I change my mind.'

'You make me sick!' Andreas wagged his finger at him. 'You think you're better than anybody else because you have Mr bloody Tempest's patronage.' He staggered backward and fell to the floor. 'Christ, you've even had Eva Barzini, when you knew I wanted her, you make me bloody sick!'

Yiannis pursed his lips as he watched Andreas get up then promptly fall over the bench that ran the circumference of the great plane tree. He picked himself up again, kicked the bench then staggered across the square cursing at the top of his voice.

With his chef Dimitra off that day, Yiannis was kept busy in the kitchen. With his mind preoccupied with the enchanting little Laura, he didn't pay much attention to the Barzini brothers when they settled down at the table nearest the entrance.

The Athena had been extremely busy all evening, buzzing with lively chatter and laughter, so when his waiters George and Manolis left the Taverna at midnight, their pockets were generously lined with tips.

Just after midnight Kostas entered the restaurant. He cautiously acknowledged Marcos and Franco then settled himself down on a barstool.

'Drink?' Yiannis said, pouring two glasses of Ouzo.

'Thanks,' he said, draining the glass. 'How long have those two been here?' Kostas whispered.

Yiannis glanced surreptitiously at them. 'They've been sat there scowling most of the evening. At least they didn't put the customers off,' he joked lightly. 'It's been non-stop all evening. I thought this was meant to be the end of the season!' He wiped the tea cloth over a glass and held it up to the light then placed it on the shelf with the others he had just washed and dried. 'Want another drink?' he asked filling the glasses before Kostas answered.

'I'm sure those two creeps are watching us,' Kostas said under his breath.

Yiannis glanced nervously at his watch. 'I wish they would go home, I could do with my bed,' he said, stifling a yawn.

A flash of lightning lit the night sky. 'Another storm coming!'

Yiannis nodded.

They both looked up anxiously at the sound of chairs scraping across the floor as the brothers rose from their table, drained their glasses then left.

'Goodnight,' Yiannis called after them. They didn't answer.

'Thank God they've gone,' said Kostas, as he flicked the lights off over the barbecue and set about clearing the table they had just vacated. Another flash of lightning was swiftly followed by a crack of thunder.

'It's okay Kostas, give me those glasses, I'll clear up, you get off before it rains. I'll see you tomorrow.'

Yiannis placed the last of the chairs under the table and cocked his head. He was sure he heard something. It must be thunder he thought, as he unhooked the door from the catch on the wall. Suddenly the door was wrenched from his grasp and Marcos had pinned him down by the throat against one of the tables.

'Do you want to guess why we're here?' Marcos hissed.

'M..Money?' Yiannis gasped, trying to ease Marcos's grasp from his neck.

Marcos tightened his grip. 'Yes money, and what else do you think you owe us?'

Yiannis felt his throat burn. 'I have nothing else to give you,' he spluttered.

'Now that's not strictly true. You have the taverna, it's yours isn't it?'

Yiannis felt his heart drop.

Marcos grinned arrogantly. 'Well it belongs to Eva as well now!'

Yiannis's eyes widened. 'Eva?'

Marcos gave a contemptuous snort. 'Don't look so surprised. You didn't think you were going to get away with it did you?'

Yiannis felt the bile rise in his throat. 'I don't know what you're talking about.'

Marcos bared his lips. 'You take her, you keep her.'

Yiannis pulled frantically at the fingers around his neck. 'I haven't touched her,' he choked.

Again Marcos sneered. 'That's not what she says.'

Yiannis was stunned into silence.

Marcos lifted Yiannis's head off the table then crashed it back down. 'I know you have been in my sister's bedroom, and I know what you did there.'

Yiannis's eyes welled up with fright. 'I didn't touch her. I swear I didn't.'

'So how come she's pregnant?' Marcos yelled, as saliva foamed at his mouth.

Yiannis bristled indignantly. 'Well it certainly isn't mine!'

Marcos grabbed a fist full of his hair. 'She says it is.'

Beads of sweat had formed on Yiannis's upper lip. 'Well, she's lying!'

Marcos lifted Yiannis by the hair. 'So not only do you use my house to have sex with my sister, but now you're calling her a liar.'

Yiannis's breathing became very shallow as Marcos stared straight at him. He was so sure that Marcos was going to kill him that he said a silent prayer as he waited for the final blow to come.

'Franco, go and get Eva,' Marcos said, pushing Yiannis down onto a chair. 'She can stay here until we arrange the wedding.'

'No, she can't!' Yiannis protested.

With that, Marcos threw a sickening blow to the side of Yiannis's head.

When Franco returned with Eva, she found Yiannis propped up behind the great oak door, his face was a pulp of swollen purple flesh and a trickle of blood ran from his nostrils to congeal with the dried blood on his split lip.

Her hands shot to her face. 'What have you done to him?' She moved towards him.

'Leave him,' Marcos yanked her back with great force. 'He's all right.'

'He's not all right! Eva screamed. 'You've nearly killed him!'

'Shut up. I've just made him own up to his responsibilities,' he said, kicking Yiannis on the shin. 'Franco, pick him up.'

'Where are you taking him?' Eva shrieked.

'Upstairs,' he grabbed Eva by the arm. 'Get your bony backside up there with him and see to him.'

Eva and Yiannis were dragged past the bar, through the back room and up the wooden stairs. At the top of the landing Marcos kicked open the first door he came to.

'Get in!' Marcos barked at Eva as they threw Yiannis into his father's old room slamming the door behind them.

Yiannis pulled himself to his knees as laughter echoed down the stairway as the brothers retreated. He reached for the wooden chair in the corner of the room and dragged himself onto it. With his head in his hands he trembled with anger.

Eva sat on the edge of the bed, smoothed her hands over the knitted bedcover, and looked around her new surroundings. The room smelt a little musty, but it was a vast improvement on the accommodation at the Ice Palace. A couple of hours cleaning would get it ship-shape. She smiled inwardly; she was going to settle here just fine she thought. It was not what she had originally planned, but it would have to do.

She glanced at Yiannis and cooed softly, 'Come over here and let me clean you up a bit.' She patted the bed, but he ignored her. 'Oh come on Yiannis, it's not the end of the world. We could have some fun you and I.' She moved and knelt at his feet. 'I'm really sorry for what Marcos has done to you. He can be such a brute sometimes.' She reached up as though to touch his face.

He swiped her hand away. 'Don't touch me.' The look he gave her was one of sheer hatred.

Eva pulled back for a moment indignantly. 'Oh dear, I hope you're not going to sulk all night, some people would be glad to be in your shoes. I'm quite a catch you know. All your friends think so, especially Andreas.'

Unable to control his anger, he picked up the chair and threw it to the wall, smashing the picture that hung there. 'Why have you done this to me? I told you I wasn't interested in you. Why did you say the baby is mine, when you know it isn't?'

She flinched slightly then began to walk around the starkly furnished room, running her fingers across the table then rubbing the dust in between her fingers. She picked up a vase on the table, looked at it with disdain then replaced it. With a pained look on her face she turned and said indignantly, 'Of course the baby is yours, I can't understand why you keep denying it.'

He rubbed the back of his neck in sheer agitation. 'You know I was incapable of doing anything that night!'

Eva smiled wryly. 'All I know is that you came to my room for sex, it happened, and *you* ruined my reputation.'

'I….,' he clasped his palm to his chest, '…ruined your reputation?' He laughed sardonically. 'You're are a scheming lying whore, and my conscience is clear when it comes to ruining your reputation. You can do that yourself without any help from me!' Shaking with rage now, he paced up and down the room, wiping the blood from his nostrils with the back of his hand.

'For goodness sake Yiannis, sit down. You can't alter what has happened. We are having a baby together and that is that.' She placed her hand on her stomach. 'So, the only decent thing you can do now is to marry me.'

'Decent! Decent! You don't know the meaning of the word!' he shouted angrily.

Suddenly the door flew open and Marcos stood in the doorway. 'Are you having trouble with him Eva?'

She glanced at Yiannis who was ridged with cold fear. 'Nothing I can't handle thank you,' she said sarcastically.

'I'll silence him if you want,' he said, pinning Yiannis to the wall by the throat.

'No Marcos,' Eva pleaded. 'Just leave us please.'

Marcos released his grip from Yiannis's neck and spat on his fist and rubbed it menacingly into his palm. 'I don't want to hear another squeak from you - we can't hear ourselves think downstairs for the racket you're making.' He slammed Yiannis into the wall and left the room.

The blow to the head made Yiannis see stars for a moment. He stood against the wall dazed and unsure what to do next. Sick, weary and incredibly frightened, he knew he must get out of here somehow.

'Come on Yiannis.' Eva moved towards him. 'Stop fighting it. You can't win with Marcos, you know that!'

He could smell her sickly perfume as she invaded his personal space. Everything about this woman sickened him. Unable to control his anger, he pushed her backwards with such force the she staggered and fell onto the bed. 'I do *not* accept this situation and you and that baby you are carrying can rot in hell for all I care!' he yelled. 'Do I make myself clear?'

'Crystal,' she said tartly. 'Marcos!' She screamed at the top of her voice.

When he heard footsteps on the stairs Yiannis leapt towards the window, wrenched it open with such ferocity the glass cracked and shattered about his feet. As the door burst open behind him he attempted to scramble out of the tiny opening.

'Grab his legs Franco,' barked Marcos.

As they yanked him back into the room, splinters of glass tore his hands as he frantically grasped at the window frame. He landed with a thud, face down on the wooden floor. They dragged him mercilessly into the middle of the room where Franco sat on him, dragged his arms up his back and held him securely.

'Get him on his feet,' Marcos snapped. 'Right hold him there.' He punched Yiannis in his stomach then caught his chin as his head fell to his chest. Blood splattered across the room as he was dropped onto the floor. He curled up in the foetal position, gasping in pain, spitting blood from a split in his gum.

'I think he'll behave now,' Marcos said, rubbing the fist he had just used. 'Won't you?' he gave a final kick in the back. Yiannis just covered his head with his arms.

'Get hold of him Franco, we'll put him somewhere he

can cool off.'

Dazed, battered and barely conscious he felt himself being dragged down the stairs - his body hurt so much now he hardly cared any more what they did to him. He managed to open one of his swollen eyes to see the familiar surroundings of the old kafeneion. He tried to grasp for the leg of one of the wooden benches, but Marcos stamped on his hand. He could hear Eva's voice somewhere in the background, pleading with them not to take him away, and then he heard a loud thwack as Eva was silenced.

Vaguely aware of where they were taking him, Yiannis braced himself as he heard the cellar door being kicked open. In one fell swoop he was thrown unceremoniously down the stone steps. As the door slammed shut behind him, he was in total darkness. Laying face down on the cold dank floor he was unwilling and incapable of movement. There was numbness where pain had once been and he felt cold, so very cold, like the blood in his veins had turned to ice. He was tired now, there was no more fight in him, and wondered wistfully, if he closed his eyes, would death come? He didn't care any more. It was clear he had lost everything. His livelihood, his possessions, and his liberty! He tried unsuccessfully to move his lifeless limbs, closed his eyes and the last thing he remembered before drifting into unconsciousness was the sensation of a soft moist kiss on his cheek, and the sound of a little girl telling him he was her best friend.

He regained consciousness when he felt his scalp prickle. He thought for a moment he was laid on a hillside amongst the scratchy undergrowth of gorse bushes – but instead of the smell of wild thyme and pine trees, his nose filled with the pungent stench of stale vegetables and damp mould. Running his tongue across the inside of his lips, he spat the filth and grime out in disgust. His eyes grew more accustomed to the dark. Shadows and movement were visible to his gritty eyes. Something pricked his scalp again.

As he moved his head a greasy brown cellar rat slithered down his face. Yiannis cried out in terror. Ever since he had been a small boy he had had a mortal fear of these disgusting animals. His blood ran cold when he felt something nip his ankle. Another rat was feasting on his flesh, pulling and tearing at him with its razor like teeth.

He wrenched his battered body onto all fours, the movement scattering a dozen such rats that had made their home amongst his warm clothing. His body shivered in horror as their sharp claws drummed across his body in frightened retreat. Fear overtook the pain as he pulled his aching body across the slimy floor towards the cellar steps, listening to the rats as they scurried away in all directions in the darkness. Taking short shallow breaths, he tried to pull himself together. He had to get out of here somehow. A sensation down his leg made him believe that blood was trickling down it, but on investigation, he felt the familiar long hard body of a rat as it tunnelled its way up his trouser leg. Whacking the vermin with all the strength he could muster, it finally dropped to the floor, but as he tried to kick it away, it clung to his sock defiantly. Pain wracked his body with the exertion, but he kicked it with his other foot again and again, pummelling it long after it gasped its terminal breath. Spent, disgusted, but strangely exhilarated at his triumph, Yiannis collapsed against the dank wall.

He gave himself a moment and then pulled his raw bruised body slowly up the cellar steps. At the top he lifted the door catch - it clicked but would not open. Through the keyhole he could see a glimmer of light from the bar, but all was quiet. He sighed, put his back to the door, and scanned the darkened room. He knew the only other way out was the delivery yard doors at the far side of the cellar, but they were secured with a padlock and the key was behind the bar. It was hopeless. He placed his head in his hands and contemplated his impending fate.

Another violent storm began to rage outside. A crack of thunder shook the old building. Rain began to pour in through the wooden slats of the delivery yard doors. Soon the rush of water from the mountains would come gushing down the hillsides. The locals would be listening for the telltale roar of the torrent of water descending. Slumbering cats would prick their ears - arched and hissing at the unseen invader, they would make ready to scale great heights to escape when necessary. Women would drag their washing from the line, and pile rows of flower filled terracotta pots inside their houses. Then the great wall of water would hammer past the whitewashed houses, transforming the narrow twisting alleyways into a rapid river of rocks and debris which flowed down to the harbour and into the sea.

He stopped mid thought. It was only a matter of time before the water came up the grate at the far end of the building and then the cellar would flood. The grate! That was it!

He hauled himself painfully to his feet and stepped back onto the slimy cellar floor tapping and dragging his foot along the stone floor until his feet found the manhole cover. He knelt down and listened, he could hear rushing water! 'Yes!' he whispered triumphantly.

There was a culvert beneath the cellar which ran the length of the taverna and out under the road to the sea, approximately one hundred yards away. He remembered once dropping a toy boat down the grate. He ran like the wind to the seashore to watch it appear from the outlet and plop into the sea. He just hoped for his sake that the culvert was large enough for a man to go down!

He dropped to his knees and pulled at the rusty ring catch on the grate but it was stuck hard. 'Come on,' he said desperately, as he grasped the ring with both hands. Tensing his aching muscles he pulled with all his strength. As the exertion prickled his body with beads of sweat, the scabs on his wounds split and bled again. Suddenly it gave way. He tumbled backwards, letting the grate fly from his hands. It landed with a deafening clatter on the cellar floor.

With bated breath he prayed the noise had not roused them upstairs. No one came. Crawling back to the gaping hole he ran his hand around its edge trying to gauge the size of the opening. It felt large enough, but in this blackness, it was almost impossible to judge accurately.

He swung his legs over the hole, dangled his feet in the rushing water and then slowly began to lower himself down into the watery darkness. Half way down he stopped, extended his elbows outwards and hung suspended across the manhole. He grimaced as the rough rusty edges of the manhole cut into the fleshy part of his underarms, but he dare not let go. There was movement again on the cellar floor. The rats were coming.

'Oh God help me,' he prayed, as he eased himself lower down into the culvert. Holding on now with his fingertips, his muscles burned with fatigue, and his heart raced as the force of the water battered him. His chest heaved as he took great gulps of air; he knew he would have to hold his breath for a long time. The power of the water was dragging him now beyond the point of no return, he could hold on no longer. When a rat ran across his hands, he screamed and let go.

He had greatly underestimated the force of the water. Almost as soon as he let go, his head was forced forward so violently that he was immediately winded. He was swept along at such incredible speed he didn't see the stone ledge that jutted out from the side of the culvert until his rib cage rammed against it. Unable to move, Yiannis endured the pounding relentless torrent of water as it pelted his body, until finally it dragged him mercilessly away from the ledge.

Barely conscious, he hardly felt the impact when his feet slammed into another stone ledge and thrust his knees to his chest. Seconds later he was pushed forwards until his arms splayed over another great rock, making him embrace the object as though it were a lover. Exhausted now, the great wall of water roared in his ears and battered his body. Slowly he forced his grit-filled eyes to open and peered wearily downstream. Could he see moonlight? He moaned involuntarily as he tried to move his body off the ledge. Gasping and choking for air, his struggle dislodged the huge rock and together they tumbled down until they crashed into the wire mesh guard at the end of the culvert.

He was now wedged tight against the wire guard. The rock he had loosened further upstream had trapped his legs, and he was now being bombarded with tonnes of rubble and debris, each piece hammering him further against the mesh. He panicked as he started to suffocate, his ribs already hurt from the blow to his chest from the collision with the ledge, and his breath came in short panting phases. He grasped the gate and shook it in desperation, but it wouldn't move! He was sure he was going to die! A boulder struck the mesh narrowly missing his leg then a wall of debris behind him shifted forwards and began to push him closer to his death. A strange wail came from the pit of his stomach as his eyes, wide open, looked around his tomb. He willed death to come then he would feel no more pain, then he heard a loud crack! The gate moved forward, followed quickly by a loud thwack as the rusty fastenings at the bottom of the grate began to break loose. All at once the wires began to rip from their casing. He felt himself move. The force of debris behind him was pushing the lower half of his body through the tiny opening. He felt the jagged edges of the wire gouge the flesh of his shins and he cried in agony. Inch by inch his battered body was slowly squeezed through the gap like steak in a mincing machine. Panic welled up in him as he felt the metal graze the skin on his thighs. A gut instinct urged him to try and protect his manhood, and he desperately tried to climb upwards, but the force behind him continued to push him down. In a last ditch attempt, he managed to push his body away from the gate to give himself enough leverage to get one of his hands down towards his groin. A second later and just before he was finally squeezed through the opening and spat out into the sea, he managed to cup his genitals in the palms of his hands before the razor sharp edge could rip them to shreds.

10

For the last thirty minutes, Richard Jameson had lain awake in the cabin of the eight-birth luxury chartered yacht, listening to the rain drumming rhythmically on the deck above him. He glanced first at the illuminated dials of the clock - it was ten past three - then at his wife Marjory who slept soundly in the next bunk. He was sure he could hear something other than the rain – as though something was knocking on the side of the hull. Rising from his bunk, he pulled on his dressing gown, grabbed his cigarette case by habit, and climbed out onto the deck to investigate. The rain was much lighter than it sounded down below. Soon it would cease and the storm would blow away over the Peloponnese. He drew a deep breath of the clean night air and lit a cigarette. Very satisfyingly he inhaled then blew the smoke out into the night. It was then that he noticed something in the water. On closer inspection it looked like a body floating on a wooden pallet. Alerting his weary crew from their sleeping quarters, he ordered them to fish the body out.

'Is he alive?' Jameson said anxiously to the crew member who had jumped overboard.

'I don't know,' he sputtered, struggling to keep afloat.

'Bring him over here and we'll get him aboard then,' Jameson instructed. With the aid of a long handed fishhook, the two men aboard managed to heave the lifeless body onto the deck.

'Richard! What on earth is going on up here?' Jameson's wife demanded, as she ascended the galley steps. Seeing Yiannis's body she took a sharp intake of breath and shrieked. 'Who on earth is that?'

'Give him some room Marjory,' Jameson shouted, pulling her out of the way with some force. 'The poor chap could be dead!'

'What? You mean to say you've brought a dead body

aboard! Oh my goodness, what on earth are we going to do with him?'

One of the crew knelt down, turned Yiannis over, checked his wrist for a pulse then put his cheek to his mouth to feel for any breath.

'Well?' Jameson inquired impatiently.

'I think he's still alive sir, but he's in a bad way.'

Jameson scratched his chin thoughtfully. 'The poor lad looks like he's been in a fight, don't you think?'

'He looks like he's been mauled by something to me,' muttered the crewman to his colleague.

Jameson knelt beside Yiannis, who was naked but for one white sock and the tattered remains of his white vest wrapped around his neck. He tried to decide what he should do in this situation. He gently touched one of the deep gashes that ran the complete length of Yiannis's body. 'He's been in the water a while by the colour of these cuts,' he said, inspecting the other wounds which were now a pale shade of grey-purple. 'Marjory, get a blanket to cover him then we'll take him ashore.'

Marjory turned in shock and went below to retrieve a blanket.

Yiannis moaned in pain. He could see strange faces above him but could not move.

'Keep still old chap, you're all right now,' Jameson shouted. 'We're going to take you ashore. Is there anyone we can take you to?'

Dazed and confused Yiannis was unable to speak momentarily.

Marjory brought the blanket and covered Yiannis, while Richard Jameson checked Yiannis for broken bones. 'Can you move your feet?'

Yiannis painfully flexed his feet in response.

'Good chap, now your fingers.'

Yiannis splayed his bloodstained hands.

'Well that's good,' Jameson said encouragingly. He lifted Yiannis's right arm and Yiannis winced. 'Sorry old chap.' He knelt back on his haunches and sighed. 'Well, I don't think anything is broken, you're just very badly bruised and grazed.' He stood up and wiped his hands down his dressing gown. 'Let's see if we can get you back on dry land.'

It was three-fifty a.m. when the Jameson's yacht sailed into Poros harbour, but the place was deserted. He looked at his crew. 'It's very late, there doesn't seem to be anyone around. Perhaps we should take him to Piraeus.'

There was a mutter of despondency between them. They'd had a busy day and just wanted to get back to bed.

Noting their reluctance, Jameson knelt down beside Yiannis. 'We're in the harbour. Can we contact someone for you? Do you have some family we could contact?'

'Charles Tempest,' Yiannis whispered painfully.

'Sorry, who?'

'Charles Tempest in the next cove.' He tried to lift his finger to point.

'Right oh.' He turned to his crew. 'Well come on, you heard the chap, start the motor and we'll take him home to the next cove.'

The sound of the yacht motoring into Amora cove brought Charles to wakefulness. As he sat up in bed, Gwen stirred beside him.

'What is it?' she asked sleepily.

'Not sure. I think a boat has just moored in the cove,' he said, as he reached for his trousers.

Charles flicked the security lights on and heard a voice call out.

'Hello there. Sorry to disturb you so late. I'm looking for a Mr Tempest?'

'Yes I'm Tempest. What is it you want?'

'Oh jolly good. We've got a poor chap here, he's been in a bit of a scrape, he says he knows you.'

'Who is it?'

'We are not really sure. We picked him out of the water half an hour ago.'

Charles scratched his head in bewilderment then cautiously made his way down the beach steps.

'Come aboard, have a look. Wait a minute I'll send the launch.'

Charles looked long and hard at the dishevelled man on the deck, but at first he didn't recognise him.

Yiannis's eyes flickered open. 'It's me, Yiannis,' he cried pitifully.

Charles reeled back in shock. 'Oh good gracious me, what on earth...?'

Jameson heaved a sigh of relief. 'Oh thank goodness, you do know him. So it's okay to leave him with you is it?' He smiled hopefully.

Charles rubbed the back of his neck. 'Well yes but, it looks like he needs to go to hospital.'

'No, no, I've checked him all over and there are no broken bones or anything. I think he just needs cleaning up.'

Charles stood for a few seconds, unsure of what to do. He glanced at the villa then back at Yiannis. 'You had better bring him up to the villa,' Charles instructed the crew.

'Well come on you two.' Jameson encouraged the crew. 'Grab the edges of the blanket. Carefully now, and lift.'

After a painful bumpy journey up the beach steps, Yiannis was placed in one of the guest rooms.

'Lord, what on earth happened to him?' Gwen declared, as she fussed around him like a mother hen.

'Goodness knows. Let's just get him cleaned up.'

Gwen carefully bathed his bruised body, each touch inducing a painful eerie moaning sound, almost like a trapped and injured wild animal.

'Take it easy my boy,' Charles whispered as Gwen carefully applied iodine to his cuts, and dressed the wounds the best she could. When she'd finished she shook her head. Yiannis had fallen into some sort of delirium. He could feel the rats licking at the blood on his leg. He tossed and turned frantically. 'No, no more!' he moaned, shaking his head, flexing his painful fingers, and flaying his legs about the bed.

Charles dragged his fingers through his hair. 'He is in a bad way. I'm going for the doctor.'

Gwen looked up in alarm.

'I'll be as fast as I can.'

Gwen threw her hands in the air as Charles left her to deal with Yiannis. He continued to fight his inner demons for almost fifteen minutes, before he finally calmed down and began to relax. When she saw that Yiannis was sleeping, Gwen heaved a deep exhausted sigh and wiped the perspiration from her brow.

'Who's that man?' Laura asked innocently, as she stood in the doorway.

'Go back to bed!' Gwen snapped, ushering her away.

'But who is it?' Laura repeated.

'Nobody, now come on, back to bed.' She shooed her back into her bedroom.

Laura reluctantly made her way back into bed and Gwen placed her teddy bear under the covers with her.

'Now go to sleep, be a good girl.'

'Will Yiannis come tomorrow?' she asked hopefully.

'Go to sleep.'

Laura snuggled down. 'He's going to teach me how to fish!'

'Sleep!' Gwen snapped.

Gwen slumped on the sofa, cupping her head in her hands. That child was trying her patience. This was not how she planned to spend her twilight years.

Deciding a brandy would calm her ragged nerves she got up and poured a large one. Standing French doors she took a sip and looked out into the night.

She had no idea what she was going to do about Laura. She certainly didn't want her here for long. It had been enough of an ordeal putting up with her, Claire and her new husband for the duration of the summer. If it had been up to her, they would not have been invited. Unfortunately Charles doted on his granddaughter, so she had no say in the matter. Now, with this turn of events she was stuck with the child for the foreseeable future.

Gwen heaved a great sigh, before taking another sip of the brandy. She knew she was being unreasonable - it wasn't the child's fault that Gwen had disliked her daughter-in-law Claire, or that Laura mirrored her mother's image and temperament, but it was because of the latter, Gwen just could not take to her.

Her thoughts drifted to her darling son Stephen. She knew he had been unhappy with Claire, he had confided in her once about how he felt, but because of Laura, he felt obligated to stay with her. Oh, he could have done so much better for himself, Gwen thought angrily. Claire was never anything than a mediocre artist with a pretty face, who saw her son as a meal ticket!

She squeezed her eyes shut - the very thought of Stephen evoked such pain in her heart. He had been her life and she missed him terribly. A stray tear escaped down her cheek which she wiped away swiftly, when she heard the sound of a motor boat approaching the cove.

*

When Dr Pachis arrived at Villa Amora he was extremely disgruntled and to Gwen's amazement, alone.

'Excuse me, but where is my husband?' Gwen inquired, as the doctor breezed past her.

An odious man at the best of time, Dr Pachis retorted. 'I have no idea madam. Now, where is this patient who so desperately needs my attention in the middle of the night?'

Gwen bristled with indignation, at his manner. 'I apologise if your sleep has been disturbed, but you will of course be compensated for your trouble,' she answered sharply.

Dr Pachis gave a curt nod as Gwen led the way to the bedroom. His bedside manner with Yiannis left a lot to be desired, but this was nothing unusual. None of the inhabitants of Poros cared for Dr Pachis, in fact, most would rather administer their own cures than call for his help. It was safe to say, everyone looked forward to the day he retired.

After checking that there were no broken bones, except for five, possibly six cracked ribs, Dr Pachis assured Gwen that Yiannis didn't need hospitalising. He administered a shot for tetanus and a large dose of pain killers that would make Yiannis sleep for the next few hours. Picking up his medical bag, he grumbled something about young men fighting and promptly left, without so much as a by-your-leave.

It was another hour before Charles arrived back, very tired and very dirty.

'Where on earth have you been?' Gwen said in a mild panic.

'The damn motor is playing up again. It cut out a dozen times. I thought I was never going to get home. How's Yiannis?'

'He'll live,' she answered wearily. 'Can we get some sleep now? I'm exhausted.'

11

At six-thirty a.m. Eva crept down the Athena stairs. Broken chairs and glass littered the courtyard as Marcos and Franco lay inebriated in the back room of the taverna. She quietly unlocked the cellar door, flicked the light on, and stood halfway down the stone steps. She screwed her eyes up in the dim light and scanned the cellar for life. Wary of Yiannis after last night, she nervously called his name. Stepping down another step she noticed the open manhole.

'Marcos! Franco! I think you had better come down here, quick!' she shrieked.

Rubbing the sleep from their eyes, they all peered down into the watery blackness. 'The bastard's escaped!' Marcos growled angrily.

'Escaped, how?' Eva said quizzically. 'Where on earth could he have escaped to down there?'

'Rats know their way down sewers,' Marcos grizzled. 'You, stay here.' He jabbed Eva. 'I want breakfast on the table when I get back. Franco, you and I are going beachcombing.'

They arrived sweating and breathless at the outlet, glanced up at the twisted grate, and then looked out to sea for any evidence of a body.

'Come on, he'll be feeding the fish by now. Let's get back. I'm starving!' Franco whined.

Marcos continued to scan the sea for a few more seconds, curled his lip in disdain and snarled, 'If he's not dead now, he soon will be when I get my hands on him. Come on Franco, we have a new business to run!' He rubbed his hands in anticipation.

Eva took the news with mixed emotions, she had rather fancied herself as Yiannis's wife, but, if he was dead, and he surely must be, she would have his business instead. No one would dare object. Especially when they found out she was carrying his baby. There would be sympathy for her, as his bereaved pregnant bride-to-be. So without shedding a single tear for him, she donned an apron and set about preparing for the day's influx of visitors.

*

When Dimitra Aronis, the Athena chef breezed into the restaurant shortly after ten a.m. he eyed the Barzini brothers suspiciously. He joined the two women kitchen hands, as they prepared the vegetables and started to light the grill.

'Ah there you are.' Eva said, entering the kitchen with an air of authority. 'What time do you call this?'

Dimitra dismissed her distastefully. 'Where's Yiannis?' he asked coldly.

'He's away for a few days,' she declared.

Dimitra wiped his hand down his apron forcefully. 'No he isn't, he would have told me.'

'I'm telling you! So, get on with your job.'

He flashed his eyes angrily. 'I don't take my orders from you.'

She jutted her chin out. 'Well you'd better get used to it, because I live here now.' She flounced out of the kitchen and back into the bar.

'I don't think so,' he said, angrily ripping his apron off.

When Eva returned half an hour later to speak to Dimitra, she stopped short and scanned the room. 'Where's Dimitra gone?' she snapped at one of the women, who pointed to the gate.

Eva was incensed. 'Why the hell didn't you come and tell me, you stupid woman.'

The woman's lip trembled. She lifted her apron to her face to stifle a wail, whilst the other woman put a protective arm around her shoulder and led her out of the kitchen.

'Where the hell are you two going, you can't just leave!' she demanded, as the two women scurried out of the gate.

Franco looked up from his newspaper and grinned derisively at her. 'Staff trouble already?'

'Oh shut up!' she screeched.

*

Without a chef or any help at the Athena, the day went from bad to worse. By five that afternoon, word had swept across the island that Dimitra and the rest of the Athena staff had walked out. Yiannis had left, and the taverna was under new management.

'It's no wonder we've been rushed off our feet!' Alexis said on hearing the news from Akis as he stuffed another handful of Drachma notes into his till.

'Papa, I'm going to find Dimitra!' Kostas announced. 'Something is seriously wrong!'

'Not yet you're not,' Alexis said, as he grabbed Kostas by the shirtsleeve and yanked him back. 'We've all these customers to see to first!'

'But papa something has happened to Yiannis,' he protested.

'Later!' he snapped. 'Then we will both go and see him,' he added sympathetically.

To their relief, Dimitra came to them, and he too was clearly worried by the day's events.

Kostas listened ashen faced, shaking his head furiously. 'Yiannis wouldn't have gone away without telling me! And he certainly wouldn't have left those maniacs in charge, Papa. Something dreadful has happened to him, I just know it!'

'I do understand your concern Kostas, but we have a business to run!' Alexis said, acknowledging another influx of visitors as they descended on the taverna. 'This should be the last of them today, and then I think you two should go and see Charles Tempest. Maybe he'll know Yiannis's whereabouts.'

*

It was late afternoon before Yiannis opened his eyes and entered his world of pain and misery. As he tried to move, he cried out in agony, bringing Charles and Gwen running to his bedside.

'Yiannis keep still my boy,' Charles said, stroking his hot forehead. 'Give him a sip of water Gwen.'

Yiannis drank thirstily, then choked, and cried out as he held his arms to his stomach. He took several shallow breaths, licked his cracked lips and tried to mouth something to Charles.

'What's that? I'm sorry, I can't hear you,' Charles said, putting his ear to Yiannis's mouth.

'I need to pee.'

'What did he say?' Gwen asked.

'Err, he wants some tea,' Charles said, leading Gwen out of the bedroom.

Yiannis groaned.

'It's okay Yiannis I heard what you said. I'll be back in a moment,' Charles assured him. He returned and presented Yiannis with an empty wine carafe. 'Sorry son, it's all I can find!' he said, strategically placing it in-between his thighs.

'Remind me not to take the wine if I dine here,' Yiannis whispered painfully.

'It's good to see you still have a sense of humour,' Charles quipped.

Yiannis grimaced with relief as he emptied his bladder into the bottle. '1980 Vintage!' he declared.

Charles grinned and quickly removed the carafe of blood red urine before the donor saw it. When he returned from the bathroom Gwen was placing the cup of tea by his bedside, but Yiannis had drifted off to sleep again.

'Come.' He ushered Gwen out of the bedroom. 'Let him sleep. We will have to wait a while longer before we know what's happened.'

Laura was sitting quietly in the lounge when Charles walked in. Unaware of her presence he walked over to the French windows. He loved this room for its light airiness. He loved the way the full-length voile curtains billowed softly with the warm breeze. He stepped outside to take in the breathtaking view beyond the sun terrace, took a deep breath of air, and drank in the heady perfume of gorse and pine. He scratched his ear lobe as he thought of Yiannis. Had he been in some sort of collision with another boat whilst out fishing? The doctor had extracted fragments of rust from his shins, which could well have come from the metal hull of a ship. But it was the bruises that troubled him most. They looked like they had been inflicted with a fist! He had an awful feeling that there was something very sinister about the whole thing. The sooner he got the full story from Yiannis the better.

He stepped back into the lounge and idly ran his finger around the rim of one of the large urns standing at each side of the French windows. His eye was drawn towards the two large white sofas facing each other in front of the unlit log fire. There was a comic book on the glass coffee table, where the usual Vogue magazines lay, and a puddle of lemonade glistened on the polished wooden floor from an upturned glass. Charles sucked in his breath. He'd better mop that up before Gwen saw it. As he moved forward, he noticed that Laura was curled up amongst the cushions on one of the sofas, hugging her teddy bear. Poor little mite, Charles thought, she looked so small and vulnerable. This house seems to be full of tragedies at the moment (he thought.)

'Laura darling, don't you want to be outside on a lovely day like this?' he said, mopping the spillage of lemonade with his handkerchief.

She jumped slightly when he spoke. 'I'm waiting for Yiannis. He said he would come and see me today,' she said shyly.

Charles sighed. 'Ah, well I'm afraid Yiannis isn't very well darling.'

'What's the matter with him?'

'He's had an accident, and hurt himself.'

'How did he hurt himself?'

He smiled gently at her. 'We don't know yet. Come on, let's get you outside.' He held out his hand and led her out into the warm afternoon sun.

'Grandpa?'

'Yes darling?'

'Is that man in the bedroom poorly too?'

'Yes he is.'

'Did he hurt himself?'

'Yes.'

Charles walked Laura to the end of the garden. Gwen was reading on a sun lounger at the far end of the terrace, but didn't look up. 'Why don't you go and explore before dinner?' he said, 'Leave your teddy bear with me.'

'No!' she said, quickly tucking her bear under her arm.

'It's all right you keep it, no problem. Off you pop then,' he said, patting her on her way.

'And don't get dirty!' Gwen shouted, without looking up from her book.

Charles made a mental count to ten and wished Gwen could be more accommodating with the child. He could not understand why she was so reluctant to help the little one settle in? He watched as Laura skipped down the terrace steps, and then turned to Gwen. 'I'm going back to work on the motor. Call me when Yiannis wakes again.'

Gwen nodded once without looking up from her book.

As soon as Laura reached the back of the villa, she reached up and pushed the teddy bear through the opening of her bedroom window for safekeeping. The first thing she was going to do was explore the square shaped white house, nestled at the bottom of the pine forest, which her grandpa had called the lodge. She'd watched intently for any signs of habitation all morning, but had seen none, and was now eager to investigate the dwelling.

When she had stayed here before, her mother hadn't allowed her to go exploring at all. They had just used the villa as a base. So, with excited anticipation she ran towards the lodge. Standing on the veranda, she glanced down to where her grandpa was working on his boat, and then tiptoed towards the front door. With bated breath, she tried the handle and pushed the door - it was locked! A few steps further brought her to a large window. With the grace of a ballerina, she jumped high enough to peer through the dusty panes. To her delight she found the house completely empty. More confident now, she skipped around the building, jumping occasionally to look through the other equally dusty windows. She desperately wanted to see inside the house proper, so she looked around to find something to stand on. Unearthing a plant pot from the back of the house, she dragged it onto the veranda, stood on it and triumphantly peered through the grimy window.

The room housed a fireplace, and a broken chair in the far corner. She could see through to the kitchen from an open door, where stood a table and two chairs, but little else except newspapers strewn across the floor. She squealed with delight, jumped off the plant pot, picked it up, and carried it to one of the back windows. From here, she could look into the kitchen and to a staircase beyond. She longed to gain entry, but when she tried the front door again, it wouldn't budge.

Looking towards the beach, the blazing sun enamelled the sea with spangles of glistening silver. Lazily she leant against the wooden balustrade, dreamily picking at the flaking black paint until she had accumulated a small dusty pile next to her white plimsolls. Kicking it away, she leant her tummy against the rail, hauled herself up and over like an acrobat, and landed steadily back on her feet. She grimaced slightly, as the impact pulled at the scar on her leg. Pulling the bandage away from her leg, she inspected her scar, covering it over when she was happy that no damage had been done. After half-heartedly brushing the large grimy mark away from the front of her yellow dress, she skipped her way to the back of the house.

The back garden was an abundance of thick bushes of faded yellow gorse. They were dry and brown from the fierce summer heat, and concealed a forgotten vegetable garden. Beyond the garden was a tiny dirt track leading up towards the pine forest. Slowly she picked her way through a soft thick carpet of pine needles until she came to a loop in the path that ran back, down towards the sea. As she walked, small birds scattered in the undergrowth, flying out in front of her, twittering crossly as they fluttered into the searing blue sky.

A few yards down the path brought her to an olive grove. She had no idea what an olive tasted like, but the small shiny fruits looked very tempting. After a few attempts at grasping one of the branches she retrieved a handful. First sniffing them, she took a tentative nibble, spitting it out in disgust. She threw the rest away, unintentionally hitting a startled tethered goat. Presently she walked further down the path until she came upon a screen of thorny branches entwined on a neglected fence which shielded a small fisherman's hut. The thicket of gorse which separated her from the hut was covered in huge bees, labouring relentlessly at the bright yellow petals. Standing on tiptoes she peered down towards a tiny sheltered shingle beach, which was strewn with drying fishing tackle. Eager to get closer, she tried to pick her way through the scratchy undergrowth until she felt something move underfoot. She screamed and scrambled her way back up to the top of the path, where she stamped her foot in panic, scraping the sole of her shoe on the dusty path. Something was moving towards her in the undergrowth and Laura took flight. She ran like the wind until she found herself back at the empty lodge. Once back on the veranda she lifted her foot to inspect the sole of her shoe, expecting to find something squashed there, but there was nothing, but she stood up and scraped her shoe again on the floor for good measure.

Panic over, she sat down hugging her knees, studying

the wild and unkempt garden beyond the lodge. It was a vast difference to the well kept terraced gardens of the villa, but Laura decided, this one was much more fun. Her eyes fell upon the scarlet petals of a single geranium as it fought for light amongst the yellow gorse. She got up and made her way through the broken terracotta pots and knelt down to get a closer look. Laura found that the geranium was growing from under an upturned blue ceramic pot. She leant closer to inspect her find, pushed her fingers under the rim, and lifted it. Before she knew what had happened, a lizard leapt from inside the pot, jumped on her shoulder, ran down her arm then immediately made its escape into the bushes. Laura's scream echoed around the hillside.

Gwen jumped as if electrified, dropped her book and fled towards the sun terrace steps, colliding with the screaming child as she came charging the other way.

'What on earth is the matter?' She shook the hysterical child. 'Are you hurt?' Gwen said, losing her patience with her. 'Laura, answer me.'

'It scratched my arm!' she screamed, pointing towards the lodge. She rubbed her arm to rid herself of the feeling from the creature.

Gwen knitted her eyebrows. 'What did?'

'A crocodile thing!' Laura wailed, rubbing her arm fiercely.

Charles appeared at the top of the beach steps, flushed and panting. 'What is it? What's happened?' He clasped his hand to his chest.

Laura ran to him with open arms. 'A crocodile thing scratched my arm grandpa!' she cried.

Gwen and Charles exchanged bemused glances, and then Charles laughed. 'It'll be a lizard Laura. They are quite harmless,' he said softly.

'It hurt me!' Laura stamped her foot indignantly.

Charles hugged her softly. 'It didn't mean to. It was probably frightened of you. Come on now wipe your eyes.' He dabbed her face with his handkerchief.

Gwen rolled her eyes and retrieved her book.

Charles threw a wearied look at Gwen and led Laura inside. 'I'll take a look at that arm of yours.' He sat her on the edge of the bath, and carefully bathed her arm, which Laura had rubbed raw.

'It stings grandpa. Will I die?' she asked in earnest.

'No darling, you'll be fine, I promise.' Charles smiled as he carefully applied antiseptic cream to her arm. 'There you go, all done and dusted.' He lifted her off the edge of the bath.

Laura grimaced, as she twisted her arm to inspect it.

'Come on, let's get you a drink.' Back in the kitchen he poured a glass of lemonade and passed it to Laura. 'There you go, hold it carefully. Are you coming back outside?'

Laura shook her head violently.

'Go and read your comic in the lounge then, it'll be dinner time in an hour.' He watched her walk slowly away, with hands clasped tightly round the glass of lemonade, and made a mental note to check for spillages later on.

12

Yiannis woke to the sound of a chair being pulled along the floor. When he felt a weight on the bed, he opened a bleary eye to find Laura beside him, her teddy bear tucked firmly under her arm.

Tilting her head she studied him intently. 'Hello Yiannis. Did you fall?' she said innocently.

Yiannis nodded painfully, swallowed and licked his lips.

'It's eight-o-clock. You've been asleep for...' She paused whilst she counted on her fingers. 'Sixteen hours!'

Yiannis sighed wearily.

'Do you want a drink?' she said.

'Please,' he croaked.

She reached over, picked the glass of water off the bedside table, and put the rim to his lips. 'Sip it slowly. It will take the nasty taste away.'

He smiled when he realised she was emulating the very words he had said to her the previous day. He drank slowly then nodded to her when he had had his fill.

Laura reached over and put the glass back on the bedside table then sat back on her haunches, studying him again with great interest. 'I didn't recognise you at first because your strawberry's gone a funny colour,' she said, pointing to his birthmark.

Yiannis just nodded sadly.

'Look!' she said showing him her arm. 'A crocodile thing scratched me, it hurts a lot, but grandpa has put some cream on it, and it's a lot better now.'

Yiannis frowned, not quite understanding what he was being told.

'Look, you can have my teddy bear if you want,' she said, carefully placing it in bed with him. Laura could hear Gwen preparing dinner in the kitchen. 'I'd better go,' she cupped her hand to her mouth. 'I'm not supposed to be in here,' she whispered, sliding to the edge of the bed.

As she began to ease herself down onto the chair, she lost her footing and grasped at the bedclothes to save herself. As the chair crashed to the floor, Yiannis lunged forward in a split second response and caught Laura before she toppled off the bed. An agonising pain shot up his arms and into his chest with a sickening force, making him gasp out loud, but he held on until she was safely back on the bed. The noise, as feared, brought Gwen running into the room.

'What's happened? Laura! What are you doing here? Get out immediately!' Gwen lifted a tearful Laura off the bed and onto the ground.

'It's okay Mrs Tempest,' Yiannis said as the pain subsided. 'Please don't be angry with her.'

'You lay still young man, you need to rest!' she scolded as she fussed around him straightening the bedclothes. When she came across the teddy bear, she raised an eyebrow at Yiannis. 'Well, you really are honoured. She wouldn't part with that bear for us.'

Yiannis smiled and cleared his throat. 'Thank you for helping me Mrs Tempest.'

Gwen nodded. 'You gave us all a fright. Charles wants to talk to you. He's down at the cove trying to get the motor working on the boat. He's been on at it all day. I *wish* he would buy a new one! Shall I tell him to come and see you now?'

'Please.' He nodded wearily.

Laura stood at the doorway and waved to him, but Gwen pushed her out of the room, closed the door behind her, and smacked her hard on the legs. 'Why can't you be a good girl? Yiannis needs rest. He doesn't want to be bothered with silly little girls like you. Now, don't let me catch you in there again, do you understand?'

Laura nodded tearfully.

'Good! Now go to your room until dinner.'

*

Laura was tucked up in bed by the time Charles emerged

from Yiannis's bedroom. In his hand, he clutched a second carafe of urine. This time, to his relief, the liquid was rosé in colour. He sat down to a late meal, deeply grieved by Yiannis's story. How anyone could inflict such injuries on their fellow human beings he did not understand. He ate in silence, his mind and stomach churning while he contemplated on how he should go about removing the uninvited guests from the Athena. Unfortunately the Athena wasn't one of the buildings which belonged to him. He had a couple of contacts in the administration department of the Piraeus police force - maybe they would know someone who could help. He would normally have gone straight to the local police, but he couldn't be absolutely sure that the Barzinis didn't hold them in their pockets - after all, they seemed to be a law unto themselves. But there was nothing he could do until morning. He sighed deeply, and shifted uneasily in his chair. He could feel the acid in his stomach burn and gave his chest a thump to bring on a belch.

'He's managed a little soup thank goodness!' Gwen said as she walked into the kitchen with an empty dish. 'Has he told you what happened?' she added.

Charles sat thoughtfully, aimlessly fidgeting with the condiments, but didn't answer her.

'Charles?' Gwen snapped.

'What?' he said crossly, as she broke into his train of thoughts.

'Has he told you what happened?'

'Yes,' he said sharply. 'I'm trying to think of how I'm going to help him, if you'll just leave me in peace for a few minutes.'

She bristled with indignation. 'Oh pardon me for breathing, I'm only the one who has bathed, fed and looked after him all day!'

'I'm sorry Gwen.' He reached out for her hand. 'I didn't mean to be sharp. I'm just astonished at what he told me. You will never believe it! Come, sit down, I'll tell you.'

Later that evening, Gwen retired to bed and Charles stood on the terrace in the cool evening breeze. He felt bloated and uncomfortable from his meal and belched loudly, automatically pardoning himself. Strolling to the edge of the terrace he looked up into the night sky. The stars were obscured by clouds, the weather was changing and rain had been forecast for the next few days. The summer was moving gently to a close.

'Excuse me sir?' A voice came from beyond the bushes.

Charles spun round clutching his hands to his heart. 'Sweet Jesus, you frightened the life out of me! Who is it? What do you want?'

'Sorry to startle you sir, it's me, Kostas Petrou.'

'Yes, yes,' Charles answered irritated. 'You nearly gave me a heart attack!'

Kostas nervously bit his lip and wished now that he had waited until morning to come here.

'Come on boy, what are you doing here so late, what do you want?'

'I'm really sorry to call,' Kostas said, clasping his hand together. 'But its Yiannis, we think he's been killed. He's not at his taverna, but the Barzini family are, and they said he's gone away, but I don't believe them. Something's happened, we know it. We just know it. It was my father who told us to come to you. He said you would know what to do. Sorry sir, sorry it's so late, but I fear for him, I really do!'

Charles gestured him to calm down.

Dimitra appeared alongside of Kostas. 'It's true Mr Tempest, he's vanished. It's not like him at all.'

Charles peered into the darkness at the young man who had just spoken. 'And you are?'

'Dimitra Aronis sir, I work at the Athena. I'm the chef, or rather I used to be!'

'So you think he's been killed then do you?' he said seriously.

They both nodded unhappily.

'I think you had better come with me.' He gestured them to follow. When they entered the house, he left them for a moment in the lounge while he went to check on Yiannis.

'Yiannis my boy, are you awake?'

Through his fug of painkillers he nodded.

'Are you still in pain?'

'A little, yes.' This was an understatement.

'I know it's late, but do you feel like receiving visitors? I have two very worried friends of yours here, who believe you to be dead!'

As Charles emerged from the bedroom a deafening scream rang out from the direction of the lounge. When he entered the room, he was aghast at the scene before him. Gwen stood behind one of the sofas, clothed in a satin nightgown, her hair in curlers, pointing one of his own grandfather's replica pistols at Kostas and Dimitra.

'Stay where you are, don't move or I'll shoot you!' she shrieked. 'Charles, thank goodness you're here, we have intruders!'

With a wry smile Charles promptly disarmed her. 'Darling we have guests. These gentlemen are here to see me. As you are up and about perhaps you would be kind enough to make us all some coffee?'

A deep flush crept across Gwen's face as she stormed out of the lounge, muttering an expletive and slamming the door behind her.

'I'm so sorry gentlemen. It's been a trying day for my wife. She's a little tired. Please follow me.'

Pale and shaken, the boys exchanged glances, and then followed Charles into Yiannis's bedroom.

Kostas was dumbfounded when his eyes fell on the mangled body of his friend. 'Oh my God, Yian?' he said, quickly moving to his bedside.

'Be careful, he is quite badly hurt,' Charles warned.

Kostas put his hands to his face to hide the shock, as

Dimitra gazed in horror at Yiannis's injuries.

'Oh Yian,' Kostas cried, reaching out towards him. 'What have they done to you? How did you get here? We thought you were dead!'

'It'll take more than the Barzini family to kill me off!' Yiannis croaked, attempting to smile.

'I'll leave you boys alone,' Charles said. 'Don't wear him out. He's been through a lot.'

*

With the taverna staff gone, Eva had been cooking and waitressing all day. The few customers who did venture into the Athena found to their cost that Eva could not cook authentic Greek food, and most left after tasting the burnt offerings of their starters and before the main course could be served. By seven-thirty that evening the place was completely deserted, with no prospect of any more customers. Eva placed a meal before her brothers and sat down to join them in the empty courtyard.

Marcos forked the food distastefully. 'I'm going to break Dimitra Aronis's legs when I see him next!' Marcos vowed baring his teeth.

'Is that after you break Kiassos's neck?' Franco added evenly.

Marcos gave a short laugh. 'With a bit of luck Yiannis Kiassos will have done that himself.' He smirked. 'Still, good of him to leave us this place! Eh Eva?' he said, slapping her hard on the backside.

'I say to hell with you,' she snarled. 'Why did you have to beat him like that? What am I supposed to do now he's gone? You've spoilt everything!'

Marcos leapt to his feet and smacked her resoundingly across her cheek, sending her spinning across the courtyard. She fell against the wall, stunned for an instant. In dazed confusion she grasped at the green and white candy striped awning over the barbecue to help heave herself to her feet, but it tore under her weight and ended up in a pile on top of her.

Franco roared with laughter and slammed his fists on the table in jubilation.

'You stupid bitch,' Marcos hissed. 'Now look what you have done! Well don't just sit there get off your backside and fetch the brandy woman.'

Eva rubbed the side of her burning cheek with the back of her hand then picked herself up off the floor, tossing the torn awning angrily aside. At the bar she lifted a bottle of Metaxa off the shelf and brought three glasses to the table.

'Oh no, you're not having any in your condition!' Marcos said, snatching the glass from her hand. 'Get yourself to bed, and take a cookery book with you, I'm not eating any more of this filth again,' he said hurling his plate of burnt Souvliki into the corner of the restaurant. 'And clean that up before you go.'

By nine-thirty p.m. Marcos was fast asleep, his head back, mouth agape and his feet on the table. His chair, precariously balanced on its back legs, rested against the barbecue. The bottle of brandy, already devoid of half its contents, lay discarded on the floor, trickling the remainder, drip by drip into an amber pool.

Franco lay in a drunken stupor across the next table. His arms crossed supporting his heavy head, a torn ribbon of awning periodically flapped at his ear. He twitched involuntary whenever the material touched him. After flicking it away several times, he grabbed the offending material, ripped it down and tucked it down the back of his chair. Satisfied that it wouldn't bother him again he reached down to rescue the discarded brandy bottle from the floor, tipped his head back and swigged the remaining dregs from the bottle. He hiccupped, swallowed hard, and then belched loudly before he fell from the chair pulling the rest of the awning from the roof until it came to rest on the dying embers of the charcoal grill.

*

It was ten-thirty when the boys said their farewells to

Yiannis. They found Charles relaxing with a glass of brandy in the lounge.

'Ah there you are. Care for a drink?' He beckoned them to sit as he poured two more brandies into fine crystal goblets. 'I take it he's told you then?'

They nodded as they accepted the drinks and settled uneasily on the sofa.

'Do you think Eva Barzini is telling the truth?' Charles asked.

'No sir!' Kostas said indignantly. 'Do you?'

'I don't know what to think. I've offered to pay her off for him, you know, set her up somewhere with an allowance, but Yiannis absolutely forbids me to do it. He is quite adamant that the child isn't his!' Charles paused to take a sip of brandy. 'But I just can't believe Eva would do this. I have known her for years. Why would she say something that isn't true?'

'Because she is a scheming manipulative little bitch, that's why,' Dimitra spat. 'She's a gold digger, she always has been, she's only out for what she can get, and Yiannis was easy prey.'

'What do you mean by that?' Charles enquired.

'Well, I believe she orchestrated this whole thing. Andreas said that she offered her services to Yiannis on his birthday. Well what sort of woman would do that except a desperate one? I think she fell pregnant with some holidaymaker and she saw Yiannis and his business as a meal ticket and took her chance at snaring him.'

'You're painting a very different picture to the Eva I know,' Charles said thoughtfully.

'Then you don't know her as we do!' Dimitra said adamantly.

Charles raised his eyebrows. 'Well, there's nothing we can do until the morning.'

'Are you going to get them out of the Athena?' Kostas asked hopefully.

'I shall certainly try. I know of someone in Piraeus

who I think can help us. I thought I would go and see him tomorrow.'

The boys sighed with relief.

'So, until the morning,' Charles said, dismissing them as he rose from his chair.

They quickly drained their glasses and scrambled to their feet.

'Thank you for the drink Mr Tempest, and for looking after Yiannis. Please apologise to Mrs Tempest for us - we didn't mean to startle her,' Kostas said, following Charles out onto the terrace.

Charles laughed heartily. 'Think nothing of it. I must say the more I think of it the more it amuses me. I really must teach her to be friendlier to the natives.'

Kostas and Dimitra grinned at each other.

'Until tomorrow then.' Charles held out his hand to Kostas.

'Hey Kostas look! What's that?' Dimitra nudged him. They all looked up at the bright red glow in the sky.

'Looks like something's on fire!' Kostas answered. 'It is, look at the sparks!' he added. 'Come on Dimitra let's get back, something's happened in the harbour.'

Charles watched as they ran down the steps to the cove, and then turned his attention towards the sky. 'Probably a flare from a boat, that's all,' he muttered to himself before walking back inside, closing the French windows behind him.

13

It took approximately five minutes for the smouldering awning to catch fire. Almost silently the flames leapt into life, licking their way across the remaining material. Paper serviettes and menus helped fuel the fire. Soon their glowing sooty remains floated gently to settle into nooks and crannies of the wooden structure of the taverna. Within minutes, tiny fires glowed throughout the courtyard, quietly crackling and spitting until they gained momentum and joined together in a great wall of orange and blue flames.

Franco coughed himself into wakefulness, just in time to see the main upright beam supporting the barbecue crash down, pinning Marcos to his chair with its weight. Marcos woke screaming hysterically as Franco staggered to help him, pulling at the burning beam in a vain attempt to free his brother. Marcos himself tried frantically to push the beam from his legs, all the while emitting long agonising screams. Suddenly he grabbed Franco round the neck, his eyes wild and bloodshot, his lips curled over his bared teeth. 'Get it off me!'

'Let go of me then!' Franco yelled, struggling to free himself from his brother's grip. A loud crack sounded from above, as the roof of the barbecue collapsed, knocking Marcos unconscious. Marcos released his grip on Franco and he fell back gasping for breath. The smoke burned the back of his throat as he gulped arid air into his lungs. He eased himself back towards Marcos, caught hold of his chin and shook it, but it was useless, his brother was dead. With burning lungs and sooty tears running down his face, he crawled about in the hot dense choking fumes, feeling for a way out. When his hands found the bar steps he cursed, realising he'd crawled the wrong way.

Waking to the sound of voices shouting and timber cracking, Eva's senses soon picked up the pungent smell of smoke and began to cough. She leapt from the bed and ran to the top of the landing, but the thick wall of black smoke fought her back. Retreating to the bedroom she slammed the door shut and made for the window, but it was too far down for her to jump. Panic prickled her body when she noticed the smoke creeping under the door with the draft from the window. As she screamed for help, the smoke burned the back of her throat, filling her lungs with arid effluvium. Grabbing a sheet from the bed, she felt her way through the bank of dense smoke towards the bathroom. The bath taps groaned and clanked as the water began to fill the pipes. 'Come on!' She thumped the taps to give water. Suddenly they spluttered to life and she sobbed in relief, kneading the sheet under the flow until it was drenched. With streaming eyes she dragged the sodden sheet over her head and made her way gingerly down the blackened stairway and into the bar. Feeling her way with her toe, she stepped down in the courtyard and promptly fell over Franco.

'Who's that, help me!' Franco groaned.

Ignoring him she scrambled to her feet, but he grabbed her ankle and dragged her back. 'Get off me!' she spluttered, kicking out to free herself.

He wrenched the damp sheet from her head, making her wretch as the smoke filled her lungs. Desperately fighting the sheet from Franco's grasp, he doggedly held on until she fell to her knees exhausted.

Only when the sheet ignited, did Franco let go of it. Flames licked at Eva's arms as she beat the material ferociously against the ground. Her face stung hot and her hair began to singe, but still Franco held her ankle.

'Let me go damn you,' she shrieked.

'Get me out of here!' he growled back in a strange guttural voice.

A splintering crack came from above them as an upright beam began to collapse. Eva shrieked as she watched the beam fall silently forward, cutting its way through the smoke towards where Franco lay. A second later the beam hit him with a slicing blow to the back of his legs. For an eerie moment, Franco lay silent. A voice in Eva's head urged her to leave him, but as soon as she moved away she realised he still had hold of her.

She tossed the remains of a tablecloth over her head, and in a last ditch attempt at escape, reached down and began to prise Franco's hand from her leg. Burning flesh engulfed her nostrils, when she noticed Franco's trousers were on fire. Suddenly the tablecloth too became engulfed in flames. Quickly discarding it, she wrenched at Franco's arm until she felt his body move. Another pull dragged him free of the burning log and she fell backwards. There were voices now and footsteps, someone grabbed her, pulling her out into the cool night air and freedom.

Marian Dopas lifted Eva's head and with a glass of water, urged her to drink. She drank thirstily, feeling the trickle of moisture cut through the thick layer of soot coating her burning throat. Coughing violently, she spluttered the liquid from her mouth, forming tiny rivulets down her blackened face. When she turned towards the burning inferno, she saw Franco lying in the street, groaning pitifully. His legs were crushed as blood exuded through his smouldering clothes. She rolled over, crawled slowly towards him, and screamed into his burnt face, 'You bastard, you nearly killed me!'

'You were going to leave me in there you bitch!' he snarled angrily.

'And you would have let me burn upstairs. You didn't even attempt to warn me,' she retorted.

'I was asleep.'

'You were drunk!'

He lashed out to hit her but she pulled away, the movement caused a searing pain in his legs. As he cried out in agony, Eva watched on with cool indifference.

When the spasm passed, he glared at her with sheer hatred in his eyes. 'Marcos is dead!' he said.

Eva shrugged her shoulders indifferently.

'I might never walk again.' He screwed up his face as another spasm cut through his legs.

Eva turned on him. 'What about me? I've lost Yiannis. My livelihood has gone up in smoke, and I will very likely lose my baby, and it's all down to you and bloody Marcos. So if it's sympathy you're looking for, you will be very disappointed. Marcos can rot in hell, and I'm sure he will. And you…' She bared her teeth at him. '…. you will just be more useless than ever now - you idle, good-for-nothing drunkard!'

Franco grabbed her by the neck to silence her, slowly tightening his grip, until her face turned purple.

The flames from the Athena licked high into the night sky, and despite the efforts of dozens of locals fetching and carrying water to the scene, the situation became hopeless. Eventually they all stood back as the old building collapsed into a glowing charred heap. Kostas and Dimitra arrived on the scene just as the studded oak door crashed into the street, showering thousands of burning embers in its wake.

'Any survivors?' Kostas asked Akis Dopas.

'Over there.' Akis pointed. 'Oh for goodness sake what the hell is he doing to her? Quick somebody stop him before he kills her!'

Kostas dragged Franco from Eva moments before she lost consciousness.

'You mad bastard!' Kostas said, throwing Franco to the floor. 'It should be me wringing your bloody neck. Look at what you've done to the Athena!' He pointed wildly at the inferno before him.

Franco clenched his fist and threw a punch full into Kostas's face, sending him reeling to the floor. He lay there for a moment, eyes wild with rage, cupping his blood-splattered nose, before he scrambled to his feet. 'Right that's it!' he snapped, but was stopped short by Dimitra.

'Allow me,' he said, calmly holding Kostas back while he aimed a swift hard kick to Franco's ribs, breaking several of them in one blow. 'That's from Yiannis!' he said, as he watched Franco recoil in agony. 'Do you know something Kostas?' Dimitra said calmly, 'my mother always said, "Two wrongs don't make a right", but then I never did listen to my mother!' They high fived with respect, then joined the others trying to extinguish the fire, leaving Franco gasping for breath and Eva retching on the road.

*

In stunned silence Yiannis listened as Kostas broke the news to him early the next morning. As he spoke, Yiannis stared blankly towards the fine white net curtains that blew gently in the morning breeze.

Seeing his despair, Kostas reached forward with a comforting hand. 'I'm so sorry Yian. Everyone on the island feels for you.'

Yiannis nodded despondently as he continued to stare at the curtains.

Presently Kostas got up. Reluctant to leave his friend in this state, but not knowing what else to say to him, he placed his hand on his shoulder and left him to his sorrow.

*

It was ten days before Yiannis was well enough to make the journey to the harbour. Ten days of agonising pain and endless sleepless nights. He would wake early each morning and push his body to extraordinary lengths to make his battered limbs mobile again. It was a long, slow, painful process and Charles and Gwen worried desperately over his mental and physical health.

He slept fitfully. Disturbing dreams tormented him. He dreamt of cellar rats and of his father, who would walk through flames towards him and call him a failure. He would dream of a birthday party and watch his father hand the key of the taverna to Marcos Barzini. Yiannis would beg his father not to give it away, but his father ignored him. Each morning he woke, soaked in perspiration. His heart was heavy with such a great sense of loss and failure he felt it would crush the life out of him.

On the day he finally stepped off the boat into the harbour aided by Charles and Kostas, he was almost unrecognisable. His battered body looked old and tired. His pellucid aquamarine eyes, now dark and empty, stared expressionless at the familiar harbour surroundings.

It was a grey miserable November day, and the fine misty rain saturated the three men as they walked slowly and tentatively towards the Athena and the devastation that Charles and Kostas feared would finish Yiannis off.

Dumbstruck, Yiannis stood in the centre of the charred remains of his beautiful courtyard, moving the scorched remnants of a table with the toe of his shoe. He looked skywards at the blackened roof timbers that had once covered his home and shook his head.

Kostas put a protective arm around his shoulder and the boys stood in devastated silence.

'This is terrible Kostas. I'll never be able to build this again,' Yiannis murmured.

Charles stepped forward and placed a comforting hand on his shoulder. 'Yiannis my boy, the first priority is to get you well again. We'll deal with this later when you feel more able to cope.'

Yiannis felt a black fug engulfing his senses. He was ruined. No amount of time could change that fact.

Sensing his despair, Charles said gently, 'Come on Yiannis, come away now.'

Yiannis held his hand up. 'No! I need to stay a while.'

Charles looked to Kostas for help.

'I'll stay with him Mr Tempest. We'll be along in a few minutes.'

'Very well,' Charles said reluctantly. 'I have some business to do in the town. I'll see you back at the harbour in half an hour.'

Slowly Yiannis picked his way across the courtyard

floor. Sooty terracotta pots stood with the limp remains of shrivelled foliage. He looked towards the shelf behind the bar at the row of black jagged spirit bottles all containing the same tar-like liquid. He picked a menu from beneath an upturned table and wiped the soot to reveal the words 'Athena Taverna - established 1935'. He sighed deeply. 'My father would turn in his grave if he could see this now. I've really let him down Kostas.'

'Yiannis don't do this. This isn't your fault. You put up with more than a lot of people would have. All that aggravation, threats and the beating you took. I think your father would have been proud of the way you fought those two for this place.'

'But I lost it in the end, didn't I?' He threw his head back. 'I should have fought harder.'

'No Yian!' Kostas snapped. 'It was out of your control.'

'How am I going to earn a living? What am I going to do, and where will I live? I have nothing - it's all gone!' He choked on the words. 'And what about Dimitra and my other staff? What are they going to do?' he added perturbed.

'Don't worry about them - it's the end of the season. You just concentrate on getting yourself back on your feet. As for Dimitra, father's given him a job.' Kostas started to smile.

Yiannis looked at him suspiciously. 'What are you smiling at?'

'Well, the fact is, since we employed Dimitra we're doing a roaring trade. We've pinched all your customers!' He winked.

Yiannis smiled weakly. 'Oh great, I'll never get him back off Alexis.'

Kostas laughed and nudged him. 'Come on I'll buy you a drink with all our profits.'

Back in the harbour Yiannis glanced at the Ice Palace. 'There's one consolation. I won't have to bother about those two thugs again. Mr Tempest told me Franco had his leg amputated.'

'It should have been his head,' Kostas retorted.

'At least Marcos got his due. Every cloud has a silver lining,' Yiannis said ironically.

'Talking of clouds, you still have a black one on the horizon.'

'Oh?'

'Eva came home from hospital yesterday, and once Andreas told her you were still alive, she wasted no time in telling everyone that you're the father of her baby.'

Yiannis faltered and reached out to Kostas to steady himself.

'Sorry Yian, I shouldn't have mentioned her,' he said, leading him to a chair in the taverna. 'I'll go and get us a drink. I'll be back in a moment.'

Yiannis sat quietly with his eyes closed. The strain of seeing the Athena and the pain of walking had taken its toll on him. He did not notice that someone was standing beside him, and jumped when a voice said, 'So, you're back on your feet then?'

Yiannis felt the bile rise at the sight of Eva, as she slid onto the seat opposite him.

'Look Yiannis, I'm really sorry about...'

Yiannis stopped her short. 'I don't want your apologies. I don't want to talk to you. I just want you out of my life, now!'

She gave him a pained look. 'Well that's not possible and you know it. There's our baby to consider. I've had a thorough check up and everything's all right with it you'll be pleased to know!'

Yiannis fought the anger welling up inside him.

Eva sighed impatiently. 'So, what are we going to do?'

'Do?' he snapped.

'Yes do, you know, where are we going to live, how are you going to provide for us? You could work at the Ice Palace if you want – we're a bit short staffed now.'

'My God!' His eyes widened with disbelief. 'You are

unbelievable. I'm not going to *do* anything and you can go to hell!'

Eva blushed momentarily. 'Temper, temper Yiannis. You have to do something, it's your baby!' she hissed.

Kostas appeared from behind her, grabbed Eva by the arm, and pulled her out of the chair. 'You're not welcome here, so get lost Eva. Can't you see the man's ill? Haven't you and your lunatic brothers done enough to him?' he snarled.

'Get your filthy hands off me!' She yanked her arm from Kostas's grasp. 'What about what he did to me?' she wailed, cradling her tummy maternally. 'I want what's due to me and our baby. It's his responsibility,' she said, pointing her finger. 'He's going to have to own up to it!'

Yiannis pulled himself to his feet, almost knocking the table over as he lunged towards her.

'Yiannis, ignore her!' Kostas said restraining him, but Yiannis pushed the table aside, grabbed her by the arms and shook her.

'You know and I know that the baby you are carrying is not mine. I will not, I repeat not, pay anything to you! Do I make myself clear?' He pushed her away. 'Go and ruin someone else's life.'

Eva, shaken by his outburst, looked sheepishly about her. A few holidaymakers at the taverna were sat open-mouthed, and Marian from the Post Office had come out to stand in the doorway to see what the commotion was all about. She looked back at Yiannis then crumpled her face as though to cry, and ran to the comfort of Marian Dopas.

Yiannis held onto the chair to steady himself, his face was pale and drawn and his head spun with a sickly headache.

'Hey, what's all this noise about?' Alexis said, running out of the kitchen wiping his hands down his apron.

Visibly shaking with anger Yiannis glanced at the onlookers. All but one of the customers looked on in disdain. In the far corner of the taverna, a well built, ruddy faced man, with a dark bushy beard and kind friendly eyes sat and smiled back at him. He nodded a friendly acknowledgement to Yiannis, and Yiannis returned the gesture. Then he glanced towards the Post Office doorway where a couple of old gossiping women had gathered to share in Eva's plight.

'Yiannis are you okay?' Charles said worriedly as he walked up to the taverna. 'What's happened?'

Yiannis shook his head in dismay.

'Come on my boy, it's been a trying day, let's get you home.'

As they watched Charles help Yiannis back to the boat, Alexis declared, 'Well I'm amazed! In all the years I have known Yiannis I have never heard him raise his voice in anger before!'

'He has good reason papa, believe me, after what the Barzinis have put him through.'

'Is it true then about him and her?' Alexis nudged Kostas.

Kostas shot his father a look of contempt. 'I'm surprised you even have to ask. You're no better than those gossiping women!' He walked away.

'Huh, sorry I spoke, I only asked,' Alexis said indignantly. 'And don't speak to your father like that. Remember who pays your wages!' he shouted after him. He turned and smiled at the ruddy faced bearded Englishman who had arrived on the island a couple of weeks previously and rented Alexis's old outhouse. 'Are you settling in the workshop okay?' He inquired.

Travis Reeves put down his sketch pad and answered that he was.

Alexis leant over and glanced at the drawing on his sketchbook. It was a fine pencil drawing of his taverna. 'I never asked, but are you planning on staying long?'

'A while, I think, if that is okay with you?' Travis smiled.

'Happy to have you here,' Alexis declared as he flipped

his tea towel over his shoulder.

14

Yiannis shut himself away in his room on his return to Amora Cove, emerging only to eat. On the odd dry day he would venture slowly down the beach steps to sit on the shoreline.

Charles and Gwen observed the boy's disillusionment of the world with dismay. 'We've got to do something Gwen!' Charles said, watching Yiannis aimlessly throwing stones into the sea.

'Yes but what?' Gwen threw her hands in the air.

'I don't know. He's lost the will to live I think.'

Gwen huffed impatiently. 'Well he'll have to pull himself together soon. I've enough on my plate with that little madam moping about!' She glanced at Laura.

Quirking an eyebrow he said, 'You've given me an idea. 'Laura? Why don't you go and see Yiannis, sweetheart? I think he needs some company.'

Laura hesitated, glancing nervously at Gwen. 'But grandma said I mustn't bother him.'

'Well I say it's okay. Off you go.'

Laura's face brightened as she skipped across the sun terrace towards the beach steps. Charles crossed his fingers in anticipation.

'Hello Yiannis,' Laura said, startling him. She giggled when she saw him jump. 'Did I frighten you?'

He smiled gently at her. 'Yes you did, you cheeky monkey.'

'What were you looking at?' she asked quizzically.

'Oh nothing,' he sighed, hunching his shoulders.

Laura frowned. 'Why were you looking at nothing?'

He gave a short laugh. 'I don't know.'

She sat down next to him and said innocently, 'You're very sad aren't you? I can tell.'

He looked at her forlornly.

She too glanced out to sea. 'I'm sad too. But don't tell

anyone, will you?' she said, widening her eyes.

'Oh Laura.' He put his arm around her. 'You lost your parents. You don't have to keep your sadness a secret.'

She shifted uncomfortably. 'But mummy and Steve died because of me!'

He narrowed his eyes. 'Whoever told you that?'

After a few seconds she said, 'Mummy and Steve had a row - a big one! Steve said I had caused it.'

'What about?' he asked gently.

Laura swallowed hard. 'I can't really remember, except it made him really angry with me. Whatever I said made them row all the way home from our holiday.' She shot him a fearful look. 'Oh don't tell anybody Yiannis will you? I'll get into trouble.'

'Of course I won't sweetheart.' He hugged her protectively. 'But look, whatever happened to your mummy and Steve that day was absolutely *not* your fault. When that tree fell on your car it was an accident and accidents happen - so no more worrying about this, okay?'

Laura gave him a watery smile and reached up for a cuddle.

Yiannis gathered her up in his arms. Whatever had happened to him over the last few weeks, paled into insignificance after what little Laura had been through. He had lost material things – bricks and mortar, which could be built again. This poor little mite had been orphaned at such a tender age - what could be worse than that?

'Laura, if you want to talk about anything I'm always here for you.'

She smiled thankfully. 'I feel a bit better now. I'll try not to be sad any more if you will,' she added.

He smiled thinly. 'I'll try, just for you.'

Laura let him go so she could select a pebble to skim into the sea. She turned and grinned when it managed three skims. 'Yiannis, when are you going to take me fishing?'

'I don't know sweetheart.'

She walked back to him and put her hands on her hips. 'Is it because you've been poorly, and your arms and legs hurt?'

He looked up at her serious face. 'Yes.'

'Well grandma says you'll never be fit and strong again, because you only pick at your food! She said she is fed up with throwing good food away.'

He felt a thickness in his throat.

Laura looked at him sternly. 'Don't you want to get better?' she asked innocently. 'Don't you want to go out in your boat and catch fish again?'

Yiannis swallowed hard and lifted his painful hands. 'I don't think I can manage the boat with these.'

Laura inspected the purple scars on his fingers then placed a warm moist kiss on each digit. 'There, that should start to make them better!' she said tenderly. She bent down to pull a lazy sock up, and then held her hand out for him. 'Come on, let's go and make a sandwich. I'm starving.

*

Within a few days of Laura's intervention, Yiannis's desperate state of unfathomable melancholy began to lift. Spending their days together, he taught her about the sea and its bounty, about the island and the culture of the Greek way of life. He watched intently as every sight and sound broke over the child in a tide of newness. Her emotions, which were bursting with life, now began to bring a new beginning to his. He could see the brightness and joy of the world through the child's eyes, and it taught him that life, nature's surroundings, and the blood in his veins, were predominantly more important than material possessions could ever be.

When the olive harvest arrived in mid December, the locals gathered at the olive grove high up on the hillside above Amora cove. Yiannis was there to help - just as he had been since he was a small boy. His place would normally be atop a ladder, raking the fruits onto the plastic sheeting below, but this year he was only able to muster enough strength to work under the makeshift corrugated hut, with the women and children. He and Laura worked side by side. His job was to feed the olives in between the two great wheels that would pummel the olives into pulp, before they were poured into a cold press. Laura's job was to keep a constant supply of sterilised bottles ready to catch the trickle of pure virgin oil. Yiannis loved this sense of community, where the locals gathered together to help each other harvest their crops when the time was right.

The olive trees at the cove normally took a whole day to harvest, and as the winter sun dipped into the dark sea and nightfall descended on the island, the tired happy group made their way down to the beach. Fires were lit and rows of sardines sizzled and spat in the glowing amber embers, before being served with toasted bread drizzled in fresh olive oil.

Laura marvelled at the whole spectacle of the event. She was tired, but far too excited to sleep, and chose instead to sit with Yiannis long into the night, huddled together wrapped in a blanket for warmth. She listened dreamily to the strange pulsating music from the eight-string mandolin called a bouzoúki, while people got up one by one to dance the slow methodical steps of the sirtáki.

A large oval waning moon rose up from behind the Peloponnese, and bathed the cove and its inhabitants with a soft ivory hue.

Laura pointed. 'Yiannis look, the moon is shaped like an olive! Would it be a good night to go moon dancing?'

He squeezed her hand. 'Not tonight Laura, but one day soon, when my hands are better, I promise we will go.'

'Next time there's an olive moon?'

'Maybe, we'll see.'

*

One evening early in January, Charles and Yiannis sat at the table after dinner, while Gwen put Laura to bed.

'You're looking a lot better Yiannis. We despaired of

you for a while.'

Yiannis smiled. 'Yes, I'm sorry. I wasn't a very good patient was I? But I am grateful for what you and Mrs Tempest have done for me. I don't know what I would have done without you, or how I can ever repay you for your kindness.'

Charles placed the palms of his hands flat on the table. 'Well, that's what I want to talk to you about.'

Yiannis's heart sank. Was he going to ask him to leave? What would he do? His hands were still not strong enough to earn a living fishing yet.

Charles caught his expression. 'Don't look so worried. I've a proposition for you!'

Yiannis offered a questioning gaze.

'I want you to come and work for me.'

Yiannis's eyes brightened with interest.

'We need someone who can turn their hand to anything, odd jobs and the like. Now I know you still haven't gained your strength back completely, so there is no rush to do anything manual just yet. But in the meantime, we need some help with Laura. Gwen finds her a real handful and you're so good with her. What do you say?

Oh and you can move into the lodge, rent free of course. It's been empty for years and needs attention, but it's yours for as long as you want it. It will give you some breathing space and a wage. You're going to need money to rebuild the Athena.'

Yiannis was taken aback by his offer. 'I see,' he breathed. 'I don't know what to say, you've done so much for me already,'

Charles winked. 'Yes will suffice.'

'Well then yes. Thank you very much, I accept.' A rush of relief washed over him.

'Good. You can take a look at the lodge tomorrow. It'll take a couple of months to get it ship shape.'

*

By the first week in March, the lodge was ready. It was clean, freshly painted, and furnished with odds and ends from the villa, and much to Laura's disappointment, she was under strict instructions from her grandparents to keep away from the lodge, unless invited.

'He needs his privacy darling,' her grandpa informed her.

Laura reluctantly agreed, until the day she came face to face with a lizard again. She'd been playing on the path adjacent to the lodge for half an hour, hoping to see Yiannis, when suddenly the creature leapt out into her path. Dumbstruck, she stared horrified at the reptile as it stared back at her, then it moved, and a moment later she burst screaming into Yiannis's kitchen, causing him to almost choke on the piece of bread he was eating.

'That lizard thing is out there again!' she wailed, running to stand behind him.

Leaving his lunch uneaten, he pulled her from behind his chair. 'Hey now, come here. He probably wanted to make friends, but you frightened him off.'

Laura scanned her eyes around the kitchen, congratulating herself for gaining entry to somewhere she shouldn't be. She folded her arms seriously. 'Well, it's no good going back out there to make friends with it, because it will have run away! So, I think it would be better if I stay here for a while until it comes back, and while I'm waiting I can have a look at your new house.'

Yiannis threw his head back and laughed.

She frowned. 'What are you laughing at?'

'You! You make me laugh! Come on,' he said, abandoning his meal. 'Give me your hand. It will be a pleasure to show you around my home.'

15

On the twenty-fifth of April, Eva Barzini gave birth to a baby boy - eight months after Yiannis's birthday! The child was named Stephano Yiannis, to the annoyance of his namesake. During her long and arduous labour at home, she screamed Yiannis's name continually for all to hear. Though the arrival of an eight-month child brought a brief reprieve to Yiannis's reputation, this was instantly quashed when Eva declared the midwife had expected her to give birth prematurely – due to the after-effects of the fire and smoke inhalation. The midwife had said no such thing, but this fuelled the few gossips that leant their sympathies to Eva's plight, and continued their condemnation of Yiannis.

From that day, Yiannis kept a healthy distance from Eva. When he escorted Laura to the local school, as he did most days, he took her through the narrow whitewashed back streets, avoiding the Ice Palace, and the inevitable scene Eva would make if she saw him.

Laura settled comfortably into school. Quickly making friends and grasping the Greek language, Charles and Yiannis were pleased with her progress and how well-adjusted she seemed to be. Gwen however was far from happy with Laura's progress. She complained endlessly to Charles that the child was becoming wild and uncontrollable, and was infuriated when Laura answered her back in Greek whenever she was scolded for anything. Gwen despaired of her. Most days Laura returned from school with her clothes ripped and dirty, and on two occasions came home with head-lice, which she promptly passed on to Gwen. On the second such occasion, Gwen was incensed on finding another infestation in her own hair. She grabbed Laura by her long blonde plait and cut it off at the base with the kitchen scissors.

Yiannis was mooring his boat in Amora cove when he

heard Laura's screams. Taking the beach steps two at a time, he was met by Charles at the top.

'Yiannis, thank goodness you're here,' he said, red-faced and visibly angry. 'It's Laura. She's run off in a terrible state.'

Yiannis narrowed his eyes. 'What's happened?'

'Gwen has cut Laura's hair off,' he said scornfully.

Yiannis turned towards Gwen, who stood with her fists balled into her hips, daring him to question her actions. He glanced at Charles for an explanation.

'She means well.' Charles rubbed his forehead wearily. 'She's just not used to dealing with children. We always had a nanny for Stephen.' He pulled a thin smile. 'Go and find her, Yiannis, will you?'

He knew where to look. Distraught and tear-stained she lay beneath the shade of a white oleander bush, high up the pine-clad hillside, next to the natural fresh water spring, clutching her long plait in her fist.

Gently kneeling beside her, he gathered her into his arms as she wept openly. No matter how good the Tempests had been to him, he could have happily slapped Gwen's face for doing such a thing. When eventually Laura's sobs subsided, he lifted her chin up and said, 'You're still my beautiful little Laura you know!'

With his handkerchief, he tenderly wiped her tears. She looked at him with mournful eyes, took his handkerchief, blew her nose, and tucked it into her own pocket.

'Do you know where we're going tonight?' he said tenderly.

'I don't want to go anywhere looking like this!' She buried her face in her hands.

'Not even moon dancing.'

Her face brightened slightly. 'Tonight?' She swallowed another sob. 'Just you and me?' Her eyes shone hopefully.

'Well,' he said cautiously. 'Grandpa might like to come as well. Come on, we'll go and ask him.'

Laura looked forlornly at the clump of hair in the palm of her hand.

'Come on, I'll show you how lovely you look with short hair. It suits you actually.'

She sniffed unhappily, pushed the clump of hair deep into her pinafore pocket next to Yiannis's handkerchief, and slipped her small hand into his. Back at the lodge, he stood her on a stool in his bathroom to look in the mirror. Pulling her hair forward so that it framed her face, he smiled at her reflection. 'See, you look like a young lady now with your new fancy haircut.'

She glanced at Yiannis's face behind her and returned a watery smile.

To his relief, the expedition was allowed to go ahead that night, and as Yiannis speculated, Charles accompanied them. Gwen however, stayed at home, smarting indignantly from Charles's reprimand of Laura's unnecessary punishment.

Sitting on the sun terrace that evening, the threesome watched the sun fall from the sky, gilding the white walls of the villa and honeycomb rocks of the bay in soft creamy amber tones.

'It's going to be a perfect night for moon dancing!' Yiannis promised Laura, as they watched in silent awe as the sun dropped into the dark inky blue ocean.

At ten p.m. they set sail. Laura held the lantern to light the way, as Yiannis rowed the boat along the narrow strait that linked the island with the mainland and out into the open sea. Yiannis glanced at Charles who sat dozing, arms folded, head nodding sleepily. The night sky obviously held no fascination for him any more.

'Look at all those stars Yiannis,' Laura whispered.

'My papa told me that when someone dies, another star appears in heaven, so that whoever they left behind can look up and feel close to them again. Look,' he pointed to a couple of stars, 'see those two there, that's my mama and papa.'

Laura craned her neck to look. 'Where's my mummy and daddy?'

'Well, which ones are the brightest stars?'

Laura scanned the sky until her eyes picked out the two stars with the brightest twinkle. 'Is it those?'

'I believe so.'

She sighed deeply.

When he was far enough out from land, he looked skywards, pulled the oars into the boat then instructed Laura to sit next to him.

The moon, three-quarters full, laid a path of silver across the inky blue ocean as Laura sat intoxicated by the sense of airy isolation. The gentle ripple of breeze teased and ruffled the surface of the water, until it danced with brilliant spangles of moonlight. Slowly she followed the path of dazzling light towards the golden moon, laid back in the comfort of Yiannis's arms, and lost herself under the huge vault of stars in the infinite night sky.

Yiannis too sat in awe of the beauty before him. He had seen this scene a hundred times before, but never more magnificently than this night. He sat with his arms protectively round this small child, who was so seduced and educated by this tiny island, and who found such joy and delight in its everyday happenings. He was never more at peace with the world than at this moment in time. Laura would forever fill his life with a richness that no other person could bring to him.

The night had cooled and he felt her shiver slightly. 'I think it's time to go home,' he said reluctantly.

He slowly rowed back in the inky darkness, leaving behind a sparkling pool of fiery phosphorescence and a night of brilliant stars.

*

As the spring unfolded into summer, the influx of holidaymakers began to flood onto their small island like a tidal wave. Yiannis settled into the idyllic comfort of life in Amora cove. The money he earned was saved to restore the Athena. But it would take years, he knew that. In the meantime, Alexis and Kostas reaped the rewards of Dimitra, the best chef on the island.

Yiannis was left mostly to his own devices, neither Charles nor Gwen setting any agenda of work for him. They were content for him to spend his days entertaining and educating Laura. So it was, that his days were filled in blissful contentment -except of course for the periodic demands of money from Eva - 'the baby's due' she called it - all of which Yiannis would promptly ignore.

16

In early July, Laura's school closed for the summer holidays and Greece was basking in a shimmering heat wave. As the days were unbearably hot, dawn was the only time it was comfortable to be out and about. Rising early, Laura would accompany Yiannis on his fishing trips. Out at sea, the air was fresher. The cooling breeze bathed and refreshed their fatigued bodies. Laura would watch in distaste as Yiannis held his live bate between his lips while he fumbled to secure it on the hook of his line. She was painfully aware that his scarred fingers were still numb, and hated to see him struggle, but try as she might, she was unable to bring herself to help him with this task. Once the line was cast over one side of the boat, and his nets laid at the other, all there was to do was sit and wait. Laura would settle herself down on a blanket on the bottom of his boat and they would breakfast silently on crusty bread and cheese, idly watching the morning break across the sky.

Shortly after nine each morning, the day's catch would start to arrive in the harbour, nets having been lifted at dawn and their contents painstakingly extracted. So at seven, Yiannis would drop Laura and some of his catch off at Amora Cove, then sail into the next cove, where he would empty the rest into a large wicker basket, close the lid and load it into Dimitra's waiting boat.

When the other fishermen arrived to unload their catch on the waterfront for sale, Dimitra would have already taken Yiannis's catch to the back yard of Alexis Taverna, where Kostas had sold it on for him. The many islanders privy to this were sympathetic to Yiannis's plight, and no lover of the Barzini family. They would swiftly and quietly appear from nowhere, and steal away, eagerly clutching their booty at a knock down price in return for their secrecy. This way Alexis always got the best catch of the day, and Yiannis made a little money without Eva's knowledge.

*

Throughout that long hot summer, Laura and Yiannis became inseparable. They would spend their mornings either sailing into tiny inlets for picnics, swimming in water as clear as glass or lazing under the shade of the oleander bushes high up above the pine forest, listening to the babble of the natural spring.

Laura's favourite place was a secluded cove, around the headland from Amora Cove. It was the one she'd stumbled across the first time she'd explored her new surroundings but had been unable to get to. It seems it was only accessible by boat and was used by Yiannis to maintain the Moondancer and dry his fishing nets.

She loved to feel the soft crunchy shingle underfoot as she picked her way up the beach path to the shade of the fisherman's hut. There she would sit, pencil poised to sketch Yiannis as he mended his fishing nets.

Yiannis was the only privileged person to see her drawings, as she left each one pinned to the hut wall, against the backdrop of old peeling paint, for him to view when she had gone. He had deeply embarrassed her when he had tried to look one day while she was still drawing, and even though she clearly had an obvious talent, and her drawings were stunningly accurate, she insisted that they were not very good and no amount of praise could persuade her otherwise. In truth, it was her grandmother who made her so sensitive about her drawings. Whenever Laura was found drawing, her grandmother would say, 'Stop scribbling child, and do something more worthwhile. You're just wasting paper, with your silly drawings.'

Most afternoons after siesta they would sit on the veranda outside the lodge, while Yiannis shared his extensive knowledge of Greek history, mythology, flora, and fauna, as Laura absorbed his narrative like a sponge. It was on one such glorious afternoon in August when

Charles called upon them to go to the harbour to meet the ferry, as they were expecting a visitor from England.

'Who's coming grandpa?' Laura asked, easing herself off the chair and slipping her small hand into his.

'It's your Uncle Jack,' he answered casually.

Laura blanched slightly at the mention of his name.

'Don't look so worried. He looked after you when you were in hospital remember?'

Laura remembered him, but she was a little afraid he had found out that the accident was her fault and had come to tell her grandparents.

Charles smiled warmly at Yiannis. 'His name is Jack Ryder. He's not her real uncle you understand, just a family friend. He's our family solicitor. He will be arriving on the five-thirty ferry. I'd go myself, but this heat is unbearable.'

*

Yiannis stood under the shade of Alexis's candy striped awnings as he waited for the late afternoon ferry to dock. He looked down at Laura who was knelt on all fours trying unsuccessfully to coax a cat from under one of the wicker chairs.

'Laura, come here sweetheart. He'll be here in a moment,' he said gently.

It was a hot, sticky day and the ferry was full of garishly dressed holidaymakers in cheap sunglasses and ill-fitting sun hats. Amongst the bustle and chaos of screaming children and harassed parents streaming down the gangplank, stood a tall, well built, pale skinned man. Visibly uncomfortable and sweating profusely in a dark grey suit and tie, he tried to sweep his dark hair from his damp forehead. Yiannis had expected someone much older, but Jack Ryder looked to be in his mid twenties.

'Good afternoon Mr Ryder,' Yiannis said, extending his hand to greet him.

'What's good about it?' Ignoring his offer of a handshake, he passed his bag to Yiannis's extended hand.

'Little Laura, come to your favourite uncle Jack!' He

moved towards the wary girl.

Laura side stepped past him and ran to hide behind Yiannis.

'Hey now what's all this? You remember me? Come and give me a big kiss,' he said, his arms outstretched.

Yiannis eased the reluctant Laura out from behind him and coaxed her forward. 'It's okay, he won't hurt you.'

'Of course I won't hurt her,' he snapped at Yiannis.

Laura looked warily at the large man, noting the beads of perspiration across his top lip, and reluctantly offered her cheek to be kissed. She quickly moved back behind Yiannis, rubbing the dampness furiously from her cheek.

'She doesn't remember very much about the accident,' Yiannis said coolly.

Jack shot Yiannis a dismissive look. 'Nonsense, she'll soon remember her uncle Jack, once she sees all the presents I've brought for her. Won't you poppet? Now let's get out of this infernal heat, before I melt!' he said, peeling his damp stained jacket from his back. 'Where's the car?'

'Boat!' Yiannis grinned, as he walked past him.

'Pardon?'

'We're going by boat. The villa is round the next cove.'

He looked at the Moondancer scornfully. 'Not in that I'm not!'

Yiannis shrugged his shoulders. 'It's either this, or you swim,' he said, choosing not to tell him there were water taxis as an alternative.

'My God, are we in the dark ages here?' he said, lowering his six feet two, fourteen stone self, into the boat.

Laura slipped her hand into Yiannis's and whispered, 'Will it sink?'

Hopefully, Yiannis thought wistfully, but shook his head as he lifted Laura into the boat.

*

Jack hadn't been at Amora Cove long, before there became an obvious coolness and a mutual distrust between him and Yiannis. The presents he had showered Laura with failed to re-establish any relationship they had shared, and he silently resented the fact that Laura wanted to spend all her time with Yiannis.

'I think you have made the right decision Gwen,' Jack said one afternoon, as they stood on the sun terrace watching Yiannis and Laura swimming in the cove.

Squeals of laughter came from Laura as Yiannis threw her into the air so that she splashed joyfully into the water. Laura voice carried as she shouted, 'Throw me again Yiannis.'

Jack lips pursed. 'It's not natural you know Gwen!'

'What isn't?'

'It's not natural for a nineteen year old man to be touching a young girl like that.'

'They're only playing,' Gwen said, as she looked down at the beach.

'Well Laura might be, but I've been watching them and its making me very uncomfortable. I'm surprised you have noticed the intimacy between them. It's quite alarming to an outsider like me. I think the sooner you separate these two the better.'

Gwen felt a shudder down her spine at Jack's revelations.

Jack gave a ghost of a smile at her reaction. 'Besides, I'm not sure a fisherman is the right sort of person to influence a young girl. She needs a proper education, with children of her own class. If you don't check her now, she could be wild in another couple of years and past redemption.'

'My sentiments exactly Jack!' She chinked her gin and tonic with his and sighed wistfully. 'Oh, it *will* be nice to have the villa to ourselves again. We're too long in the tooth to be bringing up a child. As you say, she'll be better off and safer in England. It's such a relief to think she will be staying with such a good family for the school half term holidays. The Haynes's were always good friends of my son Stephen. I couldn't wish for her to be in better hands.'

'Well I'm going to miss her,' Charles said, joining them on the terrace. 'I'm not at all looking forward to telling her.'

'It's her only salvation Charles. She'll thank us when she's older, so the sooner you tell her the better,' Gwen said firmly.

*

As the sun began to set that evening and cicadas shrilled in chorus in the undergrowth, Yiannis was working on his veranda when he heard the commotion filtering up from the villa. He frowned as Laura ran down the terrace steps shouting at the top of her voice, 'No! I'm not going, I won't, I won't I tell you. I want to stay here!' she sobbed.

She was swiftly followed by Gwen. 'You come back here at once young lady,' she shouted sternly.

Charles pushed past Gwen, and followed Laura to the lodge.

Yiannis covered the model of the Moondancer he had been working on with a cloth just as Laura scrambled up his veranda steps and ran into his arms.

Charles arrived breathless a few seconds later. 'Help?' he mouthed silently at Yiannis.

He frowned quizzically at Charles, as he carried Laura into his kitchen. Her lower lip trembled as he sat her on the table. 'Now, what's the matter with my little Laura?'

Laura put her fist to her eye and rubbed it fiercely, she could hardly speak for crying. 'They want to send me to school in England!' she wailed.

Yiannis's heart sank when he cast a sidelong glance at Charles who confirmed the news with a nod. With his mind in turmoil, he cleared his throat to compose himself. 'Oh well that's wonderful,' he said, enthusiastically.

'No it's *not*!' she said indignantly, kicking her sandal against the table.

Forcing a smile, he answered, 'Of course it is Laura!'

She pursed her lips. 'But I want to stay here with you!'

'But, I've taught you everything I know about Greece. Now it's your turn to go and learn everything about England, so you can come back and teach me.'

Looking slightly perturbed, Laura said hesitantly, 'I can tell you about England without me having to go away.'

Yiannis sighed heavily. 'I know you are a clever little girl and you know lots of things,' he declared proudly. 'But there is so much more to learn, and to do that you need to go to school in England!' As he spoke, he felt as though his heart would break. 'I thought you could write to me every week, telling me what you have learned, but if you don't want to help me, that's okay.'

This pretence was killing him. As he watched her unhappy face, his emotions impelled him to turn and leave. Once outside he closed his eyes, shocked at the enormity of how this news had affected him.

Laura glanced at her grandfather for guidance.

'Oh dear, I think Yiannis is really upset that you don't want to go to England,' he said softly.

Laura scrambled down off the table and out of the house after him.

'Yiannis?' She ran along the veranda towards him. 'I will go, if that's what you think I should do, and I promise I will write to you and tell you everything. Please don't be upset.'

He swept her up into his arms and hugged her tightly, but for a moment he did not trust his voice to speak to her.

'Can we go swimming tomorrow Yiannis?' she said, her voice wavering slightly.

'We can do anything you want sweetheart! Now I think it's time for your bed. Off you go, I want to speak to your grandpa. I'll see you tomorrow. ' He kissed the top of her head and sent her on her way.

'Thank you Yiannis,' Charles said gratefully. 'I know that was difficult for you, but you handled it very well. She's made a huge impact on all our lives, especially yours

I believe.'

Yiannis looked out to sea. He would never realise how much of an impact. 'I had no idea you were planning on sending her away,' his voice wavered slightly. 'She'd settled in so well at the local school!'

'I'm sorry Yiannis. It all happened very swiftly. We have friends back in England, Sarah and Gerald Haynes. They knew my son and his wife very well. They have a daughter the same age as Laura, who attends an excellent girls' school in Truro. They have suggested that Laura attends the same school. She would board there and receive a splendid education, with the benefit of staying with the Haynes' during the holidays. That is why Jack is here. He's been making all the arrangements for us.'

Yiannis felt a painful tightness in his throat. 'So, she won't be home for the holidays?'

'For Christmas and the summer break, yes, but you have to agree it's too far to come at half term.'

'Of course.' Yiannis nodded miserably. 'When will she go?'

'The thirty-first of August, that's a week tomorrow.'

'But that is the day before her birthday!' he exclaimed in alarm.

Charles wrinkled his nose. 'I know, but Gwen thought it would be a good idea to fly home the day before and have a little birthday party in Cornwall with her new surrogate family. It'll help her settle into her new surroundings. So my boy…' He patted Yiannis on the back. 'I'll need you to look after the place while we're gone if that's okay?'

17

During those last few precious days together, Yiannis and Laura clung to each other with the same unspoken feeling of dread of their impending separation. They filled their days visiting favourite places, gathering and storing memories which they could draw upon when the time came for them to be parted. Yiannis tried desperately to keep Laura's spirits up, even though his own feelings were in turmoil and when the day finally came for her to go, he was visibly bereft.

There was a distinct air of mixed emotions in the small party, as they sat at Alexis's Taverna drinking coffee, waiting for the ferry to arrive. Gwen had gone to the kiosk to buy some aspirin and Charles and Jack stared intently out to sea, ready to catch a glimpse of the ferry. Laura sat quiet and subdued, slowly sipping orange juice through a straw. Alexis had tried unsuccessfully to make her smile, but her face remained tragically morose.

'Is it okay if Laura comes with me for a moment?' Yiannis asked Charles.

'Where are you taking her?' Jack said sternly.

Yiannis ignored him and looked to Charles.

Charles smiled. 'Of course, but don't be long, the ferry will be here in a moment.'

Laura slid down from the table and placed her bag on the chair.

'No, bring your bag,' Yiannis said, taking her small hand in his and leading her towards his boat.

For one exciting moment, Laura thought he was going to take her back to the cove. 'Where are we going?' she asked brightly.

'I have something for you in the boat,' he replied casually.

'What is it?' She danced excitedly at his side.

He reached into the box under the seat and produced

two gaily-coloured bags. 'Open this one first,' he instructed, handing her the larger one of the two.

She plunged her hand into it and pulled out a golden honeycomb sponge! She squeezed it in her hand. 'It's a sponge!' she said, puzzled and slightly disappointed, but still grateful for anything Yiannis gave her.

'It's not just any old sponge. It's a worry sponge!' He reached over and cupped her hands around the sponge. 'If ever you're sad, lonely, or worried about anything at all, all you have to do is to hold the sponge to your heart and let it absorb all your anxieties.'

She looked up at him woefully with her big blue eyes. 'What if I have so many worries the sponge gets too full?'

Yiannis smiled gently. 'Ah well, you run it under the tap until it's full of water, then squeeze them all away.'

She looked down at the sponge and squeezed it tightly then looked shyly under her lashes at Yiannis.

'Will you promise to use it, because, I don't want my little Laura to worry about anything, okay?'

She nodded, and pushed the gift deep into her bag then threw her arms around his neck and hugged him tight.

'Now you can open this one,' he said, passing the tiny bag to her.

'Oh!' Her pink lips pursed as she lifted the tiny brooch out of the bag. It was a golden half moon with a delicate figurine of a girl dancing on the bottom tip of it. Laura lifted it up so that the sun caught its reflection.

'Do you like it? It's for your birthday tomorrow.'

'Oh yes, it's lovely,' she said, trying to pin it to her dress with fumbling fingers but had to let Yiannis help her.

'It's a moon dancer, so every time you look at it, you will think of me and my little boat bobbing about dancing under the moon.'

Her eyes brimmed with tears. 'I love you Yiannis.'

Yiannis held his hand to his chest. 'I love you too my little Laura. Don't forget me will you.'

'I won't, I promise,' she answered profoundly.

He smiled gleefully. 'You'll be back before you know it. It's only a few weeks until Christmas.'

She gave a half-hearted nod. 'Will you have the model of the Moondancer finished by then?'

'Of course I will.'

Laura's face filled with excitement. 'So, will I be able to have it as soon as I come back?'

'Oh no, I will have sent it to Father Christmas, and he'll bring it back. But only if you are a good girl though!'

'I'm always a good girl,' she said sweetly.

They both looked up as the ferry sailed into view and reluctantly made their way back to the taverna.

'Look grandpa, look at what Yiannis bought me,' she said, skipping towards him excitedly.

'Oh well, isn't that lovely. Have you thanked him?'

'Yes I have, haven't I Yiannis?'

Yiannis nodded as he gathered their luggage together and waited for the passengers to disembark from the ferry.

'Yiannis my boy, we will be away for a few weeks, we want to make sure Laura gets settled into her school. Take a bit of a holiday, you deserve one. I've left some money in an envelope on top of the fridge. Go and enjoy yourself.'

'Thank you very much sir,' he said graciously. 'I hope you have a good journey.'

'Oh and Yiannis,' Gwen chipped in. 'Sort out the garden will you, you know the bit Laura has made such a mess of.'

Yiannis frowned. 'Laura's garden you mean?' He thought of the small plot of land he and Laura had cultivated, under Laura's bedroom window. They had filled it with fragrant flowers so the smell would waft into her bedroom first thing in the morning and last thing at night. 'But…..?'

'Yiannis, sort it out please!' she retorted, as she picked up her shoulder bag, folded her cardigan over her arm and joined Charles at the gangplank.

With a heavy heart Yiannis scanned the boat to catch a last look at Laura and saw her standing on a seat hanging over the side watching the dark murky water lap against the side of the vessel. He prayed that she wouldn't be sick this time.

Charles shouted from the deck. 'Goodbye Yiannis.'

Yiannis waved and watched as the last few passengers boarded. He looked searchingly again for Laura, but she was nowhere to be seen. He stepped back ready to wave the boat off when he heard her tiny voice calling.

'Yiannis, Yiannis,' Laura called from the top of the gangplank. 'Yiannis, I didn't kiss you goodbye,' she cried.

He ran towards her, swept her into his arms, and let her put a damp kiss on his cheek.

'You take care now, you hear me? Write to me? I want to know all about your school, okay?' he said walking her back onto the boat.

She nodded woefully.

'Don't forget to use your worry sponge.'

'I won't… I think I'll use it all the time.'

'Goodbye sweetheart.' He smiled warmly as he placed her carefully down on the deck.

'Bye, bye. See you at Christmas,' she answered tearfully.

Yiannis stood and waved until the ferry sailed out of view.

'Come and have a drink Yiannis?' said Alexis, placing his hand on his shoulders.

'I may as well. I have nothing else to do,' he replied reflectively and looked wistfully out to sea to where the ferry had been moments before.

'Beer?' Alexis said.

Yiannis took the bottle from Alexis, and drank thirstily, savouring the coolness of the amber liquid as it quenched his parched throat. When he had drunk his fill he glanced about him and noticed the bearded Englishman to his left, artist sketchbook in hand, smiling warmly at him. Yiannis had found out that the man rented a small workshop owned by Alexis, but although he had seen him often, Yiannis had been too busy with Laura to make his acquaintance.

'Mr Kiassos?' The Englishman stood up and moved towards him. 'For you,' he said, handing him an exquisite pencil drawing. 'I watched you two together earlier on the harbour. She is a very special young lady to you I think? I thought you would like a memento of the two of you.'

The likeness of the drawing was stunning and Yiannis was visibly moved as he studied it. 'It's beautiful, thank you.'

'She will be missed by all who know her. I hope she returns to us very soon.'

'I'll drink to that,' Yiannis agreed. 'I'm sorry I don't even know your name.'

'Travis Reeves at your service. ' He gave a short bow before making his way back to his own table.

As Yiannis glanced again at the drawing, he did not see who approached him.

'Ah, how sweet,' Eva's voice grated like sandpaper. 'Shall I get him to draw a picture of our beautiful son as well? As you haven't met him yet!' she sneered.

Yiannis pulled the drawing from her sight, scraped his chair backwards, left his beer and walked away from her without speaking.

'When are you going to pay me, the baby's due?' she shouted after him.

'When hell freezes over!' he muttered, as he jumped into his boat and sailed angrily back to Amora Cove.

*

There was a distant rumble of thunder as he picked up the envelope left by Charles and examined the contents. "Take a holiday, enjoy yourself," Charles had told him. 'I might just do that,' Yiannis sighed. Pushing the envelope in his pocket, he locked the French doors behind him and walked slowly back to the lodge. Alone with his thoughts, he watched as a cool breeze ruffled the dazzle of the sea.

Black laden thunder clouds moved slowly across the sky, scrawling across the darkening water. The silence of the hot afternoon gave way to the rush of the breeze through the treetops, and Yiannis said a wistful goodbye to the long hot summer, as the hot parched barren earth yielded to the cascading droplets of cool rejuvenating rain.

18

Without his little Laura to care for, Yiannis found life incredibly empty. On dry days he cultivated the land surrounding his lodge, fished the fruits of the sea and spent solitary hours mending his nets. When the weather turned inclement, he sat in the shelter of his run-down fishing hut, surrounded by the beautiful drawings that Laura had hung there, proudly but secretly, for his eyes only.

His evenings were spent with Kostas and Travis in the back room at Alexis Taverna. They would wile away the late hours at Irene's scrubbed, bleached table, drinking endless cups of thick black coffee whilst playing backgammon. It was a large, warm, comfortable room. Paintings adorned the walls that were not already occupied by wooden shelves holding a multicoloured array of bottles. On the back wall stood two large fridges, between which several cats snoozed, paws and tails entwined, enjoying the heat emitted from them. In the early evening, the place would be full of cheerful elderly fishermen. Dressed in dark suits, they would toss their worry beads between thick weathered fingers, worn smooth from hard work. Together the old men would smoke, argue and drink, whilst tapping their walking sticks in time to the Greek music that played continually on the wireless, competing with the dusty television set high up in the top corner of the room.

*

When a letter came informing Yiannis that the Tempests were due back on the island in the first week of November, he decided to take the holiday Charles had advised him to do. When he returned to Amora Cove seven days later, he was invigorated with the delicious memory of the week he had spent in the arms of Katia, a young woman he had met in Piraeus who had massaged fragrant oils into his responsive body and rescued him from boyhood.

*

On their return, Charles proudly showed Yiannis a photo of Laura, in her white and green school uniform, looking coyly at the camera from under the upturned brim of her straw hat.

Yiannis gazed at her photo. She looked so vulnerable. 'Is she all right?'

'I can assure you dear boy, she has settled in well,' he said, tucking the photo back in his jacket pocket. 'She has made friends with the Haynes' youngest child Vanessa. So there is absolutely nothing to worry about. The only thing she complains about is the weather.'

Yiannis smiled thankfully.

'Gwen believes she will have forgotten all about us in a few weeks,' he said casually.

Yiannis felt a pang of dejection. He had hoped that she would have written to him before now.

'Oh by the way,' Charles said, rummaging in his other pocket. 'Sorry about these Yiannis.' He produced a handful of letters. 'Laura gave them to Gwen to post on to you, but it seems Gwen decided to save postage and bring them with her.' He gave a short embarrassed laugh. 'We very nearly threw them out with the rubbish. Gwen had accidentally put them in the bin.'

Yiannis silently took the letters from Charles. For some reason Gwen had been quite unfriendly towards Yiannis during the last few days Laura had been on the island, so he suspected that throwing his letters away had been no accident.

That evening he sat at his kitchen table and read the letters chronologically. Each reassuring letter clearly proved he had not been forgotten. She wrote wonderful simple letters about girls' school dormitory stories, lessons, and how dreadfully cold but very pretty it was in Cornwall. Some of them contained beautiful drawings of her school and its surrounding grounds, and one had been a pencil portrait of her new friend Vanessa Haynes, all of which carried strict instructions that nobody else should see them - especially her grandmother. But the one thing that touched him most of all, was that she always started the letters with the words 'I miss you,' and ended them with 'I love you,' in large capital letters.

*

As the winter drew on and Christmas approached, Yiannis had risen early as usual to fish and was now busy putting the finishing touches to the replica of the Moondancer ready for Christmas day. It was the sixteenth of December - Laura was expected back on the twentieth. He wanted it to be finished before her return.

'Morning Yiannis,' Charles said cheerily, as he stood at the kitchen door, rubbing his hands together. 'Gosh it's a bit chilly today!'

'Morning,' he replied, wiping his hands on a cloth. He watched Charles walk round the kitchen table, closely inspecting the boat he had just finished working on.

'Is this the boat you've been making for Laura, the one she mentions in every letter?' he asked cautiously.

'It is. Do you think she'll like it?'

He paused for a moment. 'Yes it's marvellous, but I thought you were going to give it to her at Christmas?'

'I am!' He laughed, and then saw the expression on Charles face. 'Why, what is it?'

Charles knitted his eyebrows thoughtfully. 'But Laura isn't coming home for Christmas.'

Yiannis's look of surprise made Charles shift uncomfortably.

'I'm sorry Yiannis, I thought you knew! That's why we sent that parcel to England two weeks ago. It had all her presents in it. Didn't Gwen tell you?'

Yiannis shook his head numbly.

Charles cursed under his breath. 'I told her you had a present for Laura! I can't understand why she didn't tell you.'

Yiannis knew exactly why. It was clearly obvious that she wanted all ties between them severed. He cleared his throat. 'Why isn't she coming home?'

'Gwen thinks, well….. we thought, it would be better for Laura to spend more time with the Haynes'. She needs more stability in her life, and when they invited her to stay for the Christmas holidays we were more than happy for her to do that.'

Yiannis shook his head. 'Laura hasn't said anything in her letters. In fact she is looking forward to coming home!'

Charles scratched his chin. 'Yes well, we haven't told her yet. It will be a nice surprise for her when she finds out. I mean, where better to spend Christmas than in a grand house on the banks of the Helford River.'

Yiannis nodded unhappily. 'Sounds wonderful, but how am I going to get this to her now? It's too late to post, isn't it?'

'I'm afraid it might be.' Charles gave him a fatherly pat on the shoulder. 'Never mind….' there was a hesitation in his voice, '….she'll have plenty of other presents to open. We've sent her all sorts,' he added cheerily.

Yiannis drummed his fingers on the table thoughtfully. He wasn't prepared to leave it there - he would try and get it to her somehow.

When Charles took his leave, Yiannis pulled on his coat, tucked the model boat protectively under his arm, and set off to the harbour. Once there, he begged a cardboard box and a few newspapers from Alexis, and carefully packed and wrapped the boat ready for posting. At the Post Office, he had to fight his way through a few sneering women, passing their time gossiping and sheltering from the rain.

'Yes?' Marion Dopas asked rudely, looking down her nose at him.

Ignoring her insolence he asked, 'If I sent this to England would it get there for Christmas day?'

A gleeful smile crossed Marion's face. 'No. It should have gone two weeks ago.'

Hiding his disappointment, he turned to walk away as a couple of the women sniggered. 'Bloody hags!' he muttered under his breath. As he moved to the door, one of them spat at his feet, just as Akis emerged from the rear of the shop.

Furiously Akis shoved the offending woman unceremoniously out of the door. 'How dare you spit at a customer? You filthy bitch!' He turned to the others. 'Go on get out, all of you!' He pushed the women until they spewed out onto the path into the rain. Dusting his hands he glared at his wife who stood open-mouthed at the ferocity of his outburst. 'And you'd better get out from behind that counter, before I do you a mischief!' he snapped. Marion cast an embittered glance at Yiannis, then in a fit of panic, lifted her skirts and made a quick exit out the back of the store, quickly followed by her furious husband.

Yiannis stood at the Post Office door for a moment, amused at the fierce row that ensued in the back room. At least something had brightened his day.

'What the hell is going on in there?' Alexis asked.

Yiannis grinned broadly. 'A little domestic trouble I think.'

Alexis nodded at the box. 'Too late?'

'Too late!' he replied, placing it on the table.

'Coffee?'

'Yes, make it strong and thick please.' His disappointment was intense.

'Excuse me, Yiannis?'

Yiannis smiled up at Travis Reeves.

Travis nodded at the box. 'Does that contain a present for little Laura?'

Yiannis sighed and nodded. 'I promised her it for Christmas, but I've just been told she isn't coming home, and it's too late to send it!'

Travis inspected the address thoughtfully. 'I'll take it for you.'

Yiannis frowned. 'But Laura is in England!'

'Yes I know,' he replied casually. 'I'm leaving tomorrow. I've a mind to go home for Christmas myself.'

Yiannis laughed incredulously. 'Well that is very kind of you, but won't it inconvenience you?'

'Not at all.' He took the box out of Yiannis's hands. 'You leave it with me. We can't let her down now, can we?' He winked at Yiannis.

'I don't know what to say, except thank you very much.' He shook his hand vigorously. 'Here let me give you the money to post it when you get to England.'

Travis held his hand up. 'We will sort it out when I return, okay?'

'Okay.' Yiannis felt an overwhelming gratitude towards him. 'Let me buy you a drink then. Alexis, can we have two brandies please?'

*

Two days later, Travis unlocked the door to his studio apartment in St Ives, cleared a space on his workbench and placed the boxed boat on the table. The studio felt cold and damp and he shivered involuntarily. He thought wistfully of the warmth of summer, and pulled his coat about him as he crawled onto his musty bed and fell into a deep sleep.

19

It had taken Laura a while to settle into her new school life, contrary to what she and her grandparents had told Yiannis. Although not unfriendly, the other pupils found her strange Greek -English accent and her wild unsophisticated manners a little odd.

Although Truro was only forty minutes from Gweek, both she and Vanessa boarded during term time. Thankfully she liked Vanessa, and her old friend Pippa Ferris-Norton was also at the school, although Pippa went home every day. Academically she faired quite well. She excelled in art, ancient history, and languages, was passable in English literature, but when it came to mathematics and science she was more of an observer and dismissed it without really trying.

She corresponded regularly with Yiannis, as he did with her, but she missed him dreadfully and crossed the days off the calendar until she could go back to Poros to see him again.

To say she was devastated when the letter came from her grandpa informing her that she was to spend Christmas with the Haynes's would have been an understatement! Faking a stomach-ache, she spent the whole day in her dormitory, in sheer misery. The prospect of not seeing Yiannis for at least another six months was unbearable. Later that evening she sat by torchlight under the covers and poured her heart out in a long letter to Yiannis, leaving him in no doubt where her sentiments lay. She sealed the envelope, kissed it, resigning herself to the prospect of Christmas without him.

Vanessa, on the other hand, was thrilled at the prospect of Laura coming for Christmas. 'We will have such fun,' she enthused. 'You'll get to meet my brothers at last. We'll sing carols on Christmas Eve around a *huge* Christmas tree. Oh and on Christmas morning, before we go to church, we'll open our presents in front of an open fire in the best front room. Oh,' she jumped about excitedly, 'you'll love it.'

Vanessa's image of Christmas at Creek House made the prospect a little more appealing. She had liked Creek House, when she stayed there briefly at half term. It was a grand imposing building, with stylish, glamorous furnishings. It was a Grade II listed building, which sat to the south of Gweek and overlooked the old Corn Mill. Vanessa's ancestors had lived there since 1490.

Set back from the main road, a steep road took them to a gravel drive, which was shaded with an avenue of mature beech trees. The first time she walked into its magnificent hall, she stood in awe at its splendour. Family portraits looked down at her from their ornate frames, and a cascade of coloured rays of light filtered down from a stained glass dome. A huge fresh flower arrangement welcomed them, set upon a large walnut table in the middle of a Persian rug.

'Goodness Vanessa, are you very rich?' Laura gasped.

'I suppose we are a bit,' Vanessa answered. 'Father makes his money from art and antiques.'

'I thought your father was poorly,' she asked innocently.

'Not poorly, disabled. He broke his back riding. But it doesn't stop him working. He doesn't leave the house, but he has contacts,' she tapped the side of her nose knowingly.

'Vanessa, don't speak of your father as though he is doing something underhand,' Sarah Haynes said flippantly, as she breezed out of the drawing room into the hall to greet them. She hugged the girls with equal affection, and then with pure sincerity she said to Laura, 'Welcome to Creek House my dear. It's lovely to have you here.'

Laura liked Vanessa's mother Sarah very much. She was a tall, beautiful, vivacious woman with shoulder length brown hair, neatly swept back off her face and flicked up at the ends. She had full thick eyebrows and long glossy lashes that emphasised her large brown eyes. Laura loved to watch her move elegantly about the house, with her cardigan draped casually over her shoulders. She was warm and friendly to Laura, always ready with a smile and a sparkle in her eyes, and would practically treat her like her own daughter. In all, she loved being at Creek House, but she was just slightly apprehensive about this trip, when she would be meeting Vanessa's elder brothers and their father for the first time.

*

The girls arrived home five days before Christmas, just in time to help the gardener choose the Christmas trees from the woods.

'We'll need a massive one for the hall, and a smaller one for the drawing room,' Vanessa said to Laura excitedly, as they held on for dear life in the back of the red pick-up truck.

An hour later they arrived back at the house, rosy cheeked and glowing with exhilaration. Sarah, with a little help from the staff, had managed to clear the hall of all its furnishing. The Persian rug had been rolled up and pushed to the wall, along with the walnut table, and in its place stood the huge red tub ready for the giant Christmas tree. Annie Bell the cook, stood alongside Mrs Strong the housekeeper, and with swiftness and ease, they all took their positions in this well rehearsed custom, and hoisted the tree into its position with the lifting ropes. The two girls helped the gardener to pack the tree with rocks and stones to stabilise it. Then bucket after bucket of water was brought from the kitchen to fill the huge red tub. When it was brimming with water everyone stood back to admire the magnificent sweet smelling pine tree.

Laura closed her eyes as her senses drank in the smell of pine, bringing back evocative memories of Poros and Yiannis.

'Come on Laura,' Vanessa nudged her. 'We've got to

get the other one in the drawing room, and then it's our job to decorate them. Isn't it exciting?'

*

Slater and Taylor Haynes arrived home on Christmas Eve, having just returned from a school skiing trip to Switzerland. Sarah and the girls stood huddled together at the door, ready to greet them from the taxi. Laura prayed the butterflies in her stomach would stop fluttering as she watched the boys emerge from the cab, laughing noisily.

'Oh my beautiful boys,' Sarah cried, sweeping them into her arms. 'Let's get indoors quick. It's freezing out here!' She ushered them into the hall.

Taylor threw his bag on the floor. 'Nice tree Van!' he said, picking her up to swing her round before planting a warm kiss on her head.

Vanessa squealed with delight. 'Laura helped me with the tree, didn't you Laura?'

Laura swallowed hard and nodded shyly at Taylor.

'Nice tree Laura,' Taylor replied, picking her up to swing her, as he had done Vanessa.

Laura blushed profusely when he put her down.

'Now calm down everybody,' Sarah laughed. 'Taylor, Slater, I want you to welcome our neighbour Laura Tempest.'

Taylor bowed graciously. 'I'm very pleased you are spending Christmas with us Laura.'

Laura blushed again and smiled as Slater moved towards her.

'Hi, I hope you're not as much trouble as Van. Girls can be a real nuisance.'

'Don't be so horrible.' Vanessa slapped him. 'Take no notice Laura, he's a pig.'

Slater grinned at Vanessa, then picked her up, turned her upside down, and shook her until she apologised for calling him a pig. When he finally let her go she stood up, furiously brushing herself down. 'Pig!' she screamed again then quickly hid behind her mother.

'Now, now you two, enough is enough, Laura will think we're all mad. Go and get washed and changed for dinner, cook will be angry if you're late for the special meal she has cooked for you.'

'Brilliant, we're starving!' the boys said in unison, as they picked up their bags and raced upstairs.

Sarah smiled lovingly at her boys as she watched them go, and then turned her attention to the girls. 'Now, let's help Mrs Strong set the table. Oh and Vanessa, don't call your brother a pig, it's extremely vulgar.'

'Yes mother,' Van sighed.

*

That evening at dinner, the family sat together in the opulent Wedgwood blue dining room.

Laura had dressed carefully, in a dark blue velvet dress. She had brushed her hair away from her face and secured it back with a matching blue Alice band, and had spat on her patent leather black shoes, and buffed them until they shone.

The table was set for six people, but only five were expected for dinner. Sarah sat at one end of the table, flanked by Laura to her left and Vanessa to her right. Taylor sat next to Laura and they all waited patiently for Slater to join them.

Sarah glanced at the clock on the dresser and sighed in exasperation. 'Where is that boy, he's always late! Taylor, be a dear and go and call him please.'

A couple of minutes later Slater breezed in, sat down without apology, and grinned broadly at everyone.

Sarah pursed her lips. 'So pleased you could join us,' she said, narrowing her eyes at him.

'My pleasure,' Slater parried.

Sarah gave him a warning look, and Slater was momentary silenced, but as soon as dinner was served, talk was loud and lively and Laura studied Van's brothers intently.

Slater was very much like Vanessa in looks and manner.

At thirteen years old, it was already plain to see that he would be extremely handsome when he grew older. He had straight blond hair, accentuated by his sun-bronzed face from his skiing trip. His blue eyes sometimes looked cold when he shot a glance at anyone, but he positively glowed with confidence, as he moved his arms to express himself.

Taylor was a year older than his brother, two inches taller, and considerably thinner. He had the same brown eyes as his mother, a fair complexion and a full sensuous smiling mouth. His attire was slightly untidy, and his thick black glossy hair, which was combed back and parted to the side, persistently flopped over his face. As he sat next to Laura and chatted to her that evening, she was overwhelmed by his warm, friendly but sensitive disposition. She knew she had made a friend for life.

After dinner all the household staff joined together in the great hall to sing carols round the Christmas tree. Afterwards, they all retired to the drawing room, where Laura and Taylor sat together on one of the large brown leather chesterfields which flanked the roaring fire. As they chatted, Laura had found to her amazement that they shared the same birthday, the first of September, though he was four years older than her. He asked her about Greece, and coaxed her into saying 'Merry Christmas' in Greek. He asked if she liked her new school and what she thought of their house. He spoke excitedly about Switzerland, describing its lakes and mountains, ski lifts to the top of the world, and waterfalls that would take your breath away. But best of all were the shops full of chocolate goodies and fancy cakes. 'Talk about making the mouth water,' he exclaimed. 'I really couldn't resist them, and stuffed my face at every possible opportunity.'

'Gosh, it sounds wonderful,' Laura said smacking her lips. 'I love chocolate!'

'Yeah, you look like you do!' Slater leaned over and pinched the flesh on her arm.

Laura baulked at his comment and immediately fell silent.

'Slater, how dare you say a thing like that?' Sarah scolded. 'Apologise to Laura immediately.'

'I didn't mean anything by it. I was just making an observation, after all she did have a second helping of dessert at dinner!' he answered innocently. 'Sorry for speaking.'

'That does not excuse you. Second helpings are for everyone, in fact I believe you indulged, now apologise at once for being rude.'

He clicked the roof of his mouth with his tongue in annoyance. 'Okay I apologise.' He scowled darkly.

Laura lowered her eyes and wished with all her heart that the floor would swallow her up. Vanessa moved over to sit by Laura and said, 'I told you he was a pig.'

Slater stuck his tongue out to her, and Sarah gave him a swift crack around the head, whilst shooting a look of disapproval at Vanessa.

'Well, I think it's time for bed, so can we all just remember that it's Christmas, the season of good will etcetera, and I don't want any silly bickering from you tomorrow when your father is here. Do I make myself clear?' Sarah said, rising from her seat.

They all nodded meekly, kissed their mother goodnight, and retired to bed.

*

At about the time Laura was climbing into bed in Creek House, Travis Reeves was just returning home to St Ives from his temporary Christmas job. He parked his car, took off his uniform, placed it in the boot, and glanced at his watch - it was ten thirty p.m. He gave an exhausted sigh as he climbed the steps to his studio, threw his car keys on the table next to Laura's boxed boat, made himself a hot drink, and took it to bed.

20

It was still dark at six a.m. when Travis rose from his bed. The light from the chapel on the island at St Ives glowed pale yellow as he stood and stretched out his aching back. He swilled his face with cold water, grabbed a slice of toast and a cup of tea, before picking up his car keys and the box containing the boat. He set off through the deserted roads for the forty minute drive to Gweek. He loved the town when all the visitors had gone home. It felt like it used to feel – a proper fishing village. Still, he couldn't grumble. The tourists bought his paintings and gave him enough money to live on.

He arrived in the village at seven-fifteen, parking his car out of sight. There were no lights on in Creek House, so he cut the engine and waited. At eight a.m. a light appeared in the main hall, then in the next room, until the whole of the first floor was ablaze with a warm yellow glow. Travis sat for another half-hour, got out and looked down the Helford River. He yawned noisily, stretching the stiffness from his limbs. The morning was still and the tide was out, leaving vast mudflats and small grassy islands in its wake. A pair of swans walked in an ungainly fashion towards the stream, and a lone egret flew from one end of the river to the other in search of breakfast. He wished that he'd brought his sketch book, but no, today he had more pressing issues. He unlocked the boot, retrieved his work uniform and began to dress at the roadside.

The Haynes household was alive with the shrieks of happy children opening their presents. Laura sat and eagerly opened hers. She had received an LP of her favourite singer, Al Stewart, from Vanessa. A beautiful hat and scarf set from the rest of the Haynes family, and a huge bar of Swiss chocolate from Taylor, which he had sneaked under her bedroom door first thing this morning. Finally she opened the package her grandparents had sent with much anticipation. Inside there were books, clothes, and sweets, but to her infinite disappointment, there was no model of the Moondancer from Yiannis.

'Well aren't you a lucky girl?' Sarah said, as she inspected Laura's gifts.

Laura nodded, trying to hide her disappointment.

'Mother, there's somebody coming up the drive!' Vanessa said, kneeling on the deep velvet cushions at the bay window seat.

Sarah glanced at her watch. 'I wonder who that could be at this time.' She knelt beside her daughter to take a look.

Vanessa let out a huge shriek and made everyone else in the room jump. 'He's here he's here!' she said, running to the door to open it.

'Vanessa, wait a moment, let me go to the door!' Sarah said, not quite believing what she had just seen coming up the drive.

All the children gathered around curiously. When Sarah pulled open the huge oak door, they all fell silent as their eyes fell on their visitor.

'Ho, ho, ho,' said Travis tentatively, as he stood on the steps in full Father Christmas uniform.

Sarah's eyes widened in astonishment, as the girls stood open-mouthed at the figure before them. Travis pulled the sack from his shoulder, reached in for the box and read the address on the front. 'For Miss Laura Tempest,' he said, handing the box to the stunned little girl. 'Special delivery from Greece, sorry it's a little late - I found it at the bottom of my sleigh.'

Resigned to the fact there was nothing Sarah could do about this unexpected visitor she urged Laura to open it.

Slowly, with trembling fingers, Laura pulled the wrapping from the box, opened it up and lifted the boat from its casing. She took one look and hugged it gently in her arms, as hot salty tears dribbled down her rosy cheeks. 'I thought he had forgotten,' she said tearfully.

'Oh dear,' Sarah said, putting a comforting arm around the sobbing child. 'There is no need to take on so.'

'Who's it from?' Vanessa said pulling a confused face.

'It's from Yiannis!' she said, hugging her prize.

'What has he sent you a boat for? Boats are for boys!'

'Because that's what I wanted,' she replied indignantly.

Vanessa laughed. 'Well, why are you crying?'

'I don't know,' Laura sobbed, grinning through the tears.

Sarah smiled at the gentleman in the Father Christmas uniform, and he threw a thankful glance back at her for allowing this intrusion.

'Well, as you can imagine it's been a long night. The reindeers are tired and it's a long trip back to Lapland.'

'Quite!' she replied bemused.

'I just have one more present for Laura here,' he said, glancing tentatively at Sarah, as he handed a small gift-wrapped box over.

Laura looked at the gift tag. It read, 'To Laura from Father Christmas.' She giggled softly, pulled the ribbon and opened the box to reveal a gold identity bracelet engraved with her name.

'It's lovely Father Christmas, thank you so much,' Laura said, reaching up to kiss his whiskery face.

He nodded happily. 'Merry Christmas to you all,' he said, flipping the sack over his shoulder. He gave Sarah a thankful smile and turned to leave.

'Merry Christmas,' they answered, not quite believing their eyes.

'Thank you Father Christmas,' Laura shouted out to him.

'My pleasure little one,' he said, as he lifted his arm to wave goodbye and crunched down the long gravel drive towards his well hidden car.

Half an hour later, Laura's Uncle Jack, along with his parents arrived at the door bearing more gifts, swiftly followed by Vanessa's Aunt Barbara and Uncle Ray.

At ten-thirty they all wrapped up warm against the cold north wind, and walked the mile to Mawgan Church for the Christmas service. When they returned home, they kicked off their boots, and ran into the warmth and splendour of the drawing room.

The drawing room was truly beautiful with high French windows and sumptuous drapes pulled back to give a fine view of the gardens and river beyond. The great open fire was decorated gaily with holly, ivy and scarlet poinsettias, and an old gramophone stood at the far end of the room playing Christmas songs.

Vanessa's father Gerald Haynes was waiting for them. He held his arms out to greet each of his children as they rushed to his embrace before sitting down at each side of his wheelchair. This was the first time Laura had seen him since she arrived at the house. A riding accident had left him wheelchair bound eight years ago and since then, unable to get about the house, he had lived and slept in the specially converted barn in the grounds of Creek House from where he very rarely ventured.

Laura had been a little apprehensive about meeting him. In her childish imagination she had felt there was something ominous and mysterious about him. She had a vision of a young, dark, brooding handsome man, broken and locked away in his own distant solitude. Instead the man that sat before her looked the same age as her grandpa. He was a proud, distinguished looking gentleman, with a face as sharp as a hatchet, and skin as dry and yellow as a withered autumn leaf. He had eyes of steely light grey, framed with small gold spectacles and his dark blond hair grew wispy grey at the temples. He was not at all the sort of man Laura expected the elegant and beautiful Sarah to be married to.

'Ah, you must be Miss Tempest?' he said, beckoning her towards him.

Laura stood for a few seconds, and then with a gentle push from Sarah, she moved towards him.

'You are the image of your mother, Laura. Isn't she Sarah?'

'Indeed she is,' Sarah replied, laying her hands on her husband's shoulders.

'Am I?' Laura asked blankly.

'Yes, pale and insipid like a ghost,' Slater whispered in her ear.

'What was that Slater?' Sarah said crossly.

'Nothing,' he lied, smirking at Laura who was fighting to keep the tears at bay.

Noting her distress, Gerald said, 'I'm sorry my dear, have I upset you by speaking of your Mother? Vanessa, why don't you and Laura pop down to the kitchen to see if dinner is ready? I'm famished.'

*

Christmas day on Poros dawned cold and dry. It felt like any other day to Yiannis. He rose early to fish as normal and returned to find Charles waiting for him on the beach.

'I'm going to the harbour this afternoon to phone the Haynes's to wish them Merry Christmas. Do you want to come? I'm sure Laura would like to talk to you.'

He nodded eagerly. No sooner had they moored at the harbour, Eva appeared before them.

'Oh Yiannis,' she spoke joyfully. 'I knew you wouldn't let us down. I knew you would come to us today.'

'Go away Eva!' Yiannis answered coldly.

'Oh but Yiannis please, for your son's sake. Please spend some time with us.' She threw herself dramatically at his feet.

Yiannis quickly sidestepped her.

Aghast at the spectacle, Charles bent down to help her. 'Get up Eva my dear. Please don't take on so. Yiannis, could you help?' he pleaded, whilst attempting to lift her.

'Absolutely not,' he said viciously. 'Don't be taken in by her.' He marched away angrily from them both.

Eva let Charles help her to her feet. 'I'm sorry Mr Tempest,' she sobbed. 'It's just that I have no money for our poor baby. Yiannis won't help me. I know he hasn't much money, and I know it was my fault he lost the Athena Taverna, but I was hoping his heart would soften today of all days. I just don't know what to do,' she cried.

Her tears, as expected, evoked sympathy in Charles. Eventually he sighed deeply. 'Come, come my dear, here take this.' He handed her his handkerchief. 'Wipe your tears.' Opening his wallet, he gave her a handful of Drachma notes. 'I'll talk to him for you.' He patted her affectionately on her arm.

Sniffing back her crocodile tears, she nodded thankfully. As he turned away, she stuffed the money down the front of her dress, 'easy money,' she congratulated herself sotto voce. She walked back to the Ice Palace, tickled the baby affectionately under the chin, feeling very pleased with herself that she'd managed to plant the seed of doubt in the old fool's head regarding Yiannis.

There was a marked coolness in Charles's manner when he joined Yiannis and Alexis at the taverna. 'Have you managed to get a line to England yet?' he snapped at Yiannis.

Alexis spoke for Yiannis. 'The Post Office is closed, but you can use our phone,' he said dialling the number. 'In fact you're connected now Mr Tempest.' Alexis beckoned him to the receiver. 'Come on,' Alexis said, 'I'll get you some coffee while he's on the phone.'

'Hello Sarah. It's Charles Tempest here. Just ringing with season's greetings to you all,' he bellowed ever so formally down the line.

Yiannis and Alexis exchanged grins, listening to his very loud English telephone accent boom throughout the restaurant. Then they heard the tone change. Suddenly the pretentious accent was replaced by a soft tender affectionate voice, and Yiannis knew at once that Charles was speaking to Laura. Yiannis shifted restlessly as Charles spoke at length to the little girl.

'Really? Well you are a lucky girl aren't you? Yes I'll thank grandma for you. Well, you can do that yourself. He's stood right next to me.' Charles beckoned Yiannis to the phone. Holding his hand over the receiver, he said, 'I don't know how you managed that!'

'What?' he said quizzically.

'She'll tell you,' Charles said, nodding at the phone. 'Oh and Yiannis, maybe a little more compassion to people closer to home wouldn't go amiss.'

'Sir?'

'I'm just saying. Go ahead - Laura wants to talk to you.'

Confused, he turned his attention to the phone. 'Hello sweetheart.'

Laura squealed with delight at the sound of his voice. 'Oh Yiannis, thank you for my boat. It's lovely. It's the best present in the world. I can't wait to sail her in Amora Cove.'

Yiannis grinned with relief. 'I'll look forward to that day too my little one. I'm glad you like it. I was a bit concerned that you wouldn't get it in time.'

'Oh I didn't get it until I had opened all my other presents, and then Father Christmas brought it to me by special delivery.'

'Father Christmas?'

'Yes, he waited until I had opened all my presents then knocked on the door with a present from you!'

'He did?' Yiannis scratched his head.

'Yes I was a little bit frightened of him. I had never seen him before. Vanessa's mother seemed to know him, but he couldn't stay, because his reindeers were tired and it was a long journey back to Lapland.'

Yiannis was totally confused now. 'What did he look like?'

'Like Father Christmas of course.'

Yiannis thought for a moment about Travis then dismissed the thought from his head. He wouldn't have done that, would he?

'He gave me a gold bracelet as well,' she said excitedly.

Charles was hovering in the background, eager to take the phone again, so Yiannis said reluctantly, 'Well I'm so pleased you got the boat sweetheart. I'm going to hand you back to your grandpa now. Be a good girl now, won't you? Yes I love you very much too. Enjoy the rest of your Christmas and I'll see you very soon. Goodbye Laura.' He handed the receiver back to Charles who talked for a while longer.

Yiannis sat at a table and fingered the coffee cup. 'Where does Travis Reeves live?' he asked Alexis.

He shrugged his shoulders. 'South of England I think, why?'

'Oh nothing,' he replied thoughtful. It had to be Travis, but why, why would he go to so much trouble for him? He smiled to himself as he thought of the joy in Laura's voice. He would be eternally grateful to that man, and looked forward to the day he could thank him in person.

'You look troubled my boy,' Alexis said sitting beside him.

'Not troubled, dumbfounded perhaps.'

'Why is that?'

He shook his head. 'Oh nothing, it doesn't matter.'

Alexis stretched his legs out and yawned. 'How is the little one then?'

'Too far away,' Yiannis answered dismally, as Charles ended his call.

'I know my friend. She'll be back soon though. You'll stay for dinner, yes? You too Mr Tempest,' Alexis extended the offer to Charles.

'Thank you Alexis, but no. I must go back to Gwen, but you stay Yiannis if you want.'

Charles bid them good day and greetings of the season, and sailed back to Amora Cove alone. It had been nice talking to Laura. He was happy that she had settled in England. He shifted uncomfortably. He hadn't the heart to tell Yiannis that she wouldn't be coming back for a long, long time.

*

Christmas lunch had just finished at Creek House when Laura and Sarah returned to the party. Everyone was playing games, and the bottle of brandy had been passed around the grown ups. Soon the adults were snoozing happily in front of the fire. It was too dark now to play out, so the children took themselves off to the indoor swimming pool, giving Laura a chance at last to sail the Moondancer. She eased herself into the shallow end of the pool and launched the boat into the chlorine waves, while the others lolled about reading on the sun chairs.

'Oh Yiannis, she's wonderful,' she whispered quietly to herself, as she daydreamed about the real Moondancer, bobbing lazily in the sunshine on the blue Aegean. Suddenly her reverie was shattered, when Slater dive-bombed the boat. Spluttering and coughing, she rubbed water from her eyes. When her vision cleared, her beautiful boat lay in splinters on the surface of the water. Slater lent against the side of the pool, his hand over his mouth in mock horror. 'Oops sorry, I slipped and fell in,' he sniggered.

'Slater! You really are an intolerable bastard. What on earth did you do that for?' Taylor said, angrily jumping from his chair.

'I said it was an accident!' he pleaded innocently.

'Like hell it was. Sometimes you really sicken me!' Taylor added scathingly. He walked to the pool steps. 'Come on Laura, bring it all here, we'll soon have it mended, it will be just like new I promise.'

Laura's eyes filled with helpless tears as she gathered the broken pieces of her beloved boat. When she glanced at Slater he stuck his tongue out at her. She emerged from the water trying to comprehend why this intense young man was so monstrous towards her.

'Ignore him,' Taylor said gently, comforting her.

21

Laura raced up the great oak staircase at Creek House and into the bedroom she had occupied during the holidays since she arrived here. Lifting the curved lid of her writing bureau, she selected a piece of white writing paper from the drawer, glanced momentarily out of the window towards the river, and began her letter to Yiannis.

It had been almost six years since she left Poros and had written to Yiannis almost every week. She longed to see him again having been disappointed so many times when her trips home to Greece had been cancelled due to her grandma's ill health. This time though the trip would not be cancelled. This time she was definitely going home!

Laura had become ensconced in Creek House. Vanessa was like a sister. Her relationship with Taylor had grown over the years into real affection, but Slater, well, he was hard to fathom. She never knew how to take him.

Taylor and Slater were now at university, though Taylor was just about to complete his final year. Normally, whenever possible, the boys had joined the rest of the family for part of the holidays, but this time Taylor was not to join them, deciding instead to prepare himself for his finals. Although unable to visit Poros, Laura had travelled extensively over the years with the Haynes's. She had toured Europe, visited America, learned to ski in the French Alps, and taken in the splendour of the pyramids of Giza. Her grandparents spent most summers in Gweek, but even then, Laura remained at Creek House.

Occasionally Laura spent the Easter holidays with her Uncle Jack and his parents. They owned a cottage at Cape Cornwall, overlooking its own secluded cove. She had grown fond of Jack. He was very sweet to her and far too generous, always buying her this or that, even though she protested strongly at him not to. Laura loved Cornwall. She loved its warm, wild, beautiful landscape and its volatile weather. Being equally happy when the coastline was lashed with rain or when the shifting sea frets blanketed the waters and engulfed the wild barren cliff tops. On dry days they would spend their days walking the coastal path, high up above the jagged cliffs dotted with evocative ivy clad mine relics. Sometimes they would pick their way down the steep coastal paths, which occasionally veered off down towards a beach, to clamber over slippery rocks, and discover tiny inlets and caves, long ago utilised by smugglers and the like. It was here she would sit and listen to the mighty roar of the Atlantic Ocean, and wish with all her heart that Yiannis could be there with her to see it all.

*

Over the years the pace of life on Poros had been as slow and relaxed as it ever had been. Alexis Petrou continued to enjoy the profits of still being the only good fish taverna on the island, while his son Kostas continued with his unstinting quest to romance every female who entered his father's taverna.

Andreas Dopas spent his days fishing with a line in the harbour and during the holidays he took Stephano, Eva's seven year old son with him. Eva adored her son, but was grateful for the free time this gave her, though she knew Andreas's motives were to win her affection. In the evenings Andreas spent his time in the back room of the Ice Palace, lusting after Eva Barzini and drinking with her brother Franco, who, since losing his leg in the Athena fire, did nothing but laze around in a drunken stupor, grumbling about his predicament.

Yiannis had long since given up hope of ever seeing Laura again, and the sound of her childish laughter filtering through the air was now a long and distant memory.

Over the years his life slipped slowly back into normality, except of course for the persistent paternity demands Eva made on him, which he continued to ignore. He fished most mornings, visited his lady friend in Piraeus whenever his manly urge took him, and found enough work in and around the Villa Amora to keep busy.

Yiannis had been busy working on the villa roof all morning. He had been filling in hairline cracks in the concrete and removing the pine needles and dead leaves that had congregated over the winter months, all in preparation for the villa's annual whitewash.

He stood up and stretched the stiffness out of his back, lifted his face skywards and felt the heat of the sun against his skin. It was the time of day when your shadow hides under your feet, and a cold drink and a lazy lunch beckoned.

He took a swig of water from his bottle, wiped his hand across his mouth and glanced down to the sun terrace, where Charles Tempest stood aimlessly staring out to the sun enamelled sea. Yiannis studied him for a while. He was quietly concerned about Charles - there was definitely something bothering that man. He had lost a great deal of weight over the last couple of years, which Charles dismissed as being a quite natural thing to happen in old age, but there was something else, something that Yiannis couldn't put his finger on.

'Mr Tempest?' Yiannis called down to him breaking his concentration.

Charles jumped as if electrified.

'Sorry, I didn't mean to startle you. I'm going into town to see Travis. Do you want anything?' Yiannis asked tentatively.

Charles's mind seemed to drift for a few moments, and then he roused himself from his reverie. 'No, I don't think so. Oh yes,' he added, 'You could pick the post up for me, if you would.'

Yiannis nodded and made his way towards his ladder.

*

Travis Reeves had returned unexpectedly to the island in the early summer of 1983 to find his old workshop transformed into a doctor's makeshift medical surgery.

Dr Aronis arrived on the island in the autumn of 1982, and after putting up with the unpleasantness of Dr Pachis for years, the islanders took to their new doctor immediately. He was a strange undersized pug-faced looking man with a cheerful affability and a voice so velvety smooth, he could practically talk his patients into feeling better. Travis had been away from the island since December 1981, and when he showed no signs of returning, Alexis cleared his workshop of brush and canvas and installed the doctor in the premises.

So when he came back, Travis found himself without a roof over his head. It was then he approached Yiannis about the Athena. Happy at last to be able to repay him for Laura's boat, Yiannis obliged willingly. He had no plans to open the Athena in the near future. He was glad that the building was of some use to someone.

Over the past four years, the two men had become great friends. Yiannis had found a soul mate - someone he could talk about Laura to, and would share the contents of the many letters she sent him. Travis seemed to understand the attachment he had formed with the child, and the loss he felt from the forced separation, more so than anyone else could.

Travis always returned to Cornwall at the end of June for the summer season, but during the winter months, between them, they had slowly made the Athena habitable again, though not to its former glory. Now its decoration was stark and minimalist, the few pieces of furniture were used to stack canvasses, paint and brushes. The only thing that remained from the old Athena Taverna was its regular visitor Papa Andreas. He would shuffle in at eleven a.m. and seven p.m. most days, stay for approximately an hour each visit, and no amount of persuasion could make the old man leave, without consuming at least three cups of strong black coffee. In the end Travis resigned himself to the fact he was part of the fixtures and fittings, and thanked the lord it was only coffee he drank.

*

Yiannis spent a couple of hours with Travis that afternoon, in the tranquil coolness of the Athena Studio, as he had temporarily called it, before stepping out into the blazing afternoon sun to walk a quarter of a mile through the deserted picturesque harbour to the Post Office. He paused for a while at the harbour wall to gaze at the brightly painted fishing boats as they bobbed lazily in the hot stillness of the marina. Most of the shops, except for the Post Office, were closed, as most Greeks were abed or out at sea at this time of day. Only Alexis was busy, straightening tablecloths and moving chairs.

Yiannis called out a greeting to Alexis as he walked past, and hesitated suddenly when he spotted Eva emerging from the Post Office with her son.

Her mouth curled into a wry smile when she saw him. 'Ah look, here's your papa,' she said, as he walked towards her.

Yiannis averted his eyes and walked past them into the coolness of the Post Office.

Yiannis knew Eva had followed him, but he continued to ignore her. 'Anything for me or the Tempests?' he asked Marion Dopas as politely as his resentment for her would allow.

Marion looked down her nose at Yiannis. 'There is one for Charles, but I'm not sure if there is anything for you. I'll have to look later,' she said, trying to look busy.

'You'll damn well look now!' Akis's voice boomed from behind the curtain that separated their living quarters.

Marion's eyes darted toward her husband as he emerged from the back room. She cowered back from him slightly and flushed as he snapped at her, 'I think you will find there is a letter for him!'

Marion pursed her lips indignantly and rummaged about for the letter she had hidden that very morning.

Akis snatched the letter from her fingers. 'Oh I see. It was waiting to be steamed open was it?' He shook it under her nose.

Marion's eyes darted towards Yiannis. 'Don't be ridiculous, I don't know what you mean,' she protested, trying in vain to stop the flush burning at her cheeks.

'I saw you hold a letter for Yiannis over the kettle last week.'

Marion bristled with indignation. 'Well,' she said haughtily. 'I think we have a duty to check what's going on between him and that child!'

Yiannis's mouth dropped open, as he physically grasped the counter to steady himself.

'What the hell do you mean by that, woman?' Akis demanded.

Marion flashed a defiant look at her husband. 'I don't believe it's proper what is going on between a young girl and *him*! I think we all need to keep an eye on him!'

Akis glanced at Yiannis who was visibly shaken, and then he turned to his wife and slapped her hard across her face. Her eyes blazed as she stood with her hand to her smarting cheek then fled behind the curtain.

Akis glared at Eva who stood in the doorway. 'And *you* can get out as well. You're behind all this!' He bellowed.

Yiannis looked around at Eva and saw her thin lips curl into a smirk as she pulled Stephano from behind her skirts and left the Post Office.

Akis looked at the letter in his hand then looked up at Yiannis.

Yiannis knew what Akis was thinking. 'Open it and read it!' Yiannis said calmly. 'I have nothing to hide.'

Akis looked again at the letter and handed it to Yiannis. 'I know son.'

Yiannis nodded thankfully, stepped out of the sunlight and tried desperately to calm his fury. He stood in the shade of Alexis Taverna and flipped the letter thoughtfully in his fingers. The thought of Eva and that hag Marion reading Laura's letters, before he ever received them, sickened him to his heart. How sordid their minds must be to read anything into the innocent words they exchanged. He slipped his finger under the seal of the envelope and read:

Dear Yiannis,

Can you believe it? I'm coming home at last. The Haynes family are to spend part of their holiday at their new villa in Rhodes and Mrs Haynes said it would be a good opportunity for me to touch base with my grandparents in Poros.

We are flying to Athens on the fifth of July. I will come straight to Poros, while the rest of the family go on to Rhodes. Mrs Haynes has sent all the details to Grandpa. We'll have a whole week together before Vanessa comes to join us.

I'm so excited. I can't wait to see you. I've missed you so much. See you very soon. I LOVE YOU.

Your best friend,

Laura.

'*Yes!*' he breathed, squeezing the letter to his chest.

Alexis flipped the tea towel over his shoulder and grinned. 'I take it she's coming home?'

'First week in July,' he nodded happily, re-reading the letter.

'Ah well, this calls for a celebration,' he said, carrying a bottle of brandy and two glasses to the table.

He raised his glass to Yiannis in a toast. 'Here's to a happy reunion.'

Yiannis lifted his glass. 'I'll drink to that.'

22

On the fifth of July, Charles and Gwen set out on the first ferry to meet Laura at Athens airport. Yiannis stayed behind at Gwen's insistence.

'I hope there is plenty of fish for dinner tonight Yiannis, you remember how much Laura loves it,' Charles said just as they were about to leave.

'Don't get too much,' Gwen said sharply. 'She may not be coming back with us. I really cannot cope with a child around the house. I shall appeal to Sarah Haynes to take Laura with them to Rhodes.'

A momentary look of despair flashed across Yiannis's face, and Charles patted his arm affectionately. 'She'll definitely be coming home. I promise.'

*

Later that morning, Yiannis walked up the beach steps towards the lodge, whistling happily, his shirt in one hand and his catch of six fish in the other. As he lifted his hand to wipe the perspiration from his brow, he caught sight of a female figure casually swishing a branch across the dusty path of yellow gorse.

He paused for a moment, shaded his eyes to identify the stranger, but the sun obscured his view.

'Yiannis,' Laura squealed with delight when she saw him.

He dropped the fish he was carrying and his heart skipped a beat when he finally recognised the vision of loveliness running out of the sun towards him. The hem of one side of her floral skirt and frothy lace petticoat was tucked into her broad scarlet waistband, revealing her long pale legs. He watched the silver rays of the sun filter through her long curly hair as she tossed it from her bare shoulders. Soft and warm like a summer's day, she looked as though she had stepped out from an impressionist painting. The vision bowled him over.

'Oh Yiannis!' She ran to his arms.

He gasped as her soft body firmly pressed against his. Drinking in the heady smell of the pine forest in her hair, he felt a shock wave pulsate through his body. He could not comprehend this transformation in her, then the frightening reality hit him - Laura was a woman now, and a beautiful one at that. The whole dynamic of their pure and innocent relationship shifted on its axis the moment he took her in his arms.

Turning her face towards his, her eyes shone vibrantly and the heat of the day had brought a rosy flush to her face. Reaching up on tiptoes she pressed her soft lips against his cheek making his body shudder with delight. Gently but firmly he moved her away from the close proximity of him.

'Laura, I can't believe my eyes. Is this really you? Where has my little Laura gone?'

With a dazzling smile, she said, 'I grew up, see?' She held out her hands to present herself, then a blush rose in her face and she lowered her eyes coyly. When she regained her composure, Yiannis had donned his shirt and was busy with the buttons.

Reaching for his hands, she entwined her fingers with his, and gazed longingly into his eyes. 'I've missed you so much Yiannis.'

Her passion caught his breath, so he gently pulled one of her hands so it sat in the crook of his arm, and patted her fingers as though to dampen the sensuality her touch was sending through him. 'I've missed you too sweetheart,' he said sincerely. Forcing feelings of desire aside, he knew he had to divert the situation. 'I'll take you fishing in the morning, like we used to, if you want?'

'That would be wonderful,' she exclaimed, snuggling against his arm.

'We'll go early, like we used to. If you can get up,' he teased. He gazed at her longer than he knew he should have, and shook his head. 'I can't believe you're here.

Come on, we have a lot of catching up to do.'

*

After a fitful night, Laura woke to hear footsteps on the path beneath her bedroom window. Sleepily she rubbed the dull ache in her stomach - damn her period, it had kept her awake most of the night. On hearing Yiannis's voice, she turned sharply to glance at the clock. Cursing herself for sleeping through the alarm, she hastily pulled on her shorts and ran downstairs. She stopped in dismay, when she heard the conversation between her grandma and Yiannis.

'Sorry to call so early Mrs Tempest, but I've been waiting for Laura for half an hour. She wanted to go fishing today. Is she unwell?'

Laura clasped her hand to her mouth in disbelief as her grandma uttered the words, 'She won't be coming today- her monthlies arrived last night.'

Beside herself with embarrassment she groaned inwardly. How could she tell him something like that? She would never be able to face him again now.

As soon as Yiannis walked away, Laura raged at her grandma. 'How could you,' she choked, she was so angry she could hardly speak. 'How could you tell him about my period?'

Gwen grabbed her arms and shook her hard. 'That's enough now young lady,' she snapped. 'I will not put up with your hysterics during this holiday. Do you hear me?'

'But the embarrassment. I'll never be able to face him again. What a hateful thing to do.'

Gwen's slap across Laura's face stung her into silence. Awash with extremes of emotions, they squared each other up for a moment, before Laura fled back to her room.

With her cheeks burning with embarrassment, she watched mournfully as Yiannis loaded his fishing tackle into the boat and pushed the Moondancer from its moorings.

Gwen returned to her stove and resumed cooking

breakfast, silently congratulating herself on doing what six years apart had failed to.

*

Laura managed to keep a low profile for the next three days, venturing out only if she was certain that Yiannis had left the cove.

The silent rift with her grandma grew daily, and Laura wished with all her heart that she had not come back to the island.

She walked despondently past Yiannis's garden, full of beans and marrows, peaches and pomegranates, dipped her hands in the tiny stream and then made her way through the mass of gorse, past the olive grove, and up towards the pine forest.

Almost as soon as she set off, Yiannis arrived back at the Lodge. He drew himself a glass of water and parted the kitchen curtain to catch a glimpse of Laura before she disappeared from sight. Within minutes he was at the top of the hill, scanning the area until he saw her.

'There you are!' he said gently, walking towards her. 'I was beginning to think you were avoiding me.'

Laura looked up from where she was dangling her bare feet in the fresh water spring, mortified that he had found her.

He moved another tentative step towards her.

'Oh please go away,' she wailed, hiding her face in her hands.

'Is this because of what your grandma said to me?'

Laura scrambled to her feet, grasped for her sandals and began to walk quickly away.

'Laura, don't go.' He began to follow her. 'Laura *wait*!' he shouted.

She paused at the ferocity in his voice, but kept her face averted from him.

He moved cautiously towards her. 'I'm not in the least bit embarrassed about what she said, and neither should you be. It's the most natural thing in the world, and all men know about periods,' he said softly, not daring to reach out and touch her. 'This is me, Yiannis! Remember, the one who has watched you grow up. There is nothing I don't know about you. Please Laura, don't be a stranger to me now, we have precious little time together as it is, and I miss you.' He watched her for a while, but there was no response. Eventually he sighed, turned in defeat and made his way back to the lodge.

With her eyes brimming with tears, she stood and watched as he walked away, until he was completely out of sight, then she sat down and pulled her sandals on her feet and followed him.

Back at the lodge, Yiannis was busy making lunch when Laura shyly peeped around the kitchen door. He knew without turning that she was there, and felt a wonderful sense of well-being run through his body. At last, she had come back to him. 'What would you like for lunch?' he said without looking at her. She slowly moved to his side and all was forgotten.

The next two days saw their relationship slip slowly back into the warm, trusting familiarity they had always enjoyed, although there was a fundamental change. Yiannis was careful in his manner with her now. She wasn't a little girl any more. Gone now were the days he would chase her into the sea or let her jump into his arms from the Midnight Rocks. Somehow, what was quite natural a few years ago now seemed totally inappropriate.

He found it difficult just to hold her hand, even when the action was just to help her from the boat. She had such an effect on him he was shocked at the intensity. It worried him deeply, how he was going to spend time with her, if he couldn't withhold these feelings.

Laura was acutely aware of Yiannis's predicament, and like him, she had known something quite extraordinary was happening between them.

As it was their last day alone together, they had decided to make a picnic and sail to the next cove.

At eight- thirty a.m. Yiannis returned from fishing. As he passed the villa he glanced at her bedroom window. Ten minutes later he emerged from the lodge, his hair wet, and his clean white shirt flowed open to the waist. Under his arm he carried a box of food covered with a tea towel. She watched as his handsome face turned again towards the villa and felt her heart leap into her throat. She checked her reflection in the mirror, dabbed a tiny bit of floral perfume on her neck and adjusted her sarong. She was ready.

As soon as she walked down the path to the beach, she knew from the look on his face that their relationship was taking on another dimension, though both parties fought the feeling they were experiencing with great ferocity.

Laura wore a white bikini, although she initially kept it under wraps beneath an apple green silk sarong, ornately decorated with hand painted white lilies.

Yiannis was in turmoil from the moment she met him at the water's edge in Amora Cove. He held out his hand gallantly to help her onto the Tempest's yacht Aglaia, and from that moment on, fought unsuccessfully to keep his eyes averted from the flimsy sarong that was patiently losing its battle to cover her pale slim legs.

She purposely sat next to him and let the fragrance of perfume tease his nostrils. She stretched her legs out towards his, until the sun glistened on her pearl painted toenails as they peeped through the light dusting of sand on her bare feet. He noted that her thigh still bore the scar of the car crash, though it had faded into a pale white line over the years. Yiannis pulled the anchor, said a silent prayer for help and guidance, and told himself over and over, she was fifteen years old and had been left in his charge, and he mustn't think of her as anything other than a friend, he absolutely mustn't!

'Is everything okay Yiannis?' Laura asked curiously.

He cleared his throat. 'Yes fine, no problem.'

She smiled knowingly. She knew that when she looked

away Yiannis was watching her, and it filled her with an amazing sense of excitement that she possessed such power over him.

They reached the secluded cove at ten, by which time the sun sweltered high in the sky. Yiannis dropped the anchor from the yacht and eyed the cool turquoise water with relish.

'How about a swim to cool down?' he suggested.

'Sounds lovely,' Laura answered as she stood up, unfastened her sarong and let it fall seductively to the floor. Yiannis watched in awe as the material fell to reveal the transformation from girl to the shape and curves of a young woman. He took a deep breath, peeled his shirt from his hot body and held out his hand for her to join him on the diving platform. They jumped together still holding hands then, after surfacing, dived again down to the seabed. Yiannis was an excellent underwater swimmer, due to the sponge diving he had done in his early youth, so Laura held his ankle as they swam down to the rocks, scattering brightly coloured rainbow fish as they went. When she thought her lungs would burst she would tug his leg and they would fight their way to the surface in a mass of bubbling foam, gasping and gulping for air. They held onto the mooring rope until they caught their breath, she with her arm about his shoulders, he with his arm at her waist.

'I'll race you under the boat to the other side then,' he challenged.

They both took a gulp of air and dived, pulling the water as hard as they could until they emerged at the other side together.

'I let you win that time,' he teased.

'No you didn't!' she said, pushing his head under water and dived again to the other side. She coughed and spluttered for a moment and waited for him to join her, but he never came. 'Yian?' she called. 'Are you there?' There was no answer. She began to tread water slowly for a minute then swam around the boat to look for him. In a panic she dived again and searched the underside of the vessel. He was nowhere. She came back up for air and scanned the surface of the water. 'Yiannis?' she screamed. Suddenly she was pulled under water, and when she came struggling to the surface, he was grinning cheekily.

'Looking for me?' he said, ducking away as she tried to strike him.

'You fool, I thought I had lost you!' she said, flaying her fists at him.

He laughed, and beckoned her to swim to the shore, heaved himself onto a rock, then reached down, put his hands under her arms and pulled her out of the water to join him. He held her tightly as they gazed into each other's eyes. They were just a whisker away from each other's face. He was mesmerised at the droplets of water which dripped from her eyelashes and ran in rivers down her skin. Still he held her, their hearts beating in unison. Time stood still.

Laura held her breath, wondering what this moment might bring, what was he going to do with her, would he kiss her?

A moment later Yiannis snapped out of the trance and the spell was broken. He looked embarrassed as he released his hold on her then smiled weakly. 'Let's eat.'

Laura's heart sank momentarily, then brushed the feeling aside and began to help Yiannis build his fire.

After feasting on sardines, succulent beef tomatoes and crusty bread, Yiannis had brought a bottle of Retsina wine, and allowed Laura her first taste of the bitter pine resin drink which she thought was disgusting. Afterwards Yiannis stretched the tablecloth over a couple of rocks to make some shade from the blazing sun and they lay for an hour in blissful happiness.

'It's so hot,' Laura said, fanning a paper plate at her face. 'Vanessa and I are going to have to stay by the pool all the time when she comes if it gets any hotter.'

'I have never met your friend, but I feel I know her from your letters. I look forward to meeting her,' Yiannis said casually.

'Well wait until you see her, she's sixteen now and looks nineteen. I've never seen anybody develop as fast as her, she is way in front of all the other girls in our year at school.'

'Well now I can't wait to meet her,' he teased.

She propped herself up on one arm. 'You might fall in love with her when you see her,' she said seriously.

His eyes glinted. 'And why would I do that when I'm already in love with the best girl in the whole world.'

Laura laughed happily, while Yiannis silently scolded himself for revealing his feelings. They lay in silence for a while longer, until the stifling heat forced them to pack up their belongings onto the boat before taking to the water again for a last swim.

They arrived back at Amora Cove in the early afternoon and as Yiannis held his hand out to her to escort her off the boat, she said, 'Thank you for a perfect day Yian.'

'It has been my pleasure,' he bowed gallantly.

'Yian?'

'Yes?'

She took a deep breath. 'Will you kiss me?'

He bent down and kissed the back of her hand.

'No, I mean a proper kiss.'

More than anything in the world, Yiannis wanted to kiss this lovely creature in front of him. He held her hand to his cheek and looked at her with his beautiful aquamarine eyes. Her lips were pouting, trembling anticipation. The voice inside his head was saying, I want to kiss you. I want to hold you in my arms forever. I want to be with you always and I want to tell you that you are the most precious person in my life and I love you. His heart was telling him to kiss her, but deep down he knew he must not. Eventually he cupped her face in his large hands and shook his head slowly. 'Laura, my lovely Laura, I will kiss you, but not today, not now, but one day soon. When the time is right, I promise I will kiss you.'

Laura smiled with sheer happiness.

23

In the shade of Alexis's Taverna, Laura and Yiannis waited for Vanessa to arrive by ferry. The candy stripe awning fluttered gently in the breeze, shading rows of high back wicker chairs, which stood in military precision.

Laura's fingers twitched with the urge to curl them around Yiannis's hand and declare her love for him for all to see, but she knew she must not. She was not a fool. Yiannis would get into serious trouble if anyone caught even a hint of impropriety in their friendship.

A black and white cat meandered slowly and gracefully in and out of the scuffed wooden chair legs. It stopped for a moment to watch a fly feast on a crust, sauntered over to inspect the morsel, turned its nose away then flopped on its side, lifted its hind leg and started the arduous task of scratching a flea from its ear.

Alexis flicked his towel at the cat and it turned and spat at him. 'Bloody scavenger, do you know it has stolen three fish from my customers' tables already this week? It would have had another this morning! We caught it pulling a red snapper out of the fridge. It had it in its mouth, but it dropped it when Irene bashed it with the broom. It isn't good for custom you know!'

Yiannis grinned at Alexis then turned when he heard the drone of the ferry.

'Here they are Laura,' Charles said joining them. Gwen remained seated at the table, engrossed in her magazine.

Vanessa squealed and waved furiously when she spotted Laura at the harbour edge.

'Oh no!' Laura said under her breath.

'What's the matter?' Yiannis asked quizzically.

'Vanessa's brought Slater with her!'

'You don't care for him much do you?'

'Well, he's okay now. He was a pain in the neck when we were younger. It's just that I was looking forward to a week with Van. I didn't know he was coming too.'

Laura grinned as Van jumped about impatiently while the ferry docked. As soon as the gangplank came down, she raced into Laura's arms and embraced her warmly.

'Is this your little island? Isn't it quaint?' She eyed Yiannis from head to foot. 'Oh,' she said appreciably. 'Who's this?'

'This is my friend Yiannis,' Laura smiled proudly.

'Well hello Yiannis. Aren't you the most gorgeous thing on legs?' She rested her hand on his arm. 'Hard muscles as well.' She winked at him cheekily. 'I think I'm going to enjoy it here.'

Yiannis quirked an eyebrow at Laura.

'Come on, we'll have some lunch here,' Charles said, leading the way. 'Alexis Taverna is the finest on the island!'

As they approached Gwen, Vanessa smiled and whispered, 'How's the ogre been Laura?'

'Her usual unpleasant self, I'm afraid,' she replied through clenched teeth.

Gwen placed the magazine on the table and held out her hand to Vanessa. 'How lovely to see you my dear, I trust you had a good journey? Did I not see Slater with you?'

Vanessa kissed Gwen warmly on each cheek. 'Yes you did, he's gone exploring. He wanted to check out the local beauty spots,' she replied.

'I see,' Gwen said, 'and will he be staying with us?'

Laura waited with bated breath.

'No, he's going back to Athens later this afternoon.'

Laura sighed with relief and began to study the menu.

'Well then, what would you all like to eat?' Charles said.

'I'd give the red snapper a miss if I were you,' Yiannis muttered, winking at Laura.

Gwen's keen ears heard the comment. 'Why do you say that then?'

Yiannis shook his head. 'It's just a private joke.'

Gwen pursed her lips. 'Well I don't think there is anything funny about making discrediting remarks about Mr Petrou's excellent fish. I'm certainly having some,' Gwen said adamantly.

Yiannis and Laura exchanged gleeful glances.

Throughout their meal, Vanessa flirted outrageously with Yiannis. 'Your spoken English is very good Yiannis,' she said, dabbing her mouth with her napkin.

'Thank you, my mother was English.'

'Really?' she pouted.

'Really!'

'So you're not a full hot blooded Greek then?'

Yiannis gave a ghost of a smile.

'Where was your mother from then?'

'Zennor, Cornwall. '

'Never been,' Vanessa said flippantly.

'I have!' Laura said excitedly. 'I was there last year!'

'Oh yes poor you! It must be such a drag having to spend your holidays out in the sticks like that, especially with 'Uncle Jack'!' exclaimed Vanessa.

'It was lovely actually!' Laura said adamantly. 'It has a beautiful church famed for its mermaid, a folk museum, and stunning cliff walks. If you take the coast road to the North you can go right to the Carrack Rocks and watch the seals basking in the sunshine, and then walk the six miles to St Ives. Or you can walk to the South towards Gurnards Head where the Iron Age Tryne Dinas cliff castle once stood. You'd love it Yiannis,' she said happily.

Vanessa wrinkled her nose. 'Sounds boring to me! Aren't there any shops?'

Yiannis said, 'It sounds lovely Laura. One day I have promised myself that I will go to visit my mother's home.'

'I can think of better places to see, if you come over to Cornwall.' Vanessa fluttered her lashes at him.

Yiannis turned his head from her.

*

Slater wandered around the harbour for a couple of hours,

before settling down for a beer at the Alexis. He had been eyeing up some French girls and was just about to make his move when Eva sat down beside him.

'Hi,' she said huskily.

'Hello,' he answered, looking her up and down.

'You like what you see?'

'What?'

'Our beautiful island - you like what you see?'

'Oh yes, I like what I see.' His eyes fixed on her low cleavage.

Eva flashed her eyes at him. 'I could show you some really beautiful places if you wanted.'

'I bet you could,' he said, shifting his seating position.

'Are you staying with the Tempests?' she asked casually.

'No!' he answered shortly.

'Oh, it's just that I saw you arrive with Laura Tempest's friend. I assumed you were staying with them. I thought you were Laura Tempest's boyfriend?'

'Well you thought wrong. I'm Vanessa Haynes's brother, if you must know.'

'I see. So you know Laura Tempest well then? I believe she lives with your family.'

'You seem to know an awful lot about me and my family.'

'Well, I don't know a great deal about *your* family, but I do know about the Tempests. Are you heir to your own estate?'

He regarded her with caution. 'No, I'm the second, more handsome son,' he said sarcastically.

'Maybe you want to reconsider being Laura's boyfriend then.'

'And why would I do that?'

'She is going to be very wealthy, come her twenty-first birthday!'

He furrowed his brow and scoffed. 'Who told you that?'

She tapped the side of her nose. 'I know these things.

She's the only heir to the Tempest Estate.'

He laughed caustically. 'I don't think a moulding old villa will bring much of an inheritance.'

Eva looked towards the harbour, her hand casually sitting on her hip. 'It's not just Villa Amora you know!'

'Oh?' His interest piqued.

'He owns most of the newly built buildings you can see on the island,' she gestured with her hands, '..and all of the land surrounding Villa Amora, which incidentally, isn't moulding. In fact it is a rather fine palatial building worth half a million pounds! The old boy never spends a penny, unless forced. I should think he has accrued a rather large fortune.' Eva smiled as Slater digested the news. 'You didn't know, did you? Maybe she kept it quiet, just in case she attracted the wrong sort of person.'

Slater glanced towards where the French girls sat, his mind was working overtime.

'Anyway, enough about the Laura Tempests of the world, what about all the beautiful places you wanted to see. I bet you like beautiful things don't you? Well we have a wealth of them on this island. Come let me show you all the things we do with gelato.' She winked, pulling him towards the Ice Palace.

Eva's son was at school, Franco had shut himself in the back room with a bottle of brandy, and the Gelateria was fully staffed. Eva had the afternoon free. Slater followed her up the stairs, watching her sashay sensually as she took each step. Once inside, she slipped seductively out of her dress revealing her voluptuous, naked body and all thoughts of Laura Tempest were forgotten.

An hour later, he lay damp and spent amongst the twisted sheets. 'Jesus Christ!' he said weakly, wiping the perspiration from his face. His body ached with exhaustion. He heard Eva murmuring something as she rested against his chest.

'What did you say?' he asked wearily.

'I said, I challenge you to experience anything better

than that. Just remember you've been spoilt now. No other woman will ever make love to you like I have. You belong to me!' she purred.

Slater snorted indignantly.

'Oh, you may sneer. You may go away and leave me, but you will always remember me, and sooner or later the urge will bring you back to me. I promise you that!'

Slater gave a short arrogant laugh. 'No woman will ever possess me.'

'We'll see,' Eva said sotto voce.

24

After two days lazing by the pool, Vanessa, much to Laura's dismay, had become bored and irritable.

Yiannis had kept a healthy distance from Vanessa, choosing instead to while away his hours with Kostas, and only approached Laura if she was alone.

'Oh God, another day in paradise...not!' Vanessa moaned, flinging herself on Laura's bed one morning.

Laura frowned. 'I thought you would really like it here.'

'There is nothing to do. It's too bloody hot. I'm being bitten to death by these bloody mosquitoes.' She inspected another angry red spot on her arm. '… and I'm desperate for some male company!'

'Oh thanks at lot,' Laura said indignantly.

'Sorry, I didn't mean that. It's just that I'm so bored! I want to lose my virginity. I'm sixteen years old and I'm still a virgin. I thought Greece would be a perfect place to do it. I bet Slater's found some willing female.' She walked toward the window and looked in the direction of Yiannis's lodge. 'My God but he is one gorgeous hunk of a man.'

Laura wrinkled her nose. 'Who, Slater?'

'No, Yiannis. You can't tell me you haven't noticed him?'

'Yes he is lovely, but I don't think of him like that.' Laura turned away to hide the truth.

'Well, *you* might not think of him like that, but I'll tell you something, *I'm* going to lose my virginity to him, even if you aren't. See you later.' She skipped out of her bedroom before Laura could protest.

Mortified at the thought of Yiannis making love to Vanessa, Laura ran to the window and watched in wretched desperation as Vanessa sauntered sexily towards the lodge.

'Oh please God don't let this happen.' She twisted the

net curtain in her palms as she watched Vanessa brazenly walk though his open door. Would he fall for her charms? Would he? She was old enough; there was nothing to stop them. 'Oh please don't let them do this to me,' she cried. She threw herself onto her bed and buried her face in the pillow, as all her hopes and dreams of life with Yiannis now lay in ruins.

Half an hour later, her bedroom door opened, and Vanessa swept into the room. 'Come on, get your glad rags on, your grandpa is taking us all to the harbour.' Checking her appearance in the mirror, she pouted her lips and then looked at Laura. 'Come on, what's the matter, why are you looking so miserable?'

Laura was too distraught to speak

Vanessa regarded her momentarily. 'For goodness sake, cheer up. It should be me who's miserable!'

Laura looked up unhappily and hoped with all her heart that she wasn't going to share all the painful details of her conquest.

'He obviously doesn't fancy women!' Vanessa hissed, nodding in the direction of the lodge.

'What do you mean?' she asked warily.

She sighed indignantly. 'He didn't want to do it! Can you credit it! I offered myself on a plate to him and he turned me down! He *actually* turned me down! Well, I give up. I'm going to the harbour. There was a rather delicious waiter at that taverna where we had lunch the other day.'

Relief swept over Laura and she sent up a thankful prayer.

'Are you coming?'

'No thanks, I'm going to stay here by the pool.' And hopefully, see something of Yiannis, she thought whimsically.

'Oh God, you are *so* boring sometimes.'

Laura gave a sardonic smile.

Half an hour later Laura stood on the sun terrace as the party set off in the motorboat. She waved until they were completely out of sight then ran up to the lodge to find Yiannis, but unfortunately he was nowhere to be seen.

With no one around, she had the pool to herself so a bathing suit would not be necessary. After applying sun lotion liberally over her skin, she poured a long cool drink, picked up her book and stepped out into the blinding sunlight. The water felt wonderful on her naked skin. Standing by the poolside, she ran her hands down the contours of her head to squeeze the moisture from her hair, adjusted her towel on her sun-bed and stretched out in the heat of the sun. Enjoying the splendid isolation, the heat dried the water instantly from her damp body.

Laura drained the contents of her glass, which was warm now. She would only lie for a few more minutes – knowing her pale skin could not tolerate too much sun. A bee hummed above Laura's head. She glanced at her wrist to check the time, but her watch was indoors. She was losing all track of time. I'll move in a moment, she decided. The bee buzzed away in the distance and Laura was alone again with her thoughts of Yiannis. The sun felt hot on her shins, so she turned on her stomach. The towel, still damp from her swim, felt wonderful on her hot skin. She turned her head to watch the swallows diving for water from the pool. The water looked inviting. Just a few more seconds and I will go for another swim, she contemplated, as she returned again to her thoughts and dozed off in the fierce midday sun.

One hour later Yiannis arrived back at the cove, hot and thirsty. He noted miserably that the motorboat had gone. He had hoped to find Laura, to spend a little time with her. As he approached the villa, he stopped dead in his tracks when he saw Laura lying by the pool naked.

He averted his eyes immediately, and turned to leave her in peace and privacy, but in his haste, he stepped backwards, caught his foot on a branch, and stumbled into a large laurel bush. He sat frozen to the spot, praying that he hadn't alerted her to his presence. What on earth would she think of him, if she found him skulking behind the bushes? He waited quietly until enough time had elapsed to assure him that his presence was still unnoticed, and then chanced a look to see if the coast was clear enough to make his escape. She hadn't moved.

Back at the lodge he couldn't get the image of her out of his mind. He was disturbed, not by what he had seen, but how he felt about Laura. The image of her moved him like never before. She's fifteen for goodness sake! He scolded himself, as he discarded his dusty plimsolls at the door of the bathroom. He pulled his shirt off and stepped out of his shorts. With the shower on at full blast, the water felt like steel rods on his head. A few seconds under the pummelling cold water was enough to cool his ardour. With a towel around his waist, he started to wonder how long she had lain out in the sun. Her pale skin would soon burn. Hopefully she had gone indoors now. Walking out onto his veranda, he looked down at the tiny white shingle beach and watched the sea as it washed the rocks, perpetually renewing its loving embrace of this beautiful island. He glanced over to the villa. From the far end of his veranda he could just about make out the pool area. She was still there. There was nothing else for it - he had to get her to move out of the sun.

He quickly pulled on his shorts, slipped his feet into his plimsolls, and ran out into the fiery heat of the day.

Trying to avert his eyes, he spoke firmly. 'Come on Laura, you're burning.'

When she heard his voice she tried to move, but her skin felt stiff and her head ached as she lifted it. He turned her over gently and she cried out when her burned skin chafed against his arms as he slipped them under her hot body.

'Stay calm sweetheart,' he said, lifting her effortlessly off the sun-bed and rushing her into the shade of the cool villa. He placed her gently on the bed, ordering her to lay still. She moaned unintelligibly as he took a pillow from the bed, ran into the bathroom, dragged a large towel from the rail and draped it over the pillow in the huge white enamel bath. He ran the water until the pillow and towel were soaked through, then carefully carried Laura to the bathroom and lowered her onto the cool wet pillow. Plunging another towel in the water, he covered her naked body with it and placed a damp facecloth to her forehead.

Taking a cool bottle of water from the fridge, he told her to sip it slowly, but to drink as much as she could. He also gave her two paracetamol to bring her temperature down.

'I'll be back in a moment,' he said and left her in the tepid water.

Laura nodded weakly.

He returned a few minutes later, with an arm full of cucumbers from his vegetable patch, and set about slicing them with the expertise of a chef.

Laura had managed to drink half the bottle of water by the time he returned to the bathroom and she was now shaking uncontrollably. He pulled the plug in the bath and let the water slowly subside away from her bright pink body. Holding a large towel to her naked body he lifted her gently to her feet. Dizzily she stepped out of the bath and Yiannis gently dabbed her raw skin dry. 'I'm so sorry Laura - this must be very embarrassing for you.'

She shook her head and closed her eyes as she savoured the gentleness of his touch over her body.

'Here.' He passed her another towel. 'You dry yourself the best you can.' When she was finished he helped her to her bedroom where he had placed the pile of sliced cucumber on her bedside table.

'Ugh! What's all that for, I hate cucumber!' she protested.

'Lay down on your tummy,' he answered firmly. 'I'm going to cover your back with it, it's a sunburn cure.' Once she was comfortable, he dealt the slices over her back with the skill of a croupier. The shivering exhilaration sent a thrill down her spine, as she began to enjoy the luxurious feather-like kisses of the cool damp slices, not to mention the tantalising closeness of Yiannis as he sat over her nakedness. He had just finished applying the last slice to the back of her leg, and was re-placing a slice which had slipped off, when a voice resounded from the bedroom door.

'What in heavens name is going on here?' Gwen said, marching over to Yiannis to drag him off the bed.

'It's all right grandma he was just putting cucumber on my sunburn,' Laura said, as she lifted her head from the pillow.

'Laura, keep still!' Yiannis ordered and Laura lay down again.

'You, get out!' Gwen screamed at Yiannis. 'You disgust me, both of you!'

'We haven't done anything wrong!' Yiannis protested.

'Then you have no scruples either. She's fifteen years old you know! A minor! If you don't think there is anything wrong with her laying there naked with you next to her, you should be locked up.'

'But grandma,' Laura wailed. 'We weren't doing anything, I promise you!'

'What's all this noise about?' Charles said, squeezing past Vanessa, who was seething with jealousy at the scene before her.

'These two have been up to something!' Gwen snapped.

Yiannis stood to address Charles. 'Laura has sunstroke. I found her asleep near the pool. I think she was in the sun for a few hours. I managed to bring her temperature down in a cool bath, but she needs to keep her skin cool. Make her drink plenty of water, and there is enough cucumber for two more applications. Oh and someone needs to watch her so she doesn't vomit.'

'Well the audacity of that man!' Gwen shouted at Charles. 'I come home to find him molesting our granddaughter, and then he has the cheek to give you orders in your own home. Well I'm not standing for it. Laura, get up and wash that rubbish off your back. You're an absolute disgrace!'

'You stay where you are Laura!' Charles said angrily.

'Vanessa? Go and sit with her, make sure she keeps drinking and apply some more cucumber as and when she needs it. Shout me if she starts to vomit. Yiannis, thank you for everything you have done for Laura. I'll come and see you later to tell you how she is getting on.'

Gwen's face turned purple with rage, and for a moment Yiannis thought she was going to explode. He glanced at Laura, who smiled weakly back at him then left the villa.

*

Yiannis sat on his veranda silently watching the afternoon sun paint a blush red glow upon the surrounding mountains. A carpet of yellow gorse blazed like fire across the dusty rocks that surrounded his house and the familiar hue of golden sunlight bathed the villa below him. He watched Charles emerge from the sun terrace and make his way toward where he sat.

'Yiannis.' He nodded to him and sat down beside him.

'Sir?'

There was a marked silence, before both of them started to speak in unison.

'Sorry, go ahead.' Yiannis said, apologetically.

'About earlier Yiannis.'

'Yes, sir, I'm sorry it must have looked a bit odd, but I was just trying to help.'

Charles tapped his mouth with his finger thoughtfully. 'Yes my boy I fully understand, but I hope you can see it from our point of view. Laura is growing into a lovely young woman, but she *is* still a minor, and well, we're all human.'

'I wouldn't do anything,' Yiannis protested. 'I'm well aware that she is underage, but I've known her for years. I don't think of her like that,' he lied.

'I'm sorry Yiannis. Please don't take this the wrong way. It's just that there has been talk in the harbour.'

'Talk! About what?'

'Oh you know, gossip,' he said awkwardly.

Yiannis looked puzzled.

'Something was said to Gwen in the Post Office.'

'Oh that Dopas woman no doubt,' Yiannis snapped. 'This is Eva's doing you know. Her and that hag, who owns the Post Office, they're just trying to discredit me in your eyes.'

Yiannis thought Charles winced at the mention of Eva's name, and then dismissed the thought.

'Believe me Yiannis, no one, least of all the Barzinis, could ever discredit you in my eyes. It's just that making a reputation is easier than altering one you know, and well, I just don't think it's a good idea for you both to be alone together any more.'

Yiannis looked aghast. 'So you do believe them then?'

'No, but I do believe that Laura's feelings towards you are more than friendly now, even if yours aren't. I would feel a lot more comfortable if you took a few days off, away from the island, just to let matters calm down a little.'

Yiannis chewed on his lip. 'You mean you don't want me to see her again?'

'No, I just think a bit of space between you two will do the trick. Just a precaution you understand?' he said, patting Yiannis condescendingly on the shoulder.

'Of course,' he answered coolly.

'Right, that's that sorted. Now, the damn engine is playing up again, so I'll be down on the beach, should you want me.'

Yiannis twisted his mouth. 'Isn't it time, I mean, surely you could…'

'Afford a new one?' Charles finished his question. 'You're right Yiannis. I can afford a new one. It's just, you see, well it gives me something to do. After fifty years of marriage, it's good to have something to get you out of the house. If you know what I mean?'

Ten minutes later Yiannis pushed the Moondancer out from Amora Cove, took the last ferry to the port of Piraeus, and turned up with his arms full of flowers at Katia's house.

25

Katia Mazarskis was six years older than Yiannis and fortunately for her, the years as a prostitute had not yet marred her looks. She was beautiful, exotic and vivacious with large brown alluring 'come to bed' eyes and long dark hair swept back into a sleek ponytail. Yiannis had visited Katia Mazarskis for the last five years, albeit too infrequently for her liking. Katia held Yiannis in great regard. He had come to her aid one night when she had been struggling to free herself from the clutches of a drunken sweaty sailor. She had taken him to her home, and as a thank you had given her services free, but on realising he was a virgin, set about teaching him everything he needed to know about lovemaking. Of all the men she entertained, he was always her favourite. He always treated her like a lady and never like a whore and therefore she never charged him. He would turn up out of the blue and she would cancel all other appointments. He always wined and dined her, brought her flowers and sweets, and after they made love, he would hold her close to him and kiss her gently and they would talk well into the night.

As he lay in her arms that night she sighed softly. 'Oh I'll miss you when you have gone,' she lamented.

He looked up and smiled at her. 'I'm not going yet.'

Katia stroked his hair softly and smiled. 'You've already gone! Who's the lucky lady?'

'What?' Yiannis answered sleepily.

'Who have you left your heart with?' she whispered quietly.

He looked up from under his lashes, frowned then turned his face away. He sighed thoughtfully. 'I'm sorry, I didn't realise it was so obvious.'

'It is to me. I can feel there is something different about you. Oh you're still the same wonderful caring Yiannis whom I know and love, but your heart is elsewhere. I envy her whoever she is. She's a lucky woman to have won the heart of someone as lovely as you. I hope she appreciates you.'

Yiannis laughed ruefully and shook his head sadly.

'What is it?' she said, trying to cajole him into talking. She eased herself into a sitting position, and asked, 'Is she married?'

'No, it's nothing like that,' he said wistfully.

'What then?'

'She's fifteen!'

'Oh dear,' Katia said thoughtfully. 'Don't wish the sadness of age on her Yian.'

'I don't!' he said, slipping his hands behind his head.

'She won't be fifteen forever.'

'I know, I know, it's just that, I've known her since she was nine and it feels,' he paused for a moment. 'oh I don't know. It just feels wrong.'

Katia stroked his face gently. 'Love isn't wrong, whatever shape or form it takes. It's beautiful and special and if it's returned, well, you need nothing else in life, you have it all. Does she know how you feel about her?'

'Yes. No. I don't know,' he said desperately. 'But I do know that I can't live without her! Look, I'm sorry I shouldn't be talking about this with you.'

'Oh Yian, why ever not? I knew you would find someone one day. I'm realistic enough to know that you wouldn't stay around long when someone special came into your life. I'm a working girl, happy to love you when you're here, but you need someone to spend your life with and I am happy for you, truly I am.'

He looked deep into her eyes as he gently smoothed her hair. 'You're very special to me,' he said softly. 'Without you, my life would have been unbearable. I won't abandon you Katia!'

She smiled. 'But you must! I won't share you, and I'm sure she wouldn't want to either. I want you to love only her, to put into practice all I have taught you, or else I will have wasted all my efforts.'

There was a pause in the conversation while they both looked at each other, then Yiannis blew a deep sigh. 'Well it may not come to that. As I say, she is very young and she will be leaving soon to go back to school.'

Katia noted the desolation in his voice. 'She'll be back, and sooner than you think if she knows you are waiting for her. What woman could resist such a wonderful prospect? Then when she does return, I'll let you go,' she said wistfully, as she cradled him in her arms.

He kissed her gently on her forehead, thankful for her words of wisdom, as Katia closed her eyes to the heartache welling up inside her.

*

It was a couple of days before the pain from her sunburn subsided, and Laura had neither seen nor heard anything from Yiannis since her grandma had thrown him out of the villa. She was also under strict instructions not to go near him for the rest of her stay on the island, a warning she was definitely going to disobey.

As Laura lay on her bed recuperating, she had ached for him to touch her again, to feel his arms around her naked body. The thought of him, as he placed sliced cucumber on her skin, sent shivers down her spine each time she savoured the memory. The image of him lulled her to sleep each night and presented itself to her each morning on waking. He was dominating her life, and unbeknown to her, she was dominating his!

Vanessa had quizzed her relentlessly about Yiannis since that afternoon, but even though Laura protested that it had all been innocent, Van didn't believe her, in fact she was eaten with jealousy. Her trip to the harbour in search of a man had quickly been quashed when Gwen insisted that she stayed with them to look around the shops. In fact the reason they had returned to Amora Cove as early as they had done that day, was that Vanessa had feigned a headache when she realised she was going to have to spend all day with a couple of 'old' people. But, she was happy in the knowledge that she had stopped Laura and Yiannis's little bit of fun. After all, why should they have it and not her!

Three days after the incident, Laura managed to get up and sit in the shady part of the sun terrace. She watched intently for any sign of Yiannis, but he was nowhere to be seen. She was beginning to fret at his continued absence. She was due to leave the island in four days time, so she must see him soon. She made the decision to rise early the next morning before anyone else had stirred, and catch him before he set off fishing.

The temperature that day had been a hundred degrees. It was far too hot to venture out, even to the pool, so she was not alone in the shade. Vanessa flicked aimlessly through an old edition of Vogue; Charles dosed most of the day; and Gwen, as always, kept her nose in a book and an eye on her granddaughter.

That evening brought no respite, making sleep almost impossible. The thermometer in Laura's room read eighty degrees when she retired at ten thirty. She tossed and turned for an hour, before falling into an exhausted sleep. Disturbed by strange dreams, thirst brought her to consciousness. This had been the fourth time in a fortnight that she had woken like this. Yiannis was dominating her thoughts. She loved him with all her heart. She had always loved him, from the first moment they had met, and he had swept her into his arms and carried her from the boat when she first came to the island. But now, now this was different; she yearned for him, ached for him, and constantly dreamt about him. She knew she had fallen head over heels in love with him.

She grasped the glass of water from the bedside table and drank thirstily, but the warm liquid could not quench her thirst. Silently she slipped out from under the mosquito net and padded softly to the kitchen. She reached for the bottle of icy water from the fridge, letting the cold air wafting out from it cool her body. When she closed the door she began to feel the stifling heat of the night surround her body again. She lifted her hair with both hands to cool her neck. The heat was suffocating. Laura listened for a moment to make sure there was no movement in the villa, then carefully turned the handle of the French windows so as not to alert anyone, and stepped out into the night air.

It was just after midnight and the huge moon shone bright like daylight across the water below her. She could see the surface of the sea ripple, distorting the moon's reflection and illuminating a figure bathing in the sea. 'Yiannis,' she breathed.

Silently she picked her way down the beach steps, barefoot but in her nightdress, feeling the sandy gravel between her toes. The sea licked her feet at the waters edge, as she looked towards Yiannis who was floating naked in the cool dark water. Pulling her nightdress over her head she immersed herself gently into the water. Like a blanket of silk she felt the sea caress her, as she swam underwater towards him.

A movement of ripples alerted Yiannis's senses that something was in the water. He swam towards the Midnight Rocks a few yards out of the cove then turned and searched the water for movement. The ripples now licked at his chest as he watched in apprehension as a shape in the darkness moved ever closer.

As Laura neared Yiannis, she reached out her fingers to his legs. She felt him jump at her touch, and then she emerged from the water until she was face to face with the man she loved.

'Laura!' He held her by the arms. 'What the hell are you doing? Someone will see you!' he cast a sidelong glance towards the villa.

His protests went unheeded as she stroked her hands gently up across his wet chest finally cupping his beautiful face in her soft palms.

'Yiannis,' she whispered.

His breath quickened. 'Oh my God Laura!' His voice was hardly audible.

In a small voice she poured her heart out. 'I love you Yiannis, I know you know I do.' She circled her loving arms around his body.

A shiver ran up his back at her touch. His heart hammered in his chest. This was so wrong. He shook his head as a fire of passion began to burn deep with him. A moment of madness urged his fingers to touch her skin. His hands hovered close enough to feel the warmth of her body. Suddenly he came to his senses. He quickly moved back from her. 'No Laura,' his breath clipped and shallow. 'I'm sorry, I'm so sorry, this cannot happen.'

Laura's eyes widened in disbelief as he dived underwater and swam ferociously back to the shore, his words of rejection ringing in her head. He did not look back at her, as she sat alone in the moonlight. He did not see the devastation in her face or the tears she cried for him. She sat for a long time on the Midnight Rocks, as waves of emotion washed over her. She sat until the salt had dried on her skin and her heart had broken. Eventually she swam back to shore. A few moments later, Vanessa moved out of the shadow of the terrace bushes, from where she had been since Yiannis had run past. She had witnessed the whole scene. Her lips curled into a wilful smile. This might just be the chance she needed to get off this god-forsaken island.

At four-thirty a.m. Vanessa was awoken by someone creeping past her window. She leapt from her bed and parted the nets to see Yiannis slipping something through Laura's bedroom window. Vanessa watched intently as he flung his fishing tackle over his shoulder and made his way to the beach. She waited a moment longer then tiptoed into Laura's room to retrieve the neatly folded note from where it lay. Back in the safety of her own room she slowly unfolded it and read:

Laura, I think we need to talk about last night! Please meet me up by the fresh water spring at two p.m.
Yiannis.

At breakfast that morning Vanessa wore an anxious face as she spoke. 'Oh Mrs Tempest, I'm so worried about Laura. She's my best friend and I don't want anything to happen to her,' Vanessa said convincingly, as she passed Yiannis's note to Gwen, watching the anger rise in her face as she read it. 'Please don't let her know I told you about last night,' Vanessa pleaded. 'I don't want to get her into any trouble. I'm sure nothing happened, as I was watching all the time,'

Gwen's anger burst into a full-scale rage as she stormed out of the kitchen and onto the terrace where Charles was finishing his breakfast. 'Look at this!' She stabbed the letter under his nose. 'Now tell me there is nothing going on between those two. They were seen together last night! What are you going to do?'

Charles read the letter and sighed. 'I'll talk to him,' he said.

'And say what? He's not going to tell you what happened, is he?' Gwen snapped at him.

'Well what do you want me to do? I'm not dismissing him!' he said, irritably.

Gwen threw her arms up in despair. 'You are unbelievable.'

'I'm being realistic. I know Yiannis would not do anything untoward. But I will speak to him!'

Gwen stared hard at him for a moment, and then swept back inside the villa swiftly followed by Vanessa, who was panicking now.

'Can I make a suggestion?' Vanessa said desperately.

'You can try,' Gwen answered sarcastically.

Vanessa took a deep breath then swallowed hard. 'Mother will be back at the Hilton Hotel in Athens now, Laura and I could go and join her today.'

Gwen's facial expression changed instantly. 'Yes, oh yes, what a good idea. Go and pack and tell Laura to come and see me.'

'You...you won't tell her I told you about last night?' Vanessa asked cautiously.

'No my dear, I won't. But whatever I do say, you go along with. Do you understand?'

'Yes Mrs Tempest,' she said meekly, relieved at last that she was leaving this island and going back to civilisation.

26

Laura stood alongside Vanessa, Charles and Gwen in the harbour and waited for the ten a.m. ferry to dock. There was an unnatural stillness in Laura's demeanour, contrary to the turmoil in her head, as she processed the conversation she'd had with her grandma that morning - a conversation she could barely comprehend.

'Yiannis has complained to us about your conduct Laura. Apparently you went to him last night?' Her grandmother had told her sternly. 'After discussing this with Yiannis, we *all* agreed that it's best that you should leave the island.'

From that moment, Laura's world imploded. Disbelief was an understatement. How could he have her sent away like a naughty child? How could Yiannis do this to her? After all the years she had known and loved him. She would never forgive him for this. Never!

Laura could hardly wait until everyone had disembarked before she scrambled aboard the ferry, and to add to her misery, Slater joined the crowd on the gangway and boarded with them.

'Where the hell have you sprung from?' Vanessa inspected her dishevelled looking brother. 'Look at the state of you! You don't look like you've shaved for days. And you're still in the same clothes as the last time I saw you!'

He winked knowingly at her. 'Let's just say I got lucky.'

'What for six days!'

'Yep.' He turned to Laura, regarded her for a moment then said, 'Hello gorgeous.'

Laura looked behind to see who he was addressing, then realised he was speaking to her.

His lips curled into a smile, as he tossed his jacket over his shoulder, and turned his face to the sun.

Laura was speechless.

*

From the balcony of the Ice Palace, Eva watched Slater sail out of the harbour - the bed still warm from his body. This time her plan would succeed. He'd been so utterly captivated by her salacious sexual appetite it had been easy to plant the seeds of her plan inside his head. Now she must sit back and wait a couple of years for it to come to fruition. She knew she could endure the wait, especially as she knew she would be seeing a lot more of Slater Haynes.

*

At the fresh water spring, Yiannis waited pensively for Laura for over an hour. When he returned to the lodge, Charles was waiting for him.

'I believe you have been waiting for Laura?'

Yiannis slipped his hands into his pockets, but didn't answer.

'Laura's gone Yiannis.'

His heart sank. 'Gone?'

'She left this morning to join the Haynes's in Athens!'

'I don't understand. Why would she go without saying goodbye?'

Charles shrugged his shoulders. 'Maybe she didn't want to see you. Has something happened between you two?' Charles asked cautiously.

'No sir.'

'Are you sure?'

'Absolutely!'

'Then it's a mystery why she left early,' Charles said casually and left it at that.

*

Yiannis waited in vain for a letter from Laura, then a few days before her sixteenth birthday he wrote to her.

28/8/87

Dear Laura,

Why did you leave so suddenly? And without saying goodbye! I hope it wasn't because of the way I left you on that last night. Please Laura you must understand, if I had stayed, then something would have happened between us, and there would have been serious consequences. You are so very young, but remember, we have all the time in the world.

It was wonderful seeing you Laura, and I miss you terribly. Until you return, my life will be empty, you know that. I enclose a card and gift for your birthday. I hope you have a happy day. I shall be thinking of you. Please write soon. All my love, Yian xxx

*

7/9/87
Yiannis,

I vowed I would not write to you after the way you had me sent away, but I find I cannot settle until I know why you have treated me so cruelly. I know I should not have come to you as I did that last night at Amora Cove, but I didn't think you would be so angry with me. All I wanted to do was love you and I thought you felt the same way about me. I thought perhaps you would have written to me on my birthday, but I did not even receive a card. It seems you want nothing more to do with me. Even if you are not willing to correspond with me in future, I would welcome your reasons for complaining to my grandma about my conduct. Would it not have been kinder to have a quiet word with me? I would have gladly left you alone if I thought I was becoming a nuisance! I await your response. Laura

*

16/9/87
Dear Laura,

I wait and wait, but I receive no letter from you! Please do not be angry for much longer, I miss your letters. Your grandfather tells me you are well and have settled back into school, but I would rather hear that from you. I wait and I pray to hear from you soon. All my love Yian x

*

24/9/87
Yiannis,

From your continued avoidance in writing to me, I must now believe that our friendship is over. I find it very hard to let go after all these years, but you, it seems, have found it easy. Goodbye.

Laura

*

4/10/87

Dear Laura,

For God's sake, please will you write to me! This situation is becoming unbearable. I wait in anticipation. Yian xx.

*

Laura's headmistress intercepted the letter addressed to Miss Laura Tempest, stamped with the Greek postmark, from the postman. Without opening the letter, she placed it inside a large brown envelope, along with all the letters addressed to Mr Y Kiassos, which she'd retrieved from the 'post out' box. She placed it in her drawer and locked it. Another few weeks and the correspondence should end. She would send the envelope, as promised, to Gwen Tempest for her perusal.

*

Laura was depressed. It was not an affliction she suffered often, but the separation from Yiannis and her broken heart had got the better of her. No matter how much Vanessa tried, she could not lift Laura from her despair. In the end, Laura requested weekend leave to spend a little time in Gweek, and Sarah Haynes welcomed her back to the bosom of her adopted family.

Sarah worried about Laura. She knew about the pain of lost love, she knew it oh so well. So, she gave her space, offered an embrace whenever it was needed, cups of tea and an open door to chat. She also told her that time was a great healer.

Early on Saturday morning, Laura walked down to the bridge near the Gweek Quay Boatyard, and leant against the granite coping stones to watch the tide rise. There was little movement in the village apart from the odd dog walker and early morning jogger. It was times like these, the quiet moments, which were the hardest. There was too much time to think. Too much time to ponder on how it had all gone wrong. The pain of first love, she laughed to herself. It had been experienced and written about for centuries. People got over it she understood, but she truly believed her heart would ache forever. Her chin trembled with emotion, her throat was sore from weeping and once again tears fell down her face. She dug deep into her pocket for a tissue, and her body shivered with cold, even though the day was warm for October.

Very gently an arm curled around her. She lifted her face to see Pippa standing beside her. More tears fell as Laura turned to embrace her friend. Pippa handed her a handful of tissues she had brought with her, after Sarah Haynes had rung her to explain Laura's predicament.

'Come and sit down.' She beckoned her towards the bus stop and once seated, Laura poured her heart out.

Pippa listened, but said nothing. She knew that nothing she said would help at this very moment. Sometimes it was just good to let people talk. She, being fifteen, and a year younger than Laura, had not yet experienced the pain of young love, and if this was the sort of state it got you into, she wasn't too sure she wanted to. She knew what Yiannis's friendship meant to her. Laura would surely have floundered after losing her mother if it hadn't been for his kindness. She'd been privy to all the letters that had passed between them. Laura had shared everything with her. So it puzzled her that Yiannis had turned on her like this. It didn't ring true that he would knowingly break her heart. Eventually calmness ensued and Laura dried her eyes.

'I have to go to work now,' Pippa said gently. She had been working at the boatyard during the summer holidays and had begged and pleaded with them to keep her on as a Saturday girl. Boats and yachts were her life, and she longed for the day she too could leave school and start to work properly. The rest of her family were veterinary surgeons, but that wasn't for her. She was going to sail yachts - big ones!

'Meet me back here at four. We'll have a cream tea at Lizzy's tea shop. Then tomorrow, if you want, we'll go down to Poldhu with the body-boards.' She smiled softly. 'I can't promise I can mend your broken heart, but it might take your mind off things for a while.'

Laura nodded thankfully through her misery, as Pippa gave her a great big hug and set off to the boatyard office.

Later that afternoon, while she was sweeping the yard, Pippa decided she must do something to help her friend. So later that night, she took out her writing box and penned a letter to Yiannis.

Dear Mr Kiassos,

I do hope you don't mind me writing to you, but I feel I must. Laura Tempest has been my best friend for many years and I know how much she valued the friendship she shared with you. She is inconsolable at the loss of that friendship, and very sorry for the incident that made you send her away. I have pleaded with her to write to you again, but she says she cannot bear another rejection. If you could just find it in your heart to forgive her and restore the special relationship you share, I know she would be eternally grateful. She misses you dreadfully and I cannot bear to see her upset. I'm sorry if this sounds terribly forward of me, but she is a very dear friend.

Hopefully yours
Pippa Ferris-Norton
Barleyfield Farm, Gweek, Cornwall UK

*

The letter duly arrived in Poros a week later. Marion Dopas looked at the postmark with interest. The handwriting was different, she noted. She craned her neck to see if Akis was about, and then gently began to steam the envelope open. She read the contents with a wry smile, and then hid the letter at the bottom of a very large pile of papers.

27

Yiannis stood in quiet contemplation in the middle of the Athena Studio as he took a moment's rest from whitewashing the walls. He'd spent a great deal of time with Travis since Laura returned to England, namely because the atmosphere back at Villa Amora, and in particular between Gwen Tempest and himself, had become a little terse to say the least.

Yiannis glanced around the room filled with canvases one against another. The bar shelves, once full of spirits, now held jam jars, brushes, oil, and acrylic paints oozing from their tubes. Even though it no longer resembled the taverna he'd grown up in, it still felt like home. One day he would restore it to its former glory, but with the meagre wage he received from the Tempests he couldn't see it happening for a couple more years at the least. Yiannis wasn't complaining though. Charles Tempest, though wealthy, had never been extravagant with money, but he had provided a roof over his head, rent free, for the last six years.

'Any plans to go to England this Christmas Travis?' Yiannis asked casually, returning to his whitewashing.

Travis laughed heartily. 'No my boy, my Father Christmas days are over,' he winked. 'Anyway I think I need the warmth on my bones nowadays.'

'Well there's little warmth here through the winter months,' Yiannis laughed, blowing on his hands.

'It's a darn sight warmer than England, I'll tell you. Anyway, I get more work done here, than in St Ives. There are too many distractions in Cornwall with the holidaymakers.' Travis gave a last theatrical brush stroke across the canvas he was working on. He stood back, admired his handiwork, then lit a cigarette and inhaled deeply.

'Any news from Laura?' he asked, picking a stray piece

of tobacco from his lip.

Yiannis shook his head and painted the wall with added ferocity for a moment. Eventually he put his brush down and sighed. 'What did I do wrong?'

'You did nothing wrong. I am so angry with Laura for tormenting you like this. I shall tell her so when she returns.'

Yiannis smiled regretfully. 'I don't believe she will ever return to the island.'

'Well I think she might,' Travis said, scratching his beard thoughtfully. 'I understand Charles Tempest is unwell, maybe she will come home to visit him.'

'Not if her grandmother has anything to do with it,' he quipped. Deep down Yiannis too was worried about Charles. These last few weeks he had begun to look very ill. Something was definitely wrong, though goodness knows what on earth could be bothering a man who had everything.

Gwen had also noticed the marked change in Charles's appearance, but she found she could not speak to him nowadays without him snapping at her. She vaguely wondered if he was still angry about this nonsense between Laura and Yiannis, and even thought about sending for Laura, but the joy of keeping her and Yiannis apart soon surpassed this idea.

Charles, for his part, sat alone most days on the sun terrace, wrapped up warm against the cool chill breezes that tripped along the sea. He wondered over and over again how he could ever have been so stupid as to get into the predicament he was now facing. He had only tried to help her! A little money now and then to help her and the child, but it had all turned so sordid, and he was at a loss what to do. Why hadn't he listened to Yiannis? Why had he not believed him when he said that Eva Barzini was evil!

It had all started so innocently the day he and Yiannis went to phone Laura, that first Christmas she'd spent in

England. Eva had played on his sensibility after Yiannis's rebuff and had stupidly given her some money. A few weeks later he started to visit her whenever he sailed into the harbour, just to make sure she had everything she needed. Her brother Franco could no longer work following his accident, and Charles sympathised with her predicament. He even tried to sort out the problem once and for all, offering money for a paternity test, which she refused indignantly. The visits had gone on for almost a year before the fateful day he arrived to find her weeping. He offered his handkerchief and a generous dose of sympathy.

Tearfully she said, 'I'm so lonely Charles. I would love to feel a man's arms around me, but no one will ever want me now I have my little boy.'

Her tears, it seemed, were real, and not knowing what else to do, he took her in his arms to comfort her. Within seconds she had turned her face to his and was kissing him. The next moment she was leading him upstairs. Her young body had felt wonderful against his, as they lay naked on her bed. Emotions he thought were long gone, flooded back as he responded to her with fire and passion. It was like a dream, until he saw the flashlight of the camera. Eva feigned shock, pulling the sheets up to cover her naked breasts, as Charles lay dumbfounded in the bed. He looked first at Franco leaning on the bedstead, then at Eva. He knew at once he had been set up.

Ceasing his visits immediately, Charles waited with apprehension for the inevitable blackmail threats, but to his amazement nothing happened - although the worry was always in the back of his mind. Life returned to normal, and he tried to forget about the incident when almost a year later the first demand note came. It had almost been apologetic! It read:

Dearest Charles,

I'm so sorry, I have tried to avoid this, but Franco now insists that you pay him for the negatives of the photos he took of us together. He requires from you the sum of five hundred pounds. If you refuse, Franco will write to your wife.

Charles felt the colour drain from his face. Sickness washed over him like a fine mist. He felt ill and old and very, very stupid. The money was paid within the week, the negatives handed over to him, and no more was said, until six months later, when the second demand came. Again it was for five hundred pounds, but this time the amount was to be paid every six months, or else Gwen would receive the photos taken from the negatives. And so it had carried on until the last demand he received.

It was the tenth of December and he had just returned from Christmas shopping in Athens. He called at the pharmacy to pick up some painkillers for Gwen, who had taken to her bed with a migraine that morning, and popped into the Post Office to collect the mail. His heart sank when he saw the familiar handwriting on the envelope addressed to him, and quickly pushed it deep into his pocket as he hurried out into the fresh air.

'Mr Tempest?' Alexis shouted over to him.

'What!' he snapped.

Alexis, shocked at his abruptness, asked cautiously, 'I just wondered if you wanted a coffee. Yiannis and Travis are here.'

'No, thank you, but no.'

'Another time then?' Alexis said, watching him rush away.

Charles stood next to where the motorboat was moored and ripped open the letter.

Dearest Charles,

You will be aware that the next payment is due. I have pleaded with my brother once again on your behalf, but to no avail. I hope you will take some comfort in the fact that the money you have already given to us, is going towards my darling boy's education, which I am sure you would approve of. However, due to my brother's ill health, the business is failing, and in order for us to run it successfully, he is demanding the sum of twenty thousand pounds to be paid by cheque tomorrow on the eleventh of December.

He has offered his assurances that the photos will remain safe and will not fall into the wrong hands, i.e. your wife or granddaughter, as long as you keep your side of the bargain.

We look forward to doing business with you soon. Eva

He re-read the letter. Sick and pale with worry, he knew this could not go on. Screwing the demand note into a ball, he set off back to Amora Cove, knowing he must now face the consequences. By the time he had moored the boat, he had rehearsed his tragic speech over and over again, and was ready to face the music, but to his dismay he found Gwen on her hands and knees retching over the lavatory. For one desperate moment, he thought someone else had told her.

'Gwen?' he spoke nervously.

'Charles, thank goodness you're home, I've been so sick, this headache is getting worse. I think my head is going to explode. You must get a doctor, quickly please!' Charles rushed to her side and tried to lift her to her feet, but she pushed him away and slumped back over the lavatory.

'Please go and get Dr Aronis.'

Within an hour of Charles and Dr Aronis arriving back at the villa, Gwen was sleeping comfortably. The doctor had given her an injection to stop the sickness and ease the pain and had left some stronger painkillers for when she awoke.

Dr Aronis ushered Charles out of the bedroom. 'Let her sleep now.'

'What's wrong with her? Is it serious?' Charles asked anxiously.

Dr Aronis pursed his lips. 'I'm not sure. I think I will send her for some tests. Has she had migraines for a long time?'

Charles laughed shortly. 'Only since our granddaughter Laura came to stay with us seven years ago. I am sorry to say that I thought she was putting them on. She was never very good with children, and found Laura quite a handful.'

Dr Aronis smiled as he packed his medical bag. 'I'll arrange for some tests. Let her have plenty of rest, and if you don't mind me saying, you too look like you could do with a rest. Are you okay?'

'Yes, I'm fine, just a little worried,' Charles answered quickly.

Charles slept fitfully that night, whereas Gwen had a perfect night's sleep and woke refreshed and pain free. He had no stomach for his usual hearty breakfast - instead he took a cup of strong coffee and stood silently drinking it on the sun terrace.

Gwen noticed his erratic mood. All day he either paced up and down the sun terrace or walked to the beach and back. It crossed her mind that the doctor had given him some bad news that he was keeping from her. She noted the anxious look on his face with growing apprehension. He looked ill and drawn, but no matter how many times she called him, he would not come inside. Finally she had marched outside and shouted at him, that if he didn't come in and sit still he would have a heart attack. He promptly turned on the spot, threw her a terrified look, and to her horror, fell at her feet.

*

Laura and Vanessa had no sooner dropped their bags in their dormitory after a fortnight skiing trip when the headmistress came to their door.

'Laura?' The headmistress spoke softly. 'Come to my office please.' She reached out and placed her hand gently on Laura's back, as an anxious glance past between the girls.

At the top of the long winding staircase the headmistress opened the huge panelled wooden door and gestured for her to go through.

'Take a seat Laura.'

Laura settled herself on the hard leather chair opposite the headmistress's desk, and a letter was handed to her.

'This came for you a week ago.'

Laura took the letter from her hand and frowned. She instantly recognised her grandma's handwriting. The letter disturbed Laura before she had even opened it. She had received a great many letters during her stay at school, but had never been summoned to the Head's room to read them before. Normally they were pushed under the door of her dormitory. Something was wrong, very wrong. She started to tremble as she unfolded the letter and began to read:

Dear Laura,

It is with great sorrow that I must inform you that your grandpa suffered a massive heart attack and died suddenly on the eleventh of December. There was nothing anyone could do. When I rang your school, they informed me that you were on a skiing trip and we made a mutual decision not to break your holiday, and to go ahead with the funeral. I hope you will understand.

Laura began to shake uncontrollably. 'No, not my grandpa,' she wept.

By the time you read this letter, your grandfather will have been laid to rest. Please don't think you must come to my side. I would prefer to grieve alone, and I think you will be happier with the Haynes's, who I know will give you all the love and attention you need.

Please take care of yourself. I will try to write again in a few weeks.'

It was just signed. *'Gwen Tempest'*.

Gwen didn't write again, not even to answer Laura's letter, but this did not surprise Laura in the slightest.

28

Laura's school days were over!

Vanessa, much to her parent's dismay, enrolled in drama school after her exams. They had hoped that she would follow her brothers to university, and when her mother raised her objections, Vanessa declared with flourish, 'Oh darling, acting is the only career that will make me truly happy.'

Slater had only just scraped through his degree in Business Studies, having only attended university for the social life. Taylor joked that Slater's only goal in life was to become an international playboy, but at present, he was working as a croupier in The Regency Casino in Athens. Much to Laura's amazement, the relationship between herself and Slater had improved immensely as they grew into adulthood. So much so, whenever he was back in England, he always sought her out to take her for dinner – an occasion she relished, as he was always attentive to her.

Taylor, having graduated in Art and History a couple of years previously, was now working with his father.

During the Easter holidays, Laura had helped Taylor in the role of his personal assistant. He even offered her a job with the family firm when she left school, but she declined. She felt that she had to make her own way in life, independent of the Haynes's. Not being a great scholar, further education held no appeal for her, although art school had crossed her mind. In the end she decided to settle for the next best thing, and set out to find work in an art gallery. Her break came as she wandered the streets of St Ives one hot afternoon.

At the T R gallery on Fore Street, she spotted a notice in the window:

Gallery assistant needed, accommodation included, enquire within.

As she stepped in through the door, a kind looking

woman dressed in a colourful array of garments with an abundance of hair protruding from a soft cream canvas hat, called out to her.

'All right my luvver? Oh be a darling, grab hold of the other end of this, will you?' she said.

Laura dropped her bag and grabbed the frame of a rather large painting, which was in danger of falling forward from where it stood against the whitewashed wall.

'Right my luvver,' she said dabbing her face with a lace handkerchief. 'Lift when I say, and hook it onto the wall. One, two, three, done!' She brushed her hands together. 'Thank you kindly.'

Laura stood back and admired the canvas. The painting was enormous, depicting a stunning life size image of a woman looking out of a window. She was dressed in only a stripy towel and wore a long blonde plait down her back. It absolutely dominated one wall.

'The artist owns this gallery. He likes painting big! No one else does anything like it here in St Ives. I'll tell you my luvver, it'll be snapped up within the day, you mark my words, and then we'll have to put another one up. Have you come for the job? Please say you've come for the job. I could do with someone handy like you!'

Laura laughed. 'I'd love the job, but don't you want to interview me?'

'Well, I suspect you like art, and particularly the art we have here, otherwise you wouldn't have stepped through my door.' The lady grinned. 'Do you want the job? It's yours if you do. Oh, tidy yourself up girl, we have a client approaching!' She moved to greet the gentleman entering the shop, adjusting her hat as she walked, leaving Laura smiling to herself. Forty minutes later they were taking the huge painting back down from the wall and packaging it ready to be shipped to London.

'See what I mean my luvver? I can't put them up fast enough. Are you up for putting another painting up? You are staying, aren't you?' She said, passing a dog treat to the wiry terrier sitting under her desk.

*

It was forty two degrees, and everywhere on Poros was closed for siesta. Stephano stood aimlessly in the empty Gelateria, he was bored, but he knew not to disturb his mother when her bedroom door was locked. He did not care for the gentleman who visited her, simply because when he came, which was quite frequent, he'd arrive on the first morning ferry from Athens and leave on the last one, leaving Stephano to his own devices for most of the day. Thankfully Andreas often took him fishing, which was more than his own father Yiannis Kiassos had done. In fact his father had never even acknowledged him, which was very confusing to a boy of eight. Stephano truly believed that he and his mother must have done something very wrong for Yiannis Kiassos to dislike them both with such equal measure. He sighed and walked into the back room where his uncle Franco sat in a cloud of cigarette smoke, drinking from the neck of a brandy bottle. The smoke caught the back of Stephano's throat, making him cough violently. He slowly backed out of the room and went to stand at the front door, hoping and praying that Andreas would come soon.

*

Laura settled into St Ives life as though she had been born there. It was a vibrant, exciting life of beach parties and social gatherings. Her colleague, the very eccentric Kimberly Townsend, was a joy to work alongside. Laura's flat above the gallery was bijou, for want of a better description. Consisting of one bedroom, a box room, a tiny kitchen, and lounge, housing one sofa and a bookcase, it was adequate for her lifestyle. It was in the box room she finally found the space to paint in private. Life was good.

She lunched with Jack Ryder at least once a month in the Porthminster Café, and as there was only fifteen years between them, the 'uncle' had been dropped some time ago. It was during one of these lunches, eleven months after starting work in the gallery that she learned of her grandma's death.

'The office received this letter yesterday, from the hospital in Athens,' Jack said, handing her an envelope. 'Apparently your grandma had been ill with a brain tumour since before your grandfather died, and had refused treatment. She is to be buried next to your grandfather in Poros, and requested that you need not attend.'

'Huh, why does that not surprise me?' Laura said, taking the news with little grief. 'She can't still be trying to keep Yiannis and I apart, because that's over, it's in the past.'

A ghost of a smile flickered on Jack's lips.

Laura drained the contents of her glass. 'She really didn't like me, did she?' she sighed.

Jack refilled her glass. 'Oh Laura, I'm sure she liked you very much. I mean, who couldn't like you?' he quirked an eyebrow. 'She was just a very private person, who adored your grandpa and was looking forward to retiring in peace - just the two of them. Then of course circumstances changed, and you came into their lives. I don't think she knew how to cope with you.'

'You can say that again. She couldn't wait to send me away from Poros!' She sat back and folded her arms petulantly. 'I was really happy there!'

'I know, but it was for your own good,' Jack argued. 'It was a joint decision between both your grandparents to make sure you received a good education.'

The waiter brought their lunch, but the discussion continued.

'But I was getting a good education at school and with Yiannis.'

Jack grimaced slightly at the mention of Yiannis's name again. 'Your grandma was your guardian, Laura. You must realise that a fisherman is not the sort of person a young lady like you should be mixing with. She was just trying to make sure you were brought up properly that's all.'

Placing a morsel of food into her mouth, she swallowed quickly and waved her fork in the air. 'What Yiannis taught me will prove to be more beneficial in this big wide world than bloody Latin ever will,' she answered bitterly.

Jack pursed his lips. 'She was looking out for you, like a mother would her own daughter.'

She dabbed her mouth with her serviette. 'I'm sorry, but she was no mother to me. The very thought of her still makes me so cross'.

There was a pause in the conversation. 'Will you be going to Poros?' he asked, breaking the silence. 'I could come with you.' He looked at her hopefully.

'I don't think so. I'm too busy at the gallery.' She lifted her eyebrows. 'Why, do you think I should go?'

'Not necessarily no. There will be things to sort out in the villa - it's still your home, though there is some new clause that you can't do anything to it, until your twenty-first birthday.' He shifted uncomfortably. 'I'm sorry to be so vague, but there was a codicil added a few months ago to the Will, and I, for some reason, have not been privy to it. High Top House in Gweek is yours now to do what you want with though. Maybe you could sell it. It should bring a good price.' He smiled thinly.

She sat for a moment as her thoughts took her back to Amora Cove. 'Is anyone looking after the Villa?'

Jack nodded. 'Your grandpa left a small retainer in his Will to keep a caretaker on until you reach twenty-one.'

'Is it Yiannis?' She asked sullenly.

'No,' Jack answered stiffly. 'He has long gone,' he lied.

Quietly turning her salad with her fork, she sighed. 'No, I won't be going to Poros.'

Smiling inwardly he placed his utensils on the plate and gestured for the waiter to bring the dessert menu - even though his waistline protested.

'So, have you planned anything for your eighteenth

birthday?' he asked, changing the subject.

She shook her head. 'Nothing for my birthday no, but Vanessa, Taylor and I are taking a road trip to America in October. Slater has just taken a six month contract as a croupier in Las Vegas. He flits about all over the place now. He was in Athens a few months back. I can't say I'm enamoured about going to Las Vegas though, but it's only part of the trip.'

Jack poured out the last of the wine. 'I didn't think you were too enamoured with Slater.'

She laughed lightly. 'That was true when I was younger. He was a real pain in the ….you know what, but he's changed now. He's always quite sweet to me. When he is home, we meet up for lunch and dinner. Sometimes he even sends me flowers!' she grinned cheekily. 'Who would have thought it, eh?'

Jack regarded Laura seriously. 'Is Slater interested in you…romantically?'

Laura wrinkled her nose. 'I shouldn't think so. He's never suggested anything.' She laughed.

Jack breathed inwardly - he wasn't so sure. He could not bear the thought of her becoming romantically entwined with anyone. She did not know it, but Jack was utterly infatuated by her. 'Well it looks like I will have to come to the rescue and throw a birthday party for you.'

'No Jack, I was just going to have a quiet night in. As I said, I'm very busy at the moment!'

'Nonsense, you leave it to me, I'm going to give you a birthday to remember.

*

True to form, Jack kept his promise. He arranged for her to have the day off from the gallery. A white limousine picked her up and inched its way around the tight alleyways of St Ives to whisk her off to The Budock Vean Hotel, overlooking the Helford River. Jack had arranged for her to stay in one of their beautiful rooms overlooking the River. He had paid for her to be pampered at their spa, before she joined Jack for a leisurely champagne lunch. Thinking she was having dinner only with Jack that evening, she was stunned to find him waiting to greet her with his arms full of flowers, having commandeered the whole restaurant. Behind him were her old school friends, and friends and colleagues from St Ives, along with Vanessa, Taylor, and Sarah Haynes and her good friend Pippa. A live band was playing in the right hand corner. Each table was decorated with white lilies - her favourite flowers - and above her was a net suspended from the ceiling full of white balloons. Laura was speechless. No expense had been spared.

'He's certainly pushed the boat out to impress you, hasn't he?' Vanessa grinned.

'He does go a bit overboard though.'

'Methinks he is trying to impress you girl.'

'I can't think why.'

'Can you not?' she chuckled.

After they had all eaten and the dancing had started, Vanessa said something to Laura which totally stunned her.

'There he goes Laura,' she said, nodding towards Jack. 'He's getting ready to make his announcement.'

'What announcement?'

'You know, you dark horse,' she said, nudging her. 'You kept him quiet didn't you? Though I must admit, I didn't think he was your type,' she added.

'What are you talking about Van? Who's my type?'

'Jack of course!'

'What?' Laura was aghast, as Jack took the microphone from the band, and called for quiet.

'Ladies and Gentlemen, please give a round of applause for the birthday girl. Come on Laura, come and join me.'

Vanessa had to practically push Laura from where she sat. As she walked apprehensively towards him, the band played Stevie Wonder's, 'Isn't She Lovely'. He held out his hand to her as she nervously smiled at him, praying that

Vanessa had been wrong.

'Have you had a nice day?' Jack spoke into the microphone.

'Lovely, thank you,' she answered nervously.

'I have a little present for you.'

'Oh?' She swallowed hard, and glanced at Vanessa, who was grinning like a Cheshire cat.

'Would you like to see what I have bought for you?'

Laura smiled weakly.

He bent down in front of her and Laura thought for one awful moment that she was going to faint. He picked up a small box and offered it up to her.

'I hope you like it. Vanessa helped me choose it for you.'

Laura's head swam as he knelt down and flipped the box lid open to reveal the most exquisite diamond ring she had ever seen.

'My lovely Laura, would you do me the honour of becoming my wife?'

A stunned silence fell.

'Will you marry me Laura?' he said, with eager anticipation.

Laura stared down at him in utter disbelief. Suddenly very lightheaded, she crumpled to the floor.

Aware of people fussing around, Laura heard Taylor offer to carry her upstairs, but when she opened her eyes slightly, she was in Jack's arms. He placed her on a bed and Vanessa placed a damp facecloth to her forehead.

Laura opened one eye. 'Get Jack out of here please!' she pleaded quietly to Vanessa.

Vanessa nodded. 'Jack, I think she will be better left alone for a while.'

'No, I want to stay with her,' he insisted.

Laura held her hand to her forehead and said gently, 'Please Jack, if you don't mind I'll be fine with Vanessa. I've perhaps had a little too much to drink. Thank you for everything, but please go back to the party. I'll talk to you later.'

'Very well, I'll go,' he said, slightly put out.

As soon as the door closed, Laura leapt to her feet and began packing her bag.

'Oh!' Vanessa stood back in amazement. 'What are you doing?'

Laura flashed her eyes at her. 'I'm leaving, what does it look like?'

'What now?'

'Yes now! How could you be privy to this Vanessa and not tell me?'

'Well, I thought you liked him….you're always having lunch with him!'

'Oh for goodness sake, just because I have lunch with him, doesn't mean I want to marry him!' She threw her arms in the air. 'I can't believe you would do this to me.' She dragged the last of her clothes into her bag. 'Do you think Taylor will drive me home?' she asked struggling to zip her bag.

Vanessa folded her arms indignantly. 'I'm sure he will. If that is what you want.'

Laura scraped her hands through her hair. 'Yes that is what I want. I need to get away from here now before he gets any more stupid ideas about marriage.'

'All right calm down. I'll go and find Taylor,' Van said, opening the door.

'There will be no need for that,' Jack's voice cut through Laura like ice. 'I'll take her anywhere she wants to go. Could you just leave us alone for a moment Vanessa?'

Laura's mouth felt dry as she agreed to Vanessa's dismissal.

Jack placed his hand on Vanessa's sleeve. 'Can we keep this conversation to ourselves?'

Vanessa glanced at Laura, who gave her approval.

Outside the bedroom, Taylor and Pippa approached Vanessa. 'What's happening?'

Vanessa put her finger to her lips and whispered,

'Come outside, and I'll tell you.'

Jack leant against the dressing table, hugging his arms. It was a stance Laura found unsettling - as though he thought he had some authority over her. He didn't speak, he just stared at her.

'Jack I...'

He held up his hand. 'Don't say anything else. I understand your feelings fully. You've made them quite plain.' His disappointment was intense. 'It's Slater isn't it?' he asked the question quietly.

'What?'

'You're enamoured with him, aren't you?

She began to laugh. 'No! Where the hell did you get that notion from?'

He shrugged his shoulders. 'All the lunches and dinners you have with him. The flowers he sends you. There was a time when you loathed him, but not any more it seems.'

She shook her head furiously. 'You are being utterly ridiculous now.'

He cocked his head slightly. 'Why else would you go all the way to America to see him?'

'For a *holiday*,' she yelled.

They stood motionless as emotions swam between them.

She could see his Adams apple move as he swallowed hard. 'I love you,' he said firmly.

She wrung her hands in anguish. 'Jack, please, I can't do this. I'm really sorry, but I don't feel the same way.'

'I thought we had something special.'

She tried desperately to hold back the tears of frustration. 'We did, we do, but, I know we dropped the 'uncle' a while ago, but to me, you are still Uncle Jack. I love you like an uncle, but that is as far as my feelings go. I'm sorry - I would not willingly hurt you, but marrying you is completely out of the question.'

'I see,' he breathed.

'I hope you do. I'm eighteen! I'm young and free, why

would I want to tie myself down?'

There came a knock on the door. 'Laura, its Taylor. Van said you might want a lift home.'

'One moment,' she called out.

Laura and Jack exchanged glances.

Crestfallen, Jack said, 'Don't go home tonight. Please stay. Enjoy the room, it's your birthday treat.' He lowered his eyes. 'I shall not repeat my proposal to you again I promise.' As he approached the door, he said softly, 'Goodnight Laura. I'm sorry in more ways than one.'

29

It was a busy Friday morning late in July at TR Gallery. Laura was busy organising an exhibition due to open that evening, when Kimberly came in with a bouquet of flowers for her, along with an airmail letter.

Laura waved the flowers away. 'They'll be from Jack. I do wish he would stop sending them.' She barely saw him nowadays, and when she did, she still found him in earnest about her. 'We'll use the flowers for tonight's opening. It'll save me buying more.'

'You're right, the flowers are from Jack, but the letter has an American postmark.' Kimberly answered.

Laura looked up. 'Let me see.' She smiled as she read:

Dear Laura,

Sorry you had to cancel your trip out here last October. Trust Vanessa to finally get an acting job, and for it to be a long run in a soap. Still, she was happy about it, so that is something. Anyway, she says she will be free in August if you want to reschedule the trip. I am finishing here at the end of August, so if you all come, I can show you the sights of Las Vegas. I've spoken to Taylor, and it's a bit short notice for him to take time off, but it doesn't stop you and Van coming. Hope you can make it. It seems ages since I saw you. Love Slater xxx

Laura looked up at Kimberly, pleadingly. 'Any chance of me taking some time off in August and September?'

*

Las Vegas was everything Laura thought it would be - brash, tacky and loud. Out of the whole American trip planned, this was the place she would have rather avoided. It was disappointing that Taylor had been unable to join them, but Vanessa's zest for life kept the whole journey on a high.

They booked into the Venetian Resort Hotel and

Casino where Slater worked as a croupier.

Tired of the noise and the falseness of the place, Slater dressed for his last night with relish. He couldn't wait to be home, mostly for the rest. This last six month stint in Vegas had filled his bank balance, but made him long for home comforts.

Vanessa and Laura settled themselves at the bar, but Slater wouldn't partake in a drink before his shift, he needed a clear head. They sat for a while, and then moved about the casino, watching the money roll away at various tables. Some people won, and won big, much to the management's annoyance. Laura watched Slater work his magic at the blackjack table. He looked slick, quick and handsome in his suit. He was obviously appreciated by the bejewelled woman at his table. So professional was he, not once did his gaze stray away from the table or players.

Complimentary champagne flowed easily that night, and when Slater finished his shift at 11 a.m. and joined them at the bar, both Laura and Vanessa were giggling like silly children.

'Here's to my final night in Hell,' Slater said raising his glass.

'What will you do now, dear brother? Father said you can't laze about at home you know.'

Slater pulled a face. 'I don't know, maybe I'll settle down,' he looked directly at Laura, who grinned stupidly.

'I was sorry to have missed your eighteenth birthday last year. I understand it was a grand affair, a real stunner.'

Laura puffed out her cheeks. 'You could say that.'

Slater winked at Vanessa. 'I understand Mr Ryder made you swoon.'

Laura rolled her eyes. 'Don't remind me. Can we talk about something else please?'

'So I take it the wedding is off?'

'It was never on!' she said, almost slipping from her seat.

Slater grabbed her arm to steady her and then gently

touched her face. 'So there's a chance for me then is there?'

The intimacy of the touch stunned Laura momentarily. She glanced at him in surprise, trying to focus on his face as he winked at her and laughed.

'Hey Laura,' Vanessa slurred. 'Wouldn't that be brilliant if you married my lovely brother? We would be…' she thought for a moment, 'sisters-in-law.'

'He's kidding Van, and you know it.' She glanced at Slater, who looked quite serious.

'Oh, I don't know.' Vanessa waved her glass around. 'He looks as though he means it to me. I think you two should get engaged. Let's have a double celebration -more champagne anyone?' Vanessa slopped the bubbles into the glasses without waiting for an answer.

'Oh God, I'm so drunk,' moaned Laura, holding her head in her hands.

'Hey, hey,' Vanessa shook Laura. 'We're in Vegas. The home of the wedding! Why don't you two tie the knot? It would be such a hoot. All you have to do is get a licence and bob's your uncle, you're married. Go on. You know you want to!'

Laura laid her head on the bar, too inebriated to answer. She felt an arm around her waist and vaguely heard Slater say, 'Let's get her some fresh air.'

The next thing she knew, Laura became aware of the sound of Elvis singing. An array of frothy wedding dresses surrounded her, and Vanessa was grinning like a Cheshire Cat.

*

Great thunderclouds hung over the Peloponnese. A few disgruntled holidaymakers sat grimly undercover at Alexis Taverna, watching the rain pour off the candy striped awnings. Akis Dopas sat at the back of the taverna, his legs outstretched, enjoying the first coffee of the day, when a piercing scream punctured the morning. Almost choking on his drink, Akis sat bolt upright, as Maria Vassos ran screaming from the post office, holding her apron to her face. Leaving his chair abruptly, Akis rushed into the dimly lit post office to find Marion's feet protruding from where she normally stood.

'What the devil are you doing woman? Get up at once.' he shouted, knowing full well that she would not be able to. He knelt down and felt for a pulse within the folds of fat at her neck. He turned to Maria Vassos who stood behind him shrieking like a banshee. 'For Christ's sake woman, stop your noise,' he yelled, pushing her unceremoniously out of the door. He glanced down at his wife without emotion and rang for Dr Aronis. An hour later, Marion was laid out in the back room. A heart attack, Dr Aronis said. She wouldn't have known a thing, he assured Akis, who nodded dispassionately. Surrounded by black clad women, Akis left them to their mourning. He set out picking up the debris of paper, which Marion must have pulled off from under the shelf as she fell. There he found a letter addressed to Yiannis with an English post mark, dated three years ago.

*

'You've done what?' Taylor gasped, when Laura rang to tell him her news. 'Were you drunk?'

'No,' she laughed. 'I wasn't drunk. Though we very nearly did it drunk one night, I admit, but Slater wanted me to be fully aware of his intentions.'

'Did he now?' Taylor could hardly keep sarcasm from his voice. 'Are you sure this is what you wanted Laura? It's all a bit sudden, isn't it?'

'Yes I suppose it is. But you know, I have seen quite a bit of Slater over the past couple of years. I must admit though, I didn't think he was interested in marrying me. His proposal came right out of the blue. We were in Los Angeles, Vanessa was meeting some film producer in Hollywood and we were on Venice beach when he proposed.'

'Just like that?' Taylor said coolly.

'Just like that! He told me he always wanted to marry me and was really upset when he thought Jack Ryder was making a play for me - devastated in fact. Anyway, I said yes. We married yesterday on our return to Las Vegas. Oh I know it sounds tacky doesn't it? But I can assure you I was a sober as a judge and Elvis was not in the equation,' she giggled.

Taylor shifted uncomfortably. He remembered Slater's reaction very well when they told him of Jack's proposal last September. He had burst out laughing. Not once had he ever mentioned that he was interested in Laura himself.

'Aren't you happy for me Taylor?'

He bit down on his bottom lip. 'Of course I am darling. It's just that, you don't *really* know him do you?'

Laura laughed heartily. 'I've known him since I was ten years old! Not intimately of course, but I suppose that's what marriage is all about isn't it - discovering each other?'

Taylor closed his eyes in despair. 'Of course it is. I just worry about you Laura that's all.' He knew his brother, and he knew his character, and that was what was bothering him most.

She smiled and blew a kiss down the phone. 'Thank you for caring Taylor. You always did look after me, just like a big brother.'

Taylor clutched the phone tightly. He wanted more than anything to keep her safe, but there was nothing he could do now. 'If you ever need anything, just call me okay?' he said seriously.

'I will. Thank you. Look, I'll have to go. This phone call is costing me a fortune. We will be in Gweek the day after tomorrow, I'll see you then. I don't think your mother will be too pleased that we've done her out of a wedding, so we'll have a bit of explaining to do. We've booked dinner at the Green Bank Hotel on Saturday, so we can have a family celebration. Can you contact Pippa for me - I'd like her to be there.'

*

When Pippa came home from work, she found two letters waiting for her, both of which brought their own share of turmoil.

The first was from Greece:

Dear Pippa,

For reasons you would not believe if I told you, I have only just taken receipt of your letter dated three years ago. I admit your letter confused me. You ask me to forgive Laura. What is there to forgive Laura for? I love her. I certainly never had her sent her away!

So, if you would be kind enough to help us again, please tell Laura, I love her and I'm waiting. Thank you for writing to me.

Yours truly Yiannis Kiassos

Pippa wore a smile from ear to ear as she pressed the letter to her chest. She couldn't wait for Laura to return from America to tell her. She picked up the second letter which contained a note from Taylor.

Dear Pippa,

Laura has asked me to invite you to The Green Bank Hotel, Falmouth, at 7.p.m. on Sat 15th of September. It's to celebrate her recent marriage to my brother Slater. We will collect you at 6.20 p.m.

Regards Taylor

Pippa felt the colour drain from her face as she sat at the telephone table in shock.

30

Yiannis pulled his boat onto the beach and hauled the fishing nets onto the rocks to dry. He looked down at his catch, glistening like liquid silver in the sun. As he reached into the slippery coolness, grabbing a fish in each hand, one of them slipped from his grip, flicking water into his eyes. 'Ugh!' he said, wiping the moisture from his face. When he opened his eyes, he caught sight of a yacht, sailing majestically into view. His body stood rigid and his skin tingled, as he looked at the woman aboard, the summer breeze blowing through her hair. Laura? Was it her? Had she come back to him?

He pulled his boat further up the shingle beach and scrambled up the dusty rocks until he could see round the headland to the small inlet of Amora Cove. Sure enough the yacht sailed into the opening, and dropped anchor in the deep water a few yards from the beach.

'Is it you?' he mouthed silently to himself. After the way they'd parted three years ago, he'd resigned himself to the fact that she would never return to him. But here she was. He could hardly believe his eyes.

He made his way quickly down the dusty hill, dragged the fish out of the boat, and threw them into the waiting basket. He gathered all his strength to push the boat back into the water, and jumped aboard.

*

From the deck of the chartered yacht, 'Cecelia', Laura gazed dreamily towards where her grandfather's yacht, Aglaia, was still moored out in the water. Her thoughts returned to that moonlit night, three years ago, when she'd swum out to the Midnight Rocks to meet Yiannis. Her heart was so full of love for him she thought it would burst. It was like a dream. It was so long ago. How her life had changed since that night. She fingered the gold wedding ring on her finger, and sighed wistfully. As she waited patiently for the crew to lower the launch to transport them to the beach, she glanced at the white lodge behind the villa. Was Yiannis there? She hoped not. She didn't really want to meet him again, not now.

*

By the time Yiannis had sailed into Amora Cove, the launch was resting on the beach. He took the beach steps two at a time and had just stepped onto the sun terrace when Laura emerged from the French doors.

'Laura…..you've come home!' He opened his arms to welcome her.

Laura, completely taken aback, took a sharp intake of breath. 'Oh my God Yiannis, you startled me. I didn't expect to see you here!' She glanced nervously back into the villa. 'You're well I hope?' she said stiffly.

'Yes I'm fine thanks, better for seeing you,' he smiled. Noting the coolness in her voice, his smile abated. Something was wrong - he could feel it in his bones. He watched her shift uncomfortably as he searched her face, hoping to see his joy mirrored. 'It's been such a long time Laura - I feared you would never come back.'

Pursing her lips, she replied sharply. 'I wasn't aware there was anything to come back for.'

Shocked at her response, he reached for her hands. 'Laura, have I done something to offend you? I waited and waited for a letter from you, to tell me why you went away. I don't understand why you left. The last time I saw you….we almost….'

She tried to pull away, but he held fast. 'Yes, the last time you saw me, you had me sent away the very next day!'

'What? No!'

'Oh come on Yiannis, don't play the innocent.' She bristled with hurt. 'You thought I had overstepped the mark, told my grandma and had me sent away.'

His face blanched. 'No, that's not true!'

'Laura!' Slater's voice barked angrily behind her. 'Is this person bothering you?' Slater moved forward, glaring at Yiannis, who was still holding Laura's hands.

Laura pulled free for Yiannis. 'Slater, I'd like you to meet Yiannis. Yiannis, this is my husband Slater.'

Yiannis stared incredulously at Slater as he moved to rest his hands on Laura's shoulders. He could hardly breathe for the intense pain in his chest. She could not have hurt him more if she had driven a stake through his heart.

'Ah yes,' Slater said sarcastically. 'I forgot you had servants. Well, now you're here, you can fetch the bags up from the beach,' he said, ushering him off the villa steps.

Yiannis sidestepped him and moved towards Laura. The tragic look he gave her pierced her heart. Shaking his head, he whispered, 'What have you done?'

Laura's eyes lowered in embarrassment and Slater stepped in-between them. 'I think it's time *you* went about your business.' He flashed his eyes angrily. 'The bags man, get the bags now!'

Yiannis ignored Slater and spoke directly at Laura. 'Tell him, I'm not his man. I'm certainly not his damn servant and he can get his own bloody bags!' With one last heartrending look, he ran down the beach steps, angrier than he had ever known himself to be.

Pushing Laura aside, Slater shouted, 'Hey you, come back here at once!'

Laura grabbed his sleeve. 'Slater, please leave him be.'

He shrugged her free indignantly. 'I'll not be spoken to like that, certainly not from a servant. He'd better not show his face here again. You're fired,' he shouted after him.

'Yiannis isn't a servant. He lives here and looks after the place,' she said, trying to calm him down.

'Not any more he doesn't. I want him off my land tonight! Do you hear me?' he seethed.

Speechless, Laura watched Yiannis as he motored away, deeply upset at the altercation.

He turned and glared at her. 'And why the hell was he

holding your hands?'

'Oh for goodness sake, it was nothing. Please just leave it for now. We probably won't see him again while we're here,' she said rubbing her forehead. 'If you'll excuse me, I have a sudden headache and need to lie down.'

He grasped her arm just as she turned to go indoors. 'Not so fast. I want to know what is going on here. Why was he was so familiar with you?'

'Excuse me,' she retorted. 'There's nothing going on.'

Grasping her by her arms he shook her. 'I saw the way he looked at you. Is he some old boyfriend? Some bit of rough in the sun you conveniently forgot to tell me about?'

'No, he is not! Now let go at once. You're hurting me Slater.'

'Not until you to tell me.' He shook her more violently. 'I want to know the nature of your relationship with him! I have a right to know. I am your husband!'

Frightened of his anger, alarm bells began to ring. 'Yiannis is a family friend that's all,' she said calmly. 'I've known him since I was nine years old! You must understand. I spent a lot of time here. We were very fond of each other.'

He narrowed his eyes. 'How fond? Were you in love with him? Are you in love with him?'

Her cheeks flushed with adrenalin. 'Don't be ridiculous,' she lied. 'I was only fifteen years old the last time I saw him.'

He grasped her tighter. 'I don't believe you. Vanessa said you were sent away from here in disgrace. You had a dirty little affair with the hired help didn't you?'

'No!' she cried, trying to disengage herself.

His lips were white with anger. 'I'll have him arrested for interfering with a minor. You just see if I don't!'

She squeezed her eyes shut to the onslaught. 'Look, you're overreacting, I wish we had never come here now,' she cried.

Suddenly he pushed her up the steps towards the

French windows. 'Yes I'm curious actually. I'd like to know *why* we came here, instead of flying straight to Rhodes, to be with Taylor and Vanessa.'

'You know why we're here. I have things to sort out. Things I should have done ages ago, when my grandparents died.'

'So why didn't you, instead of using our honeymoon?'

Laura dragged her fingers through her hair. She was hot and anxious and desperately wanted to defuse the situation. 'I wanted you to see the villa. It's so beautiful here - perfect for a honeymoon. I wanted us to spend a little time together before we met up with the other two. You were looking forward to coming!'

His lip curled into a sneer. 'Well, that was before I realised you had some lovesick lover waiting for you here.'

'Oh for goodness sake Slater, for the last time, we were friends that's all, friends I tell you.' She threw her arms up in the air in desperation. 'I'm not arguing with you any more while you're in this mood. You're just being unreasonable.'

He raised his eyebrows. 'I'll show you unreasonable.'

She saw his fist rise and the next second she felt a stinging blow to her face. Her head spun as she reeled across the kitchen floor and landed against the table, the impact causing her lip to burst, splattering blood down the front of her dress.

In stunned silence she sat under the table, wiping the blood from her mouth. Nausea swept over her in waves, as hot salty tears trickled down her cheeks, stinging the open wound on her lips. She could not believe what had just happened. This was her honeymoon! Through blurred vision, she felt her right eyelid swell and slowly close. Out of the corner of her other eye she could see Slater moving towards the table. Instinct made her curl into a ball, bracing herself for the next blow. Slater knelt down and began to crawl under the table.

'No! Please no!' she whimpered, then in a panic she

tried to scramble away from him. He grabbed her by the foot and dragged her back out from under the table. In desperation she kicked his hand away.

'Laura calm down. I'm not going to hurt you again.'

Laura trembled in terror. When Slater reached for her hand, she flinched. 'Calm down?' he whispered gently.

He carefully lifted her into his arms, and carried her upstairs to the master bedroom, placing her softly on the bed.

'Shush now,' he said, stroking her face tenderly. 'You lay there, don't move, I'll be back in a moment.'

Laura lay dead still, her mind in turmoil. Her skin felt cold and clammy, as though she had just woken from a terrible dream. Brushing her fingers across her swollen lips, the open wound confirmed the dreadful truth that it really had happened.

'Oh please God, let the anger be over,' she prayed softly. She heard Slater turn on the shower, and five minutes later he entered the room, with a towel around his waist.

He stood over her and smiled. 'Please don't do anything to make me jealous again.'

Laura listened in total bewilderment. Tears of distress began to fill her eyes as she tried in vain to contain the uncontrollable sobs as they bleated from within her.

Slater leant over her. 'You're mine now, remember that.' He kissed her with feathery gentleness. She felt his mouth skirt carefully round her swollen lips, and then his breath quickened, his mouth felt hard against hers as he parted her lips with his tongue.

Appalled at the inference, she pushed him away, but she was no match for his strength as he lay atop her.

'Oh please, no!' she pleaded, as she closed her mind to what was about to happen, but her pleas were ignored.

31

A pale yellow sunrise lifted the blanket of darkness from the sky. The cool morning dawn filtered through the voile curtains to caress Laura's hot broken face. She had not slept soundly like Slater - in fact she had not slept at all.

Inching carefully away from him, she shuddered as a wave of sickness swept over her, at the memory of the previous night. The glass of water by her bed was warm and stale, but she took a sip to wash away the awful taste of blood, which coated the inside of her mouth. Never had she felt so wretched, as she lay next to the man she was supposed to be on honeymoon with.

During the long night she recalled Taylor's words the day she'd told him of her marriage. 'Be careful,' he had said to her. 'Call me if you ever need anything.'

What a fool she'd been, she should have realised Taylor was trying to warn her about his brother. Not for the first time that night did she wonder what on earth she had got herself involved in.

Slater moved and grunted, and Laura lay very still until she felt his breathing deepen again. On her wedding day, a week ago, she'd been the happiest woman alive.

She thought of Van and Taylor at the Haynes' holiday home in Rhodes. She wished with all her heart that she had gone straight there with them. But Laura had suggested spending the first few days of their honeymoon on Poros. They had chartered a yacht in Glyfada. Their plan was to spend a few days here, then to sail to Rhodes to join the others, and then back to Glyfada. She touched her bruised face - this was some honeymoon!

Slater stirred again, sending Laura into a blind panic. Terrified of facing him, her body tensed.

Praying he wouldn't make any more unwelcome advances on her, she was relieved to feel him get out of bed. She held her breath until he left the room - her muscles aching from her motionless stance. There was movement downstairs in the kitchen, and then at length she heard his footsteps return. Her body shuddered as she felt his presence in the bedroom. She prayed again that he would not touch her.

'Laura, are you awake?'

She dared not move. He placed something on the bedside table and left the room. A moment later she heard him open and close the French windows. When she heard the motor on the launch start up, she slipped out of bed. From the terrace she watched the yacht sail round the headland. Only then did she relax. Her movements were stiff and painful as she walked back to examine the note he had left.

'Gone into town, see you later. Love Slater'

Laura laughed bitterly, mimicking the word 'love' on the note. The bathroom mirror added to her despair. The right side of her face was swollen, her eye was closed, and her lip protruded angrily with a bloody scar. Her head ached as she searched her makeup bag in vain for the packet of headache tablets she had placed there yesterday.

Glancing again at her broken face, she spoke to her reflection. 'You have got to get out of here girl!'

Locating her handbag in the kitchen, she drew a glass of cold water and searched the bag's hidden pockets for aspirin. Puzzled, she emptied the contents of the bag on the kitchen table, searching for what she knew had been there yesterday. A shiver ran the length of her spine. Her passport and purse were also missing. He must have known she would try to leave. She gathered the contents of her bag and pushed them back from whence they came and began to cry. The tears stung her painful face and the more upset she became the more her head throbbed. She pondered on what to do. She knew she couldn't sail away, she couldn't handle the Aglaia, and anyway, Yiannis kept the keys. 'Swim!' she said out loud. That was it. She would wait until Slater was asleep tonight and sneak away. She was a good swimmer. She could easily make it round to the tiny inlet which Yiannis used to sort his catch. She could hide there until someone passed by in a boat and then would hitch a lift. Somebody would help her in the harbour for sure, and as for her passport, she could apply to the British Embassy. Yes, that's what she would do, but in the meantime, she knew she must go and lay down, the pain in her head was excruciating. She retired to bed with a cold handkerchief to her forehead and slept for almost three hours.

*

Slater returned shortly after she woke. He was sweaty hot and reeked of cheap perfume. He placed a brown paper bag on the coffee table in the lounge, peeled his shirt off and threw it to her. 'I think that needs a wash,' he said.

'Where've you been?' she asked tentatively.

'The harbour - didn't you read my note?'

She sniffed the shirt in her hands and glanced up at him - he had obviously been with another woman. His mouth twisted into a smile at her countenance, before he ran upstairs to the bathroom. When she heard the shower start, she glanced at the paper bag. With one eye on the stairs, she tentatively looked inside and shuddered to find a gun. He was going to kill her!

A few moments later, Slater walked naked into the kitchen, towelling his wet hair. He knew from her face she'd looked inside the bag.

In trepidation she watched as he drew out the gun. He examined it for a few seconds before slipping his finger in the trigger. Laura was shaking uncontrollably, as he lifted the gun, pointed it at her, and closed one eye to focus. 'Bang,' he said softly. He blew the end of the gun cowboy style. He laughed mockingly. 'Your face was a picture then.'

Laura's head was pounding again. 'You're sick!' she murmured.

'If I'm sick, you're stupid! Did you really think I was going to shoot you? This is to keep lover boy off my land!'

That was the second time he had referred to Amora Cove as 'my land'! So that was it, Laura swallowed hard. He had only married her for money. Money she didn't have!

He regarded her for a moment with cold hard eyes, waiting for her to defend Kiassos. When she wasn't forthcoming, he smiled softly, his temperament changing instantly.

'Right, that's that sorted. Come on Laura. We are going to sail round the island. We need to do something to put a smile on your face.' He moved towards her, cocking his head to one side to examine her. 'Talking of which, you'd better put some sunglasses on or something to hide these marks. You made a real mess of yourself when you fell yesterday.'

Laura began to speak, but her voice was almost inaudible.

'What? I can't hear what you are saying, stop mumbling girl,' Slater berated.

Laura cleared her throat. 'I don't want to go anywhere. I have a terrible headache.'

'Nonsense, it'll soon wear off in the fresh air. You need to drink more water!' He started to pull her from where she stood. 'Come on, I won't take no for an answer.'

'No. I need to take pain killers and lie down,' she insisted.

'Well you won't find any pain killers here. You had more pills in your handbag than a chemist. I've thrown them all down the toilet. I don't believe in pumping chemicals into my body, and as my wife, I don't expect you to either - not now we are in the process of making a baby. Now come on, before I lose my temper.'

Baby? A voice in her head screamed.

'Come on,' he yelled.

Standing her ground she retorted, 'Did you put my passport down the toilet as well?'

He folded his arms. 'Your passport is safe. There are too many unsavoury characters wandering around this cove for my liking. You can't be too careful you know. Now, get your things together.'

*

Slater was a changed man in front of the crew. He gave no hint of the monster she'd witnessed last evening. Come nightfall they dropped anchor in a tiny moonlit bay. Slater lolled on plump cushions strategically strewn around the deck of varnished teak, and he beckoned Laura to join him for a gin and tonic. Reluctantly she sat down, but could not rest easy with him. She could not trust him any more, and her desire to leave him was stronger than ever since the incident with the gun. Unfortunately, all hope of swimming for freedom had been dashed with the confines of the yacht. But, she promised herself, the first chance she got, she would be gone.

'Come here.' He beckoned her closer.

She paused, her emotions simmering with antipathy for this man who had physically and mentally abused her, but with fear and repulsion she reluctantly moved closer to him.

He placed a protective arm around her shoulder and sighed. 'What a beautiful setting for two people in love to spend their honeymoon in. Have you ever seen such a moon before?'

Laura thought back to the night she had gone Moondancing with Yiannis.

Slater barked at the crew to leave them alone and Laura trembled. 'How much of this island do you own? It must be worth a packet. I should think the villa itself will be close on three quarters of a million!'

Despite herself, she smiled inwardly. So, he did think she had money. 'I don't know. I'm not privy to that information.'

He pulled away slightly. 'What do you mean? It all passed to you on the death of your grandparents. Surely that was the case.'

She shook her head. 'I'm afraid not. I don't own any of it.' Hardly able to contain her amusement she continued, 'The estate is in limbo until I'm twenty-one.'

Slater was breathing deeply. 'But it will be ours - yours and mine in less than two years?'

She regarded him for a moment, knowing full well his volatile mood, but she couldn't help herself and answered, 'As I say, I'm not privy to that information.'

*

They returned, not to Amora Cove, but to the harbour the next morning, moored the boat and walked along the sea front. A large brimmed straw hat, adorned with a white chiffon scarf to compliment the dazzling white linen dress, hid Laura's battered face. Her brown sandals clipped softly on the dusty sea front as she lethargically surveyed the scene through dark sunglasses.

They walked the length of the harbour, passing rows of darkened doors occupied with women in black dresses and headscarves. The women sat chatting and sewing whilst swapping gossip, their lives separated by an invisible screen from the tourist crowd that passed within arm's length.

They stopped at the fruit market, and despite herself Laura marvelled at the smell and colour of the scene. She had almost forgotten the photographic prettiness of this harbour, with its whitewashed houses and windows flanked with blue traditional shutters.

She remembered the walk she used to make to school with Yiannis each day, through the tiny back streets, between walls of radiant whiteness, accentuated by pots of scarlet geraniums and bougainvillaea. How simple her life had been then, so full of joy and wild abandon. What had happened to that happy little girl? she asked herself. She turned into a battered wife, that's what!

She watched her handsome husband swagger his way slowly through the market place, smiling and charming every woman who looked at him. She wondered which one he had laid with yesterday morning. The hypocrisy of the man! She touched her swollen face and could not understand his fury at her friendship with Yiannis when his own sexual philandering was dismissed as natural.

'What are you moping about?' he asked scornfully.

'I need a drink of water,' she said faintly.

He grabbed her by the arm and to her dismay, walked her towards Alexis Taverna, led her to a chair and beckoned a waiter over.

Kostas came out of the shade of the café and flung a white tea towel over his shoulder. 'Yes, sir, madam?' he said, poised with his order pad.

Laura saw him glance at her and suddenly felt very cold, although the afternoon was hot and sticky. She prayed he would not recognise her.

He lent forward to take a closer look. 'Excuse me, is it Laura? It is, isn't it?' He threw the order pad to the table and swept her up into his arms, kissing her warmly. 'Is it really you? It's been so long. How are you? Have you seen Yiannis? He's been pining for you to return all these years, and now here you are!'

Slater shifted uncomfortably in his seat. His face set hard, as anger rose in his throat like bile.

Kostas, oblivious to Slater's agitation, lifted Laura's sunglasses. 'Take these off and let's have a better look at you. Wow.' He stood back aghast. 'What happened to you? Have you had an accident?'

Laura snatched the glasses back from him and lowered her face in embarrassment. 'I.. I fell the other day,' she said, quickly slipping the sunglasses back on.

Slater banged his fist on the table so fiercely he made the condiments jump. 'Are you going to take our order or do we go elsewhere!' he snapped at Kostas.

Startled, Kostas stepped back from Laura. 'I am very sorry sir. It's just wonderful to see Laura again.' His eyes darted quickly between them.

'What's all this noise? Is something wrong?' Alexis emerged from the kitchen, flipping his tea-cloth over his shoulder.

'No papa, nothing wrong, I was just talking to Laura. You remember our little Laura don't you?'

'Of course, how could we forget her? Come and give papa Alexis a hug,' he said, holding his arms out to embrace her. 'Have you seen Yiannis yet? Kostas my boy, go and find Yiannis. He's normally about somewhere!'

'I haven't seen him these past two days papa,' Kostas replied.

'Oh yes, maybe he's away in Athens, that's a shame,' Alexis pulled a face. 'Anyway how long are you staying?'

'We're leaving tomorrow,' Laura said, trying to get a word in edgeways.

'That's a shame, Yiannis will be sad to have missed you, won't he Kostas?'

'We have seen him actually,' Laura said quickly. 'My husband Slater and I met him briefly the other day.' She gestured towards Slater to introduce him.

Alexis hesitated, speechless for a moment. Then he smiled. 'Our little Laura has got married has she? Well… congratulations. When did this happen?' he asked, trying to hold the smile on his face.

'Just over a week ago - we're on our honeymoon,' she answered flatly.

Slater grunted impatiently.

Laura tried to force a smile, but felt her lip crack open. She quickly put her handkerchief to her mouth to stop the trickle of blood.

Alexis glanced at Kostas for a moment, then said, 'Just over a week, eh? Well I hope you will both be very happy. Kostas, get the honeymooners a drink on the house.' He bowed towards them both and walked back into the kitchen.

Kostas joined him a moment later. 'Just a coffee and a glass of water for Laura, he said he doesn't want a drink.'

Alexis watched the couple from the inside of the café feeling strangely uneasy about their body language. Laura looked troubled. 'Poor Yiannis, he must be in purgatory. It's no wonder we haven't seen him for a couple of days. He'll be licking his wounds somewhere,' he said thoughtfully.

'He's not the only one licking their wounds. Laura looks like she's been beaten to me, with all those bruises on her face. It wasn't just her lip that was cut you know papa.'

'What! Are you saying he's hit her?' he said, pushing his sleeves up ready for a fight.

'Now now papa, calm down, I can't be sure. She said she'd fallen, but I don't know. I've just got a hunch that all is not well with the newlyweds. Some honeymoon, eh?'

Alexis rubbed the stubble on his chin and studied Slater for a while. 'You know I'm sure I've seen him before somewhere, and I've got an awful feeling I've seen him with the Barzini bitch!'

'I think you're right you know,' Kostas answered. 'What the hell is going on?'

Alexis scowled. 'I don't know, but I don't like it.'

Laura sat under the shade of the taverna and watched the boats bobbing gently in the harbour. Slater hadn't spoken to her, but he was clearly agitated. Gradually as the silence became oppressive, Laura could take no more. As she spoke she startled Slater out of his distant mood.

'What?' He frowned angrily, as he turned to face her.

'I said I'm looking forward to seeing Van and Taylor again. What time are we leaving tomorrow?' If she had to stay with him, she knew she would be safe with Taylor near by.

'I'm going tomorrow. You're not going anywhere looking like that!'

'Oh?' she said keeping the elation from her voice. Was he was actually going to leave her alone here?

'I'll only be gone five days, you'll be okay here, I'm sure

you won't be bothered by anyone. It sounds like your boyfriend has gone away!' he sneered sarcastically.

As will I have done, before you get back, she vowed silently to herself as she sipped her coffee and planned her escape.

32

Laura stood on the sun terrace, watching the yacht Cecilia sail away, taking with it her violent and sadistic husband. Tears of relief fell - at last she was free of him. He would be away for approximately five days, enough time to plan her escape. One thing was certain; she would be gone when he returned.

Eventually calmness ensued. The last few days had been a living hell. Not only had she feared for her life, but if Yiannis had turned up again she wasn't sure what the consequences would be.

Yiannis too watched the yacht sail away from the tiny inlet next to Amora Cove. Despondently he began to collect his belongings from the fisherman's hut, which was still adorned with Laura's drawings. He rubbed his aching back and stretched the tension from his neck. After sleeping in the hut for the last three days, he relished the thought of his own bed at the lodge again, although things would never feel the same, now that he knew Laura would never share her life with him.

Half an hour later he moored his boat in Amora Cove, ran up the beach steps and deposited his belongings on his kitchen table. Taking a much needed shower, he then shaved off his beard stubble with relish. Pulling on a clean shirt and shorts, he slipped his feet into his plimsolls and, with a heavy heart, he made his way to the villa to clean and lock up.

Just as he entered the kitchen, Laura emerged from the bathroom rubbing her damp hair with a bright yellow towel. Yiannis stopped dead as Laura twisted the towel into a turban and lifted her eyes to meet his gaze. There was a long silence before Yiannis spoke first, 'I'm sorry, I didn't mean to intrude. I thought you'd gone. I saw the yacht leave.' Suddenly he registered the bruising to her face. 'Laura, your face!' he gasped. 'What happened?' He moved swiftly towards her. 'Has *he* done this?'

Laura swallowed hard, opened her mouth to tell him it was an accident, but her eyes could not lie, as she tried desperately to hold back the tears.

'Oh my love.' He pulled her gently into his arms.

Laura buried her face against his crisp white shirt and broke down in tears. As he comforted her, he could feel the rage building. 'Where is he? I'll make him pay for this. Where has he gone now? I saw the yacht sail away!'

'He's gone to Rhodes to pick up Vanessa and Taylor,' she sniffed bitterly. 'He'll be back in five days.' She touched her bruised face. 'I think he hopes this will heal before they return,' she added.

'My poor sweetheart,' he kissed her hair. 'You *are* leaving him, right? You cannot stay with him after this!'

She lifted her unhappy eyes to him and nodded. 'I intend to leave before he returns. Oh Yiannis. I've made such a mess of my life.... of our lives.' She reached for her bag on the kitchen table and fumbled inside it. 'Look what I found in my grandma's writing desk this morning.' She handed him a pile of letters.

Perplexed, he studied them. 'These are the letters I wrote to you! Are you saying you never received them?'

She nodded. 'If you look, the letters I sent to you are there too, which you obviously didn't receive either.'

He clasped his hand to his mouth. 'This was your grandma's doing? Why did she do this? I don't understand?'

'She did it to part us forever obviously. I take it you didn't have me sent away either?'

He reached out his hand to her, and shook his head unhappily. 'Well her plan worked didn't it?'

'Oh Yiannis.' She circled her arms around him. 'Can you ever forgive me for doubting you?'

Hugging her tightly, he answered. 'There is nothing to forgive, my darling.'

'Where do we go from here?' She gazed searchingly

into his beautiful aquamarine eyes.

He reached down and tenderly kissed her bruised face. 'I know just the place.'

*

Loading the yacht Aglaia with a picnic hamper full of goodies raided from the fridge, two bottles of white wine, and a handful of fish Yiannis had freshly caught that morning, they set sail. They moored in a tiny secluded cove where the land plunged straight into deep water, dropping anchor within a few yards of the rocks in a luminous turquoise pool.

Laying a ladder from the boat to the rocks to act as a gangplank, they jumped ashore. On land, there was a static barbecue built for, and normally used weekly by the boats commissioned to take the tourists on the 'Poros Island Tour'. He lit the coals, prepared the fish and salad, and joined Laura on the rocks. There under the shade of a large parasol, with their feet dangling in the water, they dribbled juice from a watermelon down their chins, spitting the pips at the shoal of silver fish that flickered around their toes. He glanced at her several times, just to make sure she was really there with him. He smiled in contentment.

'Let's swim before lunch?'

She nodded in agreement.

The shimmering water shattered like glass as they both dived in. Down and down they swam until they touched the seabed, scattering the marine life as they went. A shoal of neon fish came between them, and they reached through them to touch each others fingertips. When they surfaced breathlessly, they laughed together with old familiarity as Laura slipped her arms around the man she truly loved.

Later that afternoon, after eating and drinking their fill, they moved to the shade of the bimini on the yacht and lay in blissful contentment in each other's arms. The afternoon was still and hot, and every now and then the boat became utterly becalmed, floating on a deep cobalt mirror, under a pale blue sky. As they listened to the tranquil slap of water on the hull, neither had ever been happier.

'If this isn't heaven, I don't know what is,' she murmured, as she gazed into Yiannis's eyes.

He smiled, lifted her chin and gently kissed her soft lips. Laura flinched slightly as he brushed her bruised mouth. 'Oh I'm so sorry darling, did that hurt?' he said regretfully.

She shook her head at his thoughtfulness, pulled him close, and returned his kiss with passion.

'Land ahoy!' A shout came from a boat in the mouth of the cove.

'What the..?' Yiannis jumped to his feet as the 'Poros Island Tour' boat with about twenty people aboard, all wearing pirate's outfits and singing noisily, motored into the cove. An incomprehensible babble of Greek was blaring through a megaphone, accompanied occasionally by parps on the ancient sounding horn.

He turned and bent to help Laura to her feet. 'Come on my love. I think hell's just arrived in heaven.'

They arrived back at Amora Cove in the late afternoon. Yiannis anchored the yacht, and then set off in the Moondancer to pick up more provisions from the harbour, while Laura went back to the villa to freshen up.

With the luxury of five whole days before Slater returned, they decided to spend three of them in relative safety in Amora Cove, before they would both pack up their belongings and start a new life together.

'I won't be long,' he said, waving at her.

'Don't, I'm missing you already.' She blew him a kiss.

The coolness of the villa felt wonderful on Laura's hot skin. She opened the fridge and loaded the remains of the picnic hamper into it. The cold air washed over her like Cornish mist on a winter's morning.

A glance at the clock told her she didn't have long

before Yiannis would return, and so she began to prepare for the evening to come.

She turned on the shower, waited until the water ran tepid, and stepped in. Washing the salt from her hair, she felt a pair of hands slip around her soapy body. She turned quickly, shocked to find Slater standing behind her.

Laura's heart dropped like a stone. 'Oh my God, what are you doing back?'

'Nice welcome, I must say,' he said, pushing her against the shower wall.

She struggled to move away from him, but he held her back. 'I've come back to check that you're not entertaining anyone.'

Her body began to tremble with fear, but the fight within her kicked in, and she pushed angrily past him.

He laughed heartily as she stumbled out of the shower, dragging a towel around her nakedness. 'Well, if you don't want to share your shower with me, make yourself useful, and get me a beer. I have a raging thirst.'

*

Yiannis steered the Moondancer around the headland, loaded with fresh bread, wine, baskets of summer berries, and a bouquet of flowers tied with a yellow ribbon. He had spent the last hour arranging to rent a house in Cape Sounion, which would be far enough away from Poros to appease Laura's worries of Slater finding them. He had also arranged to borrow a yacht to take them there. The Tempest's yacht Aglaia needed serious attention having been stood without use for such a long time. He would trust it on short journeys, but not to sail to the cape. So with everything settled, the journey home was a happy one. He could think of nothing else but his lovely Laura. This is what they had both been waiting for!

*

Laura sat on the linen basket in the bedroom, trying to compose herself. Suddenly she remembered Yiannis. Panic engulfed her. She must stop him from coming back!

She knew Slater would kill them both if he saw him here. She grabbed her bathrobe and ran onto the sun terrace to see if he had returned.

*

Yiannis ran his boat aground, jumped out and dragged it onto the shingle beach, then ran happily up the beach steps two at a time towards the villa.

Laura met him half way down the steps. She was pale and distraught, her eyes burned with anxiety. 'Go! You must go!' she mouthed, ushering him back down the steps. 'Please Yiannis go!'

He grabbed her by the arms to calm her. 'Why, what's the matter?'

'Laura!' Slater's voice shouted from within the villa.

Laura shot a terrified look at Yiannis. 'Please go Yiannis. He'll kill you!'

'Is it him?'

'Yes! Oh please Yiannis, he has a gun and he'll kill us both if he finds you here!'

He held her arms and shook her. 'I'm not leaving you with him Laura!' Yiannis said defiantly.

'You must, please, please, for both our sakes.' She kept glancing back towards the villa.

'What's he doing back?'

'I don't know Yiannis. He's just arrived. Please go, I beg you.' She pushed him away and ran back up the steps.

'Laura….' She turned, her face was ashen. 'Come with me now, leave him. Come on.' He beckoned her down the steps.

She shook her head violently. 'No! Please go, please, I beg you!' she wept.

Leaving him with no option but to agree, he threw his hands in the air in despair. 'Laura, I won't be far away. If you need me, shout, okay?'

She nodded anxiously. 'Just keep out of sight, please,' she said, before disappearing from view.

He quickly but reluctantly made his way back to his

boat.

At the French windows, Laura took several deep breaths to calm down, before walking into the lounge.

'Where the hell have you been? A man could die of thirst around here,' Slater said, emerging naked down the stairs.

'Sorry, I was outside when you called.'

He clicked his tongue irritably. 'What's so interesting outside then? A fisherman perhaps?' he muttered, yanking the fridge door open. He drained the contents of a beer can in one, crumpled it in his hand, threw it at the bin and opened another. He looked Laura up and down. 'For goodness sake woman, put some make-up on that face, you look a real sight.'

Yiannis sailed round the headland into the next cove. Once ashore he scrambled up the dusty cliff. The scratchy gorse undergrowth ripped at his hands and knees as he made his way to the summit of flat stones. From this vantage point he could see the villa, appeasing himself that he could at least make sure Laura was safe, and if need be, rescue her, although he felt cowardly for leaving her with him! Presently he saw Slater emerge from the villa, and to his dismay saw that he was naked. He then remembered that Laura had been in her dressing gown when she came to meet him. Slowly Yiannis closed his eyes to what may have occurred between them.

A moment later, Laura joined him on the sun terrace. She was dressed now, and he watched her discreetly scan the surrounding area, before taking her seat next to her husband.

'Where's the yacht and crew?' Laura asked casually, all the while keeping an eye out for any sight of Yiannis.

'It developed a fault. We were taking on water at Athens. The crew thought it would be better to get it sorted in Piraeus. I caught the ferry back to the island, but of course everyone was taking their siesta in this bloody awful place. It took me ages to find a water taxi to get me back here. So, what have you been doing all day?'

'Nothing,' she answered, trying to keep the tremor from her voice.

'Liar,' he said, holding her gaze.

She swallowed hard but could not speak.

'I saw the hamper on the kitchen floor. You've been for a picnic haven't you?'

'Yes, is that not allowed?' she asked derisively. She spoke more confidently than she felt.

'It depends if you were alone or not?' he retorted. 'You know how I feel about trespassers.'

She took a deep breath. 'I was alone.'

'That's all right then.' He smirked. 'You know how jealous I can be. I believe I would kill anyone who tried to take you away from me!' He stretched his arms and folded them behind his head. 'I would make it look like an accident of course.'

Laura swallowed nervously. 'When will the yacht be ready?'

'Why? Do you want rid of me?' he said coolly.

'For God's sake, can I not even ask you a simple question? I was just thinking about Van and Taylor,' she said crossly.

'The crew are going to pick me up at first light tomorrow so I'm going to have an early night. With a bit of luck we will catch up the lost time.' He took a swig from his can.

Laura felt her body relax slightly.

'But of course if we have any more problems, I'll be back. So, don't be far away, just in case.'

Laura's heart missed a beat.

'Come on, I'm famished. What's for dinner?' he said, rising from his chair. As he passed her he grasped her chin and turned her face to look at his.

Yiannis braced himself when he saw this and started to get up from his ledge.

'You know?' Slater said, turning her face one way then

the next. 'With a bit more make-up your face might be okay before we get to Rhodes. Maybe you should come with me.'

'And if it isn't, how will we explain it?' she said quickly.

He contorted his face in thought. 'Maybe you're right, we don't want any unnecessary questions do we? Not now we have things sorted out.' He patted her on her cheek and went inside.

Laura sat for a moment with her face in her hands, scared to go inside. She had never before felt so terrified of anyone in her life.

33

After a fitful night, Laura must have slipped into a deep sleep in the early hours, because Slater left at dawn, without her knowledge, and without molesting her again.

Yiannis stood over Laura's bed with a cup of tea and an armful of flowers. He watched in awe as the morning sun streamed through the bedroom window in slants that bathed a golden glow across her face.

Sensing a presence in the room, her eyes fluttered open, only to widen in panic at seeing him there.

She leapt out of bed, knocking the cup from his hand. 'Oh my God! What are you doing here?' she whispered, frantically scanning the room for evidence of Slater.

'He's gone,' he said picking the cup from the floor. 'I watched him go.'

Clasping her hands to her cheeks in despair, he cried, 'No, you don't understand. He came back once. He could come back again! Yiannis, you *must* leave me alone.'

Gently holding her arms, he tried to calm her, but she met him with wild bloodshot eyes. 'He's threatened to kill you Yiannis! You must leave me be.'

'Shush darling,' Yiannis pulled a chair towards her. 'Laura, sit down for a moment. You don't have to live like this.'

She cupped her head in her hands. 'Please go Yiannis. For both of our sakes, you must leave me alone,' she cried pitifully. Her headache had returned with a vengeance, impairing her vision to the extent that when she looked up at Yiannis, all she could see were flashes of light. She could feel his arms around her trembling body, but was fast becoming disorientated with her surroundings. Tiredness engulfed her, and she felt herself falling, down and down, spiralling into a deep dark void.

Yiannis caught her as she slumped forward. He lifted her into his arms and swiftly took her from the villa to his lodge. Carrying her up the stairs, he carefully placed her onto his bed, trying to make her as comfortable as possible. 'It's okay sweetheart, you're safe now,' he soothed, but she did not respond. 'Laura, wake up darling.' The sight of her distressed him immensely. 'Come on Laura, you fainted, wake up.'

As he lifted her eyelid she moved and cried pitifully. 'My head, I have a terrible pain in my head.'

Relief swept over him. 'Okay. Lay quiet now. I won't be long,' he said softly.

He took two towels from the bathroom cupboard and a handkerchief from his bedside drawer, rushed downstairs and lit the oven. He placed one towel onto the oven shelf to warm, the handkerchief in the refrigerator and the other towel he slung over his shoulder. When he returned to the bedroom, Laura was moaning incoherently. 'Shush now, I'll soon make you feel better.'

For a few seconds, Laura thought she was a little girl again, sitting on Yiannis's kitchen table after she had fallen and grazed her knee or elbow. Yiannis always had a magic potion to make it better. She opened her eyes, but couldn't make out where she was. Completely disorientated, she felt about her, grabbing at the sheets and pillows. This was not her bed, or her room! She tried to lift her head and winced as a pain seared through her temples.

Presently she felt a movement on the bed - someone sat down behind her and placed cool hands under her throbbing head. She believed she was dreaming.

Gently gathering her hair up, Yiannis proceeded to wrap a warm towel, perfumed with lavender, around her aching head. He rolled her onto her tummy, lifted her arms above her head then, with Melissa oil in his hands, he proceeded to massage her neck. After a few minutes he gently turned her onto her back, and began to massage her temples. His soothing hands worked their magic and she finally began to relax. 'My poor sweetheart,' he whispered.

She smiled as she recognised his voice. Her breathing deepened and Yiannis watched her drift into a peaceful deep sleep. Enjoying the closeness of her next to him, he stayed with her a while. Eventually he carefully lifted her head off his lap, and covered her with the sheet. Retrieving the cold handkerchief from the refrigerator, he placed it onto her brow, kissed her gently on her lips and left her to sleep.

*

It was mid afternoon before Laura opened her eyes. She lay for a few seconds, trying to take in her strange surroundings. She looked up at the black wrought iron headboard and at the picture above the bed. Even from this angle, she could make out it was a drawing of herself and Yiannis on the harbour front. The gentle breeze moved the curtains into the room, and a bee buzzed happily on the jug of flowers that stood on the dresser. Tentatively she rose and sat on the edge of the bed - at last she was without pain. She could hear movement somewhere downstairs.

The door to the bathroom stood ajar. There she found a pitcher and jug with a bar of soap and a neatly folded towel next to it. On the chair lay a dress Yiannis had brought up from the villa for her - he had thought of everything. She washed quickly, ran her fingers through her long hair, checked her reflection in the cracked worn mirror on the wall and made her way down the scrubbed wooden stairs.

Yiannis turned as she walked into the kitchen and shot her a broad smile. 'I thought I heard you stir, I've just made you a drink. Are you hungry?'

She nodded and sat down at the table.

Wiping his hands on a towel, he asked. 'How do you feel now? You look much better.'

She smiled brilliantly. 'Better than I have felt for a long time. All thanks to you.'

He placed a cup of hot coffee on the table. 'It was

nothing.'

She took a couple of sips. 'Well I don't know what you did, or how you did it Yian, but all my pains have disappeared.'

'Good, I'm glad it helped.'

'You're amazing, you know that don't you?' She laughed.

'No, if I was amazing, then I could get rid of the biggest pain in your life,' he answered simply. He placed a bowl of salad and some fresh bread on the table in front of her. 'I've made us some souvlaki, okay? I remember you used to like it.'

Laura touched his arm. 'About earlier, I'm sorry I overreacted, I...'

He placed his finger to her lips to silence her. 'It's no problem. I do understand your worries.' He knelt down at her chair and looked at her with his wonderful aquamarine eyes. 'But I won't turn my back on you Laura. I love you. There, now I've said it. I love you with all my heart Laura.'

She pulled him close; momentarily their world stood still, as they held each other's gaze, hardly daring to breathe in case the spell was broken. Their silent smiling faces spoke volumes.

'My darling Yiannis,' she said kissing him tenderly.

When evening fell, they walked hand in hand up through the pine trees, taking the gradual ascent to the top of the hill. There they sat and watched the sunset drape the Peloponnese in a blanket of gold, as the cicadas sang their shrill song.

Laura threw her head back in relief. 'For the first time in days, I feel safe.'

He reached over and kissed her gently. 'I'll do everything I can to keep you safe now. I won't let anyone hurt you like that again.'

Though uncertain, she gave him a grateful smile. She would never be totally convinced that they would ever be safe; the thought brought a shiver.

'You're cold!' he said rubbing her arms.

'No, not really, just a passing thought.'

Despite knowing she was emotionally fragile, he had to ask the question which was eating him. 'Of all people, why did you marry Slater?'

She gazed up to the darkening sky and shook her head. 'You have no idea how many times I have asked myself that very question.' She rubbed her eyes wearily with the palms of her hands. 'You won't believe me, but he was charm personified. For the last couple of years, he has gone out of his way to 'woo' me, for want of a better word,' she said darkly. 'He courted me the old fashioned way – flowers, meals – he made me laugh would you believe?' She glanced at Yiannis and smiled without humour. 'And then, right out of the blue, Jack Ryder proposed to me, on my eighteenth birthday.'

Yiannis's eyes widened.

'I know,' she mirrored his reaction. 'He really didn't want to take no for an answer either! So, when Slater asked me, I thought, well, why not. We were married within three days of him asking. How stupid am I, eh? They say marry in haste repent at leisure. Well, here I am. Married not yet two weeks, and I have a face like a punch bag.'

He smiled tenderly. 'You have a beautiful face.'

She gazed at him with love. 'Everything was fine, until we came here. He changed instantly.'

Yiannis cast his eyes downwards. 'Because of me?'

She nodded. 'He's no fool. He could see what we felt for each other. I was just so shocked at his violent reaction.'

'My poor darling,' he pulled her close and tenderly kissed her bruised cheek. 'To think, I brought this on you.'

She closed her eyes to the mess she had made of everything. 'It's not your fault my darling Yiannis. If I had put my stupid pride to one side when I left school, I could have come out here to settle things with you. How I ever thought I could be happy without you, I do not know.'

Her fingers reached for his, and the touch sent a tingle through her body. 'I could love only you, I see that now.'

That was all he needed to hear. Lifting her hand to his mouth, he kissed it, and said, 'Come, I have a surprise for you.'

The night sky was a mass of stars by the time they returned to the Lodge. With her fingers still entwined with his, her face was radiant as she turned her smiling eyes onto him. All the years of waiting and the pain of separation, dissolved as he wrapped his arms around her and kissed her with passion. She could feel his heartbeat, rapid and wanting.

'We've waited a long time Laura,' he whispered.

'Far too long,' she said dreamily.

'Can you wait a few minutes more?' His eyes twinkled mischievously as he pulled away from her.

'Why, what are you planning,' she smiled happily.

He led her to the lounge and urged her to sit. 'You'll see.' And then he was gone.

She fidgeted for a few minutes, then stood up and walked into the kitchen to get a drink of water. As she turned off the tap she heard music. Stepping out onto the terrace, the sight of dozens of flickering candles, edging the path to the beach, took her breath away. Picking her way carefully through the flickering yellow lights, soft melodious music filled the night air from the wind-up gramophone. The beach was transformed with the shimmering haze of twinkling lights, all reflecting on the clear water as it gently licked and lapped onto the shingle. The moon was out full and bright and its yellow reflection lay sleepily on the glassy surface of the sea.

'This is beautiful!' she whispered into the night air.

'Beautiful, like you,' Yiannis said from behind her, as he slipped his arms gently around her waist.

She leant her head back onto him and they swayed gently to the music.

'Shall we make the moon dance?' he suggested.

Slipping their clothes off, he reached for her hand as they stepped naked into the cool dark water towards the moon's reflection. They swam and caressed, entwined within each other's arms, until Yiannis broke free and swam towards the Midnight Rocks. He stood and watched Laura move gracefully underwater towards him, just as she had done three years ago. Like an ivory statue she emerged from the water and stood before him. Hair slicked back, shining in the moonlight, water running in rivulets over the contours of her body. She licked the salt water from her lips and whispered his name.

'Yes darling?' he answered, gently taking her into his arms.

'The last time we stood here, I asked you something.' She felt his breathing quicken, but he didn't answer her. 'Do you remember?'

'Vividly,' he whispered. 'It was the very last thing you said to me before my world fell apart. I've lived that moment over and over. Hoping that one day I would get a chance to give you the answer you wanted.'

Laura took a deep breath. 'Yiannis, would you like to make love to me?'

'With all my heart.' He sighed deeply.

They swam towards the shore, and when the water was shallow enough, he lifted her into his arms, sprinkling the night with jewel-like water droplets. Holding her as though his life depended on it, he carried her effortlessly out of the sea and up the beach steps. The gramophone continued to play as he carefully set her down at the threshold of his house. The warm evening breeze had already begun to dry their naked bodies, as he guided her through the kitchen, towards the stairs that led up to his bedroom. Laura watched transfixed as his muscles rippled under the taut skin of his legs, and water droplets trickled down his golden back. Her feet mirrored each sandy footprint he left on the bare floorboards. At the top of the stairs, he swept her up in his arms, and took her to his bed.

*

In blissful contentment they lay entwined in each other's arms. Laura smiled lovingly at the beautiful man beside her as he glistened now with perspiration. 'I can't stop smiling,' she murmured sleepily.

He kissed her hair, 'Well, I've never had a happier birthday in all my life!'

Laura's sleepy eyes opened wide and she sat up on one elbow. 'Oh no, it's not your birthday is it? I've lost track of the date. Oh I'm so sorry. I have nothing to give you.'

He laughed and kissed her tenderly. 'You have already given me everything a man could possibly dream of. I am the happiest twenty-eight year old in the world!' He pulled her back into his arms and they drifted off to sleep.

34

As they slept, several boats had passed the tiny cove and witnessed the glimmering candlelit show. Alexis Taverna buzzed with talk about it, as the fishermen laughed and debated what had been happening at Amora Cove.

'I think Yiannis has got his girl at last!' said one old man puffing on his pipe.

'It's certainly looking that way,' another agreed.

'Well if he has finally caught the catch he has been waiting for, I know someone who won't be too pleased,' said Alexis, nodding up towards Eva's balcony.

Eva kicked the balcony door shut with her foot. She'd heard enough. As a storm rumbled around the Peloponnese, she began to plan her next move.

*

A flash of lightning lit the room like a camera flash and woke the sleeping lovers.

Yiannis flexed his arm around Laura's shoulders and drew her towards him, parting her soft lips with a deep sensual kiss. When another rumble of thunder came, he sat up.

'Where are you going?' Laura said reaching her long fingers out to him.

'The gramophone is still on the beach. I'll rescue it before it rains.'

'I'll come and help,' she said, beginning to stretch.

'No problem, I'll manage,' he insisted.

The lights in the room began to flicker. Yiannis pulled a face. 'I had better see if there are any candles left out there as well.'

'Mind if I take a shower?' she called down after him.

He twisted his head and called back, 'No problem.'

Laura smiled to herself - nothing is any problem to the Greeks. She pushed the sheet from her hot body and made her way to the bathroom, avoiding the sandy footprints on the floor. The lights flickered again as she entered the room. There was a large cast iron bath at the far end of the room, a WC, and a pitcher and jug under a single tap to her right. Opposite was the shower.

Her fingers felt the water which was hot, fed by large black polyethylene bags situated on the roof and heated by the sun. She stepped under the spray just as the room plunged into darkness. A moment later Yiannis entered the room with the flicker of candlelight preceding him. She reached her soapy fingers out beckoning him to join her.

In the soft candle lit room, he wrapped her in a soft towel, infused with the smell of thyme. He tenderly dabbed her bruised face dry. Every single touch was filled with love and gentleness.

'I can hardly believe you are here with me,' he whispered, as he pulled a towel around his own waist. 'Come,' he said, gently leading her out onto the veranda.

The surrounding cypress trees bowed to the weight of the angry rain and skimmed their lower branches onto the muddy ground. Individual waterfalls cascaded from the red fluted roof tiles of the veranda, and the soft damp spray cooled the hot night air.

They snuggled together on the veranda, and though the storm raged around them a sense of calmness ensued.

'I don't want this wonderful night to end,' Laura said softly.

'This is only the beginning my darling. The day after tomorrow we will leave the island and sail to the mainland to start a new life together.'

'To the mainland?' She glanced at him enquiringly.

'Yes. My good friend Nicos has a house near Cape Sounion. We can stay there as long as we want.'

She smiled lovingly at him. 'I'll be sad to lose all this,' she said softly.

'It won't be forever. We'll come back one day.'

She shook her head. 'Not if Slater has anything to do with it.'

'He can't stop you living here!'

'Well, as he kept referring to all this as 'his' land, I can only deduct that he married me for money.' She laughed softly. 'He wasn't too pleased to find out that it isn't mine until I'm twenty-one though. It makes me sad though, it was never my intention to sell, but it seems now it must all be sold and broken up, especially if we divorce. As I say, I've been very stupid.'

'But if you divorce before you inherit, you might be able to save it,' he said hopefully.

'I have no doubt Slater will fight me through the courts for it,' she said stiffly.

'Then I shall rebuild the Athena again and we'll live there.'

Laura reached up to kiss him. 'I love you,' she whispered.

Taking a deep satisfied breath, Yiannis pulled her close and they watched the rain long into the night until Laura fell asleep. He lifted her into his arms just as the dawn broke, the rain had ceased, and the sun had begun to warm the day. Vapours of steam floated like wispy clouds from the saturated ground, and a golden yellow glow bathed the walls of his tiny bedroom as he placed her carefully in his bed and lay down next to her.

After a late breakfast of yoghurt and peaches, they walked up to the stream. The sea moved calmly below and the silence was almost deafening.

'Everything looks so much more beautiful after the rain. There is nothing better than nature's pallet,' Laura said, leaning against Yiannis.

'Do you still paint?'

'A little,' she answered shyly. 'My work involves dealing in paintings. I work in an art gallery in St Ives, or at least I did, until I decided to run away with you.' She grinned. 'Kimberly is going to kill me when she finds out I'm not coming back.'

'Kimberly?'

'My eccentric, but rather lovely colleague,' she explained. 'I shall certainly miss her.'

'St Ives you say? I have a friend who lives in St Ives when he isn't splashing paint around what's left of my taverna. His name is Travis Reeves. Do you know of him?'

'No, can't say as I do.'

'He drew that picture of us - the one on my bedroom wall. I shall have to introduce you some day. You'll like him. What about you though, do you sell your paintings?'

She shook her head.

'That's a shame, I always thought what you did was wonderful. In fact I still have all the drawings you did for me, when you were little.'

She turned to look at him. 'Do you?' she said, moved by this knowledge.

'Of course, they were all I had of you,' he answered seriously.

She reached for his hand and squeezed it affectionately.

'I could never understand your reluctance to show them to anyone else though.'

She looked down and scraped the dust with her foot. 'Grandma would have gone mad if she'd known I was wasting my time drawing. She would have ripped them up for sure!' Her voice trailed off, clearly disturbed at the memory. 'She said only wastrels become artists.'

Yiannis shook his head. 'That bloody woman.'

Laura smiled. She had never heard Yiannis swear before. 'You can say that again. Anyway, let's not think about her. Come, let's go and dip our feet in the stream, like we did when I was little.'

Throughout the morning they lazed on a blanket next to the stream. Shaded from the blazing sun by leaves, lush green from the constant moisture, they drank in the stillness of the day.

When they returned to the lodge later that afternoon, Yiannis knew immediately that someone had been there. The front door was ajar, though he knew he had closed it, and his nose picked up the faint smell of Eva's pungent perfume. He tried to stay as calm and natural as possible, not wanting to worry Laura that someone had been here, as he cast an anxious eye around the rest of the house. He made his way upstairs to check the bedroom and came back down the stairs, perplexed at the thought of Eva being in his home.

'Ugh that smell,' Laura complained. 'What is it?'

Yiannis hesitated. 'Smell?'

'It's a sickly perfume smell. I only ever smell it when I'm on Poros. Slater came home the other day reeking of it. I thought he'd been with another woman!'

Yiannis caught his breath. Slater and Eva! What the hell was going on? The sooner they were away from here, the better!

Consciously making an effort not to let Laura know he was concerned about what was going on, they spent their last evening lazing on the veranda after a meal of battered squid, and Greek salad. The pine-perfumed air hung heavy and still, cicadas chirped their perpetual song and the boats in the cove moved gently from side to side as the sea lapped at their bows. As the burning sun dipped into the inky blue horizon, they walked down to the beach to dip their toes into the cool water. The sea licked the shingle, making a gentle sucking noise as it lapped into the crystal pools beneath the overhanging rocks at the water edge, where his boat Moondancer lay.

'Are we taking the Aglaia tomorrow?' Laura asked, looking at her grandfather's yacht.

Yiannis encircled her with his arms. 'Only as far as the harbour. Slater may be able to trace us if we take it further. Anyway, the engine sounded a bit ropey the other day. I'm not sure it will make it to Cape Sounion. My good friend Nicos has a small yacht moored in Glyfada which he has offered me. I must go by ferry to pick it up. The keys to his house are in there also.'

She leant her head back against him. 'How early do we leave?'

'I'm going to go alone. It's best that we are not seen leaving the island together on the ferry. I will bring the yacht back for you as quickly as possible and then hopefully we will leave unrecognised. That way no-one will be able to trace us.'

*

At first light Yiannis left for the harbour. Laura waved him off from the beach, and he promised to be back just after lunchtime. She had a lot to do, before he returned. The villa needed closing up, she needed to pack, and, most importantly she must remove any trace of their nights of passion from the lodge.

As she gathered the towels from the bathroom and the sheets from his bed, Laura blissfully savoured the memory of the previous evenings. These last few days had been like a wonderful dream. She had never been happier. Rousing herself from her reverie, she carried the laundry out of the lodge and down to the villa to use the washing machine.

She tidied the villa before hanging the washing on a makeshift line on the sun terrace. It was then she noticed a small boy standing outside the lodge.

'I'm looking for my papa,' he said to Laura as she approached him.

Laura scanned the landscape in search of another person, and then turned back to the boy and said, 'Which way did he go?'

'He lives here!' The boy pointed his dirt-encrusted finger at the lodge.

'Your papa lives here!' she exclaimed in disbelief. Every cell in her body began to prickle. This can't be true, she told herself. Please God don't let this be true. She moved closer to the boy to get a better look at him. 'What is your name honey?'

'Stephano,' he answered nervously. 'Can I see my papa?'

Her voice waivered, 'What's your last name?'

'Kiassos. Stephano Yiannis Kiassos! Mama said I've to tell him, the baby's due.'

A pain shot through her heart like a lightning bolt and for one awful moment she thought she would faint.

'Can I see him?' the boy asked sulkily, as he moved the sandy gravel in a semicircle with his dusty sandals.

Laura swallowed and tried to speak and immediately had to clear her throat again.

'I'm sorry, but he's not here at the moment.'

'Oh, okay. You'll tell him yes. You tell him, the baby's due?'

She nodded silently as he walked back down towards the beach where his small sailing boat waited for him.

Laura stood for a long time in the searing heat, but felt as cold as the grave. Her mind was in a whirl. Yiannis has a family, and a baby due! How could this be? Endless tears trickled down her face, evaporating immediately with the intensity of the sun. She licked her lips and felt the taste of blood from the bite she had unconsciously taken out of the inside of her cheek. Sadly, she made her way towards the villa glancing over to the lodge where last night everything had been so beautiful. 'Oh Yiannis, how could you have done this to me?' She cried softly to herself.

She pulled her suitcase onto the bed and flung as many clothes as possible into it. Anger overwhelming her feelings of melancholia, she ran up to the lodge, took the stairs two at a time, and threw a hastily scribbled note on the bed that read:

'Your son Stephano came. Apparently, the baby's due!'

Sorrowfully she glanced around his room - this room where they had made love so tenderly. She screamed as she took a swipe at the vase of flowers, scattering petals and broken glass around her, as she ran out of the room, slamming the front door after her. Outside she gulped great mouthfuls of air as she stumbled down the veranda steps, to be violently sick on the flowerbed. She sat down nursing her head in her hands and sobbed until she could cry no more. Presently she went back to the villa. One by one she closed the windows, picked up her case and paused for a moment by the front door, scanned the room, then brokenheartedly she turned and left.

35

Not having sailed the Moondancer for such a long time, Laura moored her as best she could, albeit scraping a sliver of paint from the top strake as she ran alongside another boat. After the third attempt, she managed to loop the rope over a gnarled iron stay. Throwing her suitcase onto the harbour side, well away from Alexis's bustling taverna, she perched on it, and waited impatiently for the ferry to arrive.

Behind dark sunglasses, she observed the sun drenched streets of the old town. The bright blue doors of the white washed houses all stood open. Old women dressed in black sat on their wicker chairs, crochet resting on their fold down tables, babbling above the strains of Greek music coming from a wireless.

Laura stared downwards as she idly scraped the toe of her sandal in a mound of dried mud. There had been another thunderstorm late last night, but instead of washing the ground clean, there were long rivulets of accumulated mud running from beyond the cobbled ground of the narrow streets out onto the harbour front.

A musty smell of fish, seaweed, and damp wood wafted through the air. Fishing boats glistened as they bobbed sleepily in the late morning heat, their sheets tinkling against their mast with each gentle wave that lapped against the hulls. There were a few older generation fishermen sitting on their boats, thickset and weather-beaten, smoking and chatting whilst mending their nets. There was such a calm contentment in everything she saw. She sighed, this is what she longed for, but alas, it was not meant to be.

Amongst the row of boats she noticed the yacht Aglaia and swallowed hard to clear the lump in her throat. With her head buried in her hands to mask her tears, she tried to figure out what on earth she was going to do. Without her passport she couldn't leave Greece, so the first port of call was the British Consul in Athens. She was sure they would help.

Alexis Taverna was busy with waiting ferry passengers. Laura could see Kostas from where she sat, so she maintained her low profile, only lifting her head when she heard the drone of the ferry as it sailed up the narrow channel that divided the island and the mainland. As she reached to gather her hat and suitcase, squeals of laughter filtered into the morning air. Laura looked up, just as the yacht Cecilia sailed into view.

Oh my God! Laura panicked. What's that doing here today? She scrambled to her feet looking for somewhere to hide, but it was too late, Vanessa had spotted her.

'Laura,' Vanessa squealed, and all on board looked up towards the harbour. There was no escape. She had no option but to wait for them to moor.

Kostas looked up when he heard Laura's name and watched with interest as she waited to be picked up.

Slater was first off the yacht. He pulled her into a swift embrace, which made Laura's body tense.

'What the hell are you doing here you stupid woman? We could have missed you,' he hissed into her ear. 'Get on board.' He picked up her bag, and led her onto the boat.

She took a deep breath, and managed a smile at Van and Taylor, praying that they wouldn't notice that she had been crying. 'Hi, you two, have you had a good holiday?' she said, moving to kiss them both.

'Brilliant, absolutely brilliant, wasn't it Taylor?'

'Yes brilliant,' Taylor said nonchalantly. 'Though it would have been better had you joined us Laura.' He smiled warmly at her as he took her into his arms to hug her. 'It's good to see you,' he said sincerely.

'Gosh Laura, I'll tell you something, Slater must have it bad for you. It must be love!' Vanessa gushed, as she greeted her with a kiss on the side of her cheek.

Laura looked puzzled.

'He couldn't wait to get back here to you,' she continued. 'We thought we would have a night out in Rhodes with him, but no sooner had he arrived he wanted to set sail again. He's had the crew sailing through the night.'

Laura managed a strained smile.

'Come on then, let's have a look at what you've done.'

'Done?' Laura snapped impatiently.

'To your face! Slater said you fell in a drunken stupor and made a right old mess of yourself.'

Laura's mouth tightened.

'He said you were covered in bruises when he left you, and you were so embarrassed about it, you pleaded with him to come for us alone.'

Laura felt the bile rise into her throat.

'Let's have a look.' She pulled her sunglasses off and scrutinised Laura's face. 'Oh it's not that bad. You look okay to me. He was probably exaggerating as usual.'

'Most probably,' she said sarcastically.

'Laura!' Slater said gruffly as he came up from the galley.

Her body shuddered involuntarily at the sound of his voice, hardly able to hide the antipathy in her face as she stared at him.

'Over here a minute,' he commanded with his finger.

Vanessa whooped with delight as she gently shoved Laura towards him. 'Go and have your reunion. Don't worry Slater we'll keep out of your way.'

He nodded back at his sister then stood aside while Laura brushed past him to descend the galley steps.

'What were you doing in the harbour? Why weren't you at the villa?' he snapped.

Every nerve in her body was on alert. 'We had a storm here last night! Didn't you?'

'Yes, so what?'

'Well I was terrified that's what.'

'So you were terrified. That doesn't explain why you were in the harbour this morning. I told you to stay put, didn't I?'

She swallowed hard.

'You didn't need for anything did you?'

'No I….'

'So, I repeat, why were you in the harbour? Looking for someone perhaps?' His face was taut as he glowered at her.

She knew she was trembling and that he could see her fear. 'I was looking for accommodation, if you must know. I was frightened last night alone in that villa. I thought I would spend my last few nights in the harbour, so I packed up and came into town,' she said trying to steady her breathing.

He eyed her suspiciously.

Assured that he wouldn't dare hit her while Taylor and Vanessa were on deck, she hissed, 'Am I a prisoner?'

'Of course not,' he said, shocked at the tone in her voice.

'Well stop treating me like one then.' She pushed past him and ran up the stairs to the deck.

Vanessa looked round when she emerged. 'That was quick!' she said flippantly.

'It's too hot down there,' she answered, sitting on the deck.

'Well I hope you're not going to do it up here. We don't want to watch you at it, do we?' she nudged Taylor in the ribs.

'Well I don't mind watching,' Taylor said cheekily.

Laura relaxed a little. 'In your dreams,' she smiled.

'You're always in my dreams Laura,' he said whimsically, his hand on his heart.

Vanessa jabbed Taylor again in the ribs.

'Ouch, what was that for?' he cried, rubbing his side vigorously. 'That hurt!'

'It was meant to. You'll have to stop lusting after her

now. She's a one man woman, aren't you Laura?' She winked at her.

Laura smiled without humour.

Slater emerged from the galley with a tray of drinks. 'Anyone for a gin and tonic?' he asked.

Taylor watched the smile fade from Laura's face in Slater's presence.

Van was first to take a glass. 'Mmm, just the job,' she said, as Slater passed the tray around until they all held a glass. She raised her glass high in the air. 'Let's have a toast to the honeymooners.' Taylor watched with curiosity, as Laura made no response to Slater's attempt to chink his glass on hers.

'Shall we have lunch here? We could go to that taverna over there,' Vanessa said.

'No!' Slater snapped. 'We'll sail on. I don't much care for this island and its people. They're all too familiar if you ask me.'

'Oh suit yourself.' Vanessa pulled a face at him.

As they set sail, Laura sat woefully on the deck, watching her beautiful island slowly disappear forever.

'A penny for them?' Taylor said, circling his arms around her.

Laura shook her head. 'They're very private,' she whispered.

'What's happened Laura? You can tell me.'

'Nothing, it's nothing.'

'Did you see your friend Yiannis on the island?' he asked casually.

'No!' she said, violently shrugging his arms away from her. 'Why do you ask? Did Slater tell you to ask me?'

'Hey now.' He held his hands up. 'Nobody put me up to it. I just remember that you and he had a special relationship. I just wondered if you'd seen him that's all,' he said softly.

Hanging her head low, she sighed deeply. 'I'm sorry Taylor - I didn't mean to snap at you, it's just….'

Taylor knelt at her feet. 'It's just what Laura? Tell me what is bothering you? I know something's wrong.'

Her eyes watered, but couldn't answer. Suddenly she felt very peculiar. 'Oh!' she exclaimed, placing her hand on her tummy.

'What is it? Are you sick?' Taylor asked in concern.

'No, I just feel strange. Perhaps I should go and lay down.'

'Do you want me to come and sit with you?' he asked gently.

'No I'll be fine, thank you Taylor.'

'Well shout if you need anything,' he said.

'I will thanks.' She touched his hand and gave him a grateful smile. 'Thank you for being here for me.'

'I just wish you would let me help you,' he answered longingly.

No one can help, she thought wistfully as she descended the galley steps.

36

Kostas frowned as he watched Laura sail out of the harbour.

'Hello Kostas,' Travis said cheerily, placing his suitcase down in the taverna, having just arrived on the ferry. 'Boy do I need a drink. That ferry will be the death of me.'

Kostas grinned and shook his hand warmly. 'Welcome back Travis. How was England?'

'Splendid. Good to be back though.' He regarded Kostas for a moment. 'What's wrong? You look troubled.'

'I've just seen Laura sailing away with her husband,' he said, nodding in the direction they sailed.

'Laura!' Travis followed Kostas's gaze. 'Did you say, with her husband?'

'Mmm,' he answered perplexed. 'She married Slater Haynes - you know from that family she lived with. She was here the other day with him. They were here on honeymoon.' He rolled his eyes.

Aghast Travis asked, 'Does Yiannis know?'

'He does. But that's not the half of it. When she came here, she had bruises covering her face! She said she'd fallen, but…'

Travis grabbed the top of a chair and began to tremble.

Noting his stance, Kostas asked, 'Are you okay? You look like you're going to explode!'

Travis flared his nostrils. 'I'll bloody flatten him!' he said, banging his fists on the table in rage. 'Why didn't you lot do something about it, if you thought she'd been beaten?'

Kostas shifted uncomfortably. 'Well, we couldn't be sure that was what had happened - we only assumed that was the case. She did say she'd fallen. It was Yiannis who confirmed the truth later.'

'Damn it!' Travis was beside himself as he watched Laura sail out of view. 'Where the hell is she going now with him for God's sake?'

Astonished at his outburst Kostas answered nervously, 'I don't know where she's going Travis - that's what is worrying me. I don't understand what's happening. According to Yiannis this morning, he said that Laura was leaving her husband and they were going away together.' He shook his head. 'Something has gone wrong by the look of it.'

'I'll swear I'll kill the bastard with my bare hands if he harms a hair on her head again,' Travis growled, as he left his suitcase and walked purposely towards the post office.

Alexis glanced at Kostas, 'What's eating him?'

Kostas shook his head. 'A rough journey I think.'

*

As the yacht Cecilia entered the mouth of the Corinth canal at one thirty p.m., Yiannis was sailing through the narrow channel past Poros harbour and on towards Amora cove.

Kostas was busy charming a group of French girl backpackers at the time, and it was only by chance he looked up from his engagement, that he caught sight of Nikos's boat with Yiannis at the helm. He quickly pushed his way through the tables and chairs, almost unseating one of the girls he had been so engrossed in a few moments earlier, and ran to the harbour edge just as Yiannis disappeared round the headland. 'Damn, damn!' he cursed, stamping his foot in annoyance.

'Kostas!' his father yelled.

Kostas looked at his father beckoning him back, and looked back towards the headland.

'Kostas, customers, now!' his father yelled, pointing furiously towards the tables.

*

Yiannis happily moored the yacht in Amora Cove without noticing that his Moondancer was missing. He glanced up towards the villa in search of Laura, and patted the tiny box in the pocket of his shorts. Later when they had settled in Nicos's house at Cape Sounion, he would give her this special gift.

Finding the villa shuttered up, he continued towards the lodge. 'Laura darling, I'm back!' he shouted from the bottom of the stairs. He patted the box in his pocket again hoping it wasn't too conspicuous, before he ran upstairs. The broken vase crunched underfoot as he entered the bedroom. Panic engulfed him. For a split second he thought something dreadful had happened to her - then he noticed the note on the bed.

A red mist clouded his senses as he re-read the note. Stumbling back down the stairs, he stood at the threshold of the lodge, and shouted Laura's name - his voice echoed tragically around the bay, silencing the incessant noise of the cicadas.

*

Eva stood at the counter of the empty Ice Palace, casually thumbing the pages of her magazine. Happily content with the outcome of the day, she took a long satisfied drag on her cigarette. A moment later the door burst open, Yiannis grabbed her by the arms, and pushed her against the gelato counter.

Eva gasped at the force of his actions, choking desperately as she tried to exhale the trapped tobacco smoke in her lungs.

Never one for losing his temper, something had snapped in Yiannis and he was hell-bent on retribution. 'You evil woman,' he hissed, shaking her with all his might.

Hearing the commotion, Stephano ran in to the parlour, screamed in terror, and lunged towards Yiannis to drag him away from his mother. He pulled and pummelled at Yiannis's arms, to no avail. In desperation he ran to the back room and screamed at Franco, who was dozing in his greasy easy chair.

Yiannis still had Eva pinned to the counter, his grip digging into her bare arms. They were face to face. Yiannis could smell the stale, sour, smell of tobacco on her breath - everything about this woman disgusted him.

Eva's eyes glinted. 'Oh dear.' She smirked, 'I hope I didn't spoil your cosy little set up, did I?'

Incandescent with rage, he shook her violently. 'Why can't you leave me alone?' He spat the words at her. 'God help me, but I could wring your scrawny neck.'

For a split second, fear clouded Eva's eyes, until she saw Franco hobbling ungainly onto the scene. He struck Yiannis with a sickening blow with his walking stick, rendering him unconscious.

Eva gasped at the force of Yiannis's weight as he slumped on top of her. 'Get him off me,' she yelled.

Kostas looked up when he heard raised voices, threw his tea towel over a chair, and ran towards the Ice Palace, shouting to his father to follow him.

'Now where are you going?' Alexis shouted after him throwing his arms into the air in exasperation.

'Papa come quick,' Kostas beckoned.

Alexis looked at his customers, shrugged his shoulders, then threw his tea towel on the same chair, wiped his hands down his shirt and ran after Kostas as fast as his short legs would carry him.

As Franco raised the stick again to Yiannis, Kostas ran into the room and caught it before he could strike. Franco swung round, wrenched the stick from Kostas' grip, and threatened him with it. 'Get off my premises!' he yelled.

Seeing Yiannis prostrate on the floor, Alexis moved forward. 'Franco, calm down. Let's just be sensible about this. Move aside and we'll take Yiannis out of your way,' he said, as Yiannis was slowly regaining consciousness, but bleeding profusely over the rug.

'You leave him be,' Franco said, bearing his brown stained teeth at them. 'He'll stay there until he bleeds to death!' he added.

'Don't be stupid, Franco,' Alexis said, moving closer.

Franco raised the stick to Alexis and hobbled in front of Yiannis.

'Uncle Franco, look!' Stephano screamed, as Kostas picked up a chair and hurled it through the air towards them. Everyone ducked, Franco lost his balance, and Kostas grabbed Yiannis by the feet and wrenched him away from Franco.

Alexis quickly bent down to grab Yiannis by the arms and carried him out into the daylight. They struggled to carry him to the taverna kitchen, where Irene greeted them with a shriek. 'Don't let him bleed all over my kitchen floor!' she said waving them away. 'Take him to the doctor's, for goodness sake.'

As they half walked, half dragged Yiannis along the harbour, Yiannis moaned incoherently.

'We are nearly there,' Kostas said. 'You've had a nasty blow to your head that needs looking at.'

'Let me go!' Yiannis said, struggling to free himself.

'Yiannis, you need to see the doctor,' Kostas ordered.

'I could do without this,' Alexis moaned, as he struggled with his load. 'We're busy if you hadn't noticed.'

Dr Aronis's housekeeper rose from the stool where she sat in her doorway and lifted her apron to her mouth at the sight of Yiannis's bloodstained clothes.

'It's just a graze. Is Dr Aronis in?'

Kostas was forced to leave Yiannis in the doctor's capable hands as Alexis grabbed him to go back to work.

Back at the taverna, Alexis said impatiently, 'Tell me, what was all that about?'

'I don't know,' Kostas lied. 'She's probably been causing trouble again. You know what she's like.'

Alexis clicked the roof of his mouth with his tongue. 'They are all mad those Barzinis. They should be driven off the island. They've been nothing but trouble since they set foot here!'

'Excuse me,' Eva snarled from behind them. 'My father was on this island long before your family ever were. In fact, my great-grandfather owned most of this island once, including Amora Cove, but it was stolen from us, by the Tempests. I have more right than you do to live on this island. As for causing trouble, well I just want what is mine. I don't see why Yiannis should live in luxury on my land, while his son and I scrape a living.'

Alexis felt his bile rise. 'You mad woman. You don't belong here at all. Your father rued the day he went to Italy and brought your evil mother back home with him. The poor man had no peace from that woman. She nagged him into an early grave, and then promptly followed him, making sure he didn't even rest in peace.'

'Don't you talk about my mother like that,' Eva snapped.

'Shut up!' he yelled back. 'As for your great-grandfather, the land wasn't stolen from him. He lost everything through gambling. Now you don't look like you're scraping a living to me, what with your fine clothes and flash jewellery. You look like you're someone's whore. And I don't know what has gone on tonight to send Yiannis into such a rage, but I think he has had about as much as he can stomach of you and yours - as have we all! So, you had better watch your step madam from now on. Otherwise we'll have you off this island before you have time to pack. Do you understand?'

She laughed derisorily. 'You and who else?'

There was a scraping of chairs around her as Kostas, Akis Dopas, Pano from the bakery and several others all stood up. 'Us!' they said in unison.

'You can count me in on whatever's going on,' Travis said as he walked into the taverna.

Eva curled her lip in antipathy, laughed and flounced back towards the Ice Palace.

They all watched until she was gone, looked at each other, shook hands, and sat down.

*

Yiannis was still sleeping the draft off which the doctor had administered when Kostas and Travis checked in to see him later that afternoon. His head had been bandaged and his blood-stained clothing removed. He stirred when he heard them enter. 'Laura?' he groaned, holding his sore head.

'It's me,' Kostas said, pulling a chair to his bedside. 'Travis is here as well.'

Yiannis exhaled slowly. 'I've lost Laura for ever this time Kostas!' he said quietly.

'What went wrong my friend? I thought it was all sorted out.'

'It was, until Eva Barzini ruined our plans.'

Kostas sat back and folded his arms. 'What exactly did she do Yiannis? I have *never* seen you lose your temper before like that.'

Yiannis closed his eyes. 'Don't remind me. I'm thoroughly ashamed of myself. I just....' He shook his head. 'I just can't take any more of her lies. You know since that child of hers was born, she has tried to demand money off me?'

Kostas nodded.

'Well, she calls it 'the baby's due'! She must have sent Stephano over to Amora Cove with a note for Laura saying just that, 'the baby's due'. Eva knew exactly what she was doing, and how Laura would interpret it. It's no wonder she's left me, if she thinks I have a secret family I haven't told her about.' He buried his head in his hands. 'She must be devastated.'

'So you never told her about Eva?' Kostas asked in amazement.

'No, time with Laura has always been short and very precious. Eva Barzini was the last person I wanted to discuss with her.'

Kostas tutted sympathetically. 'I'm so sorry Yiannis,' he said. 'If we can do anything, just ask.' He turned to Travis who nodded in agreement.

'You can help me find her, before that mad husband of hers does.' He lifted his head off the pillow and began to slide his legs off the couch.

'Yian.' Kostas pulled him back by the sleeve as he tried to stand up.

Yiannis looked at him questioningly.

'Laura left with her husband this morning. We saw them sail off, didn't we Travis?'

Travis shifted uncomfortably.

Yiannis shook his head in denial. 'No, no she wouldn't have. She couldn't have. He wasn't due back until tomorrow!' A chill ran through his body. 'Oh no, he must have come back early! He must have forced her to go with him. I've got to go and find her. Kostas, help me up.'

Kostas remained seated and shook his head. 'She wasn't forced Yian. She went quite willingly. Believe me I saw her go. He took her by the hand, as she stepped aboard, they even embraced.'

'No….. you're wrong, she wouldn't go with him. She didn't trust him,' he snapped. He sat back down, shoulders slumped, his face downcast. 'I suppose she doesn't trust me now either.' He looked first at Kostas then at Travis, before he stood up and pushed past them.

'Where are you going?'

'Home!' he choked with emotion.

37

Laura fiddled nervously as the unfamiliar Athens doctor scanned the notes on his desk. She was there at Taylor's insistence and Slater's recommendation - this being the surgery he used whilst working in Athens. It was warm and stuffy and Laura felt quite unwell. Presently the doctor looked up and smiled. 'Well, congratulations Mrs Haynes, you're urine test is positive. You're pregnant!'

Laura blanched as his words hit her with stark sobriety. He confirmed her worst fears.

Laura stared into her lap. In her own heart she had wondered if she was pregnant - ever since the previous day - when she'd felt queasy in a ladies room, en-route from Corinth. The rest room attendant had produced a red plastic chair for Laura to sit on, then patted her softly on the tummy and asked her softly in Greek, 'when is your baby due?'

Laura looked up at the doctor. 'When is it due?' she asked softly.

'Well, from the dates you have given me, I would say don't make any plans for around the twentieth of June. Having said that, most first babies have a tendency to make you wait a couple more weeks,' he smiled kindly. 'I suggest you make an appointment with your doctor in England.' He regarded her for a moment. 'You are not happy with this news.'

Laura knew he was picking up her negative vibes. 'I don't know. We have only been married for a few weeks. This has happened too soon.'

'Mmm, pregnancies have a tendency to happen when they are least expected. It's very early days though Mrs Haynes. I suggest you give it a few days to sink in, and then see your own doctor. He will alleviate any worries you have.'

She walked out of the surgery and along the busy street

in a daze - the heat and noise of Athens barely registering through her misery.

The thought of bringing Slater's child into the world and never being able to sever ties with its violent father, filled her with dread. But on the other hand, a termination was completely out of the question. She knew it had only been seven days since she last made love to Yiannis, she wondered, could it be, was it possible, that she was carrying his baby? Much as Yiannis had hurt her by his deceit, and as much as she knew she would never see him again, she could not wilfully harm his child.

She'd arranged to meet Taylor in a nearby taverna. It had been he who had urged her to see the doctor. He'd been so kind to her these last few days of the holiday.

'Everything okay?' he asked, standing as she approached his table.

'Just a tummy upset.' She smiled, hating to lie to him. She wanted to keep this a secret for as long as possible, until she had decided what to do.

He looked at her with concern. 'Did he give you anything for it?'

She shook her head. 'It will resolve itself in time. Have you ordered?' she asked changing the question. When the coffee arrived Laura enquired as to the whereabouts of Slater and Van.

'Van's gone to find a phone box to ring her agent, and Slater's gone off to that casino he used to work at. He was muttering something about lack of finances and having to find some work.' Taylor noticed this information piqued Laura's interest.

Just at that moment Slater joined them at the table. He gave Laura a quick once over. 'Well, that's that sorted. Taylor, you and Van are going home alone. Laura, we'll have to cancel our tickets. I've secured a job here for the winter, so get off your bum, because we have to find somewhere to live, soonest,' he grinned boyishly.

Laura dropped her coffee cup, spilling it everywhere.

Slater clicked his tongue in annoyance. 'I told you she was clumsy Taylor.'

With her mind working furiously, Laura trembled as she began to wipe the coffee off her clothes.

'Leave that,' Slater slapped her hand. 'Waiter, bring some glasses.' He practically slammed a bottle of champagne on the table. 'We have two things to celebrate, haven't we Laura? Though I think I should have been at least the second person to have heard the news. I guess you have already told Taylor.'

'Told me what?' he said rearranging the upset cups.

'Huh, I don't believe for one moment that she hasn't told you we are expecting a baby.'

Taylor glanced at Laura who had paled at the revelation.

Laura gasped. Her mouth formed an 'o' as she stuttered, 'How do you know about the baby?'

Enjoying her discomfort he said, 'I asked the doctor of course. I am your husband. I'm entitled to know what is wrong with my wife!'

Laura felt her world flip - so much for patient confidentiality.

'Where is that waiter with the glasses?' he snapped his fingers rudely. 'I'm going to be a father. What do you say to that then Taylor, eh?' He nudged him roughly.

'I'm very pleased for you both,' Taylor said. 'Are you okay Laura? You don't look a bit well.'

'Oh she's fine, stop mollycoddling her. She'll expect me to carry on like that, once you've left.'

Something snapped inside. 'Stop treating me like a child, Slater!'

'Oh dear, your hormones are speaking by the sound of it.' Slater crinkled his nose.

Laura fixed an icy glare at Slater. 'You really are obnoxious. If you think I am going to celebrate this….this accident, then you are deluding yourself.' She glanced at Taylor who was sitting open-mouthed. 'Sorry Taylor, I didn't want you to hear this.' She turned back to Slater, who was visibly fuming. 'I have just spent the last two weeks in hell, because of you. If you think it is natural to treat a woman like you have treated me during our honeymoon, then you are seriously deranged. And if you think I am going to continue being married to you then you have another think coming.'

Slater's mouth tightened, as his hands balled into fists. He lunged towards Laura, but Taylor stepped in front of him. Holding his hand to his chest, he pushed Slater backwards. 'What the hell has been going on? What did you do to her?'

'Keep out of this, it's between me and her,' he hissed, slapping Taylor's hand from his chest.

Taylor, normally the most placid of men, grabbed Slater's arms and slammed him against the wall of the taverna. 'Did you hit her? Did you? When you said she had fallen. Had you hit her?' he said roughly, his calm sensitive manner forgotten.

Slater struggled under Taylor's grip. 'She got what she deserved,' he hissed, '......fraternising with that Greek fisherman. I just needed to lay down some ground rules for this marriage. I can't have her cuckolding me, a week after our wedding.'

Taylor glanced at Laura, who looked as though she was about to faint. A crowd had formed and the taverna owner was shouting for the police. 'Only cowards hit women. So I am warning you Slater, brother or no, if you so much as lay one finger in anger on Laura again, I will personally and permanently rearrange your features.' He slammed Slater against the wall, released his grip on him and left him to slide to the floor.

'You mad bastard, you nearly knocked me out,' Slater said, picking himself up from the floor. He brushed the dust from his trousers and glared at Laura. 'I'll speak to *you* later.'

Laura scowled darkly at him. 'I have nothing more to

say to you. I'll speak to you through my solicitor.'

Slater laughed derisively as he swaggered down the street.

Laura's face crumpled and Taylor quickly gathered her into his arms to comfort her.

The taverna owner stood over them, 'Please go,' he begged. 'This is bad for business, please go.'

Laura shot him an apologetic look, as they walked away. When they found a bench shaded with a plane tree he urged her to sit.

'I am sorry Laura. I'm sorry for what Slater has done to you and that you had to witness my threat towards him. But I cannot and will not stand by and see you hurt. You should have told me sooner,' he said earnestly.

'I know, but the last thing I wanted is for you brothers to be at loggerheads with each other, especially after your family has been so kind to me,' she said unhappily.

He held her hand for comfort. 'He has always been a hot-head and prone to outbursts if things didn't go his way. He was like it as a child.' He sighed angrily. 'I'll never forgive him for this.'

Taylor's kindness made the emotion well up within her again. She quickly wiped her tears, 'I'm sorry, I don't normally cry like this.'

He hated to see Laura so unhappy. 'You have a lot on your mind sweetheart.' He put a protective arm around her. 'I think the best thing is for us to go to the airport now and get a flight home. Spend a few days in Gweek and decide what to do, before you go back to work. Father isn't well, and I think Mother could do with some moral support so I'm happy to go home early. What do you say? I think some fresh Cornish air will do you good,' he added with a thin smile.

'What are your parents going to say about all this?' Laura fretted. 'And Vanessa, she'll have to fly home alone tomorrow!'

'Don't worry about anything. We don't have to tell my

parents anything yet if you don't want,' he said confidently. 'Come on, let's go and pack.'

*

Gweek wrapped its comforting arms around Laura the moment she stepped out of Taylor's car. She stood on the village bridge and took a deep breath of salt filled air. The trees were still in green leaf, autumn waiting in the wings until Cornwall was ready to give up the summer. She looked down the Helford River and drank in its tranquillity before making her way to Pippa's house. More than anything else she needed to speak to her friend.

She was greeted by Pippa's mother walking briskly down the drive, veterinary bag in hand.

'Laura!' She smiled. 'How lovely to see you, are you back for long? What a shame Pippa is away, she would have loved to have seen you. How is married life?'

Masking the huge disappointment of Pippa being away, she smiled and answered the first of her questions. 'Just here for a couple of days. Mr Haynes hasn't been very well. I've just popped down to see if Sarah needs any help.'

She furrowed her brow. 'Oh yes, I heard about Gerald. It doesn't sound too good for him does it? Is she coping?'

She gave a guilty smile. 'To tell you the truth I haven't spoken to Sarah yet. I've only just arrived. I wanted to speak to Pippa first.'

'She's out in Dubai for the winter my dear. She's working on a super yacht out there. One of her friends had an accident, and she flew out to take her place. It's something she wanted to do for a while. You know our Pippa and her love of boats.'

Laura's heart sank. 'For the winter you say?'

She nodded, 'She'll be back in the boatyard in March.'

Laura wrinkled her nose.

'Anyway Laura, lovely to see you, but I must rush, I'm on a call,' she said climbing into her Land Rover.

Laura waved her away, then with a heavy sigh, made her way back to Creek House. Unsure of what to say to

Sarah, she took a large intake of breath before cautiously opening the front door.

A waft of expensive perfume preceded Sarah, as she breezed into the hall to meet her. 'Laura, how lovely it is to see you. Taylor said you had come down with him.' She gathered her in her arms and hugged her with real affection. Laura noted that she seemed unperturbed at their early arrival. 'Are you okay my dear?' she asked quite sincerely as she scrutinised her face. It was as though she'd known what Slater had done and wondered if Taylor had mentioned anything.

'Come, we are having tea and sandwiches in the drawing room.'

At the mention of food, Laura's stomach lurched. 'How is Gerald?' she said, swallowing her nausea.

'It isn't very good news I'm afraid,' she answered resignedly.

'Is it lung cancer? Taylor said you were waiting on results?'

'I'm afraid so.' Sadness welled in her eyes and she wafted the tears away with her hand. 'Goodness, you'll have to excuse me. The tears keep coming I'm afraid.'

'I'm so sorry Sarah.'

Both Sarah and Taylor had hoped that she would stay at Creek House, but Laura needed to be alone, in her own place. She had been subdued over dinner, smiling occasionally, but small talk was not forthcoming, so soon after dinner she took her leave of them.

When Laura had gone Sarah said, 'Okay, what did he do to her, and why?'

Taylor gave her a quizzical look.

'I know something has happened!' she said evenly. 'I need you to confirm it.'

Taylor chewed the inside of his cheek, and told her what he knew.

Sarah sighed angrily. 'The stupid boy was always a hothead. I just can't understand why she married him.

They never got on as children!'

'Well, you know how he can turn on the charm when he wants something. But all I know now is that she loathes him!'

Sarah sighed heavily as she fiddled with the flowers on the dining room table. 'I suppose there will be a divorce.'

'I think the sooner the better,' Taylor said, as he bid goodnight to his mother. At his bedroom window, he could see the lights on at High Top House - he hoped she was all right. Laura had seemed so utterly broken at the turn of events and he wasn't too sure if it was all down to Slater.

*

After opening most of the windows, the musty smell of the house had been replaced with fresh air. Laura sat on the dusty leather sofa in sheer exhaustion. This was the first time she had relaxed in days, but the peace and solitude only magnified the hurt she felt. If only Pippa had been here. She was her touchstone, her leveller and trustworthy friend - her being away was a huge blow. She closed her eyes and, as she did, grief bit into her heart.

*

For the last few precious days before Laura returned to work, she embraced the calmness of the Cornish countryside. Long walks along the windblown cliffs of Poldhu Cove gave her time to think. This, and visiting Gerald in hospital to give Sarah a little respite, started to put life into perspective.

Meals with Taylor and Sarah became more relaxed, though she still struggled to keep anything down. Slater's name was never mentioned, which puzzled Laura. In truth, Sarah could hardly bear to speak of her son, after learning of his behaviour.

Not normally one to phone for a chat, he'd rung home shortly after Laura's arrival and Sarah was still smarting at the arrogance of his phone call.

'I take it my wayward wife is with you, shirking her

marital duties?' he'd said pompously. 'Tell her to get herself back out, here will you Mother?'

Sarah had to muster all her self control to speak to her youngest son. 'You have a nerve Slater.'

'What do you mean?' he said sharply.

'How could you do such a cowardly thing as to hit a woman? I didn't raise you to be so despicable.'

There was a pause for a moment. 'Oh I see. Laura has been spreading lies about me has she?'

'As a matter of fact, Laura has said nothing about it.'

He laughed caustically. 'If it wasn't her it was bloody Taylor then! Well I can tell you, whatever you have heard it's all been blown out of proportion.'

'Slater Haynes,' she scolded. 'You hit a woman, your wife of two weeks, so don't deny it.' She heard him breathing angrily down the phone.

'Look, I slapped her on the face and she fell awkwardly, that's all that happened. She was fraternising with another man! I don't suppose either of them mentioned that. Having said that, you would always favour Taylor's side of the story over mine,' he added.

'I can assure you, my information came directly from Poros.' Sarah could hear his breath falter over the phone, so she continued. 'More than one person witnessed the mess you had made of her face and noticed the fear in her eyes. That was no slap and no accident. I'm appalled at you. I'm ashamed to call you my son.'

Puzzled he said, 'Who do you know in Poros?'

Sarah considered his question for a moment, and then answered. 'You seem to forget Slater. We had a very close relationship with Charles and Gwen while they lived there. Your father and I visited many times before his accident. I have many friends there - friends who were concerned for Laura's welfare.' This wasn't entirely true, but Sarah was not about to divulge the name of her informant.

Slater snorted angrily. 'I'm not listening to this any longer. I want her back here now.'

'You astound me Slater. You're speaking as though you own her.'

'I think I have some claim on my own wife,' he snapped.

'I think you have not!' Sarah retorted. 'You will leave her be, until she decides what she is going to do.'

'What the hell do you mean?'

'I mean, whether she decides to divorce you or not - and I wouldn't blame her if she did!'

Slater laughed, 'Well she can get that out of her mind. There will be no divorce, not now she is pregnant,' he said, slamming the phone down.

*

The sea was as calm as Laura's head was in turmoil. The holiday break was drawing to a close and she needed to make a decision about her future and needed to make it fast. Laura sat amongst the dunes at Church Cove, feeling the golden grains of soft sand trickling between her toes. With her knees tucked under her chin, she circled her legs with her arms and watched the waves. They were gentle today, licking the beach, leaving a foamy line in its wake. Every soft wave seemed to be saying 'shush' as it broke, willing her frantic mind to find peace within.

The cloud split open for a second, opening its grey canopy to give a brief and tantalising glimpse of pale blue sky, but just as quickly closed again and shrouded the sea in an opal hue.

The beach was deserted. The one person in the churchyard had laid his flowers and was now walking forlornly back to his waiting vehicle. She was alone now with her thoughts.

A wave, larger than the others, suddenly broke, and the tide came a little closer. Salty air filled her nostrils and she stood up. With a swift look about her, she pulled her dress over her head and shed her underclothes. Running like the wind down the beach she plunged herself into the water. The cold stung her legs but she kept moving, opening her arms to embrace the chilly Cornish sea.

She swam hard, cutting through the water with swift determined strokes. She swam until she came to the black rocks which flanked the peninsular.

She remembered the other rocks she had swum out to, not so long ago, on a far and distant shore in the warm clear waters of the Aegean Sea. This time there was no Yiannis to greet her with a kiss, just a cold dark rock in an opal green sea.

Sharper than the midnight rocks at Amora Cove, she hauled herself carefully out of the water, trying not to graze her knees. She sat naked to the elements, enjoying the freedom it brought. Her body shivered as she closed her eyes.

'To hell with Yiannis, and to hell with Slater. I will not be a victim,' she shouted, her voice scattering the seabirds nesting in the cliffs above. She looked down at her flat tummy and placed her hand gently on her goose-pimpled skin. 'We will be fine little one,' she spoke to the tiny embryo growing inside. 'I promise we will be fine.'

She dived back into the water and swam ashore to find a dog walker studiously inspecting her pile of clothes. He turned when he heard her approach.

'Morning,' she said, smiling cheerfully.

'Oh,' he replied, averting his eyes from her nakedness. 'M… Morning,' he spluttered.

'Lovely day for a swim,' she said, tugging her dress over her wet body.

The dog walker nodded, cleared his throat and called for his dog.

She grinned to herself as she dragged her jumper over her wet hair, flipping it out to hang limp and tousled down her back. She balled her underclothes in her fist and pushed her sandy feet into her sandals. She returned to Gweek, a very different person who had left that morning.

As she said her farewells to Sarah before she returned to St Ives, Laura tentatively broached the subject of her impending divorce.

'I completely understand Laura,' Sarah answered resignedly. 'But you will still be part of this family. I always looked on you as a second daughter, and there will always be a place for you here. I am sorry for what has happened, but just remember I'm looking forward to being a grandmother.'

Laura looked at her in shock.

'I'm sorry, Slater told me about the baby, so please don't be a stranger to us.' She kissed her warmly and sent her on her way.

38

The first week of October was damp but not cold. Laura sat on the wall overlooking a deserted Porthmeor beach, pondering over the solicitor's letter she'd received that day. Slater had contested her divorce request. It was a disappointment, but no more than she expected from him. Slater was as stubborn as a mule and resented being told what to do. She would have to wait now for the courts to decide her fate.

She watched the waves lap lazily onto the damp sand. At least she was free of him - he'd been told to stay away from her flat and workplace, so she could rest easy that he wouldn't just show up on her doorstep. She slipped down from the wall, wiping the residue sand from the seat of her jeans and walked through the tiny cobbled streets of the Digey and out onto Fore Street back to work. The tourists had dwindled away, and life at the gallery had slowed to a more sedate pace.

By the third week of March, at twenty five weeks, Laura found the pregnancy increasingly hard to deal with. Her legs and back ached appallingly and her ankles were constantly swollen, the morning sickness hadn't abated either. In the end Laura decided, much to Kimberly's dismay, to leave sooner than expected. She did not expect to return to work once the baby arrived. If she was going to be a mother, she wanted to do it full time. The house in Gweek was hers and the small allowance left to her from her grandparents would allow her this luxury. So after a tearful goodbye, she packed up her belongings from the flat above the gallery and returned home to Gweek for her confinement.

The sun had real warmth in it as Laura and Sarah took coffee together on the terrace of Creek House. There was a growing tension of unease within both women, but for very different reasons. On Sarah's part it was because

Gerald was back in hospital and would probably not return home. She could do nothing about that unfortunately, but she could do something to alleviate the thing which was concerning Laura.

A robin flew onto their table and pecked at the biscuit crumbs. They watched in silence as the bird tipped its head one way then the other in a hope for another morsel.

Presently Sarah said, 'Slater is due back at the end of the month.'

Laura sighed. 'I know,' she said, as she turned her gaze towards an egret, wading on the mud flats.

'I've been thinking. Why don't you make use of our holiday home in Portugal? You are still okay to fly and the mountain air in Monchique would do you a power of good.' She glanced at Laura's interested face. 'You would be doing me a favour. I normally go around about now to check things over, but with Gerald being so ill, I just can't make the trip. Taylor is tied up with things here at the moment, and Vanessa rang last night to say she has been offered a part in an Australian soap.'

'How long is Slater going to be here for?'

Sarah shook her head. 'It won't be long. Gweek is far too provincial for him nowadays.' She gave a wry smile. 'I'll wager he'll be gone in a week, when he finds you're not here.'

*

In the warm breeze and dazzling brilliance of the pool terrace, Laura lazed the days away. Languidly soaking up some much needed Portuguese sunshine, the days slipped by on an endless sea of relaxation. Then out of the blue, Taylor arrived. When she saw him, Laura squealed with delight, kissing him with such affection, it quite overwhelmed him.

After a couple of days chilling by the pool, Taylor was restless for a different view and suggested they go down to the coast for a few days.

Laura didn't need asking twice, so within the hour they

had packed a few clothes into a case and were heading towards Lagos.

There they stood on top of the spectacular honey coloured cliffs, high above the fascinating rock formations, looking down at the tiny speedboats dodging and weaving in and out of the many caves below.

'There are some steps over here Laura, I'll just go down and take some photos, okay?'

She nodded and watched him go, then decided to follow him to get a better view herself. At the bottom of the steps, she watched in amusement as the waves sucked under the rocks and boomed against the cliffs, soaking Taylor with sea-spay as he tried to take his photos. He ran back up the steps laughing as the water dripped from his hair.

'Look Taylor!' Laura pointed to a small speedboat that had sailed through the rocks into view. 'Ask him how much,' she urged.

'Are you sure you can get on board in your condition?' Taylor asked anxiously.

'You just watch me!' she answered, cradling her lump.

Carefully helping her onto the vessel, they were soon speeding their way towards the openings of the caves. In and out the small boat sped with breathtaking closeness to the cliff walls. One minute they would be speeding out into the Atlantic and next floating into a limpid turquoise grotto. Ten minutes later they were dropped off at the bottom of the cliff steps, and they slowly began their ascent to the top of the cliff, damp and exhilarated.

A short drive took them to Praia de Luz, where they checked into a small hotel and had dinner in a beach side fish taverna, before walking arm in arm across the soft golden sand. They stood at the end of a perfect day, happy and content in each other's company, watching the evening sun bathe the crumbling sandstone cliffs in a warm glow of burnt orange.

They made their base at Praia de Luz for three days,

driving and walking a little each day.

The landscape was stark and barren on the coast path. Goats and sheep grazed on little vegetation, while large white birds pecked the ticks from their woolly backs as the animals rummaged under thickets of prickly pear and giant cacti. Thin bleating lambs trotted nervously beside their mothers, the clank and clatter of their neck bells ringing out incessantly, as they scurried across the wasteland.

As Laura and Taylor walked, they took in the splendour of the magnificent villas high above the rocky coastline with vistas far out across the sea. In stark contrast, they observed an old man with leathery skin, sitting on the dusty path at the bottom of these opulent gardens, chewing his gums and tending his flock, nodding a friendly hello to passers by. His grimy dog stretched out on the path panting in the afternoon heat, and a large snorting pig on a lead rummaged the red dusty earth where it lay in the shade of a bush.

Their last day was spent at Sagres, located on the westerly tip of the Algarve, a place known locally as 'the end of the world'. They stood on the battlements of the fortress where Henry the Navigator lived for forty years and where it is claimed that Christopher Columbus learnt his skills.

'It's so beautiful, isn't it?' Laura sighed as she looked out across the blue crescent bay towards the shimmering haze of Cape St Vincent.

'It is indeed, and I'm glad I'm sharing it with you,' Taylor answered, putting a protective arm around her shoulder.

She smiled and moved closer resting her head on his arm and sighed.

'Are you still unhappy about the baby Laura?'

Laura pulled away from his arm and looked out to sea. 'It's going to be hard on my own with a baby. I know that.'

'Mother and I will help all we can you know?'

She smiled gratefully and kissed him gently on the

cheek. 'I made a mess of everything, didn't I?'

'Forgive me for saying this Laura, but I always thought you had something special with Yiannis. I always thought you would marry *him.*'

She closed her eyes to the pain in her heart. 'It seems Yiannis already has a family!' she said, walking a few paces away to compose herself.

Taylor moved towards her and gently placed his hand on her shoulder. 'I'm sorry.'

She shrugged her shoulders then rubbed her stomach where the baby had just kicked her.

'Come on,' Taylor said, taking her by the hand. 'We had better be getting back. We have to fly back in a couple of days. When I rang mother this morning she said Slater has gone back to Athens, so everything will be fine back home.'

'Thank you for everything Taylor. Thank you for this trip. It's been wonderful.'

When they arrived back at the villa in Monchique, Laura began to feel slightly queasy. 'I think I need to lie down for an hour,' she exclaimed.

Taylor helped her up the stairs, closed the shutters at the windows and reached out to touch her lightly on the shoulder. 'Maybe we've done too much?'

'Maybe,' she smiled softly.

After an uncomfortable night, Laura felt no better the next morning and there had been a slight show of blood, prompting Taylor to drive her to the nearest hospital.

'I'm afraid flying is out of the question Mrs Haynes. You need complete bed rest. We will keep you in for a week, and then I strongly advise you to take it easy at home. Do you have anyone at home?'

Laura's mouth felt very dry. 'Home is in Cornwall!'

'Travelling is out of the question. If you want to be delivered a healthy baby, you must not exert yourself at all. Do I make myself clear?'

'Yes doctor.' She looked in desperation towards Taylor,

who grasped her hand and squeezed it tightly.

Once she was settled onto the ward Taylor said, 'Look, I have a trip to America booked - I can try to cancel it.'

Laura placed her hand on his. 'Don't worry Taylor, I'll be fine. There are worse places to spend my confinement. I have Maria the maid back at the villa to look after me, and when the time comes I'll check back into the hospital.'

'Well, if you're sure. I'll be gone eight weeks, so I'll be back in time for the birth. Just don't have my niece or nephew early!'

'I'll try my best.'

*

After a week in hospital Laura was discharged with strict instructions to rest. She took a taxi from the stifling heat of Faro back to the villa in Monchique and stepped out into the coolness of the mountain air. Maria was waiting. Smiling and helpful as always, she scooped up her bags and enquired after her health. On the telephone table, next to a vase of roses, was a letter and a postcard. Laura gathered them up and took them outside to the pool area.

The postcard was from Vanessa, living it up in Australia. The letter was from Taylor informing her that his father was gravely ill.

The doctors say Father has only a few weeks to live. He wrote. *I haven't postponed my trip to America, Mother seems confident that Father's death is not imminent. But I am on standby to return should there be any developments. Very slowly his body will close down and we have been told to expect pneumonia at the end. As usual Father is calling the shots, and has insisted on returning home, which in turn, is making a lot of work for Mother. He is attended to by his nurse and Mother so he is in good hands. I phoned the hospital to get a message to you but the person I spoke to didn't fill me with confidence that the message would be passed on - hence the letter. I hope you are feeling much better. I am sorry I can't be with you out there. Mother sends her love.*

Taylor x

Laura phoned Creek House immediately, and spoke to

Sarah, but Sarah was her usual calm self, assured Laura that all was well, and told her to look after herself.

"Well, it's just you and me Maria, and we shall manage perfectly well," she said in Portuguese.

Laura had a perfectly happy time during the last few weeks of her pregnancy. With her easel set up in the garden she bided her time painting the beautiful array of flowers which grew in the villa gardens. Her only interaction with people came via Maria and the local gardener. Most weeks she had a catch up call with Sarah, who seemed to be bearing up with the strain of Gerald's illness. Taylor too phoned from America.

One week before her due date, Taylor rang to inform Laura that his Father was gravely ill. He was in the airport at Newark awaiting a flight home. Laura immediately rang Sarah, who told her she was coping and that Slater was with her.

*

Gerald Haynes died on the 13th June. The funeral was held 20th June. Taylor and Slater were with Sarah, but Vanessa was unable to attend due to filming commitments in Australia.

Laura sent flowers, and rang later in the day and spoke to Taylor.

'Mother is having a lie down,' he said, his voice weary. 'It's all been a bit of an ordeal. Look, I'll be with you as soon as I can. I just have some loose ends to tie up here. Phone me if anything starts to happen.'

'Don't worry Taylor. If you can get here that would be lovely, but I do understand under the circumstances. Is Slater still there?' she asked tentatively.

'He left an hour ago. He said he had a pressing engagement.'

'Did he mention me?'

'No.'

'Good.' Laura felt a surge of relief run through her body.

*

A terrific thunderstorm broke in the mountains that evening. All night and through to the next day, rain pounded on the sun terrace with such force, Laura feared the pool would overflow. Rivers of water gushed from the roof into muddy pools in the garden and the smell of wet earth filled her senses. Lightning flashed periodically as the thunder rumbled continually around the mountains.

When Maria arrived, soaked through to the skin, she proclaimed that all the electricity and phone lines were down on the island. Laura immediately made her go and shower and lent her some dry clothes to put on, while Laura made her a hot drink. When the rain eased a little, Maria was sent home in a borrowed raincoat.

At four-thirty, Laura heard the sound of a car pulling up the drive. She was expecting no one. She could see a shape draped in a waterproof coat dragging a suitcase out of the boot of a taxi, but the strength of the rain blurred her vision. She stood at the door, her heart soaring at Taylor's return. She smiled brightly as the figure approached.

'For Christ's sake woman, get out of the way and let me get inside. I'm getting soaked,'

Laura froze at the sound of Slater's voice.

Once inside, he threw off his waterproof, leaving it in a wet pile on the hall floor and walked through to the kitchen. 'Where's the booze, I'm parched. I've had one hell of a flight out here.'

Laura could hear him opening and closing the cupboards. The noise of the doors slamming and the fear pumping around her veins made her quite lightheaded.

'You'll have to thank my dear brother for letting me know where you were, because for some reason Mother was keeping tight lipped about your whereabouts. Now, what the hell are these doing here,' he shook a box of paracetamol at her. 'Have you been filling your body with chemicals? If you've done anything to harm my child….'

Laura held her breath waiting for the threat that would surely follow.

'It's a good job I'm here now. I can make sure everything goes to plan. When is it due? It should be around now? It had better be soon, I've only managed to wangle three weeks compassionate leave for the death of Father. I'm not sure if I can link maternity leave onto the end of it as well.'

'You're not staying?' Laura said, her voice wavering.

With a supercilious smile he said, 'Oh yes I am.'

She swallowed hard. 'Have you forgotten that my solicitor told you to stay away?'

He raised his eyebrows. 'You seem to forget dear wife, this villa also belongs to me. Your stupid little letter told me to keep away from your flat and workplace, this….' He made a sweeping gesture with his hand. '..belongs to my family. I can come and go as I please.' He smirked as he looked Laura up and down. 'My God, you're enormous. I hope you haven't been eating rubbish all the time you've been pregnant.'

*

Laura couldn't believe Taylor had told Slater where she was - in fact, he hadn't. Slater had seen the discarded Portuguese luggage label which Taylor had ripped off his suitcase. It didn't take a rocket scientist to put two and two together to find out where he was hiding her. At the first opportunity, Laura picked up the phone to berate Taylor, but the line was still dead. In self-preservation she took herself off to her bedroom and locked the door.

39

The next morning Laura woke feeling quite relaxed, until she remembered Slater was in the villa. Quietly she made her way to the bathroom, studiously looking for signs of life downstairs. Once washed and dressed, her plan was to take the car to Faro, book into a hotel near the hospital and wait it out there. Pulling a brush through her hair, a sudden pain tore through her tummy. Grasping the edge of the sink, she gasped as a rush of water gushed down her legs and lay in a pool by her feet. She closed her eyes in dismay - her labour had started.

Gathering her toiletries from the bathroom, she packed her hospital bag. Ascending the stairs quietly, she went to retrieve her car keys from the hook in the kitchen. They had gone! Panic rose as she searched the worktops, moving letters and jars in a vain hope of finding them.

'Oh Slater, please tell me you haven't taken the car?' she moaned. The empty drive confirmed her worst fears, the car had gone. 'Damn you, where the hell have you gone?' Back in the villa she called out to the maid, 'Maria?' No answer. 'Maria, where are you?' Realising it was her day off - she picked up the phone to call a taxi. The line was still dead. A second pain made her double over in agony. Holding onto the back of the sofa until the pain subsided, she tried to assure herself to keep calm, as nothing was going to happen yet. She remembered that the midwife, at the first pre-natal class, had said she could be in labour for hours with a first baby. As soon as she could stand upright she picked up her bag and set off down the drive. Someone in the village would help. She cursed Slater - for some reason he had closed the gates after leaving and she knew they were stiff to open. Her fingers found the rusty catch, and a shiver ran the length of her body - the gate was locked. Panic brought on another contraction, causing her knees to buckle. Her breath came out in short shallow gasps as she frantically looked down the road to see if anyone was about. 'Hello,' she called out desperately. 'Can anyone help me?' There was no reply. It was half a mile to the nearest house. After calling for over half an hour, she turned and walked back up the drive.

The clock in the hall said eight-fifteen. Where the hell could Slater have gone so early? Stay calm, she told herself. Hopefully he wouldn't be gone too long. She grimaced at the irony. After making a half-hearted attempt to do some easy housework, plumping the cushions on the sofa, and straightening the fruit bowl in the centre of the coffee table, she tried the phone again – still dead. In the kitchen, she turned on the tap and reached for a tumbler from the cupboard, but dropped it as another contraction ripped through her. She fell to her knees amongst the slivers of glass.

By the time Slater arrived back at three-fifty that afternoon, Laura was knelt on the floor with her arms over the back of sofa, her clothes were soaked with perspiration.

'Where the hell have you been!' she screamed angrily.

'Out! What are you doing down there?'

'I'm scrubbing the floor, what the bloody hell does it looks like I'm doing? The baby's on its way.' She struggled without help to get off her knees.

'Sarcasm is the lowest form of wit,' he said dryly.

She looked at him with cold scorn. 'You disappeared with the car and I've been like this for over seven hours, without any help!' she shrieked. 'What possessed you to lock the gate for Christ's sake?'

Still not moving to help her he said, 'I always lock the gate when I leave the villa. I forgot you were here, that's all.'

'Like hell you did.'

Finally, without showing any emotion, he helped her onto the sofa. Once she was settled he turned to walk away.

'Where are you going?'

'To get some help, where do you think?' he answered arrogantly.

'No!' she screamed. 'Get me to the hospital!' A pain tore through her and she doubled up. She looked up when she heard Slater drive away. 'Slater, come back!' she cried out, between the panting.

To her relief he returned within a couple of minutes and helped her off the sofa, but instead of helping her out to the car, he led her up the stairs.

'What are you doing, stop, stop, I need to go to hospital!' She yanked back, trying to release her arm from his grip.

'For goodness sake woman, keep calm. Everything is under control. Help is coming. You're too far gone to make it to the hospital.' He practically dragged her up the last few steps and placed her on the bed, just as another pain seared through her body.

'Slater, I demand you take me to hospital now,' she cried.

Ignoring her rant, Slater turned as a figure appeared at the door. 'Ah good, there you are, come in then.' He beckoned the small plump woman, dressed in black, to Laura's bed.

Laura sat herself up on the bed. 'Who the hell is this?'

'This, my dear, is Luisa, she is the local midwife.'

'What? Oh no, she is not attending me if that's what you think! I've had complications. I need to be in hospital.'

'Nonsense,' he said smiling. 'I want you to have our baby as naturally as possible. You know how I feel about hospitals and the drugs they give you. Well, Luisa will help you to have as natural a birth as possible.'

Dumbfounded, Laura watched in dread as the woman busied herself about the room.

'Don't look so worried,' he said casually. 'She's delivered all the babies round here. She knows exactly what she's doing.'

Luisa started to arrange the sheets and attempted to lift one of Laura's feet. Laura shrank from her touch. She looked puzzled and turned to Slater and said in broken English. 'You said Mrs wanted me, yes?'

'Yes of course she does, don't you Laura?'

Laura leaned over and attempted to push the woman away. 'I'm really sorry, there has been a mistake. You cannot attend me. I must go to hospital. Do you understand?'

Luisa looked at Slater again.

'Ignore her,' he said unmoved.

'Oh my God,' Laura screamed in pain as the contractions began to increase.

'Have you everything you need?' he said to Luisa, who nodded. 'Good. I'll leave you two to it then.' He turned and walked out of the room.

Laura was panting to ride the pain but stopped abruptly as she heard Slater turn the key in the lock.

'No!' she screamed, struggling to her feet. She staggered across the room and hammered on the door. 'For pity's sake Slater, let me out!'

Luisa moved swiftly to her side and slapped the door with the palm of her hands shouting through to Slater in Portuguese.

Laura's face crumpled as she choked back the tears, turned her back to the door and slid down onto the floor. She looked at the old woman in desperation then cried into her hands. 'I don't believe this.' She looked again at the woman and pleaded, 'I want to go to hospital.'

Luisa knelt by her side and reached out for her hand.

'Get off me!' Laura screamed, pulling away from her.

'Mrs please, I very sorry. He told me you want me to help you have your baby. He asked me yesterday if I would attend to you.'

'What?' Laura gasped in disbelief. 'But he knew I needed to have my baby in hospital. I don't want it here!

I'm frightened!'

Luisa sat her generous bulk back on her haunches and thumped her fists into her hips. 'I do not understand. I don't think I like this.'

'*You* don't like it?' Laura asked ironically.

'Why he do this to you? Why he lock the door?'

'Because he's a bastard!' she howled, then a pain suddenly gripped her and she let out a gasp.

Quickly and expertly the woman leaned over Laura, lifted her head and started to show her how to breathe until the pain subsided. She stroked Laura's moist brow and purred, 'I will help you. Let me help you. I Maria's mama. I not hurt you,' she said soothingly. 'I help you, okay?'

Laura had no option. This baby was going to come and this woman was going to deliver it, whether she wanted her to or not. Reluctantly she let Luisa help her to her feet.

For the next few hours, Luisa coaxed and cajoled Laura until she trusted her completely. They walked the room together, panted and breathed when necessary, all through the night. Luisa lay by her side, mopped her damp brow, and sponged her body down. She held her hands as Laura screamed in pain, ignoring the sharp manicured nails digging into her hot palms. Together they counted, sang, breathed, and talked. Then finally as dawn broke, she helped her onto all fours and rubbed the small of her back when birth was imminent.

Slater tried hard to sleep downstairs for a while, but soon grew weary of the screams that came from the bedroom. He fixed himself a whiskey and settled himself on a sun-lounger by the pool, away from all the noise. He sat there with a self-satisfied smile on his face - he was back in control.

Upstairs, Laura stood in a squatting position, her arms around Luisa's neck, her body running wet with sweat. She couldn't take much more of this pain - she was exhausted and started to cry against Luisa's breast.

Luisa stroked her back gently. 'Your baby will come soon now,' she comforted her.

'I need to lie down,' Laura said, fumbling her way towards the bed. 'Oh God I think this is it!' she shrieked as the baby's head started to appear. 'I can't do this!' she cried. 'It hurts! Oh my God it hurts!' Her screams turned to pants as she gasped for breath, tears rolled down her anguished face just as the next pain ripped through her,

Slater sighed impatiently, checked his watch, and then folded his newspaper onto the occasional table by his side. He looked up just as Maria walked through the gates. He nodded at her as she bowed her head shyly. She'd always been wary of him, she didn't know why, she just felt uneasy in his presence. Another scream made her glance into the villa with alarm.

'It's all right. Your mistress is just having a baby!' Slater said nonchalantly.

Upstairs, the baby's head had made its way out, but Laura was too exhausted to be bothered.

'Okay, once more, push,' urged Luisa.

Laura shook her head. 'No more,' she wept.

'It's okay this will be the last time, please Laura one more push?'

The pain came and Laura reluctantly pushed down. She gritted her teeth and pushed and pushed and pushed. Her cries echoed through the house. Suddenly silence ensued, and a moment later a baby cried.

Slater waited twenty minutes until he was sure it was all over, drained his glass and sauntered upstairs to unlock the bedroom door.

Laura had fainted before she saw the baby and was still semi-conscious, when he entered the room. Luisa shot Slater a look of hatred, as he walked over to the bed to inspect the child.

'A boy!' she said caustically as she cleaned up the placenta.

He looked down, smiling at his new son, but the smile drained from his face as he looked closer. Shaking with rage his eyes took in the olive sheen of the child's skin, his wispy jet-black hair and..... he pressed his finger against the child's cheek and a small strawberry mark under his eye immediately told him that the child was not his.

Watching Slater's face, Luisa moved nearer as though to protect the baby, but he pushed her to the floor. In horror she watched him gather the four corners of the sheet around the boy and drag it off the bed. Struggling to her feet, Luisa followed him out of the room.

'Come back! Where you go with baby?' She tugged at his shirt, but he pushed her away again. He abruptly stopped at the top of the stairs dangling the child over the banister. Luisa held her breath and crossed herself furiously. Slater turned to face her. 'Tell her,' he said, nodded towards Laura, '… It's dead!'

Luisa clapped her hands to her face. 'No, baby is not dead, look!' She tried to grasp at the bundle.

'Tell her!' He turned and ran down the stairs and out of the house.

Maria came out of the kitchen when she heard the commotion.

'Maria,' Luisa hissed to her daughter in Portuguese. 'Follow him, quick.'

Maria rushed out onto the drive as Slater turned out of the gate. Waiting a moment and keeping as close to the bushes as possible, she cautiously followed him as he marched up the dusty road. He turned into the grounds of an empty villa. She arrived at the gate as he disappeared around the back of the building. Not sure what to do next she pushed herself into the shrubbery and picked her way through the dense undergrowth to gain a vantage point. Craning her neck to see what he was doing, she heard a plop, and a cascade of water showered the path near her feet. Maria crouched down undetected as Slater marched past her without the bundle.

40

Laura pulled herself into consciousness when Luisa rushed back into the bedroom. Noting the fear in Luisa's face, she frantically looked around the room. 'Where's my baby?'

Luisa started to weep.

Every nerve in Laura's body stood on end. 'Luisa, where is my baby?'

Slater burst into the room. 'It's dead,' he said grabbing Luisa by her arm. 'You, get out!' He pushed her out onto the landing, slamming the door behind her.

Laura watched in horror as he locked the door from the inside. She sat up and pushed herself against the bed head, her ears filled with the eerie sound of Luisa wailing outside. Her mouth felt paper dry as she followed Slater as he paced the room.

When he stopped he looked straight at her. 'I am blonde. You are blonde. The child was dark. How could that happen?'

Tearful and trembling, she answered, 'Lots of babies are born dark and grow up to be blonde.'

He started to clap in a deliberately false fashion. 'Very good answer, but it wasn't just his hair, it was his skin.' He bared his teeth. 'Now, who do we know with olive skin and a disfiguring mark on his face that could have been passed onto his child, eh?'

Laura could hear the sound of her own heartbeat pounding in her ears, as he walked towards the bed. He rolled up his sleeves and Laura instinctively curled herself into a ball.

'You know what you are?' He slapped her legs hard. 'A bloody whore, that's what! I bet I hadn't left Villa Amora two minutes, before he was in your bed. I knew there was something between you and that Greek bastard.'

Laura lay speechless.

He pulled her to her feet to face him. 'Have you nothing to say for yourself?'

She flinched as his spittle covered her face.

He pulled back his right arm and balled his hand into a fist, but this time she would not wait for the blow. With one precision jerk of the knee, she caught him full in his manhood. He dropped to his knees, shrieking in agony. Laura stumbled towards the door, and turned the key, as Slater vomited on the rug. Laura watched in disgust as he writhed about in his own vomit and hoped he would choke on it.

Once Laura was out of the room, Luisa shrieked with relief and threw her chubby arms about her. Laura tried to steady her hands so she could lock the door behind her. After the third attempt, the lock clicked and she sobbed with relief. Trembling with emotion, Luisa placed a protective arm about her shoulders and ushered her down the stairs and out of the house.

'Where shall we go?' Laura asked anxiously. 'He'll find me, I know he will!'

'Don't worry. We hide you well, so he can't find you. Come?' She led her up the dusty road just as the sun was rising.

Laura stumbled and held her stomach. She was bleeding hard and could feel a hot stickiness between her inner thighs. 'What happened to my baby Luisa?' she asked desperately.

'Shush now, keep walking,' Luisa answered.

'How much farther must we go?' Laura sobbed uncontrollably.

'We here now, this is the house of my son Carlos. He will hide you.' Luisa pushed the door open and a young man stood before them. Luisa uttered something in Portuguese to him then turned to Laura and said, 'Carlos will take care of you. I'll be back soon.'

Carlos scooped Laura into his arms and carried her up the two flights of stairs to an attic bedroom.

The room was dark and gloomy, but thankfully clean. An old woman sat near the window, humming quietly to the gentle movement of her rocking chair. She stopped abruptly as they entered and watched intently as Carlos carefully placed Laura on the bed. After covering her with a sheet he smiled, and then placed his finger to his pursed lips to urge her to stay quiet.

*

Slater wiped the vomit from his mouth with his sleeve, and pulled himself towards the locked bedroom door. Coughing and spluttering, each movement brought a stabbing pain to his groin. With his hands cupping his tender manhood, he stood up straight, stepped back a few paces, took a deep painful breath and hurled himself at the door. The flimsy chipboard gave way at the third attempt, splitting the wood around the lock. With one final wrench, Slater heaved the lock and handle until it came away in his hand and the door sprang open.

Like a warrior raging into battle, he ran towards Luisa's house. Bursting through her front door, he pushed Luisa to one side, searching the rooms one by one, knocking furniture and crockery as he went. He came back into the living room, livid. 'Where is she?' he said, grabbing Luisa by the neck and lifting her bulk inches off the ground. Slater felt a crack against his skull as Luisa's husband hit him broadside with a chair. The impact forced him to release his grip on Luisa and he fell to the floor cradling his head to mask the searing pain. A moment later he felt the force of a boot in his ribs. He scrambled to his feet and headed for the door, ducking from the remnants of the chair as it was picked up and hurtled through the air after him.

While Luisa's husband tended to his wife, Slater continued to wage war amongst the terrified community. Bleeding and furious he entered and searched every household in the vicinity for Laura, ignoring the abuse and missiles the occupants threw at him, until he finally came upon Carlos's house. Now completely out of control, Slater was a man possessed, and as this was the last house to search, she must be here!

Carlos was in the back room when Slater burst through the door.

'Where are you, you bitch? I know you're skulking here somewhere!' he shouted as he took the stairs two at a time.

Laura panicked at the sound of his voice and let out a stifled scream. The old woman stopped the motion of her rocking chair, stood up and swiftly moved towards the bed, pushed Laura under the covers and slipped between the sheets next to her. When Slater burst into the room, the old woman dragged the sheets to her chin and let out a deafening scream that made Laura's blood run cold. She was convinced Slater had killed the old woman, and braced herself for what was to come.

Slater recoiled from the room at the intensity of her scream and stepped back into the barrel of a gun.

'Out,' Carlos hissed. Jabbing him with the weapon he pushed Slater down the stairs and out into the street to where a gang of village men stood in line, brandishing lumps of wood and rocks.

Slater looked first at the mob then turned to face Carlos. 'I just want my wife, and I'm not leaving without her!' he said defiantly.

Carlos dug the barrel into Slater's belly and stared him full in the eyes. 'You will leave now! I give you ten minutes for you to collect your things, and then I set the dogs on you!'

Slater growled in fury. 'Keep her then, she's rubbish!'

'Nine and half minutes, before the dogs,' Carlos repeated his warning.

Slater turned on his heel and walked slowly past the jeering mob, with Carlos following close behind.

'Nine minutes!' he shouted at Slater as his waiting car came into view.

Twelve minutes later Slater emerged from the villa. He

stopped briefly, pulled a leather case out of his top pocket and put on his sunglasses. He picked up his suitcase and walked slowly down the short drive to where Carlos waited. He stopped at the gate, peered over his sunglasses at him and laughed.

'Minus three minutes!' Carlos clicked his fingers.

The men folk of the village who had gathered together at the top of the hill released their dogs. Slater furrowed his brow. From nowhere the sound of growling dogs appeared through a cloud of dust, as he set off running towards his car.

Carlos heard Slater's footsteps stop, and then a long harrowing scream preceded a deathly howl. Carlos waited a moment until all went silent, and then whistled the dogs to heel.

*

In the dark gloomy bedroom, Laura lay exhausted and terrified under the covers. When she was sure that the coast was clear the old woman flipped the sheets out of the way, slipped her legs out of the bed and shuffled her frail body back onto the rocking chair. She sat for a few seconds then started to rock rhythmically as she hummed and flashed a toothless grin at Laura.

Laura pushed herself deep into the bed. 'Oh Yian,' she cried softly. Sick with grief, her body felt numb to the aching void within her. Let me die, she prayed silently. Let me be with Yian's baby. Too weary to wipe away the tears, she lay desolate on her damp pillow. Her very soul had been ripped apart this time. Everything good in her life had turned to pain and sorrow. This was her darkest hour.

The door opened and Luisa made her way to where Laura lay. She was wearing a damp neckerchief at her neck to soothe the angry bruises Slater had inflicted on her. Looking down at the broken girl in the bed, she was shocked at how small and frail she looked. It was such a change from the strong-willed woman who so bravely gave birth in such shocking circumstances an hour ago.

'Mrs?' she croaked, swallowing to ease her raw throat.

Laura heard, but didn't respond. Instead, she just stared into space with glazed eyes.

Luisa cleared her throat and spoke again, 'Mrs, look!' She beckoned Maria into the room. Maria passed the bundle she was carrying to Luisa and she in turn carefully lowered it into the crook of Laura's arm.

Laura's eyes flickered, as she looked down. A faint cry preceded the appearance of a tiny hand from the blanket. Laura moved her face nearer to the bundle she cradled so gently in her arms, and the tiny hand reached up and touched its mother's face. Laura's hand shook as she moved the blanket away, to reveal her beautiful baby boy, made even more perfect with his tiny copy of Yiannis's strawberry mark beneath his right eye.

'My baby?' she cried, looking searchingly at Luisa.

Luisa nodded tearfully.

'But how?'

'Laura, your husband is a bad man. He threw baby into disused swimming pool. He could have killed baby! My Maria rescued baby just in time,' she said, proudly holding Maria's hand.

'He didn't see me,' Maria assured Laura. 'He still thinks baby is dead!

Luisa kissed Maria's hand and said, 'My Maria wrapped wet baby in petticoat, and hid in goat shed until safe. She's a good girl my Maria, yes?'

Laura broke down and sobbed. 'Oh yes, yes, thank you Maria. My thanks to all of you, I don't know how I can ever repay you.'

'No matter. You happy. We happy. Baby happy!' Luisa answered nodding furiously.

Laura lay in bed in this strange room, and stared in wonderment at the tiny bundle nestled at her breast. She grimaced at the number of times she'd screamed that she hated this baby throughout her dreadful delivery, and now here it was, cradled in her arms, the pain forgotten and a feeling of love for this child so profound it frightened her.

*

It was nine a.m. by the time Slater arrived at Faro Airport. His clothes were ripped and smeared in blood and dog saliva. There was a deep cut on his forearm from when one of the dogs pulled him to the ground, and blood trickled from the head wound he sustained from Luisa's husband. After half an hour spent in the airport lavatories cleaning his bleeding wounds, he now stood at the end of a long queue to the ticket desk, tapping his foot impatiently. The queue didn't seem to be moving and the thought of Yiannis Kiassos made his blood boil.

'Bastard!' he said out loud.

The man in front of him turned angrily. 'I beg your pardon?'

'Oh nothing, I was just thinking out loud.'

'Well don't! There are women present,' the man said, then turned back to face the ticket desk.

The more Slater thought of Yiannis the more he shook with rage. I should have shot that bastard when I had the chance, he cursed quietly to himself. Suddenly his mouth twisted into a smile.

The queue moved more quickly now and Slater soon found himself at the ticket desk. 'Destination please?' the girl said in a singsong voice.

Slater chewed the inside of his mouth.

'Sir?'

'Athens!' he said coldly.

41

Under the light of the moon, Kostas Petrou held out his hand gallantly for the girl as she stepped from the boat onto the beach at Amora Cove. At Villa Amora, the girl glanced appreciatively around the moonlit terrace, as Kostas fumbled under the mat for a key. He opened the French doors and chivalrously gestured his guest through into the lounge.

'Oh Kostas, this is beautiful,' she murmured, kissing him briefly as she passed by. He locked the doors behind him, and turned to find her draped seductively on one of the sofas. Kneeling at her feet he grinned boyishly, as she peeled off her T-shirt exposing her tanned body. A sudden noise made him pause for a moment.

'Come on Kostas!' she murmured.

'Hush a moment,' he said gently, as he moved to the window. 'I think someone's coming. I heard a motorboat!'

The moon, partially hidden by cloud, cast a blanket of darkness over the cove, making it almost impossible for Kostas to see anything, but when the cloud parted, the moon illuminated a figure walking up the beach steps.

'Who is it?' she whispered softly.

Kostas shrugged. 'I don't know, but I think he's coming here. Hush.'

The girl started to pull her clothes back on as Kostas watched the figure move closer to the villa. 'Oh God, you haven't got a husband have you?'

'No,' she giggled.

He wiped his forehead in jest. His first thought was it may be Yiannis, although since moving back into the Athena, he very rarely came here nowadays, but on closer inspection the approaching man was six-foot tall and fair-haired.

The girl touched him lightly. 'Do you know him?'

Kostas frowned. 'Vaguely, I just can't remember who….' Suddenly it dawned on him. 'Oh Christ, come on, quick, hide.' He dragged her upstairs and waited with bated breath. Minutes passed, but no one came. Kostas carefully pulled the curtains apart. He could just make out the figure of Slater outside Yiannis's lodge.

'What's he doing Kostas?'

'Don't know, but he's carrying something.' He sniffed the air. 'Can you smell petrol?'

She shook her head.

Kostas watched in astonishment as Slater first tried the door then stood back, raised his hand and fired a gun shot at the lock.

'Bloody hell! What's he doing?' He saw Slater grab the can, put his boot to the splintered door, entered the lodge and a few moments later fired indiscriminately throughout the house. Kostas spun round. 'He must think Yiannis is in there!'

The girl was trembling. 'Who's Yiannis, and why would he want to shoot him?'

'Hush now, he's coming out,' Kostas said.

Slater emerged backwards from the lodge, sprinkling petrol from the can over the sparse kitchen furniture, and out onto the veranda. He reloaded his gun, stood well back, and casually fired into the house, igniting the petrol.

*

It wasn't often Yiannis stayed at the lodge nowadays, but tonight was one of the nights he just felt he needed to sleep in the room he'd shared with Laura.

He knew now their relationship was over. He'd received a letter in April from Laura's friend Pippa, some six months after writing to her! She'd apologised for the delay in replying, due to her being away, and was sorry to say she was unsure of Laura's whereabouts. Knowing how close Pippa was to Laura, Yiannis struggled to believe this, and therefore all hope of reconciliation vanished.

The lodge held such wonderful, albeit painful,

memories, but very occasionally, his battered heart sought solace from visiting it.

As he sailed towards the Midnight Rocks, he heard what sounded like gunshots.

*

Kostas pushed the girl away from the window when he saw Slater coming back. They waited silently until they heard footsteps walking away.

'Has he gone?' she asked.

'I think so.'

'Kostas, look!' she cried, pointing at the flames, licking out of the windows of the lodge.

'Oh Christ,' Kostas shrieked. He ran down to the kitchen sink and filled the bowl with water. 'Here, take this.' He pushed it at her. 'We'll have to try and put that fire out!' he said, shoving a bucket under the tap. With fumbling fingers Kostas unlocked the French doors, ran out onto the terrace then stopped abruptly, causing the girl to crash into him, drenching them both in water.

'Ugh, what have you stopped for?' she cried, shaking the water from her body.

'I think there's another boat coming.'

'I thought you said this cove was deserted?' she hissed, looking over his shoulder.

Kostas glanced up at the fire then at the beach. 'We'd better hide. Quick, get in these bushes.'

The Moondancer ran aground on the shingle beach, swiftly followed by a heated altercation.

'Get out of the boat Kiassos!' Slater ordered.

Yiannis moved slowly, steadying the boat while he jumped into the shallow water. He glanced up at his burning house, watching the sparks fly into the night sky like fireworks. 'You're burning your own property! You do realise that don't you?' Yiannis said stiffly.

'Shut up and move yourself!' Slater said, pointing the gun at Yiannis's head.

Despite the impending danger, the sight of Slater

enraged Yiannis. He lunged at him taking him totally unawares, and Slater felt the full blow of Yiannis's fist, sending his gun spinning into the air until it landed at the water's edge.

Slater staggered backwards, cupping his blood-splattered nose as Yiannis lunged again. Grasping him by the collar, he shook him violently. 'Come on then you coward, or is it only women you hit?'

Slater attempted to punch him in the face, but Yiannis dodged his aim, and grasped his wrist to twist it down, a moment later Slater hit back with a swinging blow to Yiannis's chin with his other fist, sending him reeling to the sea.

Yiannis struggled to his feet, coughed the salty water from his throat, and then propelled himself forward, head-butting Slater in the stomach. As they fell, Slater grabbed the front of Yiannis's shirt, tearing the buttons off, leaving the material flapping in tatters, then raised his foot to Yiannis's belly and forced him backwards against the rocks. Yiannis gasped as the fall winded him. He coughed, and spat, but as he tried to move, the pain in his side seared through his body, making him gasp for breath. The gun was about two feet away from where he lay and Yiannis took a large painful breath before he scrambled for it, but Slater reached it first. He struck Yiannis a glancing blow with the butt of the gun, stunning him momentarily, and then in a frenzy of anger began to kick Yiannis in the ribs.

'You bastard, I'm going to make you pay! Nobody touches my wife and gets away with it! Do you hear me?' he roared.

Yiannis groaned in agony, reached out, caught Slater's foot and yanked it until he lost his balance, then dragged him down into the water. Slater fell flat on his back, but managed to hold the gun above water level. He kicked Yiannis until he released his grip on him. Slater scrambled to his feet and pointed the gun at Yiannis. 'Stand up

Kiassos!' he ordered.

Kostas crawled out of the bushes. 'Keep out of sight,' he ordered the girl.

'Where are you going?' She grasped his arm.

'Let go,' he hissed, shaking her free. 'I'm going to help Yiannis.'

She looked horrified. 'The other man is armed for goodness sake!'

Ignoring her, Kostas moved with stealth across the terrace, past the empty swimming pool, towards the bushes at the far end of the garden. He lay on his belly, easing forward through the undergrowth, until he came to the sheer drop to the beach. He could see Slater pushing Yiannis along the cliff path towards the summit of a precipice. Keeping his head down, Kostas moved slowly from rock to rock watching and waiting for a chance to pounce.

At the summit, Yiannis stopped and waited.

'Turn around!' Slater ordered. He stared at Yiannis, his eyes cold with scorn. 'I just thought you may like to know that my wife gave birth to a son this morning!'

Yiannis baulked at the thought that Laura was still living with him.

Sadistically pleased with Yiannis's countenance, he continued. 'It should have been the proudest day of my life, but when I held my son for the first time, I noticed its skin was a greasy olive colour, just like yours. Not only that, but it was defaced with the same birthmark as yours!'

Yiannis stood open-mouthed.

'I've killed it of course!' he said with a satisfied smile. 'I drowned it like an unwanted dog. Now I shall kill you!'

Yiannis felt his chest restrict. 'Where's Laura? What have you done with her?' He could hardly speak.

'Nothing yet, I'll deal with her later. I have a lot of unfinished business with that bitch!' Slater smiled sardonically. 'But for your information, the last time I saw her she was on a blood soaked bed weeping for the loss of her child.'

'You sick bastard,' Yiannis shook his head in disbelief. Suddenly he felt the ground crumble away under his feet. He tried to move forward to safety.

'No you don't!' Slater said, holding the gun to his face. 'Goodbye Kiassos. Go and join your dead son!'

Slater squeezed his finger on the trigger, but before he could fire, the ground gave way and Yiannis disappeared over the edge.

Slater roared with laughter as he inched forward to look over the cliff, and then turned suddenly as Kostas leapt from his hiding place and hurled a huge rock at him.

The rock hit Slater with a glancing blow to the head. He staggered backwards, falling to the floor, dropping the gun as he landed. He frantically grovelled on the dusty floor, searching for the weapon, blood oozing from the gaping wound above his eye. In the frenzy to retrieve the weapon, he accidentally knocked it over the cliff. He lunged forward in an attempt to catch it, but the cliff gave way beneath him and he began to slide over the edge. Panic-stricken, Slater grasped for a handhold, found one and began to scrape his way back up.

Kostas threw himself onto his belly, clenched his fists and thumped at Slater's trembling fingers, until Slater finally let go and fell into oblivion.

Cautiously, Kostas eased himself forward to look over the edge. To his relief, he could see Yiannis a few feet down. He had fallen feet first onto a ledge and was clinging to a shrub growing from a crevice in the rock face.

'Yian?' Kostas hollered down the cliff.

'Kostas is that you?' Yiannis said in sheer amazement. 'Oh thank God you're here. Help me, I'm slipping.'

'Hold on, I'll get some rope,' Kostas said, shuffling his body backward to safety. Back at the villa, he shouted to the girl for help, but she was nowhere in sight, so he dragged the sheets and mosquito nets from one of the beds and began to knot them together as he ran back towards the cliff.

Twice Yiannis almost lost his grip as he clung to the cliff face. His fingers ached, as he urged himself to hold on and grasp tighter. He edged his left foot inwards, but the stone ledge began to loosen.

'Kostas?' he yelled desperately. He lost his footing, kicked at the cliff, and found it again. 'Where the hell are you? I'm going to fall!'

His thoughts turned to Laura and the son she had borne him. My son, she had given birth to my son, and he had killed him! For a split second he plunged into the depths of despair and considered letting go of his grip on life. Only the thought of Laura brought him back to his senses. My poor Laura, she must be in purgatory somewhere. He had to find her. 'Kostas,' he yelled again.

'It's okay my friend, I'm here.' Kostas lowered the knotted sheets down over the edge after securing the other end to a tree. The makeshift rope was short by two feet and as Yiannis reached for it, the branch his right foot was standing on snapped under him. He pulled himself closer to the cliff, grasping desperately at clumps of soil as each handful crumbled and filled his eyes with grit.

'Yian, what happened, did you get it?'

'It's too bloody short!'

The rope was quickly pulled away and Yiannis silently prayed. He could see the rocks around him move and loosen under his weight. 'Kostas, hurry please!'

The rope was dropped again and Yiannis laughed at the absurdity of what he saw. Dangling from the end was a pair of trousers.

'What the hell are you laughing at you bloody fool, grab it!' Kostas snapped.

Yiannis grabbed them as the wall of the cliff gave way, pelting him with debris. As quickly as Kostas pulled, Yiannis climbed up the makeshift rope. His hand came over the top of the cliff, flailed around to find his friend, their hands locked and Kostas pulled and pulled, ripping at

Yiannis's shirt, grasping and dragging at his clothes until he caught the waistband of his shorts and hoisted him clear of the edge.

*

At the mouth of Amora Cove, a few yards from the bottom of the cliff, a motorboat lay anchored in the darkness. The vessel moved gently from side to side as the water licked and slapped softly against its hull.

Eva, her breath bated, hung over the side of the boat, her eyes skimming the water for movement. Suddenly Slater's hand surfaced and tapped the side of the boat. She stifled a scream. 'My God you nearly gave me a heart attack!' she said, holding her hand to her chest.

'Shut up and help me out!' he hissed.

Eva pulled him until he found his footing on the mooring rope and then flopped unceremoniously into the vessel.

'I saw you fall - are you okay?' Eva whispered.

'No I'm not okay!' Covering the gash above his eye with his hand, he looked up at the cliff just as Yiannis was being hauled back up. 'I thought I'd killed that bastard. If I had the gun I'd shoot him from here! '

'No!' Eva's lips curled into a smile. 'I have a better plan.'

'Well?'

'He has a whore in Piraeus, she's called Katia. I believe they are very close. Maybe you should pay her a visit.'

Slater peeled his wet clothes off until he stood naked on deck, then looked at Eva thoughtfully. 'Special is she?'

'Very. She's the only woman he has ever been with,' she paused and smiled. '…except of course your wife!'

Slater lifted his fist to strike her.

'Don't even think about it!' she warned. 'You need me, just remember that. Now, let's get the hell out of here. I'll come back and deal with Yiannis Kiassos.'

*

On top of the cliff, Yiannis and Kostas lay exhausted.

Yiannis reached again for his friend's hand and squeezed it in thanks. 'How long have you been here?' Yiannis asked breathlessly.

'Long enough to hear everything. I'm so sorry my friend."

A large crack from the burning house made them look up and they wearily got to their feet and ran back to the lodge. When they reached the beach path, the young girl was busy filling buckets from the stream and then running to the lodge to douse the flames.

'Who's that?' Yiannis said, picking up a bucket.

'My date!' Kostas said embarrassed. 'We came here for an undisturbed night of passion! I can't remember her name.'

Yiannis slapped him playfully. 'Always the romantic, eh?'

They worked in rotation. Drawing the water from the stream, carrying the buckets and dousing, until soon it was too much for the three of them to fight. The upstairs windows had blown out and the left side of the roof had collapsed. Sparks were flying high in the sky, and an orange cloud was drifting in the direction of the harbour. The heat was becoming unbearable. In the end they turned coughing and choking from the flames, only to find crowds of locals coming up the beach path, armed with buckets. In the end, their noble efforts were in vain. When the last dying embers were extinguished, there was very little left of the lodge. Yiannis stood back with the rest of the crowd, shaking his head in desperation at his ruined home.

'Mr Yiannis Kiassos?' An official voice came from the crowd.

Yiannis turned to face two police officers. 'Yes?'

'Is this your house?' one of them asked.

'No, but I live here occasionally.'

'Who owns it?'

'The Tempests. I worked for them.'

'Excuse me,' a shrill voice butted in, 'but the house and villa belong to someone called Mr Slater Haynes actually. The man *he* murdered tonight!'

Yiannis turned in the direction of the voice.

'Who said that?' The police officer ordered. 'Come forward and reveal yourself.'

Eva stepped out of the crowd. 'I'm Eva Barzini and I saw Yiannis Kiassos set fire to Mr Haynes's house, then murder him!' she said calmly.

The crowd gasped in unison and all eyes were on Yiannis.

Yiannis and Kostas groaned in unison.

'Mr Kiassos, what do you have to say to that?' the police officer asked.

'She's lying.' Yiannis snapped.

'I know what I saw!' Eva tossed her head confidently. 'I was out fishing.'

'You! Fishing? Fishing for lies more like,' Yiannis retorted incredulously.

'Be quiet!' the officer ordered. 'Go on Madam.'

She gave a slight head wobble. 'As I say, I was out fishing when I heard shouting from the cove. I saw Mr Haynes quarrelling with *him*!' she pointed at Yiannis.

'Go on,' the officer urged.

'I could hear them. Mr Haynes was angry about an affair Yiannis had had with his wife. I heard Mr Haynes order him out of the house and off his land.' She sniffed haughtily.

Yiannis's face tightened.

'Did you see him set fire to the house?' the officer asked Eva.

'Oh yes, I saw it all. First he hit Mr Haynes and then he ran up to the house. The next thing I saw was flames licking out of the windows.'

The waiting crowd listened intently.

'You lying bitch!' Yiannis lurched forward, but one of the police officers quickly stopped him. 'Don't take any notice of her. I came home to find the house on fire.'

Yiannis was ordered to keep quiet and Eva urged to continue.

'Mr Haynes followed him, and tried to put out the fire, but Yiannis came up behind him, hit him with a huge rock and knocked him unconscious. I began to panic then, and decided to sail back to the harbour to get help, but just as I turned the boat around, I saw Yiannis dragging Mr Haynes up to that cliff!' Eva pointed in the direction where Slater had fallen.

This time Kostas shouted, 'She's lying.'

'Shut up!' the officer ordered, reaching for the pistol in his holster. 'And then what?' he asked Eva.

Eva stood for a few seconds enjoying the anguish on Yiannis's face. 'He threw him off!'

The crowd took a simultaneous intake of breath.

'If you go up to the cliff, you will see evidence of a fight there,' she added.

An officer was swiftly despatched to cliff, to take a look at the scene of the crime.

'Look!' Kostas said, grasping the officer by the shirt. 'That is not what happened. It was Slater Haynes who tried to kill Yiannis. He set fire to his house thinking Yiannis was inside, I saw him do it. Then just as he was sailing away, Yiannis came home and there was a fight and....'

Eva butted in. 'Well, he would say that, wouldn't he? Thick as thieves those two. I know what I saw,' she sneered.

Yiannis cast an anxious glance at Kostas.

The officer waded back, climbed onto the rocks, and shouted, 'I can't see anything in the water, but there's evidence of a landslide!'

'You won't find anything in the water,' Eva said calmly. 'I sailed over there straight away to try and rescue the poor man, but he'd gone - drowned I expect.'

The officer nodded, before turning to Kostas. 'Have you any witnesses to your story?'

'Yes I have.' He searched for the girl. 'There was a girl with me, a blonde English girl. She'll tell you. She saw it all too.'

All eyes scanned the crowd, but no blonde girl was forthcoming.

The officer raised his eyebrows and said to his colleague. 'Arrest Mr Kiassos.'

Held by each arm, Yiannis was escorted down the path, past the condemning crowd and an ecstatic Eva.

'Kostas?' Yiannis shouted, as they got into the patrol boat. 'Get in touch with Jack Ryder in London. He's Laura's lawyer. Tell him what you saw and heard. He'll know what to do.'

42

Jack Ryder tore yesterday's date off his desk calendar to reveal the twenty-second of June 1991. He opened his diary at the appropriate page and was beginning to prepare to see his first client of the day when his secretary buzzed him. 'Yes Melanie?'

'I have Laura Haynes on the line - can you take it.'

He hesitated - the very mention of her name gave him a rush of adrenaline. He cleared his throat. 'Yes of course, put her through.'

'Jack?' Her voice seemed distant,

'Laura, this is a surprise. ' He tried to hide the hurt in his voice. 'I haven't heard from you in months. I believe you got married!'

'Yes.' She inhaled deeply. 'Jack, I need your help.'

He shifted uneasily in his leather chair. 'Why, what's the matter?' he said gravely.

'It's Slater.' She began to cry. 'Oh Jack I'm terrified. He tried to kill my baby!'

'You have a *baby*?' A tiny part of him died inside at this news.

'Please help me,' she sobbed.

'Hush Laura, don't cry, of course I will help. Where are you, still in St Ives?' He started to stand.

'No, Portugal.'

'Port…..Oh!..' He rubbed his face, consciously planning how to get there. 'Well…that might take a little longer to get to you.'

Her sobs became louder. 'I'm so sorry to have to ask, but I've no one else to turn to. I'm in a village called Caldas de Monchique in Portugal. Please come and get me.'

'Where's Slater now?'

'I don't know Jack. Please come for me, I'm frightened.' The phone began to beep and the line went dead.

'Laura. Laura!' he shouted down the handset.

He hit the intercom. 'Melanie, get me on the next flight to Faro today!'

'Yes sir, when do you want to return?'

'Leave it open, cancel my appointments for the rest of this week. I'm taking some holiday leave.'

*

Half an hour after Jack had left the office, Kostas rang.

'I need to speak to Jack Ryder please,' he said anxiously.

'I'm sorry, Mr Ryder is out of the country, can someone else help you?' Melanie said in her singsong voice.

'No. When is he due back please?'

'He's on holiday, but if you would like to leave a message, I will pass it onto him if he calls in. I'm afraid that's all I can do,' she said calmly.

Panic began to well in Kostas voice. 'But it's really urgent!'

'I'm sorry, I have no forwarding number. Do you want to leave a message?'

'Yes please. Tell him, Yiannis Kiassos needs his help. Slater Haynes has set fire to a house on the Tempest estate in Poros Greece. Yiannis confronted him, now Slater is missing, believed dead, and Yiannis is in prison, wrongly charged with arson and murder. Yiannis is also concerned that Laura Haynes is in danger. My name is Kostas Petrou, and it's imperative that he can contacts me on Athens 3224-632. Have you got that?'

Melanie quickly scribbled the note. 'I promise I'll pass this message onto Mr Ryder as soon as possible, good day,' she said, putting the phone down.

*

Jack landed at Faro Airport late that afternoon. He was hot and sweaty and his throat felt parched and raw. He hired a car and drove for an hour through the unfamiliar mountains of Monchique, until finally he arrived at the tiny village of Caldas de Monchique by dusk.

Not knowing where the Haynes villa was located, he asked at a local restaurant for directions. It was dark when he managed to find it. At the villa door, he tentatively pushed it open and shouted, 'Laura, are you there?' Someone jumped from the shadows, struck him a fearful blow to the head and Jack fell to his knees.

He woke to a monumental headache, in a strange bed, and an unusual smell of goats in the air. He tried to sit up but his head hurt.

'Lay down Jack,' said a familiar voice.

'Laura?'

'I'm here.' She stroked his bruised head.

He heard a small whimper from a child, and then squinted up at Laura. 'What the hell hit me?' He held his sore head.

'Sorry about that, Carlos thought you were Slater.' She turned to the young man behind her. 'I think I'd better introduce you two,' she said, 'Jack, meet Carlos. Carlos, I'd like you to meet my good friend Jack Ryder.'

Carlos stood with his hands on his hips. 'Welcome. I give you a thousand apologies my friend. I do not know what else to say.'

Jack nodded. 'What did you hit me with?'

'This!' Carlos lifted the gun in the air and Jack shrank back into the bed.

'Well I'm glad you just hit me with it, and didn't aim it at me!'

Carlos gave a short snort. 'Yes, you are lucky I didn't disembowel you with it!' he said proudly.

Jack shuddered at the thought.

'I will leave you now, you have someone to stay with you,' Carols said, resting his rifle over his shoulder.

'Thank you for everything Carlos,' Laura answered,

When he'd gone Jack said gingerly, 'I'm glad he's on our side.'

'Thank you for coming Jack. I can't tell you how relieved I am. I've been so frightened.' Pools of tears swam in her eyes.

'Think nothing of it.' He gently touched her damp cheek. The child whimpered again in Laura's arms. 'He's lovely Laura. What the hell happened? I can't understand Slater doing what he did. All men want a son!'

Laura lowered her eyes. 'I'm afraid he got someone else's son.'

Jack glanced at the baby's skin. 'Yiannis Kiassos's by the look of it!'

Laura nodded sheepishly.

Jack twisted his mouth. 'Why didn't you send for him, instead of me?'

'It's complicated.'

'Mmm, it always is.' He smiled gently. 'It's funny you know, Slater rang me shortly after you came back from your honeymoon. He wanted Yiannis evicted from Amora Cove. I told him Yiannis was part of the fixtures and fittings and came with the property. He slammed the phone down on me. I did wonder what was going on.' Jack tightened his lips. 'So, what do you want to do?'

'I'd like to go home.'

'To Greece?'

'No.'

'What about his father?' He nodded toward the sleeping child.

'He has a family of his own.'

Jack sighed happily. 'Well, it looks like I'll have to look after you both then.'

'Thank you Jack.' She began to cry again.

'Hush now. It will be my pleasure darling.' He stroked the boy's face. 'What's his name?'

'Yiannis,' she said proudly.

Jack pursed his lips. 'Maybe a more English name would be appropriate. We could call him Ian perhaps?'

Laura frowned at his suggestion, but perhaps, this was

not the right time to object.

*

Taylor replaced the phone and began to drum a tattoo with his fingers on the telephone table.

'Is everything all right?' Sarah said, walking into the hall. 'You look pensive.'

He turned to his mother. Her face was etched with grief. He didn't want to bother her with this, but it worried him. 'It's Laura. I've tried several times to phone the villa but the line is dead. The baby should be due any day now.'

'Maybe she's at the hospital.'

He shook his head. 'I've just phoned the hospital in Faro, but she hasn't been admitted yet.'

Sarah placed a comforting arm on his shoulder. 'Taylor, I'm fine you know, if you want to go out there.'

He pulled his lips into a tight smile. 'I don't like leaving you, so soon after…Maybe I should get Slater to come home for a few days.'

'Slater phoned this morning to tell me he's gone back to our villa in Rhodes. I'm fine. Go and give her my love.'

Taylor dropped into the offices of 'Ashborne, Ryder, and Bains' Solicitors in Truro en route to Gatwick.

The secretary was on the phone in Jack's office, and Taylor laid his coat over the back of a deep-buttoned leather chair in reception. He casually glanced around the book-lined walls to pass the time, and eventually his eyes fell on the secretary's untidy table. He cocked his head to read the scribbled piece of paper by the phone, and then looked closer when he saw the name Laura Haynes. He glanced through to Jack's office where the secretary was still engrossed in her phone call, then carefully turned the memo enabling him to read the whole message:

Yiannis Kiassos is in Athens prison for murder and arson. Both he and, Laura Haynes need help. Something to do with Slater Haynes. Phone Athens 3224-632 urgently .

He pushed the memo back in its place when he heard

the secretary enter the room.

'Good morning Mr Haynes. If it's Mr Ryder you're looking for, I'm afraid he is out of the country. He didn't tell me he had an appointment with you?' Melanie said smiling warmly at Taylor.

'No Melanie, I'm just dropping off some papers he wanted. Out of the country, eh? That's strange; he doesn't normally like travelling abroad. When did he go?'

'It was all very sudden. He wanted a flight to Port..,' she stopped mid sentence then smiled.

'Portugal?' he asked casually.

'Oh dear, I wasn't supposed to tell anyone.'

'It's all right, it's only me, I won't say a word,' he whispered, then added casually, 'has he gone to help Laura Haynes?'

The blush on Melanie's cheeks intensified.

'Thank you,' he winked, as he picked up his coat.

Taylor walked back onto the street, stood for a moment on the pavement, then set off almost running down Lemon Street towards the telephone boxes on the Piazza. He punched the Rhodes villa phone number into the phone.

'Slater? It's Taylor.'

'Yep.'

'Is everything okay?' he asked calmly.

Slater gave a short acrid laugh. 'Is everything okay?' He paused for a moment. 'Well, apart from the fact that my wife gave birth to a baby that wasn't mine, I'm taking anti inflammatory drugs to combat the infection I picked up after being savaged by a pack of mad Portuguese dogs, and not to mention surviving a forty foot drop after being thrown off a cliff by one of my wife's boyfriend's, and having six stitches to a cut over my eye - yes everything's fine!'

'What do you mean the baby wasn't yours? Whose is it then?'

'You mean whose *was* it? Remember the greasy

fisherman, always sniffing around Laura? Well, it was his! And you know what? He was really cut up when he found out the brat was dead?!'

'The baby's dead?'

'Yep, died at birth! Well, I think it's for the best all round don't you?'

Taylor was flabbergasted. 'How do you know this? Have you been to Portugal?'

'Yep. You know Taylor, if you want to hide someone, you really should have been more careful disposing of your flight bag labels.'

Taylor felt an uneasy lurch in his stomach. 'Where's Laura now?'

'Who knows, and I don't bloody care.'

Taylor stiffened. 'You'd better not have hurt her.'

Slater laughed caustically. 'No, but I did manage to settle a few scores with her boyfriend.'

'What are you talking about?'

'I burnt their bloody love nest down and had him take the blame. Let's just say the Greek won't be siring any more brats for a while. In fact, by the time he sees the light of day again he'll be a very old man.'

'You're despicable Slater. I disown you. You are no brother of mine.'

Slater laughed and put the phone down on him.

*

Yiannis had been in Athens prison for four days, with still not word from Jack Ryder.

Kostas visited him every day, and with each visit he was visibly shocked at his wretched appearance. His tanned skin looked sallow, a rough beard accentuated his haggard looks and his hair was pulled back into an untidy greasy ponytail. Kostas guessed he had lost at least half a stone in weight, as his prison garments sat across his shoulders like clothes on a coat hanger.

'Ryder isn't going to help me, is he?' Yiannis asked wearily.

Kostas shook his head. 'I'm sorry Yian. I've rung everyday but he's never there.'

Yiannis gave a short laugh. 'I don't know why I'm surprised, he never liked me anyway. Did you tell them Laura needed help?'

'Yes of course. In fact, when I rang today, his secretary told me Laura was okay.'

Yiannis's shoulders fell in relief. The guard came across to their table and nodded that their time was up.

Yiannis pressed both palms on the table and got up wearily. He looked at Kostas with haunted eyes. 'I need to get out of here Kostas.'

'I tried to get bail for you. I rang Travis and he offered up the money, but they've refused. He's flying out as soon as possible to see what can be done. We are trying everything, I promise,' he said, watching desperately as Yiannis was ushered through the door back towards his cell.

*

Kostas stood with his tea towel over his shoulder, staring into space. Alexis came and stood beside him. 'You have a heavy weight on your shoulders my son?'

'Not as heavy as Yiannis has,' he answered wearily.

'It's all *her* fault!' Kostas nodded towards Eva's house. 'How could she do this to him? Why did she tell all those lies?'

'You know what they say about a woman scorned.'

'Well I could kill her for this, in fact I think I will!' he said, making to go.

'Calm down Kostas. The best thing you can do is prove her to be a liar, so she can't show her face here any more!'

Kostas gave a short laugh. 'I wish I could, but how?'

'The truth always comes out in the end, you'll see. Anyway come on, there's work to be done,' he said, nodding towards the late afternoon ferry as it approached the harbour.

Kostas busied himself seating holidaymakers at the taverna. He was always polite to everyone and always charming with the women, making them laugh and flirting with them.

He had just finished taking his last order and was on his way to the kitchen when a voice from the far table spoke up.

'Hello, Kostas, remember me?'

'One moment please,' he replied, and then stopped dead in his tracks. He knew that voice. He spun around and there she was - the miracle he had been waiting for. He ran to her table, scooped her into his arms and kissed her passionately. 'It's you! It's you! Oh thank you lord for this miracle.'

'Heck!' she said flabbergasted. 'I didn't even think you would remember me.'

'Remember you, of course I remember you. Where have you been? I've been searching everywhere for you, in all the hotels and apartments on the island. I've even waited in Athens airport in a hope to catch you before you left Greece.'

'Gosh,' she said in bewilderment.

He held her by the arms. 'Where did you go after the fire?'

'I had to catch the early morning ferry with my friends. So once I knew the fire was out, I hitched a lift on one of the boats back to the harbour so I could collect my things from my apartment. I'm on an island hopping holiday!' She laughed, 'I'm amazed I made such an impression on you.'

'Oh, you misunderstand me,' his voice faltered.

She frowned. 'I'm sorry, you've lost me now.'

'Sorry it didn't mean to come out like that, it's just, I needed you and I didn't know your name. You just disappeared.'

She looked totally confused now.

'Sorry, I'll start again, by the way what is your name?'

Kostas said.

'Karen Mason.'

'Well Karen Mason, you remember Yiannis, the one whose house was on fire?'

'Yes I do. Did they arrest the man who set fire to your friend's house?'

Kostas shook his head. 'He's dead!'

'Dead?'

'Yes, you didn't see it, but there was a struggle and he fell off the cliff, it was while you were dousing the fire. The body hasn't been found yet, but Yiannis has been charged with his murder and...'

Karen butted in. 'Wait a minute, he's not dead! I saw him the next morning, he boarded the same ferry.'

Kostas was aghast. 'Are you sure?'

'Absolutely, he was with a woman with short dark hair and a young boy.'

'Oh Karen, you're wonderful, this is marvellous news. This will get Yiannis out of prison, especially if you testify that it was the Englishman who set fire to the lodge as well.' He dragged her to her feet and danced around with her. 'Come on let's go now!' he said looking up at the ferry just about to set sail.

43

Yiannis lay in the stark prison cell, his haunted eyes staring blankly into space. He blinked slightly when he heard footsteps outside his door. With a clink of keys, the guard opened the cell door.

'Kiassos?'

Yiannis blinked again and looked up.

'Get your things, you're on the move.'

Escorted down the corridors and through the security gates, he wondered pensively if they were sending him to a different prison. He hoped not. Not that he had any wish to stay here, but he had got used to the routine and felt reluctant to change. Presently they stopped outside the door of a side room.

'In here!' the guard said roughly.

Yiannis was surprised to see Kostas waiting.

'What's happened?' Yiannis said puzzled.

'A miracle,' Kostas said smiling brilliantly.

'What do you mean?'

'The girl turned up again. Haynes isn't dead. She saw him the next morning. She's given a full statement to the officer in charge and you're free to go!'

Yiannis reached for a chair and sat down.

'Get up, we're going home!' He dragged him back off the chair.

Outside the prison, Yiannis sucked feverishly at the fresh air. It felt so good to feel the sun on his face again.

'Yian, I'd like you to meet your saviour,' Kostas said, pulling him towards Karen.

Yiannis moved towards her, cupped her hands with his, and kissed them affectionately. 'I am extremely grateful to you. If I can do anything for you, let me know,' he said sincerely.

Karen smiled happily at him. 'I'm just so glad I could help.'

'I think this calls for a celebratory drink,' Kostas said, eyeing the taverna behind them.

Yiannis faltered slightly. 'Kostas my friend, can we do it later? I need to go and see someone. I'll catch up with you both this evening, if that's okay?'

'No problem,' Kostas winked at him knowingly.

When Yiannis reached Katia's apartment, he immediately knew that something was wrong.

The air hung heavy and musty. Her normally neat bed was an untidy mess and flies hovered hungrily round a plate of rancid food.

'Katia?' he spoke, consciously knowing she would not answer. He asked after her in the taverna downstairs, but no one had seen her for days. He ran the length of the harbour one way, then the other, calling in at all the places he knew she frequented. When he returned to Katia's apartment block, Christina, one of her friends, ran out to greet him.

'Yiannis, I have been trying to contact you. Is Katia with you?' she said anxiously.

'No, I'm looking for her as well. I haven't seen her since the twenty first of June, when did you see her last?'

Christina placed her hands on her hips. 'It was the day after *you* had been here. I remember how happy she was. She was always like that after you had visited her.' She sighed deeply. 'It's so out of character. She never goes anywhere without telling me!'

'Come on,' Yiannis beckoned Christina. 'We'll have another look in the apartment. She may have left a clue to where she has gone.'

They walked up the narrow alleyway and up the back stairs to Katia's apartment, cupping their hands to their noses to mask the stench from the refuse bins.

Yiannis coughed. 'Don't they ever empty those bins?' .

'The refuse workers have been on strike. Thankfully, they have returned to work today,' Christina mumbled from behind her hand.

Once in the apartment they searched all the rooms.

'All her clothes are still here, her toothbrush, everything. I don't understand it,' Christina said.

Yiannis moved towards the window and watched as the refuse cart trundled noisily up the main road. Two men jumped from the back of the cart, whistling and joking as they walked together towards the alleyway. A few moments later they dragged a large metal bin out onto the main road, ready for emptying. Yiannis watched with distaste as both men, clearly retching at the smell, lifted the lid, and stepped back several paces as a swarm of bluebottles emerged to fill the sky with a great black shadow. Yiannis smiled inwardly - serves them right for going on strike.

There was chaos below, as taverna owners shouted abuse at the refuse workers, whilst running about, swotting the insects that had settled on their customers' food.

Christina balked at the sight of thousands of flies, still feasting on the contents in the bin. They both watched as the bin was moved into position, then as it knocked violently against the refuse cart, the remaining flies lifted like a blanket to reveal the source of their banquet.

'Oh my God,' Yiannis whispered, as he saw a woman's body flop forwards into the refuse cart.

Outside on the street, Yiannis stood ashen faced, comforting Christina, as she sobbed noisily in his arms. He watched numbly as the emergency services wrapped the decaying stinking body of his lovely gentle Katia in a large grey plastic body bag.

Of all the people questioned by the police, no one had seen her with anybody. No one except Katia and Eva knew that the tall blond handsome Englishman had been her very last client.

In a daze of misery, Yiannis made his way back to Poros. He grabbed a bottle of brandy from the shelf at the Athena studio, and drank himself into oblivion.

*

Taylor was at his wit's end trying to find the whereabouts of Laura. He'd called Jack's office every day to try and speak to him, but Jack was working away from the office, and not taking any calls. Pippa in particular was also desperate to speak to her, knowing how much she would need a friend, when something like this happened. In a last ditch attempt, Taylor invited Melanie to dinner, and after a couple of red wines, her tongue loosened and she told him that Jack would be back in the office briefly the next day.

*

When Taylor walked into the office the next day, Melanie buzzed through to Jack's office. 'Mr Ryder I have Mr Taylor Haynes to see you!'

'Tell him to go away. I'm not seeing anyone.'

'Sorry Jack, but I insist,' Taylor said, bursting into his office.

'I'm sorry Mr Ryder, he just pushed past me!' Melanie glared at Taylor.

'Where's Laura?' Taylor said, slamming his hands on Jack's desk.

'That will be all Melanie,' Jack dismissed his angry secretary then looked at Taylor with cold eyes. 'Safe from your family,' he said evenly.

'For Christ's sake Jack, this is me, Taylor! I wouldn't hurt her, you know that.'

'Is that why you told your sadistic brother where she was?'

'I didn't tell him, why would I?'

'Well Slater told Laura that you did, and because of you, he put her life at risk by stopping her giving birth in a hospital. That poor girl went into labour in a locked room, without pain relief or proper medical assistance for over twelve hours until she gave birth. Then, when she lay exhausted in her bed, he took the child from her and threw it in a disused swimming pool!'

'What?' Taylor reached blindly for a chair to sit down. He hung his head in shame, sickened at this revelation.

Jack pursed his lips. 'So, you see why I'm not at liberty to tell you, or any of your family, her whereabouts. I don't think she will ever trust any of you again. I have of course informed the police, regarding Slater's attempted murder of the child. Hopefully they bring him to justice.'

Taylor looked up in dismay. 'I'm deeply grieved at what you've told me. I had no idea what happened, except that the baby had died.' He shuddered involuntarily. 'Please tell Laura how dreadfully sorry I am for my brother's actions. I have disowned him. He is no longer my brother. Tell her that Slater found my discarded luggage label, that's how he knew where she was. I would never have told him.'

'Tut, tut, tut Taylor - as they say carelessness costs lives,' he said stiffly.

Taylor got up wearily. 'Ask her to forgive me Jack, and if she ever needs to contact me…..'

'She won't!' Jack snapped.

Jack watched Taylor leave the room. He would not be telling Laura of his visit.

*

Travis shook Yiannis into consciousness.

Yiannis woke to his misery. 'Travis my friend, leave me be,' he pleaded.

'Drink this.' He pushed a cup of strong coffee under his nose. 'It will sober you up.'

'I'd rather be drunk, it numbs the pain.'

'Drink the coffee,' Travis sighed. 'I know what has happened.

'You don't understand how much it hurts, Travis. I've lost everything now - Laura, my son and Katia. I just want the hurt to go away!'

'I understand more than you think. I too lost a child, not like you though. I wasn't allowed to be a father to her.' He paused reflectively. 'The woman I loved was already married, and rightly or wrongly she decided my daughter should be brought up with her and her husband. They had money, and I was just a young artist, struggling to make ends meet.'

Yiannis sat up to listen. 'How old is she?' he said humbly.

'Oh she's grown up now.' He smiled.

'Do you know where she is?

He scratched his chin. 'Not at the moment, no, but I've seen her occasionally over the years. She doesn't know my identity. I can't tell you how much it pains me to see things happen to her and not be able to help her.'

'Bad things?'

'Sometimes,' he said sadly.

'But if she's a grown woman now, why can't you step forward?'

Travis fell silent and picked at a blob of acrylic paint on his fingernail. 'It would ruin her life. I can't explain further.'

'I'm sorry Travis, I had no idea. To look at you I would have said you haven't a care in the world.'

'That's because I have a very happy face.' He grinned. 'My heart grieves, but my face smiles - life goes on. You have to make the best of it. Believe me Yiannis, even bad luck runs out in the end! You mark my words.'

Yiannis lay back on his bed and thought of Katia and all the hopes and dreams he had shared with her. How she had listened to his troubles and had always been there for him and then to die so horribly. He should have been there to help her. He should have taken her as his wife, when all hope of a relationship with Laura was lost. His heart ached then at the thought of Laura, and how her baby had been killed by Slater because of him. Suddenly his heart turned to ice, and in his mind's eye he could see Slater Haynes with his lovely Katia.

'Oh God Travis, I think I know who killed Katia.'

*

Taylor searched in vain to find Laura. He had an inkling she would be somewhere in Cornwall, and was desperate to find her to make amends for his brother's appalling behaviour. He had even followed Jack home a couple of times, but he never led him to her. Wherever she was, Jack had her well hidden.

Slater had been ostracised from Creek House, not that he wanted to come back. He had settled himself quite comfortably at their holiday home in Rhodes. The Haynes family were divided about the allegations Jack brought against Slater. Taylor and his mother were estranged to him, but Vanessa took an altogether different view of the allegations made against her brother. Even going as far as saying she was proud of him for standing up for himself over Laura's indiscretions.

As the search for Laura became fruitless, Taylor turned his mind to making amends with Yiannis. He'd made enquiries back in June about Yiannis's arrest and imprisonment, and had found to his relief that he had been released without charge. He had written to him via the Post Office at Poros, expressing his regret at what Slater had put him through, but he felt this was not enough, and decided to make the journey to Greece to apologise to him in person.

It was late in November before Taylor managed to make the journey. The sky hung heavy with grey cloud, casting a steely sheen to the surface of the Aegean. He sat down in Alexis Taverna and ordered a coffee.

'Are you here to walk?' Kostas asked inquiringly. 'It's late in the season for holidaymakers.'

Taylor smiled warmly. 'No, I'm looking for someone - Mr Yiannis Kiassos. I believe he lives somewhere around here with his wife and family. Could you give me his address?'

'Who's asking?' Kostas said bluntly

Taylor laughed. 'I am.'

'And who might you be?'

Taylor sighed uneasily. 'My name is Taylor Haynes. Do you know where I can find him?'

'Haynes.' Kostas quirked an eyebrow. 'Well, Mr Haynes, for your information Yiannis isn't married nor has he got a family, and I know *you* are the last person he wants to see. So, I think you had better leave, while you can still walk!' Kostas threatened.

'But it's important that I see him!'

Kostas picked up the coffee cup he had just served Taylor with and placed it on the table behind him. 'I said leave!'

Taylor's face twitched nervously as he glanced at the ferry he had just arrived on. 'But I must see him,' Taylor protested.

'Over my dead body!' Kostas growled.

There was nothing else for it. Taylor picked up his rucksack and began to walk towards the ferry, fully aware he was being escorted from behind. He stopped at the gangplank and turned to address Kostas. 'Will you at least give him a message from me? I'm staying in Athens and he can contact me on…..'

'No!'

44

Yiannis wore his grief like a heavy overcoat. He had informed the police of his suspicions about Katia's death, but as yet Slater had not been brought to justice.

He still fished most mornings - it took his mind off what had happened. Occasionally he stopped at Amora Cove and would walk up to the burnt ruins of the lodge and aimlessly kick about in the charcoal debris. It was on one such day he was rummaging around in what used to be his kitchen, when his foot kicked the metal ring on the cellar trap door. He moved the blackened dust away and lifted the handle. It was more like a cache instead of a cellar, just big enough to house a couple of dozen bottles of wine. Yiannis had used it mainly to keep important documents in, and had forgotten that this was where he placed the ring he'd bought for Laura, before she had fled to England. He knelt down and searched until he found the tiny box. It was charred and reeked of smoke, but otherwise it was intact. With trembling fingers, he opened the lid and nestled deep in the burgundy velvet, the solitaire diamond sparkled back at him. He pushed the boxed ring deep into his trouser pocket and then turned to walk wearily down the beach steps.

*

It was the fourth of May, and Melanie found herself without employment. She had been dating Taylor Haynes for several months now, unbeknownst to her employer Jack Ryder. When he became aware of their relationship she was given two options. Either to end the relationship and continue as receptionist or to leave the establishment forthwith - she took the latter.

Taylor immediately employed her, and now under no obligation to Jack Ryder, she gave Taylor news of Laura Haynes.

*

In early June, Akis stopped Yiannis outside the Post Office. 'Letter from England, Yiannis!' he said, handing him the envelope.

Yiannis scrutinised the English postmark, nodded thankfully, and folded it into the pocket of his shorts. He walked to the harbour edge, jumped in the Moondancer and started the motor, not really knowing where he was going. The postmark troubled him, and he toyed with the idea of ripping the letter up unread, but curiosity got the better of him. He manoeuvred the boat into the tiny cove where he had spent many hours with Laura, settled down on an upturned bucket and ripped open the letter. A pang of disappointment jabbed him when he checked out the signature. Just another letter from Taylor Haynes, expressing his regrets for his brother's action no doubt, he sighed, as he reluctantly skimmed the letter. It read:

'Dear Mr Kiassos,

I have no idea if this letter will reach you, as all my other attempts at contacting you have been in vain. I travelled to Poros in November last year to see you, but was driven away by a well-meaning friend. My reason for visiting you was to apologise and make amends for all the pain and trouble my brother caused you.

My reason for writing now is that I have news of my sister-in-law Laura. I am now led to believe that she is living with Jack Ryder in Botallack, Cornwall. I was dismayed to learn that Jack plans to marry Laura as soon as her divorce is settled. This news troubles me greatly. When I was in Poros, I found out that you are not married as Laura believes. If this is the case, I beseech you to come to England as soon as possible and find her, before it is too late.

Mr Kiassos, I know you have no reason to trust or believe me, but you are her only salvation! She loves you, I know for a fact that she has always loved you, ever since she was a little girl. Please come! I can't bear to see her make another mistake and waste her life on such a man again. I have enclosed the sum of two hundred pounds, an open return air ticket for you, and a single ticket to take Laura

back to Greece. I hope and pray you will go to her. You belong together.
Yours sincerely,
Taylor Haynes.'

Yiannis inspected the plane ticket and the money enclosed in a separate envelope, felt for the trinket box still nestled in his pocket, folded the letter, picked up his fishing lines, and pushed the boat out into the water.

*

The weather in Cornwall was extremely hot for June. Pink Thrift blossomed profusely amongst the bright yellow gorse bushes on the cliffs high above the wild Atlantic, and a lone cuckoo could be heard in the stillness of the afternoon far across the fields towards Pendeen.

Since settling with Laura and her baby in a cottage near Botallack, Cornwall, Jack Ryder had commuted to work by car to Truro. The commute made it a long day, but Jack didn't seem to mind. As long as he had Laura to come home to, he would have travelled to the moon and back every day. Laura had been with him for almost a year now and her son Yiannis, or Ian as Jack insisted on calling him, was about to celebrate his first birthday.

When Jack arrived home one evening with an early birthday present for the little one, he noticed Laura had set the table with flowers and candles. 'What's this then, are we having an early birthday party?'

'No this is just for you and me,' Laura said happily, passing him a gin and tonic.

Jack raised his eyebrows. 'Mmm this is a treat. Where is Ian?' he said, looking around for the child.

Laura bristled slightly at Jack's insistence of calling Yiannis, Ian. 'In bed, I've managed to keep him awake all day so that he will sleep tonight and let us have a civilised meal without interruptions.'

Jack smiled warmly and kissed her on the cheek. 'Something smells good!' he said, sniffing the air.

'I've made something special for you, it won't be long,' she said as she vanished into the kitchen.

Ten minutes later they sat down to their meal and Laura raised her glass of white wine. 'A toast!' she said.

'To what?' he enquired.

'To you - for all you have done for us over the last year.'

'The pleasure is *all* mine!' he answered, chinking his glass on hers. 'I can't believe it's a year. Doesn't time fly when you're enjoying yourself?'

She smiled at him. 'I don't know what I would have done without you. I can never repay you.'

He looked seriously at her. 'Yes you can. You can marry me and make me the happiest man on earth.'

'I am still married remember? You said yourself that Slater is adamant that he will not agree to a divorce. I can't understand it. The man hates me as much as I hate him!'

'Things may alter in the next few months,' he said, casually topping up her glass of wine. He knew full well that Slater was waiting until her inheritance came through on her twenty-first birthday.

'How come?'

He shrugged his shoulders and gave a wide grin. 'It's just a feeling.'

Her face lit up.

Jack put the bottle down and gazed at her. 'Very soon you'll be free to marry again. I promise,' he said, gently lifting her chin to kiss her lightly on the lips.

She closed her eyes. It felt strange being kissed after so long - not unpleasant, just strange. He kissed her again, then pulled her to him and held her close. 'Oh Laura, I've wanted to kiss you for so long,' he whispered in her ear. He held her for a long time, almost too frightened to let her go. 'I love you Laura. I love you and I'm in love with you. I always have been, you know that,' he murmured. 'I wish you could love me the same way.'

'Jack, I...'

'Don't say anything. I know that you love me, just not in the same way as I love you.'

'Jack, please?' she said awkwardly.

'Sorry, I'm pushing you again aren't I?' He released her from his hold. 'We'll take things slowly and see how it goes from here,' he said hopefully.

Please don't depend on it, she thought to herself.

He woke her the next morning with a kiss and cup of tea and set off to work.

She rose, dressed, and lost count of the number of times she sighed. The day was grey and misty and seemed to match Laura's mood exactly. She looked around at her surroundings. The house was perfect, she was in a beautiful part of the country, she was safe, had a stable, happy child, and a man that loved her unequivocally. What more could she want? She looked around again at the beautiful things that made this house a home, but material things in life didn't really matter to her. All she really craved was love, the passionate love she had shared and lost with Yiannis. Once you had experienced pure love, with someone you truly adore, nothing would ever come close to matching that.

She looked wistfully down at her child. It was little Yiannis's first birthday, and the child had been grouchy all day and had fallen into a fitful sleep just as Jack arrived home.

He presented her with a large bunch of white lilies and kissed her warmly on the lips. 'Where's the birthday boy?' he asked, placing several boxed presents on the hall table.

'Not in the mood to celebrate I'm afraid. I think he is cutting more teeth!' Laura explained. 'I've been so busy with him all day, I'm afraid I haven't made dinner yet!'

The child woke and began to scream and they both exchanged a weary smile. 'You go and get him and I'll make us something to eat,' Jack said. 'Then he can open his birthday presents.'

Jack had bought the boy everything a one-year-old

could possibly want - far too much in Laura's opinion. In fact he only played with the wrapping paper for a couple of minutes before he became grouchy again.

'He's tired,' Laura said, scooping the fretful child into her arms.

He touched her arm. 'Have you thought any more about what we spoke about last night?'

'As I said, I've been busy all day,' she answered, swiftly running up the stairs.

Jack sighed and watched her go, then went about picking up discarded wrapping paper.

The next morning the mist had cleared and the sun blazed down on Laura and her son as they sat on the blanket in the middle of the front lawn. The air was filled with the heady scent of honeysuckle. Little Yiannis stood unsteadily before her as she pulled his T-shirt down and brushed the grass from his shorts. When satisfied with his appearance, she kissed him softly on the cheek, turned him round and patted him gently on the bottom. She watched as he crawled away from her. He stopped to pick a daisy from the lawn, and pushed it into his mouth.

'No darling, don't eat that!' She picked the petals out of his mouth while he blew raspberries at her. A butterfly caught his attention as it fluttered in the buddleia bush. He pointed and mouthed the word, 'Ah.'

'Yes darling, it's a butterfly,' she answered.

He looked back at the bush and crawled towards it as it took flight. 'Ah,' he said pointing to the bush.

The sun made his dark glossy hair shine. It was really long again and needed cutting. She couldn't believe how quickly it grew. She thought of the first locks she had cut off and placed in a tiny silver trinket box. She wished with all her heart that she could keep everything about him in a tiny box, so she could keep him a baby. She marvelled at this little person who brought such joy to her sad, strange life. Each day she could see a little more of Yiannis in the child, and her heart would ache. It ached for the child who would never know his father, and it ached for herself because she knew she would never again feel the pure and perfect love that this little boy had been conceived with.

Laura lay back on the blanket and closed her eyes for a second as the child cooed and rasped noisily beside her. The sun was hot on her skin, and as she reached for her hat to fan herself, a shadow fell across her face. She lifted her hand to shade her eyes and tried to make out the dark figure obscuring the sun. In a panic she sat up, just as the child was crawling towards the figure. 'Darling, come back to mama!' she said, standing up and brushing the grass from her skirt. By the time she had reached the child, he was at the feet of the stranger. She looked up at the tall, handsome man and her heart leapt. For one long minute she could not speak and her breathing became so shallow, she thought she would faint.

'Hello Laura.' She looked at him dumbstruck. 'Laura, speak to me?' Yiannis pleaded.

Eventually she shook her head and said, 'I can't believe my eyes! How did you find me?'

His mouth twisted into a smile. 'With great difficulty!'

'Ah.' The child gurgled and tugged at Laura's skirt, and they both looked down at him.

Yiannis bent down to pick him up and Laura bit her lip as Yiannis looked the boy full in the face. The strawberry mark under his right eye said it all.

'Oh my God Laura,' Yiannis gasped in astonishment. 'My son?'

Her silence spoke volumes as her eyes filled with tears. She nodded.

'How can it be, I don't understand. I heard that... Hell Laura, why didn't you tell me, why didn't you write to me about him?'

'What difference would it have made?' she brushed away her tears. 'You obviously have no regard for your other family. Why should this one make any difference!' she snapped, hating herself for her cruel words.

'You're mistaken Laura. I don't have another family,' he said softly.

She shook her head angrily. 'Please don't lie to me anymore. I saw Stephano with my own eyes. I spoke to him. You should have told me Yiannis. Why did you let me let me find out from your son?'

The child began to cry in Yiannis's arms and reached for the comfort of his mother. As he passed him over to her he said, 'You ran away from me before I could explain. You keep running away from me!' he said in desperation. 'Laura come, sit down, I have a long story to tell you.'

Reluctantly she followed him to the blanket on the lawn. There she sat in silence in the warm afternoon sun, her son close by her, while Yiannis told her about Eva and her lies. About Slater burning the lodge down, and telling him that his son was dead. He spoke about his false imprisonment, and how he had been frightened for Laura's life. The only bit he missed out was Katia's death. He would explain that when they finally arrested Slater.

Laura listened intently, shaking her head in disbelief. 'Oh Yiannis, I've put you through so much pain, I'm so sorry,' she said desperately.

Yiannis shook his head. 'It doesn't matter, as long as you are okay.'

'But if I had just waited, none of this would have happened.'

'Perhaps I would have done the same in your shoes.'

'No you wouldn't Yian. You're full of kindness. You don't judge me like I judge you.'

He put his fingers gently to her lips. 'It doesn't matter.' He reached down for her hand and gazed into her eyes. 'I never thought I would see you again.'

'Nor I you,' she said, letting him kiss her hand.

He looked at the boy who had fallen asleep on his mother's lap. 'Our son!'

Laura nodded. 'He is beautiful, isn't he?' she said, stroking the child's head.

'Just like his mama,' Yiannis answered as he cupped Laura's face gently. 'I was so worried about you sweetheart while I was in prison. Kostas phoned Jack Ryder but he wouldn't return his calls. It was Jack's secretary who finally said you were okay, and then Taylor Haynes wrote to me to confirm it.'

'Taylor wrote to you?'

'Oh yes, if it hadn't been for him, I would never have found you.'

Suddenly terrified she said, 'You mean to tell me the Haynes's know where I am?'

'Only Taylor. He sent me the air ticket and money to come and find you. He thought we should be together!'

'Did he?' she said thoughtfully. 'And you say Jack wouldn't help you?'

'Well, he wouldn't return the calls,' Yiannis said, watching Laura's countenance.

She was visibly angry as she tossed his words about in her head.

Suddenly Yiannis stood up. 'Come on, it doesn't matter now. Are you going to show me around?'

They walked down the lane to the coast, taking turns holding the boy. Once on the coast path they veered right and walked down towards Crown Mines perched precariously on the cliff edge. There they stood against the wall and looked out towards Cape Cornwall, as the sun shimmered across the sea in spangles of silver lights.

'Doesn't it look wonderful Yian?'

'Yes, and very cold!'

'That's all part of its beauty. It's wild and passionate.'

Yiannis grinned. 'Just like me!'

Laura laughed and kissed him tenderly on the cheek.

'Zennor is over there Yiannis - isn't that where your mother came from?' Laura pointed to her right.

He nodded. 'I was there yesterday. It was very beautiful!'

'Yesterday? How long have you been in Cornwall?'

'Not long, two days. I came here yesterday evening, but I could see Ryder with you,' he said casually. 'I wanted to speak to you alone. I am staying at the taverna up the road.'

Laura smiled to herself. She didn't suppose 'The Queens Arms' at Botallack had ever been called a taverna before.

He put his arms around her shoulders and held her tightly. 'Now I've found you, I'm not going to let you go again,' he said firmly.

45

When he arrived home that evening from work, Jack found the happy trio playing together on the rug. He froze instantly at the sight of Yiannis in his sitting room.

Both Laura and Yiannis stood as he entered the room. 'Jack I…' she began.

'Kiassos!' he said coldly. He glanced at Laura, visibly irate at the scene before him. 'This is a surprise. What brings you to this part of the world? As if I didn't know,' he growled. He shot a damning look at Laura. 'Did you tell him where we were?'

'Of course not!' Laura flushed angrily.

Jack pursed his lips - as bile rose in his throat. 'I don't believe you.'

Laura blanched with indignation.

'After all I have done for you, to keep you safe from these…' - he looked angrily at Yiannis - '….these unsavoury characters you seem to attract. Now you go and repay me like this! I just don't understand you.'

'I said I did not tell him!'

'Then how?' he shouted.

Yiannis squared up to Jack. 'I found out from Taylor Haynes.'

Jack laughed without humour. 'No you didn't.' The tone of Jack's voice turned to sarcasm. 'You're a liar Kiassos. Nobody knew we were here.'

'Jack!' Laura scolded. 'Don't be so rude!'

He turned to Laura and shook his head. 'How could you?'

Little Yiannis began to whimper, reaching up to Laura's skirts to be comforted. She pulled him into her arms and covered his ears. 'Jack stop this at once,' she hissed, 'You're frightening the boy. I have told you, this is as much as a surprise for me as it is for you.'

'Here,' Yiannis pushed Taylor's letter towards Jack.

He snatched it from his hands and scanned the letter. As he did, Laura saw his shoulders visibly droop.

'You're surprised to see me in more ways than one Mr Ryder?' Yiannis said stiffly. 'Maybe you thought I should still be detained in a Greek prison?'

Jack's face coloured at his accusation. 'I have better things to do with my time than deal with criminals.' He moved to touch Laura and felt her shrink from his fingers. At this inopportune time, an unpleasant smell filled the room, as the little boy smiled and filled his nappy. Reluctant to leave the two men together, Laura had no option but to dash out of the room and up the staircase to see to the child. Yiannis stared at the door Laura had just gone through, wanting to follow her, but conscious that this was Jack's house.

Jack's eyes narrowed. 'I think it would be better if you leave now.'

Yiannis remained where he stood.

Softening his voice he said, 'She's mine now Kiassos. I suggest you let her go. She has suffered enough! They are happy here with me.'

'The child is mine you know? They both belong with me!' he said calmly.

'Ah yes, but you let her down, didn't you?'

He fixed Jack with a steely gaze. 'I did not let her down. It was all a misunderstanding. I have told Laura what happened and she believes me. That's all that matters.'

Jack sighed impatiently. 'For God's sake, be reasonable man. What can you offer them? You have no home now or so I understand. No real work and no money.'

'I love her!' Yiannis said passionately.

'As do I, and we are to be married,' Jack retorted.

They squared each other up for a good few seconds, until a cry from the child broke the silence.

Exasperated, Jack said, 'Look, please leave. I am needed elsewhere.'

Yiannis picked up his rucksack. 'They belong with me,'

he said defiantly as he walked out of the front door.

Jack was sick to the stomach as he watched him leave. He had won this battle but he knew in his heart he would have to work hard to win the war. The child cried again and Jack ran upstairs. He called out for Laura, but she was nowhere to be found. 'Oops a daisy,' he said, as he lifted the boy from his playpen. 'My you smell a deal sweeter then you did a few minutes ago. Come on, let's go find mummy.'

*

Whilst Yiannis and Jack argued, Laura slipped quietly out of the back door. With mixed emotions, she ran as fast as she could down the rubble path towards the coast. As she turned down to the Crown Mines she stumbled and fell, grazing her knee on a rock. She sat on the grassy earth, surrounded by tufts of pink thrift. Her long blonde hair, wild and dishevelled, blew about in the strong warm south-westerly wind, as she dropped her head into her hands and sobbed. Her mind was in turmoil. Her head told her she must stay with Jack. He had been so kind and done so much for her, but oh, her heart, her poor bruised heart was telling her a very different story.

*

It was nine-thirty that evening when Laura finally returned home. She walked wearily down the hall and into the sitting room where Jack was waiting.

Angry but relieved she had returned to him he snapped, 'Where the hell have you been? I've been so worried.' He noticed how tired and drawn she looked and that she had been crying.

'I'm sorry - I needed to walk for a while.'

'On the coast, at night, are you insane? You could have fallen down a mine shaft!'

She flashed her eyes angrily. 'I said I was sorry!' She walked to the window and looked out for a few seconds, trying to make out the outline of the garden in the twilight. She sighed heavily, and then turned to face Jack. 'Is

Yiannis all right?' she enquired.

'To which Yiannis are you referring?' he answered caustically. 'If it's the child you mean, he went to sleep an hour ago crying for his mother.'

She nodded miserably.

'Laura we need to talk.'

She looked at him sadly.

'You still love him, don't you?'

She hesitated a little too long for his liking.

'You do don't you? Answer me truthfully.'

She could feel her own heartbeat thumping. 'I don't know what I feel, except perhaps very confused,' she said fiercely.

Jack flung his arms in the air and paced about the room. 'I don't believe you sometimes. This is the same man who failed to tell you about the wife he already had, the same one who broke your heart and got you into all this trouble.'

'Yes I know, but he's explained all that, it was all a misunderstanding.'

'Oh! So now what? He breezes back into your life, and all I have done for you is just swept aside, is that it?'

'No, I don't know. Please Jack this has been such a shock, can we just leave it for tonight?' she said desperately.

'No Laura, we can't leave it. I must know where I stand with you!' he insisted.

'I'm still here aren't I?' she said, more harshly than she had meant it to sound.

His face paled and the hurt showed tragically in his eyes. With the tone of her voice still ringing in his head, he said quietly, 'I'm going to bed.'

Laura sat for a couple of hours in the window seat, staring out at the moon. Eventually she tiptoed upstairs, checked on little Yiannis, and then lay fully dressed on top of her bed covers.

In his own bed, Jack's mind would not let him sleep.

He pushed the sheets away and moved with stealth to her bedroom door. From there he watched over Laura for a long while. From the light of the moon filtering through the open curtains, he could see that she too did not close her eyes for sleep. She lay on her back and stared at the ceiling, and every now and then, he saw her move to wipe her eyes. When fatigue overtook him, he returned to his own bed, but when he woke in the early hours, he checked on her again, only to find she had gone. His heart dropped as he moved swiftly and apprehensively along the landing towards the nursery, relaxing with relief when he saw her sitting there. She had moved the rocking chair to face the window and was gazing out to sea. Quietly, he stood and watched her from the doorway as she hummed softly to herself. At the end of her tune, she sat in silence for a few seconds then her whole body shuddered. He turned away, walked despondently back to his room and climbed back into his lonely bed. A few minutes later he heard her footsteps on the stairs and the back door close quietly. He didn't follow her. He knew there would be no point.

Outside under the cover of darkness, she leant against the granite stone ruins of a tin mine and took a deep breath. It felt good to be out of the house - the walls had been closing in around her. Out here she could think more clearly. She shivered with the chill night air and pulled her coat tight about her. The wispy dark clouds moved slowly away, to reveal the pale yellow moon. The same moon she had danced under now shimmered across a cold dark sea. She felt sick to the heart for hurting Jack. She could never fall in love with him, she knew that. She felt so wretched, how could she be so heartless. He didn't deserve this. He had been so good to them. So kind, considerate, and loving, and she had been safe with him. 'Safe,' she laughed as she spoke aloud. What happiness is there in being safe? Could she really live the rest of her life with someone she just felt safe with? Could she really marry someone she didn't love when she knew Yiannis was somewhere in the world? 'Oh God, what am I going to do?' she shouted aloud. The suddenness of her voice sent seabirds crying and flapping into the air.

'I think you must follow your heart,' said a familiar voice.

Her scalp prickled as she spun round. 'Who's there? Who spoke?'

A figure came out from behind the old tin mine engine house and the moon filtered down to reveal his face.

'Yian! I thought you had gone!' she cried.

'I'm not leaving without you Laura.' He pulled her towards him. 'I'm not losing you again.'

Laura sank her head in her hands. 'But what about Jack?' she cried. 'I feel an obligation to him. He took us in, hid me from Slater, and kept us safe.'

Yiannis cupped her hands in his hands. 'What about me? I've waited years for you. We have a son and I love you Laura,' he said, covering her face with tender kisses.

His touch made her shiver with anticipation. 'Yiannis, my Yiannis,' she whispered, as she slipped her hands gently under his shirt and ran her cool fingers across his warm lean body. It felt so good to be close to him again.

He quickly shrugged off his jacket and placed it on the ground for them to lie on. 'I never dreamt I would hold you in my arms again,' he said, sensually covering her face in soft feathery kisses.

She returned his kisses with passion, and whispered the words he thought he would never hear again. 'I love you too, my darling Yian,' she said.

Afterwards they held each other as though their life depended on it. Neither wanted to move away from what they had found again. It was only when the air turned icy cold did they realise a huge bank of sea mist was rolling in onshore.

'We must get off the coast path before it comes,' Laura said, scrambling to her feet. They made their way across the rubble of the ruined mine, as the great bank of fog gained momentum and engulfed them. Soon they couldn't see where they were going. The lighthouse at Pendeen a couple of miles down the coast sounded its fog horn, which gave Laura an indication of their bearings. 'I think we are nearly on the top road,' Laura said, pulling Yiannis by the hand. Suddenly she stopped to listen. Beads of moisture ran down her face, and her hair hung uncomfortably damp down her back.

'What is it?' Yiannis asked.

'I thought I heard someone calling,' she whispered.

'Laura.' The voice filtered through the fog.

'It's Jack!' she whispered.

The outline of his figure came into view. 'Laura, there you are. What the devil are you doing out here. I've been out of my mind with worry since I heard the fog horn sound. Come on back to the house at once, you're wet through.'

Laura glanced around nervously for Yiannis, but he had gone.

*

Although reluctant, Jack forced himself to go to work that week. Laura had been in a happier, albeit quiet mood, since the night of the fog and he decided that she must have just needed time to think things through. Thankfully for Jack there had also been no sign of Kiassos, so he truly believed that life had begun to return to normality.

'Laura, I've been thinking,' he said, as he finished his breakfast.

Laura took a bite of toast and looked attentively at him.

'I know how much you like it here, so I've decided to put in an offer for the house, so we can spend the rest of our lives here.'

'Jack, I really don't think..'

He saw the flicker of alarm cross her face. 'No!' He held his hand up to silence her. 'Just think about it, okay?' He smiled happily. 'This will be the start of a new life for us all - something solid to build on.' He kissed her on the cheek, picked up his coat and briefcase and left.

*

Jack arrived home at six-thirty that evening, confidently clutching a bouquet of flowers in one hand and a bottle of champagne in the other. He had done the deal and put an offer in on the house. Knowing how much she liked this house, he was confident she would never want to leave, once she owned it. He walked through the front door into the long entrance hall.

'Laura, I'm home.' He placed the flowers and champagne on the hall table while he struggled out of his jacket, then gathered them up again and breezed into the kitchen. It took him a few seconds before he realised there was no smell of cooking, no usual childish noises coming from the parlour, and the house had an uneasy stillness, as though it had been burgled and was waiting to be discovered. 'Laura, where are you?' he said, placing the flowers on the kitchen table. He took the stairs two at a time, the bottle still firmly clutched in his hand. The beds were made and the room was unusually tidy. He declined to look in the wardrobe for fear of finding it empty, instead he went back down the stairs and out of the front door. He placed the champagne on the outside windowsill and stood out in the lane, first looking up then down.

'Evening Mr Ryder.'

Jack spun around. 'Oh, good evening Mrs Pasco. You haven't seen Laura have you?'

'Not since this morn when she got into the taxi.'

'Taxi?' His heart sank.

She nodded. 'Her and the little one and the foreign gentleman, 'twas about ten o clock I think. They've not come back yet?'

Jack was momentarily speechless. 'With a foreign gentleman you say?'

'Aye, 'twas the same one she been with these past few days.' She screwed her nose up and smiled. 'Sightseeing I expect. They've been doing a lot of that.' She paused for a moment to examine Jack's expression, before saying, 'Charlie Drago said they were over at Sennen the other day. Then my husband, Zak, spotted them, didn't you Zak? Over yon they were, having a picnic overlooking the cape.'

Zak moved to his wife's side, lifted his hat slightly with his fingers, and scratched his head. He had actually seen them having more than a picnic, not that he had told his gossiping wife that. He had been clearing the path, just below where they were yesterday lunchtime, when he had stumbled across them. He'd seen the boy first, curled up asleep on the grassy bank, and then he noticed the couple. In all the twenty-six years of married life, his wife had never looked at him like Laura had looked at her gentleman friend.

'They have probably just gone further afield today,' Mrs Pasco said. 'Nice gentleman that foreigner - Greek I think, 'andsome as well. He's been staying at the Queens Arms. Been frozen stiff in the evenings the landlady said! Been huddled round the fire to keep warm - I reckon he finds the climate a mite chillier than Greece. Staying long is he?'

'Not sure,' Jack said, collecting his thoughts. 'Please excuse me.'

Mrs Pasco nodded, and then watched as he marched up the lane in the direction of the Queens Arms.

46

The intercom crackled and the seat belt signs illuminated as the stewardess told them first in Greek, then in perfect English, that they would be landing shortly at Athens airport. The local time was ten-fifty a.m. she added, and the weather was fine with a temperature of ninety-eight degrees.

It grieved her the way she had left Jack, but there was just no other option. She loved Yiannis, and felt it only right that her child should live with his natural father. She thought of the heartfelt letter she'd left Jack and envisaged him finding it on the mantelpiece. Even though the letter thanked him profusely for his love and kindness, she knew her leaving would wound him deeply

Laura glanced out of the aircraft window. Below, swathed under a gossamer veil of shimmering heat, lay a beautiful array of vividly coloured boats, bobbing lazily in the sweltering port of Piraeus. As the aircraft began to circle, little Yiannis began to cry. The poor child had been desperately airsick throughout the flight. Yiannis took him from Laura's arms and held him tight to his chest, softly smoothing his dark glossy baby curls. Laura's eyes swam with happiness at the sight of them reunited. From the window, the Aegean ocean disappeared from view, and in its place the mountainous region of Athens, ravaged and scorched by the relentless sun, stretched extensively before her with biblical austerity. They were home.

The blast of hot air as the plane door opened at Athens airport caught Laura unawares. Suddenly her dress was soaked in perspiration and her hair prickled as sweat trickled uncomfortably down her neck. Yiannis however, seemed unaffected by the heat, as he cautiously descended the aeroplane steps with his precious son in his arms.

The journey to Piraeus was almost unbearable. The taxi smelt of sweat and stale tobacco, and everything Laura touched felt sticky. She had completely forgotten how desperately hot Greece could be in the summer.

Yiannis glanced at Laura. 'Are you all right?'

She nodded. 'I worry about little Yiannis in this heat though.'

Yiannis squeezed her hand tightly. 'Our son has Greek blood, he'll be fine.'

At Zea's marina, they relaxed in a taverna, under the shade of a candy striped awning. Little Yiannis fell asleep as Laura and Yiannis shared a cool glass of ouzo and a seafood platter. Two hours later, they wearily boarded the Flying Dolphin for the final stage of their journey back to Poros.

Alexis and Kostas stood with their tea towels over their shoulders, ready to welcome the influx of visitors to their taverna, but when they saw Yiannis and Laura their customers were forgotten, as they rushed to welcome them home.

*

From the balcony of the Ice Palace, Eva Barzini clenched her teeth at the scene unfolding before her. Her hands balled into fists as she pondered her next move.

*

Sarah Haynes sat quietly on the lichen covered seat on Gweek green, contemplating the letter she'd received that morning from Ashborne, Ryder and Bains solicitors.

Several artists shared the green with her, all busy painting or holding up their brushes to get the correct angle of their subject. The Gweek Quay boatyard was quiet in the hot afternoon sun, and the tide, full when she had seated herself, now ebbed slowly back across the mud flats. It had been a year since her husband Gerald had died, but it was not only him she grieved for that day. The letter she'd received that morning had sparked memories of nights long forgotten when life had been fun and filled with passion. Her reverie was broken when Pippa appeared at her side.

'Hello Mrs Haynes. Mind if I join you? It's too hot to sit inside today, so I thought I would bring my lunch over here. You never know, I might get my portrait painted at the same time.' She nodded towards the artists.

'I would welcome the company,' Sarah smiled, patting the seat beside her. 'So how are you?'

'I'm good thanks.'

'Any plans to go back to Dubai?'

'No, I'm really happy working in the boatyard for now. My wanderlust days are over for the time being,' she said with a satisfied sigh. She offered up her box of sandwiches to Sarah, who declined.

Silence ensued for a few moments. Then they both spoke together. 'Sorry Pippa, you were saying?'

'No, you first.'

'I was going to ask if you had heard from Laura.'

'I have yes,' Pippa answered awkwardly.

Sarah looked directly at her and she asked, 'Is she well?'

Pippa nodded slowly.

'And the child?'

Pippa nodded again.

Sarah looked wistfully down the river. An egret had landed, spooking a pair of swans in its wake. 'I was so relieved to find that the child had survived, but I will never forgive Slater for what he did though.' She looked back at Pippa who had stopped chewing her sandwich. 'I don't blame her for finding solace in another man's arms you know. God knows Slater must have driven her to it with his behaviour.' She laid her hands on her lap. 'I was rather looking forward to being a grandmother. When you speak to her next, tell her I understand and that I miss her.' Sarah stood up and smoothed down her summer dress.

'I'll tell her Mrs Haynes, I'll tell her.'

As Sarah walked away from the centre of the village, she felt relief and sadness in equal measure. The letter she'd received today would alter life as she knew it. Questions would be asked and hearts would be broken.

Oh what a tangled web we weave, as they say. Some serious thinking time and a small village in the Portuguese mountains of Monchique beckoned, where she also had a few bridges to build on behalf of her errant son.

*

By mutual decision Laura and Yiannis decided not to live at Villa Amora. The horror of Laura's time there with Slater and happy memories of Yiannis, evoked mixed emotions. In truth she was scared of its isolation. She didn't trust Slater to stay away. After hearing about his last visit to the island, she knew he would stop at nothing until his revenge was complete. So it was decided that they all move back into the Athena.

Travis more than welcomed them into what had become his home for the last few years. He doted on little Yiannis and was immensely kind to Laura, and Laura in turn quickly became very fond of Travis.

'I have heard so much about you Travis,' she'd said, when they first arrived. 'I feel as though I know you already.' After seeing one of his many paintings, and noting the inscription, she'd looked puzzled. 'But I know this style of painting! You're the artist TR!'

He'd bowed gallantly. 'At your service ma'am.'

'I worked at your gallery but I never saw you,' she'd said flabbergasted.

'Well, I'm a bit of a recluse,' he'd winked. 'Like to keep myself to myself you know.'

'But, I am sure I have seen you before. Have we met already?' she'd asked earnestly.

Travis had glanced surreptitiously at Yiannis. 'Perhaps, we may have met when you were younger.'

Their first couple of weeks back on the island were idyllic. Days spent catching up with old friends, and picnics in secluded coves.

Yiannis taught his son to swim in the clear warm waters of the Aegean. Soon his little body turned nut brown and they could hardly keep him out of the water. Now more than ever Yiannis felt the need to get the Athena Taverna back in business. He had a family now and no other means to support them. The small retainer Laura received only just tied them over, so Laura had decided to sell the house in Gweek. The money from that, coupled with what Yiannis had saved, should set them up on their new life together.

Once settled, Laura wrote to Taylor, thanking him for instigating her reunion with Yiannis. She also offered an invite to visit, offering Villa Amora for as long as he wanted. It was to be Laura's twenty-first birthday at the beginning of September, and as she and Taylor shared the same birthday, she thought it would be wonderful to celebrate together in the warm Greek sunshine. Taylor needed no encouragement, and he and Melanie arrived in the middle of August for a two week holiday.

The day before their birthdays, during lunch at Alexis Taverna, Akis Petro delivered telegrams to both Laura and Taylor.

Laura furrowed her brow. 'It's from Ashborne, Ryder and Bains solicitors in Truro. Apparently they are sending representatives over, and request that I attend my father's Will reading in Athens at eleven-thirty a.m. tomorrow. Oh no, I hope they aren't sending Jack!'

Yiannis placed a comforting hand over hers.

'How strange, Daddy's been dead these past thirteen years! Damn it,' she threw the telegram on the table, 'this is going to spoil all our plans.'

Taylor read his telegram. 'The strange thing is they've requested that I attend too. Why would they do that?' he puzzled.

Laura pulled a face. 'Maybe to represent your family, after all your mum and dad acted as loco parentis. You would have thought they would have asked your mum though, wouldn't you? Laura sighed wearily. 'Do we have to go?'

'I'm sorry Laura. I think we have to attend. But don't

worry, we should be back here by mid afternoon,' he added.

*

Eva listened intently to the conversation below. She picked up some loose coins and made her way to the phone box in the Post Office and dialled a number in Rhodes.

*

Jack glanced nervously out of the aircraft window. As the aircraft began to circle, he squeezed his eyes shut. He was desperately airsick, and swallowed hard to stop the nausea rising from his stomach. When he opened his eyes a moment later, the Aegean ocean had disappeared, and the scorched earth of Athens and its surrounding areas came into view.

'Bloody God forsaken place!' he muttered, leaning wearily back into his seat.

Next to him, his colleague Arthur Bains raised an eyebrow.

Jack had no idea what this meeting was about. Arthur would only say it was a reading of a codicil of Stephen Tempest's Will. Irritated beyond belief, because he'd always represented the Tempest family, he should have known what was written in the codicil. He was told by Arthur, that because of his strong attachment to Laura Tempest, which had gone back a long time, he added, it was decided that Jack was not to be party to its contents.

The intercom crackled and the seat belt signs illuminated. Jack closed his eyes and gripped the armrest. He hated flying, but especially hated landing. He felt himself start to perspire. He switched his thoughts to Laura. He didn't want to be on this plane today. He certainly didn't want to be reacquainted with Laura and the romantic entanglements that still haunted him. He stared absently out of the plane window. Just the thought of Laura evoked a pain deep in his heart. 'Damn the woman!' he said sotto voce. He had given her everything she could possibly want, and she'd thrown it back in his face and betrayed him.

He felt the thud of the undercarriage drop, tightened his grip on the armrest and prayed silently as the ground raced upwards to meet them.

A blast of hot dusty air hit him as he stepped out of the jet. He glanced nonchalantly at the sparkling Aegean to one side and Mount Hymettos on the other, then at his watch to confirm the time.

*

Taylor had hired a speed boat to take Laura and himself to Piraeus. They now sat in a small law office in the centre of Athens, awaiting two associates of Ashborne, Ryder and Bains solicitors.

They sat quietly together hand in hand in the musty office as Laura surveyed her surroundings. The lopsided bookshelves on the wall behind the desk housed a dusty collection of law books, and the filing cabinet to her left was piled high with files, probably from clients long since divorced or dead.

'What a strange place to celebrate our birthdays,' she whispered. 'I wish they would hurry and get here, I'm so looking forward to our party this afternoon.'

Taylor squeezed her hand. 'Shouldn't be long now, I think I can hear them coming.'

They both looked up when the door opened and Laura blanched as Slater entered the room, swiftly followed by Jack Ryder. Laura began to tremble uncontrollably.

'What the hell are you doing here Slater?' Taylor knocked his chair over as he stood up.

'Sit down and shut up dear brother. As *her* husband, I'm entitled to be here, isn't that so Jack,' he sneered.

Jack mouthed an apology to Laura, who, though visibly shaken, managed to flash him a look of utter disbelief.

It took great effort for Jack to speak to Laura, but he knew he had to explain. 'I didn't bring him. He was outside when we arrived.'

Slater settled on the chair next to the window, folded

his arms and stared intently at Laura.

Taylor sat and reached for Laura's hand for comfort, which made Slater laugh at the gesture.

'And how is my darling whore of a wife? Have you given birth to any more bastards recently?'

'Shut up Slater for Christ's sake,' Jack snapped, shifting uncomfortably in his seat.

The door suddenly opened and a small podgy man entered the room, holding a white handkerchief to his red bulbous nose. He nodded a cool acknowledgement to his fellow colleague Jack, and glanced around the room. 'Oh good, good, you are all here, please be seated,' said Arthur Bains to the already seated group.

He pushed his rounded belly around the back of the desk and settled himself on a deep-buttoned green leather chair. 'Good, good,' he said to himself, as he shuffled the papers retrieved from his attaché case onto the desk.

He looked up at the group, smiled broadly at them all, took a deep breath and began to read: *I Stephen Tempest, a citizen and resident of the United Kingdom, being of sound mind and body, do hereby make, publish and declare this my last Will and Testament, hereby revoking all other Wills I have formally made.*

'This was dated the third of January 1974, two months before his untimely death.' He addressed Laura sympathetically.

..and declare my last Will and Testament…etc, etc. He repeated as Slater sighed noisily. *I devise and bequeath my estate as follows. According to the rules that were laid down by my father's father, the estate, consisting of High Top House, Gweek, United Kingdom, three hundred acres on the island of Poros, upon which the Villa Amora stands, sixteen businesses in the harbour of Poros and any monies due and saved will be divided as such.*

To my first born, I declare that on September the 1st in the year nineteen ninety two, all real estate on the island of Poros plus a sum of one million pounds will be deposited into their bank account.

Mr Bains looked up at the group as though to ask if that had been understood but received no response, other than Slater's face which held a wide smile. He sighed and said, 'Good, good. Now, attached to this Will is a codicil for Laura, with a request that I read to you.'

To Laura, It is with great sorrow that I find I must write this letter, but medical reports confirm I have a brain tumour and have now approximately three months to live. I now find myself with the awful task of getting my affairs in order and tying up loose ends. You may or may not be aware that the Tempest family estate, namely the house in Gweek, which will have been given to you already, Villa Amora, land and sixteen other buildings on the Greek Island of Poros, has been handed down the generations. If the executor has read out the first part of my Will and Testament you may now be aware that a substantial amount of money should be due to you payable on the day you become twenty-one. It is with great sadness that I must now tell you that you are not my biological daughter, and therefore will not collect the inheritance. Blood tests at your birth confirmed that I was not your father, and because you could not possibly take the blame for your mother's indiscretions, I accepted you into my home and brought you up as my own. I hope you have never wanted for anything.

I trust now your real father has made his way in life sufficiently to take over his duties and accept his responsibilities, though I feel sure he has kept his distance until now, in case he, like your mother, thought me ignorant of the true facts of your conception.

A gasp of disbelief followed by an angry eruption as Slater hurled towards the desk. 'What the hell are you saying?' he said, slamming his hands on the desktop. 'This is a set up, isn't it?'

Arthur Bains took a deep breath, and then spoke in a calm, collected voice. 'Mr err…'

'Haynes,' Slater spat, '…her husband!' He pointed wildly at Laura.

'Mr Haynes, please be seated while I continue with the rest of the codicil.'

Laura watched Slater pace the room, before returning to his seat. His face was puce as he flashed a look of hatred towards her.

Taylor looked at Laura and squeezed her hand tightly to comfort her, but noticed her expression showed all the signs of amusement.

Laura was shocked of course and wondered who the hell her real father was, but like the Will said, she had never wanted for anything. As for not inheriting Villa Amora, well, she had never felt like she belonged there anyway. She glanced back towards Slater and gloried in his fury, it took all her self-control not to laugh out loud.

Mr Bains cleared his throat and read on: *Except for the house in Gweek, which was bequeathed to you on my parents' death, the rest of the estate will now fall to my first-born son, who up until now is unaware of his correct parentage and will remain so at his mother's wishes until his adopted father's demise.'*

Mr Bains retrieved a piece of paper from the desk, cast a quick glance over it, and then looked up. 'As the aforementioned person is confirmed as deceased, I am instructed to continue,' he said solemnly. *Mr Taylor Haynes is my biological son. He was conceived during a loving and sincere relationship I had with Sarah Haynes before I was married. As Sarah was herself married, it was a joint decision at the time that the boy would be brought up within the bosom of her family and on his twenty-fifth birthday, providing Gerald Haynes had passed on, his rightful inheritance would come to him. Gerald Haynes, I might add, had no knowledge of Taylor's real parentage. I am sorry Taylor if you were looking forward to becoming master of Creek House, but I hope Villa Amora and its surrounding properties will more than compensate.'*

Taylor was dumbstruck - 'conceived during a loving and sincere relationship' what the hell was going on?

There was a hushed silence while the stunned group digested this latest revelation.

Slater was the first to speak. 'To think I have put up with you and your dirty little affair,' he snarled at Laura.

'Don't you dare speak to me like that,' Laura snapped back. 'It just proves what an unscrupulous bastard you are.'

Slater moved towards her, but Jack restrained him. 'Slater, leave her alone for God's sake man!'

'Yes leave me alone. Get out of my life once and for all,' Laura cried.

'My pleasure,' he sneered. 'I've wasted enough time on you, and if I never see you again it will be too soon. Enjoy your poverty dear wife.' He turned to Taylor, '…and I want *you* out of Creek House. I don't want any bastards under my roof.'

'Gentlemen please, this behaviour is quite unacceptable,' said Bains, pulling at the neck of his shirt.

'Don't worry, I'm leaving,' Slater said, wrenching the door open and slamming it behind him.

Arthur Bains cleared his throat in embarrassment. 'Nasty piece of work!'

Laura raised her eyebrow at this understatement.

Taylor squeezed Laura's hand and said sincerely, 'I don't know what to say, I feel as though I have robbed you.'

Laura smiled. 'No Taylor, don't ever think that, you are welcome to it. I have never felt that I belonged at Villa Amora, my grandmother made sure of that! Come to think of it, it makes me wonder now if she knew of my real parentage. That would explain a lot of her ill feeling towards me.' Laura looked at Mr Baines, 'Did my grandmother know?'

He moistened his lips. 'She did, but your grandfather did not.'

She turned to speak to Jack. 'Did you know about all this?'

'I did not,' Jack answered acidly, turning to Arthur Bains. 'Even though I am meant to be the family solicitor,' he added.

Arthur Baines sat at the desk, his fingers steepled. 'You were too involved with the family, my friend. We could not guarantee your discretion.'

47

Outside the office Jack turned to Slater. 'I'm surprised you dare show your face. You do know the police want to question you.'

Slater laughed caustically. 'Oh really? I don't think the police are they going to arrest me for burning a hut down. Do you?'

'There is also the question of attempted murder of a child,' Jack said stiffly.

'No case to answer,' Slater snarled. 'As far as I'm aware the brat ails nothing. I just gave it its first swimming lesson that's all.'

'You are despicable!'

Slater snorted a laugh.

Jack looked scornfully at him. He didn't like the idea of him being anywhere near Laura so he asked, 'Taylor said you've been living in Rhodes. Are you flying back there now?'

Slater regarded him for a moment, as he mulled over the question. 'Not yet. My flight isn't until four p.m.' he said, hailing a taxi with a wry smile.

Jack watched him drive away. It was time someone took him down a peg or two. He turned to Arthur. 'I just need to make a phone call before we set off,' he said.

During the taxi ride to the airport, Jack stared quietly out of the car window, resigning himself to a future alone. Pushing his trolley into the checking in queue for the Gatwick flight, he began searching for his passport and tickets. Confident he had them safe and sound, he glanced at his watch then scanned the flight times for the Gatwick flight - it came up at three fifty p.m. Good it's on time, he said to himself, then unconsciously checked the flight time for Rhodes. He lifted a quizzical eyebrow - there were no checking in times for another Rhodes flight that day. He double checked, and felt a chill down his spine - Slater had lied to him. Pushing his passport and tickets back into his pocket, he manoeuvred the trolley out of the queue and back out of the large glass sliding doors.

'Where are you going?' Arthur shouted. 'You'll miss the flight!'

Ignoring him, Jack hailed a taxi and set off towards Piraeus harbour.

'On holiday?' the taxi driver said. 'This is nice place, I show you the sights yes? It cost you not very much Drachma.'

'Piraeus harbour please as quick as possible,' Jack answered.

'We take scenic route past good bars, Tavernas, yes?' the driver asked hopefully.

'No! Take me straight to the harbour, and before you try anything I know my way around, okay?' Jack growled.

The driver shrugged. 'Okay, I take you straight there. I am only trying to help.'

The Flying Dolphin was just pulling out of the harbour as the taxi pulled up. Jack cursed as he paid the indignant driver, pulled his bag out of the car, and watched desperately as the ferry sailed away with Slater clearly visible on deck. He looked around for the nearest payphone.

'I need to speak to Police Inspector Kokkotos please, it's urgent,' Jack said.

After almost a minute a voice came on the line. 'Hello, Inspector Kokkotos speaking, how can I help?'

'Hello, this is Jack Ryder again. I spoke to you earlier about Slater Haynes.'

'So you did,' the inspector said casually.

'I told you that he was in Athens and would board a flight to Rhodes this afternoon, but my information was wrong. He's now heading to Poros. I believe he is about to harm a member of the family I represent - I'm a solicitor you see.'

'Thank you Mr Ryder, rest assured we've been keeping

an eye on your Mr Haynes since he arrived in Athens. We are just waiting for the police boat to come back from another call and we'll follow him as soon as possible.'

'Oh thank God for that.' Jack began to relax.

'We've had a dossier on him for several months. We know his movements. Don't worry Mr Ryder, we're on the case.'

Heaving a sigh of relief, Jack replaced the receiver, picked up his bag and walked back to the harbour to check the time of the next ferry out to Poros.

*

It was mid afternoon and while the celebrations continued at Alexis Taverna for Laura and Taylor's birthday and the latter's good fortune, Eva Barzini found herself sprawled across her bedroom floor, nursing a bruised and bleeding face from the beating she'd just received from Slater Haynes. 'That will teach you to keep your harebrained ideas to yourself,' Slater said as he stormed out of the door.

Stephano stood next to the open gun cache, his face white with anger at the sight of his battered mother. In a trembling rage he ran down the stairs after Slater.

'Stephano leave him, Stephano no, come back,' Eva screamed, as she struggled to her feet.

*

In the warm afternoon sun, champagne flowed in abundance.

'So, how soon can we expect a wedding Yiannis?' Travis said jovially.

'The sooner the better' he said, pulling Laura into his arms. He produced the velvet box from his pocket. 'If she'll have me,' he said slipping the solitaire diamond ring on her finger.

She gazed with love into his aquamarine eyes. Suddenly, there was a loud bang and every nerve ending in her body prickled. There was a terrible searing pain in her left breast as a second bang echoed in her ears. Screams sent a shiver down her spine. Only aware of the terrible pain, she looked down at her pretty cream summer dress and frowned as it glistened with blood. Her mind was numb, she looked for Yiannis, but he was no longer at her side. Something heavy fell at her feet and her eyes followed the blood down her dress to the floor where her darling Yiannis lay.

She fell to her knees, gathered him into her arms, and looked into his glazed eyes. 'Oh no,' she whispered, 'Yiannis...my love.' Her throat began to constrict as she shook uncontrollably. 'Yiannis,' she kissed his blood-stained hair. The morning sun glistened on the thick crimson liquid pumping from a wound in his chest and a gash to his head. She stemmed the flow with her hand but the blood trickled through her fingers over her engagement ring.

Her screams echoed around the sleepy sun drenched hills of the Peloponnese and each guest at the gathering felt their hair stand on end.

*

Laura woke in hospital, after an emergency operation on her breast to find Kostas and Travis at her bedside. She licked her dry lips. 'Where are Yiannis and my baby?'

Kostas grasped her hand. 'Laura it's me, Kostas. The little one's fine, he wasn't hurt, my friend Karen is looking after him back on the island.'

'And Yian, is he all right?' she said, scrutinising Kostas's face, but Kostas could not speak. 'Oh God no,' she sobbed, 'Please no!'

'Laura,' Kostas said quickly. 'He's not dead. He's had an operation, but he is very, very ill.' Kostas wiped the tears from his face. 'The bullet entered you first, passed straight through and then punctured Yiannis's right lung. When he fell, he banged his head. He's in a coma. I'm so sorry Laura.'

At her insistence, Laura was taken to where Yiannis lay in intensive care. Tubes and drips entered his inanimate body. There she sat for a long time, in grief stricken silence, holding Yiannis's hand. Her eyes stared intently at him hoping for a miracle, watching and praying for him to open his eyes. No amount of coaxing by Travis and Kostas would make her leave his side. She crawled onto the bed beside him to cradle his face tenderly. 'Yiannis?' she murmured softly to him. 'Yiannis I'm frightened. Please don't leave me. You can't leave me. Not after all we have been through. I love you and I need you, please don't leave me.'

As she wept, her own tears tumbled onto his face and she kissed them gently away, then nestled into his neck, and drifted off to sleep. Travis and Kostas looked on miserably until the nurse advised them to leave her for a while.

*

Travis and Kostas were joined by Jack, as they sat in a taverna, half a mile from the hospital, all nursing a drink they didn't want. Cicadas shrilled in the heat of day and traffic rumbled noisily down the dusty street.

'Anyone know where Taylor is?' Jack asked eventually.

'He's been with the police all day.' Travis answered. 'I believe his mother Sarah, is flying in tomorrow.' He twisted the beer glass aimlessly in his hand. 'Much as I hate Slater for what he has done in the past, this must be an awful ordeal for any mother to face. I feel for her, I really do,' Travis said quietly.

'There is nothing else we can do here today.' Jack said. 'I suggest you two catch the last ferry home and I'll drop back in to check on Laura. I am booked into a hotel nearby, so it's no problem.

After they said their farewells, Jack returned to find Laura still asleep beside Yiannis. He watched for a long time. His heart ached to see such love and devotion. He wished with all his heart that it was aimed at him.

She woke when he touched her arm. As she lifted her tragic face to find Jack at her side, she was too grief stricken to think why he was there.

'Come on Laura, there is nothing you can do at the moment. You need to be back in your bed, otherwise your own wounds won't mend,' he said tenderly.

She glanced at her darling Yiannis, but he was still and silent, except for the hissing of the oxygen mask and the machines which were keeping him alive. Her limbs felt stiff and she was in a great deal of pain, as Jack helped her to her feet. With his arm protectively round her, he slowly led her back to the ward where she fell into an exhausted sleep.

*

When Laura woke the hospital was in semi darkness. Almost immediately, the aching grief engulfed. She needed to be with Yiannis, he needed her. Dragging her legs off the bed she tried to stand, but the pain in her breast caused a wave of nausea which brought her to her knees. Taking great gulps of air to combat the nausea, the smell of disinfectant caused an eruption in the pit of her stomach and she began to wretch. Each involuntary convulsion ripped the stitches on her wounds. Crawling on all fours, she spat the bile from her mouth. Her rough cotton hospital nightgown stuck to her damp shaking body, and traces of blood began to spot through her bandages.

'Yiannis,' she cried pitifully, watching her tears congeal with the pool of saliva on the grey linoleum. A nurse lifted her onto the bed. 'I need to see Yiannis,' she pleaded, as a doctor came and administered a powerful drug sending Laura back into oblivion.

*

Travis arrived the next morning with an arm full of flowers, only to find Laura drugged and dazed in her bed. After an angry altercation with the nurse attending her, who insisted that Laura was disruptive to the other patients with her erratic behaviour in the middle of the night, Travis had her moved to a private room and her sedation lifted. By the time Jack arrived, Laura was once again lucid, and her first request was to go to Yiannis's side in intensive care, where she sat in vigil, oblivious to Travis and Jack.

*

Eventually Travis took his leave for some lunch, but Jack continued watching Laura as she rested her head on Yiannis's bed, her eyes staring blankly into space.

'Laura?' he spoke gingerly.

She lifted her head, but the movement made her wince in pain. She squeezed her eyes tight shut until the pain subsided. 'Why are you still here Jack?'

The question hurt him beyond belief. 'Because I care about you!' he said stiffly.

She lifted her hand in apology. 'Sorry, I didn't mean it to sound like that Jack. I meant that I thought you were leaving after the Will reading.'

Jack tapped his finger to his mouth. 'Well I had an inkling that Slater meant to harm you. So I had the police follow him. I couldn't leave until I knew you were safe.'

'So Slater did this?'

'Indirectly yes.'

She looked puzzled. 'Where the hell is he now?'

'He's dead Laura. He can't hurt you any more.'

She dropped her head in her hands in relief. 'Was he killed by the police?'

'No, Stephano Barzini killed Slater, and unfortunately you and Yiannis were hit by his first missed shot.'

She looked aghast.

'Apparently Slater went to Poros to deal with Eva Barzini. They'd been lovers for many years and schemed together over your inheritance. Because their plan failed, he took his revenge on Eva with his fist, and in turn Stephano revenged his mother.'

'Well I'd guessed that Slater had married me for my inheritance, but what the hell had Eva Barzini to do with it?

'She believes she is owed something, particularly from

the Tempests.'

'Why?'

'Are you sure you want me to keep talking? You look washed out,' he said concerned.

'Yes, tell me everything, I need to know why.'

'Well I only know what Kostas has told me. It all started back in 1910 when your great-grandfather Norman Tempest came to Greece with the Royal Navy. His ship docked at Piraeus, and he hitched a ride with a local fisherman and came to the island of Poros. It was here that he met Pano Kokkotos, Eva's great-grandfather.

Apparently, Pano owned land on Poros, lots of it, but he was a compulsive gambler, as was Norman Tempest! They spent all that day playing cards in the back of Pano's house. After losing a vast amount of money to Norman, Pano, sure that his luck would change, began to gamble first his property, then his land. Norman Tempest urged him to give up, but the locals kept egging Pano on. At the end of the day your great-grandfather found himself to be a very wealthy man. The locals congratulated him, but he shrugged off their congratulations and made it clear he would not make Pano honour his debt. What use had he for land and property in this far away island in Greece! He was a seaman and always would be. He had no land legs. Unfortunately, before he managed to tell Pano his decision, Pano pointed a gun at him and shot him in the thigh. Pano went to jail and died there, leaving a widowed wife and fatherless son called George.

With an injured leg, your great-grandfather was forced to leave the Navy, and having nowhere else to go, settled on the land he had acquired on Poros.

To his credit, he gave everyone who lived in his inherited properties a chance to buy them over an unlimited amount of years, and he and local builders began to build the town and harbour as it now stands. The most poignant thing he did - and the locals still talk of it today - was that he provided a house free of charge for Pano's widow and made sure her son Spiro was well provided for.

Shortly after, your great-grandfather married an English girl called Elizabeth and Villa Amora was built for her in 1913 and your grandfather Charles was born shortly afterwards.

The Tempest family lived there in peace for twenty years, until Pano's son, Spiro Kokkotos's brought home Maria Barzini, a young ambitious woman, from his travels in Italy. She ruled Spiro's life with her dominating ways, set up the Italian gelateria 'Ice Palace', and worked the poor man into an early grave, though not before he fathered three children. All three children kept their mother's surname of Barzini - apparently, Maria had no wish to associate her fine children with their spineless father. Maria decided the family would be a force to be reckoned with. She knew of the gambling debt, and poisoned her family's mind into thinking they had been cheated. As they grew up, Marcos and Franco set out to make the locals pay with their protection racket and I think Eva has been no exception to this rule.'

'But why did Eva target Yiannis in her catalogue of hate?' Laura asked.

'No one knows. It could be that she was jealous of his friendship with your grandfather or 'hell hath no fury like a woman scorned'. She was a gold digger and Yiannis said she set her sights on him, because he was a taverna owner. She had been very free with her body, offering it up to all and sundry Yiannis believed she got pregnant with a holidaymaker, and then put the blame on him.'

'How old is Stephano?'

'Twelve, he was born in April 1981,'

Laura closed her eyes as the last argument her mother had with her step father Steve, suddenly jumped into her memory. They were waiting for the Flying Dolphin, in Poros harbour and Steve had been approached by a woman he clearly knew. There had been a short hushed conversation between them, but Laura heard the woman say to Steve that she was pregnant. As they waited to board the plane at Athens, Laura had asked her mother what the word pregnant meant, because a lady wearing horrible perfume had told Steve that she was pregnant. From that moment on, the argument erupted and Laura could not put back into the bottle what she had let out.

Jack watched Laura with concern. 'Are you okay?' he asked.

'I believe the father of Eva Barzini's son, was Steve - mum's second husband. That was what they were rowing about when the tree hit us.'

'Oh Laura, I'm so sorry.' He placed his hand on hers, and she let it lay there.

'Where is Eva Barzini now?' she asked stiffly.

'Don't you worry about her; she and her brother have been driven off the island once and for all. You won't have any more trouble from them! Now, rest! I'll be back tomorrow.'

'Yes but where is she?' Laura insisted.

'At the moment she lives on the island of Agena, and travels back and forth to Athens to visit her son who is in a young offender's prison. As I say, I will make sure she won't bother you again! Now, I think it is time I left you to rest.' He got up to leave.

'Before you go, I want something done Jack. Can you arrange it?'

'If it is in my power, I'll do it. What do you want?'

'I want a paternity test done on the Barzini boy. I want Yiannis's name cleared forever.'

Jack nodded. 'Consider it done.'

'Thank you Jack,' she said sincerely, as he took his leave. She laid her head on Yiannis's bed and closed her eyes.

48

Sarah Haynes struggled to hold herself together on the long journey to Athens, but seeing Taylor at the airport, her resolve crumpled.

As he comforted his mother, Taylor noted she had visibly aged since he'd last seen her. Her perfect chignon fell untidily about her face and her clothes were creased from the flight. His heart broke to see her so distressed.

Nestling her head in the crook of Taylor's arm, she cried softly throughout the taxi journey, only recovering when she was ensconced in her hotel bedroom, and cold water had been splashed liberally on her face.

The morgue was the next port of call, at her insistence; she requested to see Slater's body alone.

She circled his body slowly, waiting for his response to her presence. She moved her face closer to his, searching for a movement, a twitch, a breath. 'Slater?' she whispered. His handsome face showed no signs of the pain inflicted from the bullet which brutally ended his short life. He wore a pale blue shroud, which looked bizarre on her fashion conscious son. Unable to understand the enormity of what she saw, she whispered, 'What demons possessed you to cause so much heartache to so many people Slater? What demons brought you to this?'

Touching his soft blond hair, her fingers moved down to caress his cold damp cheek, and then her weary eyes travelled the length of his body. He looked shorter than his five foot ten inches. Taking hold of his cold lifeless hand, she warmed it in her own. A great heaviness settled on her heart that she truly believed would never ease. Tears blurred her eyes as she gazed for the last time at the son she had given life to twenty four years ago.

*

In a small taverna in Plaka, the old historical

neighbourhood of Athens, set around the northern and eastern slopes of the Acropolis, Taylor and his Mother picked aimlessly at a plate of pork souvlaki. They sat in silence among the throng of people making their way between the labyrinthine streets and neoclassical architecture.

Eventually Sarah spoke. 'I think I owe you an explanation.'

Taylor shrugged. 'No explanation is necessary yet.'

She smiled thinly. 'You're a wonderful son, but I feel I must speak.' She cleared her throat. 'I was at Falmouth College of Art, when I met Stephen Tempest. He was part of a huge circle of friends, including Travis Reeves and Claire Moore, as she was known then.

Taylor's eyebrow rose. 'You know Travis Reeves?'

'I do yes.'

'I was doing pottery, Claire was into fashion, and Travis was a fine artist. Stephen and his friend Steve, who bizarrely were not related but shared the same surname, were doing a graphic design course. Stephen was my boyfriend throughout our time at Falmouth and we were very much in love. When we graduated in 1963, Steve urged my Stephen to go travelling with him before getting a job. Personally I didn't care for Steve and the feeling was mutual, so I had no intention of going travelling with them. We reluctantly parted company and Stephen promised he would only be gone for a few months, but he didn't return. I used to ask Gwen and Charles for news, but they had none. I gave up hope of ever seeing him again, and eventually I met and married Gerald Haynes.

Our union was looked on unfavourably by Gerald's parents, and by mine. As you know he was almost thirty years my senior, but he was kind, charming, and charismatic and he loved me.' She sighed affectionately. 'I left all dreams of becoming a potter behind and became mistress of Creek House. Gerald, being an art dealer, was away a lot, which I coped with admirably for a while. The running of Creek House was a full time job. When Stephen returned home in 1966, he stayed at his family's house in Gweek. Because of the proximity of both dwellings, it became increasingly hard to not see each other every day. He was full of remorse for leaving me for so long, and devastated to find that I had married someone else.' She laughed without humour. 'Of course with Gerald away, old feelings rushed back, and one Christmas, just before Gerald was due home, I invited Stephen in and the inevitable happened. Shortly after I found out I was pregnant with you,' she hesitated slightly – 'I ended our affair there and then. I wasn't prepared to leave Gerald.'

Taylor sat back in his chair and drummed his fingers on the table as he digested the story. Presently he asked, 'Did you tell Stephen about me?'

'No, I didn't, but he obviously knew when he saw you growing up. You were the image of him.' She took a drink of wine and nodded knowingly. 'Now I think about it, I believe that is why he married Claire Moore. It was so he could be near you to watch you grow up. I was amazed when he married her. I always thought Claire would marry Travis. They were made for each other. But Claire wanted more security than Travis could give her. Alas she and Stephen were not particularly happy. We all made a real mess of things in the end.'

Taylor flicked a fly away from the bowl of bread. 'Did father know about me?'

Sarah shook her head. 'Not to my knowledge no,' she sighed heavily. 'Thankfully Stephen was kind enough, when he wrote his Will, not to let the truth be known if Gerald was still alive on your twenty-fifth birthday. For that I am eternally grateful.'

Taylor leaned over and placed his hand gently over his mother's and Sarah's throat grew thick with emotion as her heart filled with love for him.

*

As the days passed, Laura constantly defied her doctor's

orders and instead of resting, sat with Yiannis. She was not alone. Travis too, sat quietly willing his friend to recover.

'Do you still paint Laura?'

Laura lifted her tired eyes to Travis. The last thing she wanted as her darling Yiannis was fighting for his life was small talk. She sighed and answered, 'Sometimes.'

'It's just that I've seen some of your early work, it was really very good.'

She turned back to gaze at Yiannis then registered what he had said. 'How come you have seen my work?'

'Yiannis showed me the ones in the fishing hut.'

Laura frowned. 'He promised he wouldn't show them to anyone.'

Travis laughed quietly. 'I'm sorry. Yiannis and I shared a lot of secrets over the years, we've been good friends. We both missed you a lot.'

Laura lifted her eyes to meet Travis's gaze. He looked uneasy as he bit at his lower lip. 'You didn't know me. Why would *you* miss me?'

There was a long pause as they both studied each other intently.

'Travis?'

He could feel his heart hammering in his chest. 'Because Laura, you are my daughter!' He felt as though his heart would burst as he said the words.

Laura felt her jaw slacken. 'I'm *your* daughter?' she said incredulously. 'You are the father who abandoned me?' Her voice was almost inaudible.

'Abandoned is a strong word,' Travis said defensively.

Laura sat bolt upright now. All the anger she felt at the injustice of Yiannis being shot, bubbled to the surface. 'But abandon me you did, you can't deny it!' Her face turned puce with indignation.

Travis's eyes stung with tears as his mind whipped him back to the day Laura was born. 'I didn't know your mother was pregnant with you until she sent word from the hospital. We'd been lovers at art school, and afterwards, well, I was a penniless artist, struggling to make a name for myself. Claire wasn't prepared to wait until that happened. She yearned for a comfortable life where she didn't have to work, so in the end we parted and the next thing I knew she had married Stephen Tempest.' He glanced at Laura and thankfully her face told him her anger was abating. 'Out of the blue, I was invited to a Christmas party at High Top House, along with some of our other friends from art school. I don't mean to speak ill of your mother, but we all thought she just wanted to show off her new found wealth. So we decided to go, even if it was to only drink them out of house and home.' He smiled wryly, but Laura didn't return his emotion. 'No sooner had I arrived, she pulled me outside and into the summer house.' He shook his head. 'I never could resist her.' He lowered his eyes. 'We made love there and then between the overwintering palms. When it was over, she casually went back to her party as though nothing had happened. After the party, I heard no more from her until I was summoned to the hospital a few hours after you were born. I could see you were clearly my little girl. She wanted me to see you, but then she sent me away, assuring me that you would want for nothing. She had no plans for another child and fully expected you to inherit the Tempest fortune. She did ask me to name you though, which I thought was strange at the time, so I named you after my mother.' He paused for a moment, drew in a deep breath. 'Please believe me Laura. I didn't want to leave you, but I had nothing, no home, no money, and no prospects at the time. So I reluctantly said goodbye to my little girl!' He licked his dry lips. 'I know you won't want to hear this, but I thought it was probably the best thing for you.' His shoulders sagged. 'I didn't realise Stephen Tempest knew you weren't his. If I had, I would have been at your side in a heartbeat.'

Laura turned her attention to the window but her eyes

saw nothing and her face was void of emotion.

'Laura?'

She turned to face him.

'Say something,' he pleaded.

'I don't think I like you,' she said evenly.

Travis lowered his eyes. 'If it's any consolation I don't think I like myself.'

Laura glanced at Yiannis. 'Did anyone else know?'

He nodded. 'Sarah Haynes knew. She saw us when we emerged from the summerhouse, though I suspect she didn't say anything for her own reasons. She also saw me leaving the hospital the day you were born. It seemed Sarah had her own secret to keep though, and that was why she kept ours.'

Laura felt a great emptiness within her. 'What heartache these secrets and lies bring.' She lifted her eyes to meet with Travis. 'Does Yiannis know?'

He shook his head. 'He knows I lost touch with my daughter, but no, he doesn't know it's you. When your mum died, I followed you here, just to be close to you. When you returned to school in England, I too went back home. But apart from hanging about outside the school gates like a dirty old man, I knew I had to let you be. When I returned to the island, Yiannis thankfully took me in and together we shared the letters you sent him, so I was able to follow your progress through school. Yiannis has been my salvation.'

Laura blinked. 'And mine,' she said wearily. She glanced at Yiannis then turned her gaze to Travis.

'You were Father Christmas weren't you?'

'I was.' He smiled.

She reached out her arms to him and immediately he was by her side, where they shared their first embrace as father and daughter.

*

Later that evening, the door to Laura's private room opened and Sarah Haynes popped her head around. Laura noted that although she was immaculately groomed, her beautiful face was etched with sorrow.

'May we come in?' Sarah asked.

Laura nodded with great trepidation. She entered with a waft of expensive perfume and Taylor brought up the rear.

'My darling girl.' Sarah reached for her hand and held it to her cheek. 'I have no words to express my sorrow at the horrors my son inflicted on you. I am at a loss to comprehend what has happened, but I am truly sorry.'

'I'm sorry for you Sarah. To lose a son must be the worst thing for a mother, and so soon after losing Gerald.'

Together they cried. 'Thank you Laura, after all you've been through, your kindness shines through as always.' She dabbed Laura's wet cheek with a handkerchief. 'My little Laura, you were always special to me. You always felt like my daughter.'

Laura smiled through the tears. 'Is Vanessa with you?'

'No, she's eight months pregnant and living with an Australian surfer. She's taken Slater's death hard. I'm afraid she doesn't actually believe what he did - they were always very close.'

'Have they released Slater's body for you to repatriate?' Laura asked awkwardly.

'Yes, but after consulting the British embassy, we decided to have a cremation here in Athens. As you can imagine, it's going to be difficult explaining to all our friends back home, how and why he died. We thought to keep everything as low key as possible. It'll get out, I have no doubt, but for now, we will just say goodbye quietly.' She blinked the tears from her eyes and smiled her perfect lipstick smile.

'And you? How are you my darling girl?'

'In all honesty, I won't mend until Yiannis wakes up!'

Sarah nodded. 'I'd like to meet my adopted grandson if that is possible?'

Laura's lip quivered slightly. 'Of course, I'd like to see him too, but they won't let him in the hospital. He's apparently being spoilt to death with Travis, Kostas and Karen. If you are going to Poros, give him a big hug from his mummy won't you?'

'I will darling. We're staying in Greece for a while, until we sort things out, but we'll leave you in peace now. I think Travis is coming later.'

They shared an emotional embrace, and after they had gone, Laura donned her gown and slippers and made her journey once again to Intensive Care. She'd only been there an hour when the nurse called her back to her room, where a couple of policemen were waiting for her.

'Mrs Haynes, we are sorry to disturb you. Are you well enough to speak to us?'

Laura nodded wearily.

Inspector Kokkotos continued. 'It's about your husband. If he hadn't died, he would have been imprisoned for murder.'

'Murder?'

'Yes, we thought you may want to know that the skin sample tests taken from under Katia Mozarski's nails at the time of her death, matched your husband's.'

Laura looked puzzled. 'Who is Katia Mozarksi?'

Inspector Kokkotos pursed his lips. 'She was Yiannis Kiassos's girlfriend. We think it was a revenge attack. Mr Kiassos always believed that Mr Haynes was responsible for her death. You were very lucky Mrs Haynes - you could have ended up like the Piraeus prostitute.'

Laura was dumbstruck. With all her heart she willed the policemen to leave her alone.

*

When Travis arrived, he found Laura quiet and subdued. She had witnessed every single emotion possible since the police visit that morning.

'Katia Mozarski!' she said, before Travis had a chance to sit.

Travis pursed his lips. 'What about her?'

'Katia Mozarski was a prostitute!'

'Yes she was.'

'Why is a prostitute linked to Yiannis?'

'Katia was his friend,' Travis answered carefully. 'He had a great respect for her. She was an enormous comfort to him in your absence.'

'He used a prostitute?' she gasped incredulously.

'Katia was his friend,' he reiterated. He could see the disgust in Laura's eyes. 'Yiannis is a man, with manly needs.' His cheeks flushed as he spoke. 'He could have had the pick of any woman, but he loved you Laura. He didn't want to start a relationship with anyone else in case you came back! Katia helped him. She gave love without commitment. He felt her loss keenly.'

Laura lowered her eyes and plucked absently at the bed sheet. 'I see.'

Travis sat back in the chair. 'Why do you ask about Katia?'

'The police believe that Slater killed her as well.'

'Hmm.' He tapped his mouth with his finger. 'It was what we thought.'

She put her hands to her face. 'He was a monster Travis.'

'Yes he was darling, but he's gone now. He can't hurt anyone else.'

'If Yiannis dies, I shall never stop hurting.'

'Don't speak like that. Don't give up hope Laura.' Travis moved to sit on the bed. 'Look, I've spoken to the doctor. He says you can come home tomorrow.'

Panic filled her eyes. 'I can't leave Yiannis.'

'We'll come back every day, I promise, but you need to come home. Little Yiannis is missing his mama. I do have some good news for you though,' he said brightly.

Laura looked up and waited.

'Kostas and Karen have got engaged.'

An involuntary tear fell down her cheek. 'I'm happy for them, truly I am.'

*

Laura and Travis stood silently on the quayside in Zea harbour, Piraeus waiting for the ferry. This was the same journey they embarked on these past three weeks now. Day after day they sat in vigil at Yiannis's bedside, hoping and praying for a miracle. They spoke to him, played music, Kostas came when he could and spoke of boyhood memories, all to no avail. Today, by special permission, Laura had been allowed to bring little Yiannis to his side, in a hope that his childish presence would pull him out of his darkness. The child sat on his bed, his little hand reaching out to Yiannis. 'Pa –pa wake,' he said, gently patting Yiannis's face, but still there had been no reaction. But being disruptive, as any eighteen month old child is, Travis eventually took the boy out, leaving Laura, bereft at her lover's side.

Because of the child, they left early that day, catching the two-thirty ferry back home. The day was cool and grey and thunder rumbled around the mountains of the Peloponnese. Laura had lost weight and her bones were clearly visible through her clothes. Travis fretted constantly for her. Her thin body trembled relentlessly in the chill breeze. She stared out into the rough Aegean, which slapped noisily against the harbour wall, firing glistening globules of oily water high into the air to land in vast puddles at her feet. Masts clanked as redundant pleasure boats rolled and smacked against the wooden jetties. Sun-lotion bottles and newspapers, dead fish and plastic flip-flops, congealed in an oily scum on the surface of the water, and the air hung rancid with fuel, fish, and hotdogs. Everything looked ugly and hopeless.

She glanced at the slow trickle of passengers as they began to queue for the boat. There were twenty-seven passengers waiting by the time the ferry droned into sight, as Travis bent down to pick up the child. Patiently they all waited until the ropes and lines were secured and a dribble of passengers began to disembark.

Laura's senses picked up a strong pungent perfume. The same sickly sweet combination of chocolate and patchouli she'd noticed on Slater's shirts. Then she closed her eyes, remembering the woman who had approached her step-father Steve, all those years ago, the woman who'd said, 'I'm pregnant, what are you going to do about it?'

Laura shuddered and opened her eyes and there she was, the stony-faced woman with the cruel thin lips and short-cropped black hair. This was the very same woman who had sparked the argument that had led to their car accident, and who had plagued Yiannis's life with her lies, and schemed with Slater over her inheritance. A prickly iciness ran down her spine. Laura gasped, stepped back and grabbed the sleeve of Travis's jumper.

'Are you unwell?' he asked, trying to steady her while juggling with the child in his arms.

'That's her isn't it? That's Eva Barzini!'

Travis followed her gaze and sighed heavily. 'Yes it is. She isn't worth fretting over any more Laura. Leave her now to stew in her own juices. You do know that Jack ordered a paternity test on her son, and the results showed that Yiannis was not his father? Well, because of that, there is no reason for her to live in Greece any more. I believe Jack requested that she and her son be deported back to Italy. The Italian courts will decide what to do with Stephano there. Jack thinks that because of his young age and the fact he was trying to defend his mother, the courts will be lenient. But it will be best for everyone if they are sent back to Italy.'

'Amen to that,' Laura whispered to herself.

*

In the quietness of Intensive Care, Yiannis lay still and helpless. He could not move. Terrified and trapped in this nightmarish existence, everything was out of his control. He knew that Laura, Travis and little Yiannis had left, and a deep unfathomable loneliness engulfed him. A presence caught his attention, but he could not move. In his mind's eye he could see a huge white room, without walls, just a floor that seemed to sparkle. Suddenly his bindings seem to loosen enough to move. Now he stood at the beginning of an endless corridor with locked doors to either side. He struggled past people he knew from his childhood, and customers from the Athena, but try as he might, he could not make anyone see him. Moving slowly down the endless bland, white corridor, he found a door which opened. Many steps rose up before him and he climbed and climbed until his legs ached. When he could climb no more he rested his hand on a door, which opened onto a roof and a starless night sky. He lay down and longed to feel the sun on his face and the wind in his hair. Someone was by his side, dark, exotic, and beautiful. She smiled sweetly, softly whispering his name. He felt a calm peacefulness. 'Katia, is that you?' he mouthed.

*

The next day, the ferry was over two hours late due to rough weather. Knowing how important it was to keep up some routine when sitting with a coma patient, Laura raced into the hospital.

'I'll just grab us a couple of coffees.' Travis said, stopping at the vending machine, but Laura had gone ahead towards Intensive Care. She pushed the door open and strode in with purpose.

'Mrs Haynes, *Laura* I must speak to you,' the nurse called out from reception, but Laura was on a mission and never heard her. The nurse quickly moved from her work station and ran after her calling her name, but it was too late.

Laura stood stock still in shocked bewilderment. The tubes and machines lay still and quiet, only the sound of her heartbeat thrashed inside her ears. She began to tremble uncontrollably, as her eyes scanned the bed which was stripped and empty. She sank to her knees with only one thought in her mind. Her beautiful Yiannis had gone.

49
One year later

The Athena Taverna was decked out in its finery. Tables full of flowers were swathed in ribbons and the great oak doors, between walls of radiant whiteness and splashes of bougainvillea, were pushed open wide to welcome guests.

A hundred yards down the road, in the middle of a wide paved square dominated by colossal plane trees, stood the chapel in photogenic prettiness.

'Where do you want these?' Alexis asked Travis, struggling into the kitchen with a box of flowers. He smacked his lips when his nose picked up the delicious aroma of braised lamb and potatoes. The suckling pig was roasting on a spit near the back, and rows of spinach and feta pies lay waiting alongside glistening baklava. 'There is nothing like a Greek wedding to tickle your taste buds,' he said, pinching a pie.

Travis inspected the box of flowers and asked, 'How's the groom this morning?'

'He's nursing an ouzo hangover - as are we all,' Alexis grinned. 'He's just about to be shaved by his best man.' Squeals of laughter filtered down the stairs. 'How are things here?'

Travis grimaced. 'The place is full of damn women. I'm sick of the smell of perfume and I can't get in the bathroom!'

Karen called down from the bedroom, 'Travis, is that Alexis with the flowers?'

'Yes.'

'Good. Have you got your suit on yet?'

He pulled a face. 'No. Do I have to wear it? I'm an artist, I don't dress up.'

There was a pause then she shouted back, 'Laura says yes you do!'

Travis blew out an exasperated sigh at Alexis. 'Now I

know why I didn't get married.'

The happy bride-to-be smiled at her reflection. Her long, elegant, embroidered ivory silk shift dress, along with the garland of oleander and rose-buds in her hair, looked wonderful.

Stepping out into the Greek sunshine, she drank in the air, perfumed with gorse and thyme. As she took the first steps towards her new life, the local musicians serenaded her all the way to the chapel.

At the gates she saw Kostas grinning boyishly, as he stood by the blue and white chapel door. She smoothed down her dress, ready to make an entrance. Immediately to her right stood a beautiful shrine, heady with the scent of fresh flowers. She bent to read the inscription:

Katia Mozarski
A friend and confidant, whose eternal light shines through the darkest days.

Plucking a flower from her bouquet she offered it up. 'I promise I'll take care of him,' she whispered.

'And I promise I'll take care of you for the rest of my life,' Yiannis said, moving to her side.

Laura's fingers reached for his hand. The last difficult year was behind them. Yiannis's rehabilitation was almost complete; today was their new start.

Yiannis gazed with love at Katia's shrine. She had led him through the darkness, he knew it for sure. Her beautiful, dark, exotic face had come to him, calling his name.

'Have you come for me?' he'd asked in quiet resignation.

'No my love,' Katia had whispered. 'I told you - when the time comes, and you find your true love, I'll let you go. Your Laura is waiting for you - you must go back to her.' As her image faded, Yiannis had opened his eyes to find a nurse standing over him. She smiled, checked his pulse and welcomed him back to the world.

Laura squeezed Yiannis's hand. 'We have a lot to thank

your Katia for.'

'We certainly do.' Yiannis nodded gratefully. He turned to gaze lovingly at Laura. 'You look beautiful my love.' He brought her hands to his lips and kissed them.

Travis, smart, but uncomfortable in his Sunday best, cleared his voice behind them. 'Time to go in,' he said, proudly standing at his daughter's side.

In the chapel, Kostas left Karen holding their month old baby girl Casta, flanked by doting grandparents Alexis and Irene, as he moved to stand beside Yiannis. Pippa, in a large feather hat, holding a box of confetti, beamed with happiness for her friend. Kimberly from the gallery, stood at the back, also sporting a newly purchased hat. And Melanie, Taylor and Sarah had their hands full, charged with minding a rather boisterous two and a half year old Yiannis for the day.

*

Jack Ryder sat in his office in quiet contemplation. Today was a difficult day. He could have gone, he'd been invited, but his heart was sore. He knew he had to move on, he just didn't know how. He looked up to see Jenny, his new secretary, at the door. She looked different today in her bright summer dress and her hair loose about her shoulders. He smiled at her. 'You look nice. Are you going somewhere after work?'

She nodded shyly.

'Anywhere good?'

She smiled with her eyes and walked towards him. 'That all depends where you take me,' she said softly.

*

The evening sun gilded the walls of the taverna in soft creamy amber light as the wedding party continued. The exclamation 'Opa' was shouted at regular intervals.

Laura stood in Yiannis's arms. 'The Greeks certainly know how to party. Will it go on all night?' she asked.

'I'm afraid so, don't worry, we won't be here tonight. We'll be on our honeymoon.'

She laughed. 'Honeymoon! Where are we going?'

He tapped his nose knowingly.

After a noisy procession escorted them down to the harbour, the guests shouted their goodbyes as the newlyweds climbed into the Moondancer.

'You're not spending the night on that thing are you?' Taylor shouted down to them. 'I though you wanted the yacht Aglaia!'

'Later,' Yiannis turned to Laura. 'We have something special to do first.'

They motored out of the harbour, to shouts of, 'I ora I kali.' Eventually the noise of the harbour drifted away on the night air and the Moondancer approached the Midnight Rocks. The moon laid a path of silver across the inky blue sea, and the gentle breeze ruffled the surface of the water, until it danced with brilliant spangles. Together they lay under the huge vault of stars in the infinite night sky.

'What does 'I ora I kali' mean?' Laura asked dreamily.

Yiannis tenderly took her face in his hands and kissed her. 'It means 'here's to the good time to come.'

ABOUT THE AUTHOR

Ann E Brockbank was born in Yorkshire, but has lived in Cornwall for many years. On a Distant Shore is Ann's third book. Her first book, Mr de Sousa's Legacy, was published in July 2013 and her second, The Blue Bay Café, was published in May 2015. Her inspiration comes from holidays and retreats in stunning locations in Greece, Italy, Portugal, France and Cornwall. When she is not travelling, Ann lives with her artist partner on the beautiful banks of the Helford River in Cornwall, which has been an integral setting for all three of her novels. Ann is currently writing her fourth novel.

Follow Ann on Twitter AnnEBrockbank1
Facebook Ann-E-Brockbank-Author

Printed in Great Britain
by Amazon

50167458R00236